ABANDONED DENTAL CLINICS

DAVID MATHEW

MONTAG

First Montag Press E-Book and Paperback Original Edition April 2023

Montag Press ISBN: 978-1-957010-28-1
Design © 2023 Amit Dey

Montag Press Team:

Cover: Rick Febre
Author Photograph: Sabrina Lake
Editor: Charlie Franco
Managing Director: Charlie Franco

A Montag Press Book
www.montagpress.com
Montag Press
777 Morton Street, Unit B
San Francisco CA 94129 USA

Montag Press, the burning book with the hatchet cover, the skewed word mark and the portrayal of the long-suffering fireman mascot are trademarks of Montag Press.

Printed & Digitally Originated in the United States of America
10 9 8 7 6 5 4 3 2 1

By the Same Author

——•◦•——

Fiction
Paranoid Landscapes
O My Days
Creature Feature (with M.F. Korn)
Ventriloquists
Sick Dice
The Parry and the Lunge
Dreadnought Flex
Panic Soup
Nostalgia's Boat
Torso Redux (*forthcoming*)
The Concrete Blush (*forthcoming*)

Academic
Fragile Learning: The Influence of Anxiety
The Care Factory
Psychic River: Storms and Safe Harbours
in Lifelong Learning
Learning and Long-term Illness: Saturated Spaces
(with Susan Sapsed)

Writing as Tom Lockington
Blush
Inspections of the Wounded
Pungent Verbs: Interviews with Genre Writers
at the End of the Twentieth Century

"And I am genuinely taken ... with a potential literary greatness here that deserves far more attention than just mine."

—D.F. Lewis,
The Des Lewis Gestalt Real-Time Reviews

"David Mathew creates a world that's familiar but seen through a deviant lens. There are shades of Clive Barker and JG Ballard in [his] stories – fiction that's all the more unsettling for having its roots in the everyday – but Mathew has his own voice and vision for the twenty-first century."

—Julie Travis,
author of *We Are All Falling Towards the Centre of the Earth*

"Stunning—an intricate and intriguing web of relationships! An ever-morphing story, tightening its grip as it expands, this novel melds the psychological and philosophical."

—Soramimi Hanarejima,
author of *Visits to the Confabulatorium* (on *Nostalgia's Boat*)

"Mathew is happy to leave us guessing about right and wrong/ good and bad in a paradoxical world ..."

—Dr Alan Bainbridge,
Psychoanalytic Psychotherapist &
Co-Editor of *Psychoanalysis and Education: Minding a Gap.*

"Mathew leads the reader into stories of calm and controlled prose, which contrasts with the unsettling way in which he turns our world slant and hallucinatory."

—Iain Rowan,
author of *One of Us*

"Mathew is a master of subtle unease. His characters, inhabiting a world that is always an inch off kilter, walk the margins of moral ambiguity ... sadness, surrealism and slow-burning mystery."

—Neil Williamson,
author of *The Moon King*

"A top-notch and unnervingly dreamy thriller from an author who really knows how to get inside your head."

—Nick Gifford,
author of *Erased* and *Piggies* (on *Nostalgia's Boat*)

DEDICATED TO DES LEWIS.

Not the villain in some of my fictions,
but the *real* Des Lewis.

A gentleman, a scholar and an acrobat,
if ever I knew one.

"Uncle Des."

Thank you.

CONTENTS

BOOK ONE

RAULTON & THE VILLAGES

I may say that I shall continue to repeat these things for the rest of the time that I'm coming. You may not recognise it because it may sound different, but it won't be. It will be the same thing, which I shall repeat, but it may appear to be different. I'd like to point out also that so far, I haven't said a thing (I think) which everybody here doesn't already know.

Wilfred Bion, *Los Angeles Seminars and Supervisions*

It just goes to show that you can bury yourself in the country and still somehow acquire a vocabulary.

P.G. Wodehouse, *Right Ho, Jeeves*

ONE YEAR OF MOTHS

———•◎•———

"In our Year of Moths, we must learn to expect no butterflies."

Brother Joe

CONDUCTOR AND CAVITY

If Twennyfour lowered his eyelids and tried to dream his way out of the vehicle, he could transform the worrying noises leaking from the engine into a piece of music. With a gentle smile pulling at the nook of his mouth, he could pretend that he was not in the back of a hot van that smelt of unwashed men and flatulence, which was bumping down tracks and lanes.

In his fantasy, Twennyfour is clean and shaved; he wears a tuxedo, and the orchestra hangs on the merest twitch of his baton.

The disappointment when he returned to the waking world was as intense as depression, but for moments and the passing of miles he would have been in a better place – and a better life.

When the vehicle banked suddenly, two of Twennyfour's fellow passengers swore at the driver. From the front, Brother Joe called out, "Sorry, brothers! Road's worse than ever!"

"How long till the next piss stop?" Twennyfour shouted back.

"Not until you're desperate, brother!" was the hollered reply. "I'm nervous about stopping the engine in case I can't get her started again!"

"Keep the engine running and stop. I can't keep my legs crossed anymore!"

There were five men in the back of the van and one more up front with Brother Joe – seven in total. Those in the back had to wait for someone to open the doors because the fastening mechanism had broken two days earlier, and the doors were held shut with a piece of broom handle wedged diagonally between the lip of the step that helped people climb aboard and a bullet hole in the door on the right.

Roger Billie slid out of the passenger side door and walked around the side of the van. Inside the vehicle, even these few seconds were difficult: no breeze entered through the windows; the temperature outside had risen.

The sound that Roger made when he dislodged the broom handle was a perfect chord, thought Twennyfour; the creak of the door as it opened was a sweet open A string on the violin.

The men climbed out into a scorched and silent environment; they withered under a punishing midday sun. Without a sound they walked off in different directions, some following the road, some staying to the sides, into the parched silver soil and throttled shrubs that were the only forms of vegetation visible.

Although they had travelled together for nine days, any element of familiarity when it came to matters of bodily waste remained absent. The men preferred to do their business in private, out of sight of anyone else. Back in John Hodgins – the village that Twennyfour had once called home – it was considered bad luck to see another man's genitals.

For Twennyfour, the urge to urinate was not as dire as he had made out. Away from the vehicle and his fellow passengers, he urinated quickly; and hearing the words "Ten minutes, brothers!" behind him, he strolled across the dust and sand, convinced that he could feel heat radiate up through the soles of his boots. It was *fresh air* that Twennyfour craved; fresh air and a sense of freedom, however fleeting this sense would turn out to be.

Because the land had seemed flat from where Brother Joe had parked the van, Twennyfour was surprised to feel a decline in the terrain. He descended a slope that could barely be discerned. Similarly, Twennyfour was intrigued to see a small cuboid building in the distance, below, its stonework or plaster the same colour as boiled shrimp.

Having nothing further to do in the ten minutes that had been allocated for the stop, Twennyfour approached the building, curious to know what it might be (or once have been), so far from civilization and with no road or path to lead to its entrance.

An unexpected odour met his nostrils when he was ten feet from the nearest side of the building: something medicinal. He walked on. More puzzled than before, he leaned into one of the rectangular spaces that must once have been a window with glass. From within, the smell was stronger: something that made him think of the hospital back in John Hodgins.

Inside were wooden chairs arranged in rows of three, such as might be seen in a waiting room. That the building had once been a place of medical treatment seemed likely.

Twennyfour skirted around the building. He found a space where a door used to be. Though wary of wild animals having made this place their lair, Twennyfour was too driven by curiosity to stop himself from crossing the threshold.

Inside it was musty and gloomy, but cooler than it had been in the open air. That was reason enough to linger for a few moments, while he explored the four rooms leading off the waiting area that he had seen from outside.

The first two rooms gave him no doubt that this building had once been a dental clinic. Each boasted a large reclining leather chair and a counter on which tools – some sharp, some with small mirrors on the end of metal sticks – had been abandoned.

The smell must be anaesthetic, Twennyfour reasoned; but other questions pressed in to fill the space in his head. What population had this clinic once served? In the van, on their journey, the men had not encountered human habitation in the past two days, so who could this clinic have been *for*? And why had all this expensive equipment been left behind?

The third room was divided into a kitchen area with an overturned circular table in the middle of the floor, and a door that led to three toilet cubicles. In the kitchen, on the counter farthest from the door, a microwave had been left wide open and a few bowls remained in the sink. The room was dirty with dust but not filthy, and Twennyfour noted the suggestion of haste in the departure – a hint of poorly-concluded business. It was a wonder that no flies were attracted to the scene.

Twennyfour did not want to push his luck: it was time to return to the van. And yet he would remain disappointed if he did not glance into the fourth room.

It was the only room with a closed door. As Twennyfour pushed down on the handle, he was more aware of the anaesthetic smell, concentrated (he was certain) on the other side of the wood...

From a distance came the sound of the van's horn: the warning that departure was imminent.

The room was larger than the other two treatment areas, but its function was identical. A leather chair was centre stage, and the counter tops were strewn with tools and pieces of clinical machinery. The major difference that this room had from the other two was that it had a mattress. The mattress lay in the far corner; there were blankets upon it, and a figure sat cross-legged on top of the bedclothes. Her blue eyes twinkled, despite the paucity of natural light.

"Who are you?" the girl asked as she rose to her feet with the fluidity of gymnastic youth.

Too stunned to offer anything but facts, Twennyfour recited his name.

It was as she nodded that Twennyfour noticed the uneven surface of the skin on her face; it was as if she had developed scales – or more realistically, pale-hued boils or blisters.

"You're the twenty-fourth child," the girl asserted.

From outside the building (though it sounded from outside a dream) the van's horn sounded again: three long blasts.

The sound unlocked a compartment in Twennyfour's brain. The word that he had been struggling to locate in his lexicon – the word that stood for the antiseptic aroma – occurred to him suddenly. The word was *ether*.

"No, not the twenty-fourth child. I have two brothers and three sisters. I'm the twenty-fourth in line to the crown." He compromised with himself and added: "Though I'm technically twenty-*third* now; my sister died. But we keep our original names."

Mentally he shook himself.

"Where are your parents?" he asked, agreeing to say something that would not seem threatening. What he *wanted* to ask was what was wrong with the girl's face. And could it be contagious?

"They went into the Saturated Spaces," the girl replied with a shrug, before simplifying her response. "They went away."

Approximately nine years old, the girl was of average height and slim build. She was dressed in blue trousers and a sensible pair of brown sandals; her lightweight cotton top was long-sleeved, and showed on the front a cartoon squirrel, holding a red balloon. Her small hands – Twennyfour noted – were bumpy with the same affliction that was prominent on her neck and facial features. Her dark hair was shoulder-length, and although a little tangled it was hardly filthy. Nor did the girl smell. This was not a child suffering from neglect; in fact, a wild child would have been simpler for Twennyfour to comprehend – someone who had survived against the odds, on her wits and will.

"Someone's calling you," the girl told him.

Though Twennyfour had not heard his name being shouted, he had no doubt that she was telling the truth. Furthermore, it felt like a good sign. Surely one of the other men would also see the building – and would deduce that Twennyfour must have entered it.

"Who looks after you here?"

If only he could establish that the child was in someone's care, Twennyfour could return to the work party. No doubt his name would be mud for several miles (especially if the van's engine sounded worse than when they had stopped), but the men had not been friends to begin with. In all good conscience, he could not leave an unattended child out here in the middle of nowhere.

"The Dentists."

"The dentists who used to work here? Where are they?"

"They still work here," the girl replied. "They protect me." She stepped towards Twennyfour and raised an open palm to the side of her head; she was indicating what had now turned out to be the decorations to her skin.

Embedded into the girl's face and neck – and indeed into both hands, the one she'd raised and the one that remained by her side – were hundreds of *human teeth*. They had been pushed into the skin so hard that they stayed put, like pebbles in mud.

This time Twennyfour heard his name being called, outside.

"*Twennyfour! Where are you, brother? We're waiting!*" It was Brother Joe's voice.

Torn between pragmatic acceptance of the situation and a desire to keep the secret in his paws for a few moments longer, Twennyfour succumbed to the lure of reality. Sucking in a lungful of the intoxicating air, he prepared himself to shout "*I'm in here, Brother Joe!*"... when a sudden wooziness overtook him.

"I'm in here…" he croaked.

The little girl smiled.

Waves of green lapped at the edges of Twennyfour's eyes. Briefly, he imagined the building that he'd visited as a rotten tooth.

Violin tides sipping… a sweet open A string…

An echoing cello belly.

A discordant crash of cymbals and kickdrum; (the van door opening and closing)?

Twennyfour stands on a platform the area of a dining table, a baton throbbing in his grip and a gentle smile pulling at the corner of his mouth. From here, he can lead the orchestra, his eyebrows writhing; or from here he can make all of his future mistakes.

This is the sum total of Twennyfour's thinking. The tension is as dense as an earache.

Open one eye at a time, the man thinks. The symphony swells like clouds condensing. The power shrinks and elongates; it roars and thrums…

Twennyfour woke up.

He gasped like a fish out of water; his lungs vibrated with the same melody as his unconsciousness had convinced him was of his own making. The cymbals in his dream were the clanking from the van's engine.

The back of the van was no more and no less crowded than it had been before they had stopped. Gradually adjusting the position of his head, Twennyfour was able to see a few of the other men. They appeared as tired and bored as ever.

Bruno Amitrano was plumply established, cross-legged on top of a structure of cuboid fuel barrels and small boxes of bottled water and tinned fruit. The cans of beans and soup were on a pallet between Paper Jake O'Donnell and Rick Shawdon, who both had their backs to the side of the van and were being roughly massaged by the vehicle's progress along yet another uncared-for stretch of road. Roger Billie and Twennyfour himself were near the rear doors. Gray (or *Professor Sir Grayson Twivy*, to give the man his due respect) rode up front with Brother Joe, in deference either to his senior years or his societal authority – or maybe to both.

Remembering the brief interaction with the girl in the dental clinic (whose name he had not so much as questioned, it occurred to him now), Twennyfour sat up straight.

"What happened to the girl?" he called out to the front of the van.

Brother Joe had a saying: *You can drive when I'm dead.* He would not let anyone else take the steering wheel, and today was no exception.

"You're awake, my brother!"

"I'm awake! What happened to the girl?"

Brother Joe laughed. "You were stricken by heatstroke, brother! We found you passed out! We gave you water and salt tablets and let you sleep!" he called back. "We put your trousers back on when they were dry! You had a little accident!"

Twennyfour touched the crotch of his trousers: bone dry. Even in the oven-like temperatures in the back of the vehicle, the drying of clothing would have taken a while.

"How long have I been asleep?" Twennyfour asked Bruno Amitrano.

"Since yesterday," Bruno answered. "We've been driving non-stop since then. And we haven't seen a thing."

Twennyfour remembered a night when he'd been a child of approximately the same age as the girl in the dental clinic. The family had still held together in those days; it was before his father had become sick with chickenpox. Bandits had broken into their home in John Hodgins; it was three in the morning. They had not hurt any of the family, however desperate they might have been. Instead, they had eaten every morsel of food in their home, holding Twennyfour's older sister at gunpoint. They had said that if anyone stopped them eating, they would kill Twennythree and then roast her to eat *her*. Though no one in the family believed the threat, the muzzle of a gun is convincing: the family had watched the bandits eat, and no one in the village had known that they had been targeted and attacked.

Twennythree had hanged herself from the side of the bridge that spanned the gap between John Hodgins and the next village. The bridge was called Feast Bridge.

The feeling that Twennyfour had experienced on discovering his sister's suicide, and the feeling that raged through him at the thought of having abandoned the girl in the dental clinic, were identical. Not so much shame as an acceptance of helplessness – even idleness.

"Brother Joe!" called Twennyfour. "I need a piss, brother!"

"Lord save us from leaky bladders!" cried Brother Joe, in response, as he slowed the van. "It is night, brothers! Whose turn is it to cook?"

The evidence suggested that the workers in the van had been travelling for eleven days, but the *other* Twennyfour, who awoke on the floor of the abandoned dental clinic, was not aware that a version of himself had moved on through time, while he had stayed put, with the girl. For the Twennyfour who had *first* discovered the clinic, only nine days had elapsed since the seven men had left John Hodgins. It was *this* Twennyfour who awoke as if from fever, and said, "Where do we go from here?"

"The Dentists have left us supplies," the girl told him. "Basic but nutritious. Come!"

Twennyfour climbed to his feet; he noticed a wet patch at the front of his trousers – he had had an accident. His sinuses were clogged with the aroma of ether, and he was aware of an anaesthetic hangover revving in his temples, as he watched the girl exit the room.

"What's your name?" he asked.

"Carey. Come!" she repeated, her voice exhibiting an emotion – excitement – for the first time since the two of them had met.

Twennyfour followed Carey out of the room and into the area where patients would have waited for their appointments. The girl skipped into the room that Twennyfour had mentally labelled a kitchen; again, Twennyfour followed her across a threshold.

The table remained inverted in the middle of the floor; the microwave oven's door was still wide open. Whoever had visited while Twennyfour had been asleep was no more house-proud, it would seem, than the girl knew how to be. Yet the fact that someone had paid a call here seemed hard to refute. The counter on which the microwave stood was busy with four glass jugs of milk and a selection of plates with foil stretched across them, their contents impossible to guess.

To Twennyfour, it looked home prepared; it was as if he and Carey had been invited to a picnic on the recreation land in the village. While Carey removed the foil, Twennyfour experienced a nostalgia as powerful as it was sudden.

Children, squeaking with pleasure, climbed the summer air on swings, and then returned to where they had started from, with a plummeting sensation in the belly. A shuttlecock was knocked over a makeshift net in a game of mixed doubles, for the prize of an apple and cinnamon pie. Conversations revolved around the family; speculations about fledgling relationships; or the maturational processes that would take certain children to the ritual that would transform them symbolically, with the village looking on.

The reverie felt like hunger to Twennyfour; it made him almost faint with expectation. The days had been happy, by and large. No one, then, had needed to talk of crop failure or bandits. The smells had been of curried goat and garlands; it was only later that the nostril had twitched at the scent of kerosene, at the stink of burning straw...

"*Ta-da!*" announced Carey, stepping aside from the counter with a showy flourish to reveal what was on offer for their meal. Although the selection was not ostentatious in terms of quantity, it contained items that Twennyfour had not seen for months. There were chunks of hard white cheese; leafy greens, apples, carrots, almonds, and celery; there was yogurt.

The girl pointed first at her mouth and then circled her forefinger, to indicate her whole head. "Very good for the teeth. Would you like an apple first?"

Twennyfour was starving; the abundance of questions that echoed around his skull could wait a few minutes more. "An apple and a long drink of milk would be wonderful," he answered. Standing by the kitchen counter, they ate in silence. Twennyfour's stomach received the nutrition with gratitude. A debt formed in his bones – he was heavier in the body because of it. Whatever else happened, he could not leave this girl alone here.

As he ravished a stick of celery, he noticed memories that were endeavouring to be thought through; the ether fug was dissipating.

"The van," Twennyfour muttered.

"What about the van?" Carey asked him.

Brother Joe had pulled the vehicle over to the side of another ramshackle track. The sky was a checkerboard of impending night and oddly cooperative clouds.

In the sepia-toned scrub to the left of the road, Roger Billie had made a small fire. Smoke rose in dreadlocks. The provision of flame and heat would not impact the choices available from the limited menu, but the warmth would be welcome; it always was.

Twennyfour regarded the blaze.

"Where's Brother Joe?" he called to Bruno. The latter waved a hand as he drained a bottle of water. As Twennyfour walked off in the direction indicated, Bruno tossed the plastic to the side and spat.

Elsewhere but close, a dog howled – a coyote, perhaps. A bat flickered in the gloaming like TV screen interference.

Brother Joe was praying, forty feet from where he had parked the van. Seeing the man kneeling in the near distance, Twennyfour approached with trepidation. When Brother Joe gave a sign of spiritual satiation, Twennyfour searched his conscience. He cleared his throat and called:

"Brother Joe!"

The smile that Brother Joe offered was lambent.

"I would like to discuss an issue! May I move towards you?"

"Always, brother!"

The bat flapped adjacent to them, slicing the warm evening air that would soon cool.

Brother Joe intimated that Twennyfour should take a seat on the ground beside him. "What ails you, brother?"

"My memory. When we stopped and I went into that building, there was a child there – a girl of about nine years old – and she had teeth all over her face and hands." Twennyfour paused for effect. "Pushed into the skin. And I was close to asking her why she had done this to herself when I ..."

"Fell ill?" suggested Brother Joe.

Twennyfour nodded. It was as good a euphemism as any.

"I was the one who found you, brother. I sounded the horn several times."

"We heard that."

"... and then we took a different direction each and looked for you. No one had noticed where you went after we stopped." Brother Joe shook his head. "There was no child in there, Twennyfour. If we'd seen a child in there with you, I promise I would have done something about it. You were alone. Flat on your face on a mattress in the corner."

Twennyfour lit up. "And didn't that seem strange to you, Brother Joe?"

"Indeed it did. I'm not saying the building had *never* been somebody's home, I'm merely trying to assure you there was no girl we left behind." Brother Joe shrugged. "Maybe she was an angel. If she was sent to test us, we failed."

Sensing that this private communion was drawing to a close, Twennyfour prepared himself for one final question. However, his thoughts were demolished by a single gunshot, elsewhere. His body rocked with shock... and he took in the powerful brightness of Brother Joe's unforced smile.

"Maybe it's rabbit tonight," the latter said.

"I heard a coyote before I came to find you," Twennyfour replied.

"Someone'll know a good recipe for coyote. Shall we go back?"

"A moment longer, Brother Joe," said Twennyfour. "I feel I *left* something there, in that clinic, with that girl."

"You did, brother. Half a gallon of urine."

"I'm serious. Ever since I woke up, I've felt I'm living here *and there*."

To Twennyfour's surprise, Brother Joe showed signs of giving the statement its due consideration. The response was reasoned.

"The concept makes sense, but the pragmatic execution is impossible. Whatever it was you saw – and I believe you, brother, you saw *something* – it was not a child in a clinic."

Twennyfour knew that he had to accept this rationally: there was little chance of a nine-year-old girl surviving on her own, provided for only by beneficent dentists. Where would she bathe? How would she fill her days?

If she had *not* been present, what had Twennyfour experienced? Heatstroke might make a person unwell; it might create dream-strength hallucinations; but heatstroke did not explain the sense that he had *remained there*, clinging onto an existence.

"There are things I know that the girl told me after I woke up," said Twennyfour.

Both men were now on their feet.

"Her name. It's Carey. She is nine. She wears other people's teeth in her face because bone and teeth decay slowly. The Dentists have told her to look after the teeth and they will look after her. She thinks she's protecting herself."

"From what?" Brother Joe demanded.

COLLECTOR AND TOOL

Five months "pregnant" (so to speak), emotional, tired, and edgy, Claire drove around the Raulton Estate, searching for Feast Bridge Road. She was ten minutes late – and counting.

The Raulton Estate felt etiolated and desperate with low energy. Few walls had escaped the attention of a graffiti provider whose tag was Spyblood. Such traffic as used the roads this afternoon moved either too fast or too slowly. To Claire, it seemed that the drivers were either posing for attention – or bolting away from a disadvantageous scene. On entering the estate, Claire had heard a decrepit van backfire; she had talked herself out of the possibility of a gunshot.

Her vehicle fit the scene's demands; it did not stand out. Though eleven years old, a trifle scarred, Claire's Fiat ran obediently over short distances, and the Raulton Estate was a mere fifteen miles from the flat. The problem was, the cigarette lighter had long since broken, which meant that there was nowhere to plug in the navigation device. Its collected power had haemorrhaged; consequently, Claire was lost. Having viewed Feast Bridge Road on an online map before she'd left, she was driving, now, on a pigeon's instincts. She would have to stop and ask someone for directions.

Claire indicated left and pulled into a diagonal parking space in front of a row of shops and businesses. She silenced the engine. As a committed practitioner of mindful breathing, she took a moment to close her eyes and acknowledge her surroundings. *An unfamiliar setting is nothing to be afraid of...* All the same, her palms were slippery; by leaning sideways, she was able to dry her hands on the fabric of the passenger seat, on which her large and heavy backpack perched, secured (as ever) by the seatbelt.

Deciding to leave the backpack where it was for as long as it took to request directions, Claire climbed out of the Fiat. Her choices of who to approach were plentiful. Directly in front of her was a place that served chicken and pizza. It was flanked by a loan company on one side and a funeral director on the other; the words *Holy Trinity* sprang unbidden to Claire's mind. A few doors down, there was a bicycle shop, next to it an establishment that would buy unwanted gold. Behind a low fabric barrier and unoccupied white plastic tables was a café. It was called Back to the Eggy Bread, and Claire thought it would do nicely.

Inside, a rough-and-ready count suggested twenty tables to Claire, some for parties of two, some for larger. One of the three family booths was occupied by a group of six women in matching beige headscarves, laughing at something with thunderous glee. Elsewhere, the tables were employed in unpredictable patterns. A cuboid postman, his delivery shift completed, ate *shwarma* and falafel with his fingers, his back bent forward in gustatory concentration. Three young men from a building site (or so Claire guessed) were engaged in a conversation about the United States that might have been of interest to Claire if she had not already been fifteen minutes late. A boy-and-girl couple sweet-talked over a family meal. A girl-and-girl couple kept control of what Claire took to be anger as they ignored the pizza that was cooling before them.

Claire approached the well-lit counter, stepping through a cheese-and-oil-flavoured breeze caused by the front door hanging open (slowly swinging shut on fire escape hinges) and an unseen door to the kitchen, also wide open for the benefit of the workers backstage.

"I was hoping you could help me with directions," Claire said to a man who had offered her a "Howdy!" in a Polish accent, knocking the beak of his cap up an inch or so. The badge on the right of his chest identified this front-of-house man as Zbig.

"Directions?"

From memory, Claire articulated the address that she sought. However, if Zbig's carpet-underlay of a beard so much as twitched, Claire did not discern it. She held her phone out to her interlocutor; the address was on the screen.

As if addressing the back rows of the Gods, Zbig shook his head. "I don't live here. Perhaps you'd like to order something."

"I would. A coffee with chocolate sprinkles, please."

"That chair won't get warm without you."

Smirking, Claire took her seat. Should she call the vendor and explain that she was running late? As yet, she was not *very* late (and on the phone both women had repeated *one-thirty-ish* several times); but as she waited for her beverage to arrive, a nervousness settled upon her. The vendor had told her that she would need to go out later: she would have to pick her daughter up from school. Business would have to be concluded promptly.

Giving in to temptation as her coffee was set down on her table, Claire pressed the number that was stored in her phone as: AMANDA DENTAL TOOLS.

"Hello Amanda," she said. "I'm sorry, I'm lost. I can't find you."

At the other end of the connection, a woman that Claire pictured as older than her own twenty-six years chuckled. She spoke with a deeper voice.

"How far have you got?"

"A café called Back to the Eggy Bread."

"I know it. I'll walk over and collect you."

The woman who entered the café was clearly looking for someone, so Claire assumed this new arrival to be Amanda. She was probably in her late thirties; they were roughly the same height of five-six or five-seven, but Amanda was broader in the beam – the heavier of the two. She wore comfortable clothes and a pair of grey trainers. Her dark hair framed her wider face, whereas Claire had tied her longer, lighter hair back in a ponytail.

"You must be Claire."

Claire had stood up to shake Amanda's hand. "Would you like something before we get down to business?"

Amanda smiled. "That's very restrained of you; I'm sure you want to see the egg burnisher I've got for you." Then she laughed quickly. "We're going back to the Egg Burnisher! Not just back to the Eggy Bread!"

Claire copied her vendor's smile. "I probably shouldn't seem too keen as a potential buyer, but the money's burning a hole in my pocket." She stood up and added: "I've already paid the bill."

Outside, children had collected in pockets around some of the precinct's benches. In passing, Claire wondered why these children were not at school.

"Shall I drive us?" She indicated the parked Fiat. "That's me."

Amanda gave the question a moment's consideration. "You can do, but we're only a five-minute walk away, and it can be a bit sticky to park there. As long as you don't mind leaving your car unattended…"

"I'll just need my backpack."

They had taken only a few steps before Amanda advised her buyer that her stepdaughter would not be in school, despite their previous conversation. "She's under the weather," Amanda summarised.

It was none of Claire's business; she changed the subject as they strode. "How long have you been selling?" she asked.

"About five years. It's a decent occasional income with no heavy lifting. Plus, I stay at home – I can read and think." Their steps had synchronised: left-right, left-right, like a pack drill. "I do some freelance editing and proofreading, as well. Between Roger's salary and what I peck at… we get by. Roger sends me what he can from his alternative timestream."

Uh-oh...

"Or that's what it looks like sometimes," Amanda clarified, "the way he describes his working conditions in his emails – and some of the photos he sends. *Primitive* does it no justice whatsoever. But you didn't come here to discuss my war stories."

Claire was about to ask where Amanda's partner or husband worked when Amanda closed the topic. "We're nearly there. Next street."

To Claire, stepping foot inside the bungalow smelt like a walk in Nature; the building's interior was an artificially created environment of odours, but it was pleasant. The entrance space, which gave straight onto the lounge, was tastefully decorated and kept clean and tidy.

"She's in there," Amanda informed Claire, gesturing towards one of three closed doors that surrounded the lounge area. "She shares your name, by the way. She's nine."

To the closed door, Amanda called, "Honey, I'm back!"

"Welcome home!" the younger Claire called in return.

"Do take a seat, Claire. Would you like a refreshment?"

"No, thanks. Just one or two coffees a day for me." Claire removed her coat and seated herself at the end of a three-person sofa. "Do you mind me asking what's wrong with her?"

"Chickenpox. I asked her to stay in her room until you'd gone, just in case she gave it to you. Her skin looks like a pork scratching... Can you hear us okay, darling?"

"I can hear you!" the girl's voice replied from beyond the closed door.

"Have you got drinks and snacks?"

"I have everything a girl could want."

Feeling that she would like to offer something positive, the adult Claire called out: "I hope you're feeling a bit better, Claire!"

"Just itchy!" was the response.

"Bless her," Claire added in a lower voice. "I remember missing school when I was her age. Then I went back too early, and the French teacher made me feel guilty about infecting the other kids!"

Amanda smiled. "Missing school with chickenpox, you mean."

"Yes. *Exactly* her age, funnily enough. My mum and dad took me to a Chickenpox Party. Do you know what that is?"

"Yes."

"…Why are you laughing?"

"Claire caught it at a Chickenpox Party on the other side of Raulton." Amanda raised her voice. "Whose party did you go to, to get the disease, darling?"

"John Hodgins!"

"A friend from school," Amanda explained – though Claire had inferred as much.

(*On a momentary thermal, the face of a different, more senior John Hodgins soared up from her memories, like a bird of prey: the face of a man she had used to know, half a decade earlier. The flash passed and his face descended away, scarcely glimpsed and already forgotten.*)

"We had the better part of a week to get ready – and to prepare Claire. We told her why it's good to get chickenpox when you're a child, rather than later. We had pep talks about how she'd cope with the itchiness. Roger was online when he could get a decent signal…"

Amanda lowered her voice. "The full thumbs up and a broad grin. All going to be positive."

Claire also dropped her volume. "And what happened?"

"She burst into tears when she got to the lad's house. The front garden was full of older kids with spots on their faces. It turns out, John's family had decided to cash in a group ticket. The boy's older brothers' friends were also there, some already infected and some waiting to be. An orgy of acne! It freaked her out. They were trying to give chickenpox to everyone in the borough."

"Well," Claire resumed, her voice at the same level as it had been before the non-disclosure clause had been breached. "She must have been a very brave girl."

"She was. We managed to convince her to go in and play with her friends."

An uneasy feeling had seeped into Claire's frame. Was it something to do with Amanda's repetition of *we*? If Roger was working elsewhere, away from home, what *we* could Amanda mean? *To whom does Amanda refer?* Claire translated into an example of the syntax in her PhD thesis.

"You'll be wanting to see my egg burnisher," Amanda announced. "It's in the kitchen."

When she returned, she was carrying a thin silver implement with an even thinner head. "High-grade stainless steel," Amanda almost *sang* in a mock sales pitch. "Burnish amalgam to your heart's content to ensure your adequate condensation.

Blend your material for final contouring, to achieve sculpting in grooves and fissures. Twenty years old, approx."

Claire took hold of the dental tool. "It's beautiful." She made an expression that conveyed a message of: *No further questions necessary.* "You said forty pounds in the email."

"Yes. With a discount available for multiple purchases."

Immediately, Claire understood that the discussion up to now had been a second leg of the suitability interview that she must have passed while they'd communicated online. Claire felt flattered.

"What else have you got in the kitchen?"

"Nothing. I don't keep merchandise here, as a rule. I hope you don't mind I was checking you out; you can't be too careful."

"I don't mind at all. I'm happy to drive if we go back to the Eggy Bread."

"It's a walk away. We can all get some fresh air." Amanda raised her voice again. "Do you fancy a stroll to the lock-up, Claire?" Then she looked again at the older namesake. "Assuming you don't *mind* being with a chickenpox-riddled child. You said you'd had it."

"I'll be very happy to walk with you, Claire," Claire stated. Then, while standing up and reaching for her coat, she added: "In what way were you checking me out?"

"Questions so subtle you didn't know I was asking them! I'm joking. I just wanted to know you were serious. I get a few time-wasters."

"Oh, I'm serious all right."

"Understood," said Amanda; "but I'm not expecting you to buy anything you don't want to buy; I'm in no rush to sell.

All I want is for it to go to someone who really *desires* it. I'm not looking to retire on the proceeds from recycled dental tools."

Bicycles whirred past, on a pavement that sounded studded. While Amanda locked her home, Claire counted seven bicycles… and eight children in a high-speed chase upon them. One of the bikes had a rider on the saddle and a friend or sibling on the handlebars.

Don't the children around here go to school?

Hand in hand with her stepdaughter, Amanda led the twenty-six-year-old Claire through a *linguini* of interconnected passageways and courtyards. A couple of times someone called out a friendly greeting.

Amanda shouted *Hi!* – or waved her free hand – to return the goodwill.

Claire remarked, "You know a lot of people, Amanda."

"I suppose so. Well enough to wave to and say hello; not many of them more than that. Perhaps it's because of the history of the place: we stick together to form a protective barrier. Guard against the outside world and all that."

"I don't think I follow. The estate's got a history?"

"Well, you can't have failed to notice that we don't live in Bel Air. We'll walk by Feast Bridge in a moment, and I'll tell you a story."

"I'm intrigued."

Little nine-year-old Claire had started to hum a tune that the older Claire recognised as something streaming currently. She had heard it on the Fiat's radio on the way here.

"By the way, I can't tell you how relieved I am to see my *instincts* were correct," Amanda continued. "My instincts about *you*, I mean. I did some light research on you. I hope you don't mind."

"I don't mind. If anything, it lends you the same sort of credibility as I hope your searches for me provided... otherwise I wouldn't *be* here, I suppose."

"You're a PhD student."

"That's right." Claire attempted a moment of levity. "And you don't need to ask: the bank won't refuse the transfer; I have funds. I teach part-time at the University. I waitress a bit when I need the hours. I work a few shifts in an off-licence and sometimes a pub. It all adds up. Or I have cash if you'd prefer."

"Well, cash is king, someone said; but that's not what I was getting at. I was interested in what you're researching. I had to withdraw from my studies. Years ago."

Claire paused before responding.

"*Collectors*, in a word; the psychology of collecting. I'm looking at what makes a collector a collector. What need does it satisfy? That kind of thing. For sixty thousand words."

"... So you're writing about *me*."

"In essence, I suppose I am – yes."

"I feel flattered. And what have you come up with so far? Do I accidentally speak a universal language of greed?" Amanda asked through a smile that Claire only caught by glancing sideways as they continued walking.

Is she joking, teasing, or serious?

Choosing to take the question at face value, Claire answered: "No. I don't think it's a matter of greed."

"Acquisition is usually concerned with greed. I certainly *feel* greedy," Amanda persisted.

"I'm not sure how to respond to that."

In her mind, Claire returned to Amanda's previous point about having conducted some research on her – on Claire. Only a few sources of information seemed likely. Claire Carey was named as one of four co-authors of a paper lead-authored by Dr. Alex Gordon – Claire's PhD supervisor – which had been taken on a tour of academic conferences the previous year. Gordon had presented at a handful of universities proximate to the south and south-west coasts, and once in Japan. The proceedings from some of those conferences were on the Web, but a more likely headwater of information was in Claire's mind.

"You saw my page on the University website, I'd imagine."

Amanda nodded. "The Institute for Applied Social Research… Impressive. Nice photo too. You've changed your appearance a bit since then…"

"The photo was two years ago." Claire summoned to mind what she referred to as her *standard academic pose*: a picture that had been taken by a fellow PhD candidate, a middle-aged woman named Phyllie Reydman, with whom she had become friends. The photo showed Claire outside the Postgraduate Centre; the University's logo stretched out of Claire's cranium like red horns. For the purpose of her picture being taken (a requirement of the Institute, for external publicity to attract applications), Claire had worn one of the respectable white-blouse-and-dark-knee-length-skirt combos that she wore when waitressing or pulling pints.

"You're not wearing your glasses today," Amanda noted.

True. Her vendor had certainly paid attention to the photograph! In the picture, Claire had worn some hipster horn rims that she had eventually left unrepaired after she'd sat on them accidentally. She'd decided that they didn't suit her. These days she might wear a lighter pair for reading; her distance vision was good enough.

Claire nodded. "I only put them on to appear pedagogically *suitable.*" A mild sense of discomfort worried through her. By now she was used to explaining what she "was doing" for her PhD. In fact, she had her response down pat, in a way that she believed would prove useful – eventually – after she'd submitted her thesis and was invited to defend it at the oral examination. Dr. Alex Gordon had stated that a likely early question was: "Tell us about your research in a couple of sentences." It was a technique favoured by viva examiners, deployed to invite the candidate to focus but also to relax. An easy one to start with, in other words.

She might have preferred questioning along such lines. *I'm exploring the psychology of collecting and collectors. I hope to explain the nature of the lure and the hook. Why do people want things to complete the whole set? What does it say about us, as a species?* A conversation about her eyewear, in a photo two years old, was less familiar territory to defend. On any given day, Claire did not have much of a thesis to discuss her fashion choices.

"Your hair's blonder now too," Amanda added. "Here's Feast Bridge."

The construction arched over one of the river's wider spots. Nearby was a pub named The Pilgrims. Swans and ducks glided in every direction.

"Unusual name," Claire mentioned. "Where does it come from, do you know?"

Amanda's answer did not miss a beat.

"It's because of the human sacrifices that took place here," she answered coolly. "That's the legend at least. Urban folklore. The water had stopped flowing for the seventh week, or something like that. The headwaters had stopped talking to the sea, hundreds of miles away. Breakdown of communication; no current flowing…"

"Wow. The river was arguing *with itself*?"

"Kind of. The compromise reached was the occasional human sacrifice – for the water to feed on and keep the current moving. Hence… Feast Bridge."

"That's amazing; I've never heard anything like that. You'd think there might be cause to *bury* a legend like that, wouldn't you?"

"How do you mean?"

"Well, I assume the area grew up and developed in the Sixties and Seventies. The story must pre-date the naming of the estate by centuries."

"Not at all, Claire. Corroborations exist as recently as the Second World War."

"That's just… frightening. I can hardly credit what I'm hearing."

"Of course… then there's the plaque," Amanda added quickly.

Given the context and her interlocutor, Claire's first thought was of dental equipment and the build-up of plaque on a patient's teeth. Try as she might, however, she could not square this information within the frame of the tale that Amanda had told.

"What plaque?"

"The little blue plaque on a post leading up to the bridge itself. The one that gives a different point of view."

"Why, what does it say?"

"The bridge was originally built on the donation from a local entrepreneur. James Feast. But there's no rule about which version we should believe, is there?"

The slipstream pulled Claire in several directions at once; if she'd worn a dress it would have tugged at its hem. By exploring Amanda's face, eye to eye, Claire felt the tension of a smile as it dragged open her own features and allowed light to splash inside.

"You were *bullshitting* me?" Claire asked, almost in awe.

Her acceptance unlocked the moment. Amanda burst out laughing; almost immediately Claire joined her – together they acknowledged the power dynamic inherent in the weaving of a story or a joke.

"Oh my *life*, you had me going there. Talk about poker faced! You could be an actor."

"I was, funnily enough, once upon a time," Amanda continued.

"…No you *weren't*."

"No I wasn't; you're right. Just a couple of minutes on from here."

"Here's the treasure trove."

Amanda, Claire, and Claire had arrived at a row of storage boxes, two horizontal rows of twelve containers, each approximately the size of a two-car garage.

"Box G3."

Although there were other people present, paying attention to other units, there was nobody close to Box G3. Amanda's fingers typed through a density of keys and fobs. A metal door opened with a squeak, and Amanda let them into the cuboid mausoleum. A musty smell slipped out from the unit.

While the lights flickered on, Little Claire knew exactly where she wanted to go. She skipped to her right and followed a path through shelving that groaned with boxes and dust.

"I'm going to play with *Awesome Load the Toad*," the girl stated.

"Some clockwork toys at the back," Amanda translated.

"I picked this up – believe it or not – at a car boot sale about fifteen years ago. With my mum and dad," Amanda added.

"You must have been very young to be a collector," Claire replied.

"Well, that's it exactly – I wasn't one. I had no idea what I'd picked up. Neither did the seller. It was on a small plot selling annuals and paperbacks and rock 'n' roll 45s. There was an old… what do you call 'em? Sort you'd use to paste wallpaper on. A *trestle* table?"

"It might be – I don't know."

Amanda smiled. "No, why would you? You've never put up wallpaper."

Although the comment was presumably a reference to Claire's comparatively tender years, the recipient felt mildly abashed at the insinuation that she would be unable to decorate a room. Claire noted her reaction and filed it in a section of things that were annoying about Amanda.

"It looked like a collection of brass bits and chromium steel. You can imagine why the seller might have thought it was junk."

"But if it was junk – or perceived as junk – why was he selling it?"

"For a profit, I suppose." Amanda shrugged. "It cost less than a cup of tea."

"What drew your eye to it?"

"A magpie's instinct. Shiny, shiny…"

The object under discussion was called a spoon excavator. When Amanda had shown it to Claire, the latter had impressed the former by exhibiting her knowledge of the tool's use. "It removes carious dentin," Claire had offered; Amanda had nodded in appreciation.

Less than an hour later, so encouraged was Claire on her egress from Amanda's presence that she stopped at Kirsty's Heels, near where she had parked the Fiat, in order to buy a pair of French shoes. Throughout the transaction, she smirked and kept hold of the backpack, inside which her new pieces (protected in bubble wrap) were stored.

She felt rich.

SESSION 7

I'm at a huge wedding celebration. There's food everywhere; I'm trying to eat.

John Hodgins walks past, and I ask him where he's been all these years (since we were children). He talks in a thick accent he didn't have when we were kids. He's depressed because his team is losing the game.

"Whose wedding is it? Can you tell?"

"...That's not what I was expecting you to ask."

"What were you expecting me to ask? 'Who is John Hodgins?' You've mentioned him before, Phyllie; and I don't doubt he's important, but for now – whose celebration was it? Could you tell?"

"No. No, it wasn't clear."

"Could it have been your own, from the past – distorted."

"Mine was nowhere near as big or grand as this one."

"That would be the distorted bit," the psychoanalyst, Dr. Chaz Bruce-Sange, explains to her analysand, Phyllie Reydman.

"I suppose it's possible. I didn't feel it was my own wedding," Phyllie replies.

"John Hodgins' wedding?"

"I don't know."

"Does the amount of food disgust you?"

"Not that I can recall. But something is preventing me from eating. Perhaps it's the sheer volume of it all – you may be right."

"Do you remember ever eating with John Hodgins?"

Phyllie shrugs. "Not at all. We probably swapped bites from our packed lunches. I don't recall much from my childhood days, to be honest. Bits and pieces."

"Let's go back to something most people can recollect," Chaz suggests. "What's your earliest memory of what you wanted *to be* when you grew up?" Chaz asks Phyllie.

"I was already grown up when I first had an inkling. I was going to be a teacher. The thing is, I was already training to be a teacher."

"And you don't recall any childhood dreams about your future profession?"

"No, I don't. Is it significant?"

Chaz mirrors Phyllie's earlier shrug. "At this stage, I can't say; but I would imagine there's a good reason why you're dreaming about a boy you left behind thirty-odd years ago."

Phyllie smiles. "What were *yours*, if you don't mind my asking?"

"My earliest career ambitions? That's an interesting *pas de deux*, Phyllie."

"Why do you suppose I might have asked the question?"

"You wanted to know what early impacts lead someone to become a psychoanalyst. The earliest thing I remember was wanting to be a fighter pilot."

"Seriously?"

"Older brothers. Very influential…" The smile on the psychoanalyst's face disappears gradually, like an aircraft's vapour trail. "Why do you think you dream about John Hodgins so much recently?"

Phyllie waits a long time before replying. She turns the words over in her mind, as if she is fumbling the good fortune from a lucky stone. *Are you trying to entrap me?* a part of her wishes to demand; but she knows the answer to such a question.

Not in the slightest, Chaz would respond. *What made you think that?*

Dr. Bruce-Sange would answer her question with another question. Phyllie is a link in an interrogative chain.

Now you're confusing me, Phyllie might complain. *What made me think John Hodgins was the key part of what I said or what made me think you were trying to entrap me?*

Throw your net wide, Phyllie, Chaz might reply. *Answer what you want to answer.*

During a previous therapy hour (in Session 4 or 5), Chaz had changed the subject abruptly, and Phyllie had told her that she – her analyst – was in a *twisty-turny mood.*

No, I'm not, Chaz had spat back at her analysand. *You are.*

But it's you who's asking the questions!

Exactly, Phyllie. The questions are merely the road. You're the one in the driver's seat. It's up to you which journey we take.

"Why do I think about John Hodgins these days? Because I abandoned him, I suppose," Phyllie forces herself to answer. "We all did."

DILUTING MAN

Bristling with a sense of localised disappointment, Twenny-four had decided that he wanted a second opinion. If the spiritual response had proved insufficient, perhaps something from the other end of that spectrum would be more to his taste: the *voice of science*.

He had decided to talk to Gray. The fact that Gray was in the grips of a skin condition, which – although very different from Carey's – was visually striking, was a connection that Twennyfour made later. Had he imagined (on an unconscious level) that Gray would know more about Carey if they both presented unconventional appearances?

Gray.

Oldest by far among the workers in the van (oldest, it had been mooted in private, by at least two decades) was the man known as Gray. Perhaps it was this maturity that lent Gray his air of wisdom and serenity. A softly-spoken man of slight build, he was known for his patience and his instinct for finding the right moment to drop his intellectual anchor; to proffer the donation to the ongoing conversation, around which the other men would swim for the duration of the discussion or debate – sometimes for the remainder of the evening, until the first to concede decided that it was time for bed.

Only one man, among those travelling in the van, knew that Gray's unfortunate skin condition was unrelated to his more advanced years. This man was Twennyfour; and the reason that Twennyfour knew that Gray had worn his skin complaint for many years was that Gray had paid a visit to the school that Twennyfour had attended from the age of five to the age of sixteen. Even then, when Twennyfour was nine, Gray's face had been changing colours. Coin-sized irregular patches on the man's face, arms, hands, and legs (the latter in evidence due to his wearing of knee-length khaki shorts) were thinning in colour, from the rich dark brown of wet fertile soil, to the colour of cloud cover.

Two decades later, of course – now, this evening – the effect appeared less remarkable than it had to a room full of nine-year-old children.

Twennyfour had overheard the occasional conversation on the subject of Gray. A theory had been propounded several times: that "Gray" was a long-held nickname, a reference to the shade that a high percentage of his skin had turned to. Twennyfour had not felt it his place to correct the suppositions under discussion.

"We had a man come to school today, Mama," Twennyfour had announced at the time. "A scientist."

"What did he talk about?" his mother had asked, making sure that her son knew he had her unalloyed attention. They drank warm milky tea together while the boy told his mother about his day in class. Mama feigned surprise: the parents had been advised of the scientist's educational visit weeks earlier.

"Viruses," Twennyfour had answered. He had practised the visitor's job title on the bus home from school; he had rolled the world around his mouth like a tough mint. "He's a *virologist*. He studies viruses and the diseases caused by them." Twennyfour had raised his left thumb: his sign to show that a list was underway. "He's worked on dengue fever, chickenpox, and rabies." A thumb and two fingers had been raised by this point. "*Plus...*" – a third finger – "he's *met the Queen of England*. He was made a Sir."

Mama had smiled. "Did *you* call him Sir?"

"I did... but he invited me to call him Gray. He said everyone calls him Gray. He said he doesn't stand on ceremony... and Koyrun made a joke and said *you knelt at the ceremony*, and some of us laughed, but some of the div kids didn't get it."

"Don't call your schoolfriends div kids, Twennyfour!"

"Sorry, Mama."

"...Did *Gray* laugh at the joke?"

Twennyfour had nodded his head. Months later, he had learned that Mama had already been aware of Koyrun's joke from Koyrun's father. Koyrun was a girl whose family had lived in the house five buildings down the street.

Twennyfour had placed down his mug of tea and fetched his schoolbook from his bag. While in class he had carefully copied a virus name that Gray had written in squeaky blue pen on this whiteboard. Standing before his mother, Twennyfour had proudly read his own research to Mama. "And the links he made with Japanese *encephalitis* virus." He had continued to read aloud what he had learned in class. "They are usually transmitted by arthropods, like mosquitos or ticks."

Mama had smiled broadly. "All this," she had said, "and you haven't even told me your guest teacher's name."

"Oh... *Professor Sir Grayson Twivy*. He's English."

"He *sounds* English!" Mama had replied. "I can't imagine how he could sound any *more* English! Or Scottish, for that matter..." The grin on Mama's face had been worth a king's ransom. "Come here, Twennyfour..."

Schoolbook in hand, Twennyfour had stepped in his mother's direction. They had embraced. (To the present day, Twennyfour could remember his mother's aroma. Mama had carried about her, at all times, the scent of dried herbs and spices.)

"I'm very proud of you, Twennyfour," Mama had mentioned.

"...Why?"

"For not mentioning Gray's skin condition first. For your enthusiasm, your keenness to learn."

Twennyfour had disengaged himself from the hug.

"How did you know about his skin condition?"

Mama had smiled. "The word got around," she had replied enigmatically...

Twennyfour remembered the piece of music that he and Mama had listened to together, directly after this discussion. It was Franck's *Symphonic Variations*, all sixteen minutes of it, with the Royal Philharmonic Orchestra, and Jorge Federico Osorio on piano. Twennyfour and Mama had played the piece twice. During the first recital, Twennyfour had conducted Mama, watching with acute attention her long brown fingers as they had tickled notes and struck chords from the edge of the kitchen sink. For the encore, they had swapped roles and responsibilities: Mama's conductor's baton was a toothbrush, and Twennyfour had played a plump arm of the family sofa.

Two decades later, Twennyfour had decided to talk to Gray. He strolled through a gloaming muggy and ticklish with evening insects.

The older man was reading by the light thrown out from a torch that he had balanced on his left shoulder. It was kept in place by the hood of his sweatshirt, with the drawstrings pulled tight. In addition to his having found an innovative way to read, Gray had also found an interesting place to rest his bones before going to sleep. He was sitting on one of the fold-away chairs from the van, and he had his feet up. His footstool was an abandoned piece of farm machinery, turned on its side; in the dimming light, the metal appeared a deeper shade than dark red – it seemed as black as spilled oil.

"I wish I could offer you a pew," Gray said, smirking. The light from the torch made his cheeks seem hollow, his face skeletal.

"You look comfy. What are you reading?"

"The *Journal of Virology*. I've subscribed for years now. I only read the *Journal of Virology* and Samuel Beckett these days. Do you happen to know what this thing is, by the way?" Gray tapped his heels on his metal footstool.

"It's called a towed roller," Twennyfour replied. "It flattens the soil. Obviously, this one has served its purpose."

"Didn't it deserve a civilised burial?"

"Apparently not. Coincidentally, the subject of abandoned things is what I wanted to talk to you about, as a man of science."

"Shall we walk and talk? I could do with a stretch of the legs."

"… Do you need a hand?"

"I do not. Let me wrestle my way to my feet." Watching Gray do so made Twennyfour uncomfortably guilty. "Do you know your Beckett? *Now that we know where we're going*, he writes in *Molloy*, *let's go there. It's so nice where you're going, in the early stages. It almost rids you of the wish to go there.* I'm ready, my brother; let's stroll."

"For a moment," Gray offered, after a long pause, "consider what you'd *like* to be true – and by *what criteria* you'd like it to be true."

"*Explicate*, brother."

"You do not doubt the evidence of your senses; am I right? What you see is present. What you hear is audible to others if they happen to be in the environment."

"Yes," said Twennyfour.

"Then it seems to me that you either accept what's presented to your sensory apparatus and say *she really was there*, with all of the implications of that reality; or you accept *she was there, but nothing to do with my senses*."

"Thank you for not doubting that I saw her."

"I don't doubt for a second there was something," Gray expanded. "What I believe you experienced was a *residue*. Something left behind in the abandoned dental clinic."

Gray smiled.

"Though a girl with teeth pushed into her skin is pretty *specific*," he continued. "Is it *possible* you were overwhelmed and lost consciousness?"

The two men were some distance from where Brother Joe had stopped the van for the night. In one direction – the direction that the men would continue to travel tomorrow – the night was not troubled by the least hint of light. In the other, the vaguest of brown tints flecked through the visual display.

"Allow me to mention your sister," Gray continued.

"It's fine to mention Twennythree," said Twennyfour. "It's nice to be reminded of her."

"What was she like when she was the same age as the girl in the dental clinic?"

Marking time and stalling, Twennyfour kicked at stones in the road. Had he been on stage, baton in hand, about to lead the orchestra, undoubtedly the spotlight would have been on him.

All other lights have dimmed. The rally of syncopated coughs in the audience has come to an end. Twennyfour faces the musicians and taps his baton.

"She had a friend called Koyrun at that age. They were inseparable. Where we lived in John Hodgins there was no real friction, at that time. As far as I can recall, the two girls played ... like two girls. Except for one thing ..."

Gray waited.

"She developed a gum disease. They thought she was going to lose all her teeth. They started to collect them. From others, I mean."

"To do what with them?"

Someone in the orchestra has bummed a note. One of the violinists – as beautiful as a sunrise over the mesa, for all violin players are beautiful – has strayed into an adjacent musical neighbourhood. Perhaps there is no turning back.

"The girls had a plastic doll," said Twennyfour. "They took turns looking after it – like parents in a custody battle."

"Do girls still play with dolls at the age of nine?" Gray asked.

To Gray's surprise, Twennyfour answered: "No. No, I don't think they do."

"Violin players are always attractive," Twennyfour states calmly to his audience through a microphone. "And this young lady is no exception." He smiles for several flashes in the darkness; strangers take his photograph. He is famous enough to warrant people wanting a picture. Each flash resembles a tooth in a maw, the size and depth of an auditorium.

"Ladies and gentlemen, may I introduce to you my older sister, Twennythree."

The round of applause is respectful.

As Twennythree crosses the stage, she smiles at her brother. Her mouth is empty; she has lost all her teeth. Will she be able to play the violin?

Everyone knows you need teeth to play the violin!

On opening his eyes, Twennyfour scratched around for a grip on reality. Soft light was in the sky; dawn approached. Twennyfour could see (and hear) the colleague who was physically the closest to him. Nearby, on an inflatable mattress similar to his own, Bruno Amitrano was snoring, lying on his back. At some point during the night, a corpulent *rat* had joined Bruno, and was now perched on the man's broad chest, warming itself on top of his sleeping bag.

Twennyfour blinked, trying to dislodge the image.

The corpulent rat now turned to Twennyfour… and *waved at him.*

The words that Twennyfour spoke seemed to come from another place; they did not seem his choices. He asked the rat: "How did you know my name?"

Giggling shallowly, Bruno stirred and mumbled: "What did you say?"

The rat took its cue and leaped off the man's chest and onto the ground. It scurried away as Bruno sat up and fumbled inside his sleeping bag for his glasses. After a few seconds, he opened the case and donned his specs.

"Why are you awake so early?" Bruno asked Twennyfour in a whisper.

"You had a rat on your chest."

"Is that a euphemism? Was the old chap big and proud?"

Twennyfour did not follow Bruno's flight of fancy, but he knew what *euphemism* meant. "No, brother; an actual *rat*. It waved at me."

"Yeah, right it did. Have you got any water?"

The two men walked towards the van so as not to wake anyone up. They shared half a bottle of cool water, and while they were doing so, Bruno added:

"You must have got in my head when you asked us about the girl you saw. I had a dream about an ex of mine and *she* was called Carey too."

"In the dream?"

"No; I used to go out with a girl named Carey," said Bruno.

INK ON AN EMPTY STOMACH

———•◦•———

"It is best to think of us, if at all, in sepia tones –
with a slight blur on the lens. That's what memory
is, after all: a changing of the hues and the accuracy
of our vision."

Brother Joe

THE BUDGERIGAR HARNESS
(BRUNO AMITRANO'S STORY)

"Sheelagh Carey," Bruno continued. "*She* for short. *She* to her friends…"

Bruno stopped talking: for one banana, two banana, three banana, four. A grin crept up on his features; it *sidled in*. He had remembered something about the woman in question.

"She was *quirky*, to say the least. Unexpected things would wind her up. Like, she got a real bee in her bonnet about the word *outside* – in the Christmas song "Let It Snow"? 'Well, the weather outside is *frightful*…' – and so on. She said the word *outside* is totally redundant. 'Where else would the weather be? Weather's *always* outside.' And of course, I'd smile along to start with. 'Tis the season, you know? – it was Christmas. But then she'd keep going *on* about it. Kept singing the line, over and over. 'Of course, the *bloody weather's outside*' – and you could feel her getting *meaner* as the day went on. By dinner, she'd be silent. She'd stew herself into a combat she was having with herself… As a mere *example*, you understand."

Twennyfour exhaled. "A point of order, if I may? Weather is *not* always 'outside'... though it might be frightful. We have emotional weather as well."

Bruno acknowledged the point with a sideways dip of the head. "That's a philosophical stance for another day." Having fetched from a pocket the various required accoutrements, he set about constructing a cigarette. "Want one?"

"No thanks."

"I'm not helping you understand your vision, though, am I?" Bruno continued. "But maybe this will. Do you know what *pseudologia fantastica* is?"

"It sounds medical – but no, I don't."

"Compulsive lying, in a nutshell." Bruno exhaled with a hiss that reminded Twennyfour of how his sister Twennythree had used to smoke. "Not an honest thought crossed Sheelagh's mind. Used to lie to me all the time. On a *sociopathic* scale." He laughed.

Although he was by no means certain that he wished to wander down this particular Memory Lane (he was getting tired), Twennyfour knew the rules of polite discourse.

"Do you want to tell me about it, brother?" he asked, attempting to rinse the weariness from his words.

Bruno's grin bloomed. "She'd swear to you black was white, just for the sport of it. She'd forget what she said and trip herself up – and I mean *often*."

He shrugged. "But what do you do? I loved the girl. I listened and learned. Even when she was tricking me. You see, I'm basically a gullible man."

"But you're going to tell me something went wrong," said Twennyfour; "otherwise, what's the point?"

Amusement washed through Bruno's features. "Tell me. Are you one of those who enjoys people-watching?"

"I must be. Aren't we all collectors of people's stories? Isn't that why we're here?"

Bruno smiled. "I'm not entirely *sure* why we're here, but that's a different story. I'm talking about watching – only watching. Interaction *verboten*. Collection *verboten*."

"Creating our own stories from what we observe."

"Not even that. Just looking."

"Then I'd have to say no, brother. By that criteria – no, I'm not much of a people-watcher," said Twennyfour."

"*She* was – Sheelagh, I mean. She loved nothing more. Apart from lying."

"We met at a tattoo convention in a town in the southeast. You could smell the ink in the air, half a mile away. If tattoo ink was addictive, you'd have about a thousand people getting high or overdosing for a weekend – not including the people who live nearby."

Bruno appeared apprehensive and twinkly.

"We both worked in the industry, though I didn't know it at the time."

At which point, Twennyfour spoke. "If it's not asking the obvious... what's a tattoo convention?"

"It's where you have artists and fans together in a big venue – some people there for business, selling their wares (like I was); some people there to show off what they'd had done. There's no such thing as modesty at TattCon, believe me! The organisers have to keep the temperature sky-high – just to cope with all the nudity on display."

"Not *total* nudity, surely?" asked Twennyfour.

"No, of course not; but plenty of beachwear – that kind of thing. Women showing off the artwork on their breasts and lower backs… Anyway. I was doing a demo. All miked up, talking to an audience of about *twelve* – about blends and feathering: the tricks of the trade. I was buzzing a budgerigar onto a man's left shoulder – he was getting it for free, to be part of the demo. He bit my hand off."

"Sheelagh was in the audience?"

Bruno nodded. "Watching me like a sparrowhawk."

"Asking questions?"

"Yes. Making the exhibition *work*, to be honest."

A pause had descended. Taking initiative as a compass, Twennyfour offered: "What lie did she tell you, brother? It's clearly on your mind."

"She told me about the budgerigar harness."

Twennyfour smiled. "I can't help but be obstructive. There are two words in your answer – two words at least! – I don't understand."

"…Do you know what a budgerigar is?"

"That's *one* of the culprits."

"A small exotic bird. A house pet," said Bruno Amitrano.

"And the harness?"

"…How do I describe a harness, mate? It's like a straitjacket. If *that's* any help!"

"Oh. Well, I know what a straitjacket is!"

She is Bruno's new girlfriend and expectations are high. Bruno has put her through a period of training – identify and name – using photographs and cards that he has paid to have laminated near his tattoo studio.

She has learned fast. Shown a photo of Jacqui, she can say: "Jacqueline. Your second cousin on your father's side. Married to Gavin. Two grown-up children. Ronni – Veronica – and Fulton. She works in a dentist's reception office."

On the long runup to the wedding that they must attend, She has stopped bothering to ask why she must be script perfect about Bruno's family, all the way down to married changes of surname and children's ages.

"A wedding's a big deal for us," Bruno has explained a dozen times. "We're an old-fashioned family. Conservative's an *under*statement… especially with my mum and her sisters. Now, who's this?"

He would show her another photo.

By the day of the wedding, She is ready to recognise – and converse with – the relations of Bruno with whom she is not yet acquainted, believing that she knows them better than her own far smaller, and considerably more left-wing, clan. (She has a sister named Claire and two parents in two separate towns.) She feels as though she has resat her Finals seven times in the previous week. Not only does she arrive at the Registry Office exhausted, she is irritable in a formal dress a shade too tight for her large frame, and her forearms itch as a result of the grey jacket that she has felt obliged to wear to cover her tattoos.

The ceremony passes beautifully; hymns are sung, and the Lord's Prayer is recited as a reminiscing hum. "You're doing grand, Sheelagh," Bruno whispers during the happy couple's signatures; and She replies, "I really need a cigarette."

Not even Bruno is aware of how much water She has had to pour on the flames of her fondness for alcohol since they started out; but he understands her requirement for nicotine. To a certain extent, as an ex-smoker himself (for the time being, at least), he empathises with his girlfriend's desire. "Can you wait till the reception?" he whispers. "It'll look strange."

"I know."

The celebrants in the two hundred-strong party mainly travel on foot from the church to The Hotel Harlequin, three-quarters of a mile away. This is where the celebrations will take place and where most of the guests have stayed the previous night and will stay tonight.

Somewhere between the unveiling of the buffet and the DJ's opening address, She acknowledges that if she cannot have a third glass of wine then she must be able to light up a smoke outside.

Although it is not as dark as she might have preferred, it is a relief to step into the comparative cool. As she strides away from the building, searching for a place where she might hide, She tastes the salty flavour of nicotine expectancy. Ago-nizingly, it is like approaching a station while aboard a slow moving train. In the end, with desperation coagulating, she hikes over to a far corner of the car park, beyond the wedding limousine, where she casts a glance over her left shoulder and, seeing no one in her wake, rams her way into a threadbare copse of six-foot vegetation.

She sighs.

It is while enjoying her third consecutive smoke, with the dependency withdrawing like a tide, that she glances down and spots what has lain by her right foot all along. Snug on a pillow of dropped leaves is a mobile phone, which she picks up. As soon as she is ready to do so, she carries the phone back to The Hotel Harlequin.

The DJ's announcement of a lost phone having been located produces no takers. The object remains on the table, adjacent to She's dinner plate, for the next half-hour, before she tells Bruno that there might be clues in its photo gallery, at which point she turns the old model on and waits for the screen to fill up with icons.

"Do you know where there *really* might be clues?" Bruno enquires. "At Reception, babe. Hand it in. The Reception staff might have been told."

"All right, I'll hand it in. If this doesn't work."

Many times – even in their short relationship to date – has Bruno stood among the foothills of an uphill climb of daunting gradient – a visual metaphor that he adopted to represent how it is to convince She of a contradictory viewpoint. With little conviction, therefore, he tries again:

"It's not *yours*, She."

To which Sheelagh grins. "Well technically, it's not *anyone's* right now, is it?" she asks him, at which point Bruno abandons his appeal to fair play and turns to the practical.

"You'll need a *password* at least, *surely*," he suggests; but this caveat turns out not to be the case. It seems that the phone's owner is not security conscious.

On the brink of opening up the photo gallery, however, She is interrupted by one of Bruno's uncles. ("Uncle Maurice. Second-time married to Simone. Two grown up from the first marriage. Boy of four from the second. Works in something to do with aviation fuel.") Uncle Maurice invites She to dance to an Abba medley of substantial length and acoustic volume. Although Sheelagh's musical tastes lean towards darker material, she knows her place on this happy occasion, and accepts the offer.

For the time being, the phone is forgotten.

Two hours later, full of finger food and with She on the acceptable side of inebriation, she and Bruno retire to their tiny room upstairs. It rocks and squeaks as they make love. It is not until after midnight that She runs a bath, with Bruno snoring soundly beneath a sheet and a towel (the room is too hot for the duvet). While the bath fills, She turns the phone on again, hoping that its battery will endure.

Bathwater crashes as She sits on the edge of the tub, a fine warm spray teasing the sparring mitts of her amble buttocks. As she opens the photo gallery, she is glad that she chose to take the weight off her feet: the pictures drain her legs of strength as swiftly as the bathtub swells with its scented tide.

"Why, brother? What did she find?" asked Twennyfour.

The photographs show the first dead body that She has ever seen.

She makes no sound as she thumbs her way through the collection. The victim was stabbed repeatedly, presumably using the same knife that sticks from her sternum in the majority of the captured poses. Her throat has been slashed. She was in her late thirties, in She's opinion. When she finally utters something, it is not a word in any language; it is a grunt of sickened recognition, about to be repeated when She jumps at the sound of Bruno knocking on the other side of the door.

"Can I come in?"

Bruno enters the bathroom and waves at the steam. "Don't burn yourself," he adds. "You could boil a lobster in that." With which he stretches his penis briskly and urinates like a race-horse. "You look as white as a blizzard."

"Tell me I'm not going mad," She implores him. "Take a look at these. But brace yourself first."

"Did you take them tonight?"

"It's the phone I found in the bushes. I don't know what to do."

Bruno walks the phone into the bedroom. Sheelagh abandons the hot breath of the collected water and stands beside Bruno, who has perched on a stool in front of an *escritoire*. He is strumming through photos, a noncommittal expression on his face.

"It was about the fourth picture," She explains. "The one taken from further back?"

"...Yes?"

"Well, don't you recognise it, Bruno?"

"I must be drunker than I thought." Bruno turns the phone in Sheelagh's direction so that she can see what is on the screen. "They're on holiday, babe. I think it's Venice."

"… I need a burn. I can't handle this," says She.

"You can't handle *what* exactly?"

"The murder pictures," Sheelagh replies calmly.

"…The *what* pictures?" Again, Bruno starts thumbing, slowly, all the while providing a commentary on his interpretations. "Venice – yes. Venice, Venice – it's the canals, She!"

"Keep shuffling, Bruno," She continues.

"Are you sure this can't wait till the morning? You were about to have a *bath*."

"I saw some photos, Bruno – on *that phone* – of a woman who looked a bit like me – with a knife in her front and covered in stab wounds."

"Well, I'm sorry, She, but I see… a cat, cat, cat, cat… statue, train, bloke who looks like me but with massive sunnies on, cat…"

"I must have started at the back of the gallery then," She tells him.

"Show me."

"I don't think I can look at them again." Sheelagh seems to snap herself out of something that had pinched her tight. "It was just the shock, Bruno – sorry. It's bath-time for Bonzo."

Nodding his head, Bruno answered: "I think that's best. You won't mind if I have a doze, will you? I'm knackered. Too much brandy."

Sheelagh smiles. "Doze away, mate. I'm still too wired up from the Abba medley."

"Good girl. And that phone's going under my *pillow*, by the way. We'll do what we said we'd do and hand it in at Reception, but when we wake up, okay? We should have done it before we left the dancing and the barbecue."

"I forgot to," Sheelagh lies.

Neither Sheelagh nor Bruno closes the curtains before dropping into bed, and when the phone rings under Bruno's left ear, the hour is early and the mercury light of pre-dawn is nudging into the room.

Bruno wakes up with the following words in mind.

Budgerigar harness.

"I need to explain the budgerigar harness reference," said Bruno to Twennyfour.

"I think that would be helpful."

"It started as one of Sheelagh's fibs. We hadn't known each other long, and we were walking in a park. She was trying me out. Little fib. Slightly bigger fib."

"Like what?"

Bruno smiled. "Like *both* her parents had been keen amateur boxers. Her brother ran a hemp farm in Pakistan. And then we moved to the budgerigar harness. She said, when she was a girl, during the summer months, she used to go into the back garden of the family home and read a book. Her mum used to take the budgies out there as well, for the fresh air."

Twennyfour nodded.

"And *I* said, quite reasonably, I thought, *I'm surprised they don't fly away.* And Sheelagh didn't miss a beat. She said, *Oh, we put the birds in a little harness on a lead. They can fly around in a circle to get some exercise, but they can't get away.* And *I* said something like, *That's amazing. I never knew that existed.* And of course, She *erupts* with the chuckles. Turns out, there's no such thing as a budgerigar harness. She meant, they took the birds outside *in their cage*, with the door firmly fastened. Well…

"…It got me thinking. What if the stuff about the murder photos was another budgie story, shoving me towards a boundary? Never mind the *why* for the minute. What if Sheelagh was having me on, for reasons of her own."

"And then the telephone rang," Twennyfour prompted.

Bruno nodded his head; with one single-syllable exclamation, he seemed to clear both his throat and the path back to the memory.

LEWSEY FARM is displayed on the phone's screen.

Bruno sits up and swings his legs to the side. "Hello?"

"I'm calling from Lewsey Farm," a woman's voice informs him. "You're late."

Bruno looks over his shoulder at Sheelagh; she's been fossilised in a complicated sediment of duvet, bed-runner, damp white towels, and discarded clothing. Her exhalations are heavy and regular. As is her frequent preference, She had left the bath and moved straight to the sheets, naked and wet. Such skin as Bruno can see is either milky white in the pre-dawn glow, or darkly mysterious with tattoos as hard to decode as hieroglyphs. Bruno decides not to move off the bed in case he wakes her. He will keep his voice low and sit still.

"I'm not who you think I am," Bruno tells the voice, having inferred that the caller had indeed expected a man to pick up the call.

The protest goes some way to amusing his interlocutor. With a lightness in her voice, she responds: "Well, none of us are!" and chuckles gaily. "Not here we're not."

Bruno tries again. "I mean to say, I found your friend's phone. Or *someone's* phone. I'm at a wedding for the weekend. My girlfriend found the phone."

"I'm calling from Lewsey Farm," the woman repeated. "Doesn't that mean anything?"

"We're at The Hotel Harlequin. Whoever you're trying to reach is either here now or was at some point recently. The phone was in some bushes."

For the first time, Bruno wonders what Lewsey Farm might be. The caller had said that she was calling *from* there: it is not the name of a person.

"Where are you now?" the caller asks… and does Bruno detect a subtle change in her tone. "You're late – and they'll be here any minute!"

"I'm sorry, but I'm not the one you think you're talking to!"

"That's what they all say," the caller responds, her voice having altered once more. She has gone from angry to panicked to disappointed, all within the space of a few exchanges.

Taking this turn to the conciliatory as an invitation, Bruno grows in confidence.

"I can leave the phone at Reception," he offers, "or I can meet you at Reception and hand it to you directly. Then you'll see I'm not who you think I am."

The caller laughs. "Hark at *Bruno,* so masculine all of a sudden!" she scoffs.

"...*What* did you say?"

"We know *exactly* who you are, Bruno, so lose the testosterone and the peacock feathers, would you? *I am calling from Lewsey Farm.*"

"Yes, you said that. Who *are* you?"

"Get some clothes on. Walk upstairs to the Dorothy Anthony Room. Right now."

Although Bruno's half of the conversation had not woken Sheelagh, his movement in the hotel room does.

"What's going on?" She wants to know.

"Someone rang me on the phone you found. She wants to meet me."

"*Now*? It's not even five a.m." Sheelagh straightens her spine; it crackles like crossed wires. Sitting up and rotating her way from under the duvet is as smooth a movement as any performed at a competitive gymnastic level. "You are *not* going on your own, mate."

Bruno's chest is an orchestra. The kettle drums are enthusiastic. For a moment he halts and takes stock of his action of dressing. "Why not?"

"Because it's *odd,* that's why not!" Sheelagh tells him. "Have you checked the pictures this morning?"

Not many minutes earlier, the call had pulled Bruno from a comfortable sleep. Until now he has cushioned himself against the conversation of a few hours prior.

"Check the gallery, Bru," Sheelagh says quietly. "There were stills there, straight out of *The Hills Have Eyes*."

Despite the fact that the reference means nothing to Bruno, he is attuned to his girlfriend's impension.

"The caller said *now*," says Bruno.

"And *I'm* saying, slowly slowly. Catchee monkey..." She has left the bed and is taking the few steps necessary to the door into the bathroom. When Bruno had got around to booking their accommodation for the wedding weekend, The Hotel Harlequin's larger rooms had long since been taken by members of the wider family. The room that Bruno and Sheelagh are sharing is on the poky side.

Experiencing nostalgia, Bruno watches his girlfriend step into the bathroom. She leaves the door wide open. Under the insistent glare of the room's illumination (as bright as a sunset), Sheelagh stands nude in front of the sink. She leans into the mirror.

"...But what if there's *not* a monkey?" Bruno asks, having spent a few seconds wondering how best to articulate his doubts.

Could it be that Sheelagh has arranged one almighty prank to play on her boyfriend? And if so, *why* would she do it, and why now? Bruno is aware that She had not much enjoyed the weeks of training that he'd put her through. Could this stunt be some sort of revenge?

(Why didn't she wake up when I was on the phone?)

Sheelagh shrugs and squints for better clarity before she inserts her contact lenses. "Then we'll catch the budgie instead. There's *something* to catch, wouldn't you agree? I need five minutes." Sheelagh faces Bruno: full frontal, big-boned, and beautiful; her skin marked in the most wonderful ways, with hours of dedication and pints of tattooists' inks...

"To do what?"

"Christ, Bruno. To use the lav and put on some fresh underwear."

Sheelagh closes the bathroom door.

"I don't want you to come with me!" Bruno calls in her direction; and then, inspiration strikes. "*She called me Bruno.*"

"Wonderful. So what?" Sheelagh calls back.

"It's one of my cousins, having a laugh! It's bloody Violet, that's who it is!"

"Violet was as hammered as the rest of your brood, mate. She'll be sleeping it off right now. As *we* should be! Check the phone's gallery. At least let me know I'm not losing my marbles."

Instead of moving to do so immediately, Bruno completes his dressing.

Sheelagh flushes the toilet. She will emerge in seconds.

Bruno opens the phone's photo gallery.

Twennyfour was tired and part of his brain was ferreting and snuffling for sleep; it wanted to close down for the night. But *another* part of his brain – the inquisitive part, the section that contained his instincts for preservation – was keen to hear the conclusion of Bruno Amitrano's anecdote. Why was this? Not least because Twennyfour liked to observe patterns and signs. Bruno had described Sheelagh's observation of photos that depicted a stabbing. The group in the van was *en route* to a town named Scent of Knife. Twennyfour was known to read such coincidences as signs. They seemed important.

"What did you find?" Twennyfour asked… though a part of him already knew the answer to the question.

"I found something hard to look at," said Bruno, in a distant, dreamy manner.

"They were there all along, She. Sorry. After the cats and the statues."

"Sorry you doubted me?"

"…If you like," Bruno replies, recognising his girlfriend's need to win.

"How many did you see?" Sheelagh asks.

"How many photos?"

"No, how many *pixies* – in the woods. Yes, photos."

"About five."

"And you saw her clearly. I wasn't imagining it."

"You weren't imagining it. Are you ready?"

"I think so." Sheelagh's voice betrays her indecision and nervousness.

Bruno asks, "Have you got your phone?"

"You're holding it."

"No, *your own* phone. Have you got *your* phone?"

Sheelagh picks her phone up from the *escritoire*. "Why will I need a phone?"

"We don't know what we're going to find up there; that's why."

"Up where?"

"She said, go up to the Dorothy Anthony Room. *Up* to the room, She. So she knows where I am, wouldn't you say?"

At this point – with the two adults wobbling on this precise pivot – the telephone in Bruno's hand rings again. In no way is Bruno surprised to read the words LEWSEY FARM.

He answers the call and thumbs the megaphone icon to operate the speaker function. He wants the conversation to be heard by Sheelagh as well.

This time the woman's voice is combative.

"Dead women are no more patient than living ones, you know," he is told.

"*Dead* women?" Bruno repeats, noting the alarm on Sheelagh's face.

"Well, *stabbed* women, specifically," the caller continues. "It really *stings*."

Bruno's breathing has deepened; pinpricks of sweat have appeared on his forehead. Beneath the clothes that he had worn for the wedding – hastily pulled on again in recent minutes – his skin feels stuffy and dirty.

"Are you saying she's there with you upstairs? The woman in the photos."

"Silly goose! I'm *saying*, I *am* the woman in the photos! You did me in good and proper, copper!"

Helplessly, Bruno repeats: "Copper?"

The months of training have not been wasted or spent in vain. Sheelagh processes the information in seconds. A copper is a policeman, therefore...

"Your Uncle Vincent," She offers. "Divorced from Geraldine. Four children."

Bruno and Sheelagh have moved to the door. Realising his mistake as he articulates it, Bruno protests into the phone's smooth surface: "I'm not Vincent! I'm Bruno!" Immediately, he knows that he might as well have skimmed a stone across a lake.

The caller laughs at him – and disconnects.

"We travelled north, as it were, through the building."

And then... thought Twennyfour. An image fluttered on his mind's breeze. He wondered if he could press pause on this story and recommence it after he'd slept, as if Bruno might be a recording made for their leisure hours. It was an oddly persistent image.

"May I join you, brothers?" asked Paper Jake O'Donnell, from a few metres to their side. The young man displayed the body language of one who had already calculated that he'd be made welcome.

"Sure," said Bruno Amitrano.

"I'm just about going to bed," said Twennyfour. It was not meant as a knockback to Paper Jake; more, as a hurry-up to Bruno Amitrano. *Get on with the story!*

"What are you lads chatting?" the new arrival wanted to know.

"A hotel story," Bruno answered.

Don't ask him to start it again!

"Oh, I've got one of them," said Paper Jake. "*More* than one. Were you sleepwalking, by any chance?"

"Nothing like that. Moving towards a room we were told to visit."

"What do we do when we get there?" Sheelagh asks.

"We go into the room," Bruno answers. "What else?"

They have reached the right floor. The door cannot be far away.

"She might not let us in."

"Then I'll break down the bastard. What are you getting at? She *invited* us."

Footsteps are smudged in the beautifully carpeted hallways. Other sounds are non-existent. Sheelagh and Bruno might as well be walking on the Moon.

"This is the room," says Bruno. A nameplate reads "The Dorothy Anthony Room" in a style of ornate font that customers sometimes ask him to needle into their skin.

The door has been left wedged open by a pair of socks; although a crack of light is visible from the carpet to the top of the door, it is too narrow to reveal anything.

If they want this story to end, they will have to enter.

"I went in first."

Paper Jake O'Donnell was swift to interrupt.

"Was there an aroma about the room? What did it *smell* like?"

Twennyfour felt mildly affronted. The other man had taken over the responsibility of a participative audience member that he, Twennyfour, had been executing, a matter of seconds earlier.

"I don't remember a particular smell. Like blood, do you mean?"

Paper Jake straightened his head on his neck. "No, I didn't mean *blood*. What on earth've you guys been discussing? I just remember noticing a smell that made me realise: *this is not my room*. When it happened to me, like."

Both Bruno and Twennyfour were confused. "Not right now, though," Paper Jake added. "Sorry to poke my oar in. You were saying…"

The woman on the rumpled, dark-stained bed linen is the woman in the photos on the phone: both Bruno and Sheelagh recognise her immediately.

Fully dressed and awkwardly posed, she is on her back, her legs slightly spread; her right arm reaches up for a spiritual high five and the other has been left with her forefinger pointing at the bathroom. Over her black tights, she is wearing only one of a pair of flat purple shoes. She might have attended the wedding. In fact, she *must* have attended the wedding: a fascinator is on the bedside table nearest the woman's head; on what other occasion might a woman wear a fascinator?

"Oh my God," Sheelagh breathes near Bruno's ear.

Even from half a room away, it is clear to Bruno that the fasci-nator has been dotted with blood. Blood is furthermore smeared on her face, on her wedding-appropriate attire; blood colours the lemon-hued bedclothes. There is blood on the wallpaper; blood even on the ceiling at which the victim sightlessly gazes.

The knife that presumably made the hole in the woman's midriff is on the bed. It points in the same direction as her life-less left forefinger: at the bathroom.

"Call the police, She," says Bruno.

"No, *don't!*" shouts the woman on the bed – at the same time as the bathroom door opens…

"She was *alive?*" asked Twennyfour. "After all that?"

"Consider yourself well and truly *pranked,* they told us," said Bruno. "I was furious."

Twennyfour was nonplussed. "All a *joke,* brother?"

"One massive set-up from start to finish," Bruno agreed, nodding his head.

"But why? What were they trying to prove?"

"Nothing! It was a *game* for them, mate. They couldn't even be sure anyone would find the phone, could they?"

While the two men exchanged Q&A, Paper Jake O'Donnell shook his head. In a voice too quiet for the moment, he added, "I can't *tell* you how close this is to something I want to share."

"They were part of the wedding party, then, after all?" Twennyfour continued.

"No. *They lived at the hotel.*" Bruno shrugged, as though acknowledging his moral defeat. "They took out long-term leases in hotels around the country and devised stupid dares with long odds, to up the ante every time. They were *bored with only having money*. The task was to belittle people – *ensnare* people. If Sheelagh hadn't found the phone that night, *someone else would've* found it a different night."

Twennyfour paused for a moment.

"But wait a minute. She called you Bruno, you said. She knew your name."

Again, Bruno shrugged. "When I say *lived* there, I mean they had *jobs* there as well, sometimes. Light duties around the grounds; that kind of thing. They were a couple of wealthy troublemakers, with nothing better to do. The *husband*? – he's the one who put together the Abba medley! How hard would it be to mingle and ask a few questions? We'd been to Reception to make enquiries. All they had to do was *check*."

Twennyfour rose to his feet.

"What did she look like?" asked Paper Jake O'Donnell. "The woman pretending to be dead. How would you describe her?"

In his fantasy, Twennyfour is clean and shaved; he wears a tuxedo, and the orchestra hangs on the merest twitch of his baton.

What did you think when you entered that abandoned dental clinic?

Twennyfour breathes through the question; he does not wish to rush his response. At length, he seems to agree with himself and nods his head.

I thought it one of the saddest places I've ever seen, *he answers.*

Good, *the voice tells him.* That's what you're supposed to think.

"PLAY LIKE A MAN WITH TEN THUMBS"

"I'm clumsy," he answered. "I play like a man with ten thumbs."

Play what? she wanted to ask him. *What exactly do you play?*

Claire Carey awoke with this silly sponged-up dream in her consciousness. It looked and felt messy; it seemed even more incomplete than many of the fragments that she was often left with. Parenthetically, she wondered how much had not made it over the consciousness parapet. How much was still back there, where the grass grew down, and the wipe-out blankness was something to see.

Someone in her dream had spat at her, "You querulous little *twat!*"

A different person had told her, "Last night I dreamed of a girl made of teeth."

Engagement with the decryption process took Claire from the bedroom to the shower. One of life's reluctant pleasures was a scalding shower during the days of menstruation. For one more month, she could dismiss her menses in a wave of heat. *Be gone!* Claire watched some of her blood dilute and swirl. *Good riddance to bad rhubarb chutney.*

She was set to meet her PhD supervisor this morning. At one of their initial meetings – when they'd circled one another, neither of them confident to be traversing the terrain ahead – the supervisor had advised Claire not to seek perfection.

"Play like a man with ten thumbs, would be my suggestion."

"A *man* with ten thumbs?" Claire had repeated.

The supervisor had not picked up on the nuance. He had nodded his head. "Be clumsy; make a noise." He had been on a roll by this point. "Forget about pitch for the moment. Say *balls* to adequate tuning!"

"Yes, I think I get the idea," Claire had interrupted.

"Good. Until next month then?"

They had been engaged in conversation for a mere twenty minutes.

"What should I do in the meantime?" Claire had asked, her voice a trifle panicky. In her journal that night, her entry would reflect her status of travelling on a ship at sea, where she was a passenger who had paid for a first-class cabin... and the captain had jumped overboard, in a huff.

The supervisor had seemed displeased with the question.

"If you think supervision is about instructing you, Ms. Carey, I'm afraid I'll have to disabuse you of the notion. You will read until your eyelids feel heavy. You'll write gobbets of wisdom – and gobbets that will seem like gibberish the following day. You will..."

"Play like a man with ten thumbs," Claire had interrupted.

"Exactly. Or woman," the supervisor had belatedly reconsidered.

Having driven to the university town, Claire met her PhD supervisor at the agreed time, on the customary bench, near the bank of networked computers for postgrads that were rarely used, on the third floor of the Postgraduate Centre.

"I hope you don't mind if I eat," said Dr. Alex Gordon, in a manner that had become (to Claire) familiarly fidgety. "I had to rush out before breakfast."

Although the two of them had settled on the hour of the day for their monthly progress meetings, it did not seem to make much difference to Dr. Gordon's eating habits. Every time they met, he excused himself for what he was about to receive – without awaiting a response from Claire – and then cracked open a plastic 3D triangle containing a sandwich. The truth was, Claire resented her time being thought of as an academic pit-stop; a quick way to refuel between seminars, exam boards, and department meetings.

"Of course, I don't mind," Claire answered. "Shall I begin by explaining what I think has happened since we were last here?"

"What you *think* has happened. That's good," said Dr. Gordon, ripping into the packaging.

There's probably a study available – somewhere – on the choices we make while eating on the go, Claire would think later. For Alex Gordon, it was always the grey sausage, sliced lengthways, and laid to rest in the plastic coffin's white bread shroud. "The Sandwich as the Death of Ambition," Claire would consider. "The Sausage Sandwich as Defiance of Class Ideologies." "The Sausage as a Symbol of Freud's Reality Principle."

"Why do you say *think*?"

Claire wanted to answer with a phrase like "a reflective stance", but the words that she had prepared were pulverised by the sight of her supervisor's temples filling and then hollowing out while he chewed. At the beginning of their academic relationship, so alarmed had Claire been at the way the man's temples turned from concave to convex when he ate, that she had tested herself by eating a sandwich in front of a mirror at home. She had wanted to be certain that her own temples did nothing of the sort. Although she knew that it wasn't Gordon's fault, the sight was repulsive.

"I'm trying to keep a distance," Claire replied, "between my various states of perception and reality." *Yeah, that'll do*, she added internally.

"I'm pleased to hear this. Tell me more."

In truth, there was nothing to add: Claire had saddled up and ridden the old bullshit bronco – and now it had thrown her off its back. Simply for something to say, she decided to relay the story of her most recent visit to Amanda Billie.

Two days earlier, Amanda had gotten in touch by email.

Hi Claire!

I'm just about to list some items on the site. I thought I'd get in touch to offer you first refusal. Let me know if you're in the market for a Gingival Margin Trimmer and/or a Binangle.

Love,

Amanda xxx

Their business concluded, Amanda had offered to buy Claire a drink at The Pilgrims. "It's too nice a day to sit inside," she had said. "Let's chat by the water…"

Feast Bridge was busy that afternoon. Although the air was cool at best, the day was bright; saucers of luminosity bobbed and wrinkled on the surface of the river. Nearby, a Cuban band – of all things! – dished out tunes that it took Claire a while to realise had once been performed as heavy metal. It was while Claire tapped her toes to an overhauled "Run to the Hills" that Amanda told her:

"I'm a collector of other things too. Stories, mostly."

They had opted for zero-alcohol mocktails (Claire would still have to drive). Claire's libation was of a Kermit-green hue, with the viscosity of porridge. While dabbing some of its residue from her upper lip with a paper napkin, Claire volunteered a reply.

"Well, aren't we *all* that? Collectors of stories? We do it all our lives. We base our memories on the stories we've heard – or maybe learned. My thesis is only one example."

"I don't disagree," Amanda replied, "but I meant something different. I'm the sort who finds it hard to let a detail slide."

"How so?"

"I'm sure you can imagine. Do you *really* want to know all there is to know about a boyfriend's past, for example?"

"No, I never do. I make it a point of saying I'll never ask them about their history – it's none of my business – and I'll expect the same courtesy from them."

Amanda nodded. "I envy you. Having to know it all is exhausting – and time-consuming!" The addition was offered in a slightly raised pitch that suggested that it had come as a complete surprise, even to the speaker.

"Expensive too. The cost of knowledge is rarely cheap, in one way or another."

Amanda nodded again. "Nothing *vaguely* out of the ordinary is ever inexpensive."

"I'm not so sure about that."

"Take the stories my husband tells me, for instance," Amanda continued. "They are all about someone's success over difficult odds, or failure and sinking. The human cost is hard to measure."

"But that's the story itself. The *telling* costs nothing," Claire countered.

Amanda shrugged. "Roger goes away to help people in towns and villages I haven't heard of. That's a *nice* thing. But while he's doing good work *there*, things cost me more *here*. Not that I'm complaining. If he hadn't gone away this time, there's a reasonable chance I wouldn't have bothered to advertise the dental tools. Our paths might never have crossed."

"Indeed. So when you say *cost…* "

"Maybe *consequence* is a better way of saying it," Amanda agreed. "Would you like another mocktail?"

"Yes, please," said Claire. "You choose for me. What kind of stories does he send from abroad?"

Amanda had risen to her feet. "I feel I know more about the group's leader – Brother Joe – than about most other humans on the planet."

"*Brother* Joe? Is it a religious expedition?"

"Not as far as I know. The alpha male goes by the name of Brother Joe. He drives the van and he's cock of the walk, in Roger's estimation."

"What does Roger say about him?"

"Brother Joe collects *people*."

"My husband's ex-wife," said Amanda Billie, "is doing her PhD where you're doing yours."

"Really? What's her name? I might know her."

"Phyllie Reydman… Your grin tells me everything."

"I was in a study meeting with her at the start of this week. We get on well."

"So do we: she and I, I mean. It's a distant relationship, about as cordial as these things ever become, I suppose. Roger takes Claire to see her every third Saturday."

Claire smiled at what she was about to say next. Not only did it seem friendly and something akin to a gear-change in the conversation; it also cancelled out any sense of discomfort that she had begun to cultivate at knowing too much about Phyllie through channels of which the other woman might disapprove.

"It's a bit odd the two girls being Claire, isn't it? Do they get on okay?"

Amanda shook her head. "Sorry, you've lost me. *What* two girls?"

"Phyllie's daughter Claire and *your* daughter Claire. I've never known if that makes them half-sisters or stepsisters."

"No, Claire…"

"With Roger in the middle, I mean. As a father to both."

In the following moment, Claire understood that she had read the situation incorrectly. If Roger was the father in common, why would he have given both of his daughters the same forename, like a tribal branding?

"I might've given you the wrong impression, Claire," Amanda offered. "We are talking about the same girl. The same Claire. There's only one – the one in her bedroom right now."

"Sorry. I hope I didn't cause any offence."

"Of course not. The fact is, Phyllie had issues to resolve, way before I was involved with Roger. She basically said: I can't cope. And I think she originated the idea: the domestic arrangement. Claire would live with her dad. You see, Phyllie had a traumatic experience nine years ago – I can't see any point in sugar-coating the situation."

"I've never felt it my place to ask for clarification."

Amanda smiled. "I don't think Phyllie would get stroppy about anyone asking her to share her story. She's been candid about her emotional difficulties – and that nightmare at the Edlesborough house, nine years ago."

At the same that Claire and Amanda were discussing Phyllie Reydman, Phyllie Reydman was discussing herself – *with* herself.

The self in the mirror stares straight at Phyllie in the bedroom. The mirror image has a few words to say about the sloppiness of Phyllie's unmade bed. For now, however, the other draft of Phyllie holds her tongue.

*Exiting the bedroom – thereby turning her back on the twisted
bedclothes – Phyllie runs through what she hopes to achieve today.
It is just after eight in the morning; Phyllie has been awake for two
hours. It is time for her weekday half a grapefruit; she will eat this
(in a dispirited fashion) while listening to the news on the streaming device in her kitchen. She might add a dollop of Greek yogurt.*

*At nine-thirty she is due to meet Clare Carey at the university.
They will have a coffee and discuss the meeting with their fellow
postgraduate students that they will co-chair after lunch. Between
the meeting with Claire and the meeting with the university's other
students, Phyllie will walk for twenty-five minutes – from the campus to the home and workplace of her psychoanalyst, Dr. Chaz
Bruce-Sange.*

"Do you ever get the feeling that there's more than one
version of you occupying the same physical space?" *Phyllie
imagines the Good Doctor enquiring.*

"I hear voices in my head sometimes," *Phyllie answers – in
her head.* "I know that's not what you asked, but it's probably as
close an example as I have."

"Describe the feeling."

"It's not a *feeling* as such. I think of where I am and I'm
aware of someone else looking in on the scene. But not a *ran-
dom* anyone else. It's myself with a slightly different perspec-
tive. Older, younger… wiser, maybe. Always giving advice;
not quite in the first person and not quite in the objective third
person either."

"She doesn't say *you*? Or *we*?"

"She doesn't speak. I can sense her presence. Or smell her
coat or something."

"Her *coat*?"

"Little details like that. Hear her blinking. And it makes me wonder. Do we have finite space and infinite versions of ourselves to fit into it? How do we decide how to take turns with ourselves?"

"Do you mind if I raise a small objection to your theory?"

"Not at all: I want to be wrong."

"We have *loads* of space available – geographically speaking, I mean. Why would we crowd together?"

"But we *don't* have loads of space available. We can't expect our characters to live on the side of a cliff: we all have the same basic needs of food, warmth, safety, and so on. Or you might as well say we can live on the ocean floor!"

SESSION 9

It's a hotel in the country, somewhere. I'm there to find John Hodgins' "shredded" DNA (whatever that means). I'm in a messy room. A blonde woman's wearing pink pyjamas. We go outside. My daughter Claire is wielding a fifteen-foot dreamcatcher that keeps snagging on branches. Then I'm in a room with three elderly women presenters with strong Midlands accents. They are trying to teach me Geography techniques, but I can't understand them. They get nasty; the whole group turns on me.

Phyllie Reydman laughs briefly. The way she holds up a hand to cover her mouth puts Dr. Chaz Bruce-Sange in mind of a Japanese geisha, theatrically feigning modesty.

"The only thing conceivably unusual about him is where he would take me on dates. Everything else was what I've come to regard as *commonplace*."

Into the ensuing silence, Chaz adds: "I'd expect to be curious about your use of *commonplace*, but first…"

"You'd like to hear about the dates."

"I would indeed," Chaz agrees.

"He was into *waiting rooms*," Phyllie answers. "Medical and healthcare waiting rooms. For doctors' surgeries; opticians; dentists – the room turned him on."

"How did it work?"

"It was different every time. Sometimes we'd go for a drink first; other times, it was going in bareback – as he'd put it. Turning up at a dentist's or a doctor's or whatever, and taking our seats among the ill and inconvenienced."

"And you'd do what there?" asks Chaz. "Just wait to get busted?"

"In a manner of speaking. If you go into a larger clinic, there's a waiting room servicing the cancer specialist and the phlebotomist. We'd stay there for *hours*."

Chaz shifts in her seat. Phyllie can hear the older woman's discomfort – a rare show of the psychoanalyst's grubby feathers.

"I'm not sure I understand. You said it turned him on. Did you mean sexually?"

"Nothing obvious," Phyllie answers. "He wasn't getting hard, or anything like that – or at least, not as so's you'd notice. It was more a frame of mind. A comparison with the other waiting room."

"...And whatever became of him, do you know?" Chaz continues.

"Just another set of facial features I left behind. Bruno, his name was. Bruno Amitrano, bless him. What happened to him indeed."

Phyllie waits. She closes her eyes. She shifts gears and changes the subject.

"Nine years ago," she continues, "I didn't want to be defined by something negative. What happened in the Edlesborough house... happened. I can never reverse it. But I can – I knew I *could* – dislike it with the energies built into positive achievements. I spent a year on sick leave, which I managed to convince myself was a continuation of the torture. I don't even know how many times I tried to resign. I wanted to run away – even if the school had nothing to do with what had gone on."

"How would you have supported yourself?" Chaz wants to know.

"Emotionally?"

"Financially, I meant. I presume you were drawing a salary."

"With an enormous sense of guilt, I must say; but yes. It didn't hurt to be a subs-paying member of the Teaching Union, either. You'd think I would've been happy! But I just wanted to be left alone – to grieve."

"To mourn a life you thought had ended?"

Phyllie shakes her head. "To mourn a life that *had* ended. Yes. And although my *marriage* also came to an end, I have nothing but respect for Roger for while we were together. He tried his best. If the Teaching Union hadn't thrown its weight behind the school keeping me employed, Roger would have kept us going financially – to answer your question. He was a social worker in those days."

"And what is he now?"

"Same industry; higher up the ladder. He also goes on... missionary trips overseas. But I'm not sure what he does there, to be honest. We separated and agreed to sell the house. Fifty-fifty split of all goods and chattels."

"With the exception of your daughter. She lives with Roger and his second wife."

Nodding her head, Phyllie puts on a brave face of being fine with this line of questioning. "Fairly ancient history," she offers. "I miss her when I can't see her outside of designated times; but it was for the best. I couldn't cope."

Making the church-and-steeple of her hands and fingers, Dr. Chaz Bruce-Sange nods gently. A few beats of time pass. She seeks out light in the murky countertransference that exists between her and the analysand, and then she drifts into a new lane.

Phyllie continues to speak.

"Roger moved into the Feast Bridge area to spring clean his life – and to keep his bills low, presumably. It's a cheaper area than where we'd lived. We were both starting from scratch. Financially *and* emotionally."

"How were you informed that Roger was going to remarry?"

Phyllie snickers. "Pragmatically enough, by text. He texted me one day to say he hoped I didn't mind but he'd met someone he liked when he made a house call in the line of work."

"I'm not sure that's in the rules, is it?"

"Oh, he didn't fall in love with the old lady hoarding ice cream tubs! It was someone complaining about the conduct of one of her neighbours…" Phyllie shrugs. "Good luck to him, I say. Always trying to help someone out of a jam, that's Roger; and as far as I'm concerned, it was me who let *him* down, not the other way around. He's been a good dad to Claire."

"And Roger's second wife?"

"Amanda. Claire has nothing but nice things to say about the domestic set-up," Phyllie answers. "Everything's satisfactory."

Phyllie smiles. Briefly, Chaz smiles too.

"*Satisfactory* is less than a glowing endorsement," the psychoanalyst states.

"If you haven't already noticed, Chaz, after eight sessions together, I'm less than a glowing individual."

Although Phyllie is proud of the remark and her quick wit, Chaz's expression had returned to its former composure, and it remains set on professionalism now. Knowing the expression of old, Phyllie understands that she is expected to say more.

"Roger has a theory,' Phyllie continues, "that all women eventually marry their fathers."

"With respect, I think Freud might've come up with something along those lines first."

"Well, in my case, he was right, whoever it was. I married my father when I married Roger. They've even got the same name! That should've been a clue. I've been punishing myself for something ever since."

Phyllie is struck by a bolt of *déjà vu*. She is certain that she has said this before. Not just the general message, but the actual words in the order that they emerge.

"In what way, punishing yourself?" Chaz asks.

"Taking risks. Not settling to much of anything."

An image at the back of her mind slowly clears into an oneiric focus. She'd been talking to Vig! Her work colleague, her fellow teacher, her friend; the man she had loved from afar. Nine years before today – maybe closer to ten – Vig had made it big on the Lottery, and had bought a nice country pile, complete with a birdkeeper named Donald.

"What's amused you?" asks Dr. Bruce-Sange.

"I've just remembered a barbecue that a friend invited me to, before what happened at the horror house." Phyllie straightens her spine. "Before I was taken captive."

Dr. Chaz Bruce-Sange is thinking about the coordinates of psychoanalysis – how every encounter, during every fifty-minute therapy "hour" can be considered as the plotting of a node on a complicated graph. Once upon a time, she had intended to write about this; to decode the sensations to which she was subjected into a paragraph or two – or a chapter, perhaps, or an academic paper... *But when, Chaz, when?* The idea of the graph had occurred more than a decade earlier.

With the fountain pen weighty in her hand, she writes: *The x-axis demonstrates the progress of time, from the lowest recorded value (with t=0); and the y-axis demonstrates an ideation of counter-transferred happiness in the analysand.*

She glances up from a galaxy of ink spots sprayed onto the page of the hardbacked notebook, into which she routinely deposits her thoughts and reflective statements.

When Phyllie Reydman had offered the dream about John Hodgins' shredded DNA, what had she – Chaz Bruce-Sange – experienced?

No doubt about it: there had been something that felt like *jealousy*.

Relief is what Chaz experiences when her landline trills. She stands up and crosses the office to take the call. Her feet feel numb. She has sat still for hours. Noting the identity of the person calling in – DOUG STEGMEYER – she smiles at a recollection that swarms her consciousness. No doubt the association arrives because Chaz had discussed the graph on many occasions with Doug, but the image in her mind as she lifts the receiver is from a time even earlier than the graph's inception. Maybe *three decades* earlier – or not far from such a milestone – Chaz had asked Doug about negatives. They had lain between sheets clingy with exertion and perspiration. In those days Chaz had smoked. She had ignited her cigarette and said, "Right at this moment – what do you feel about Bion's notion of negative capability?"

"You filthy squaw," Doug had replied. "Foul-mouthed as usual with your dirty talk."

"I'm serious, Doug."

"I don't doubt it. What about it?"

"Bion talked about how we cope with not knowing something – the skill involved in abdicating the throne of knowledge, as it were."

"Negative capability, yes," Doug had agreed. "Following Keats. You seem keen to expand on your theme, so why not? By the time you've finished, my breathing should be back to normal."

"What do you do about *negatives*?" Chaz had enquired. "Not just negative capability: negatives in general. Bartleby the Scrivener: *I would prefer not to*. What do we ignore – or negate – when we offer our interpretations? It occurs to me, a parallel existence probably exists at the same time, where the opposites are true. Where what we *didn't* say in *our* reality was *actually said*, and the analysand developed in a completely different way."

"Good evening, Doug," Chaz says now.

"Hi, Chaz. How are you?"

"Not too bad. Without a word of a lie, I was just thinking about you. Do you remember when we discussed the possibility of anti-reality?"

"We discussed it more than once. I was developing my idea of saturated spaces. What's made you think about it now?"

"I'm trying to write."

At around the same time as Chaz had thought about the graph, she had typed the following words onto her computer screen: *Slipping through holes in the woodwork.* Then she had made the phrase into a title by capitalising some of the words. (A decade on, and she remains unclear about whether the *through* should have a capital letter or not.) Since that moment – when the phrase became a title – Chaz has had a name for the autobiography that she tries to start composing, every year or so. Warily viewing the approach of an important birthday – she'll be seventy in November – she has started the book once again.

"How's it going?"

"Twenty-one thousand words of scintillating gibberish," Chaz replies honestly. "My big bad insight this afternoon was – and I quote from memory – *The psychoanalyst's life is not for external consumption.* Then I thought: *So who's going to read this book, then? Why am I bothering?"*

Chaz carries the phone back to her desk. "How's your day been?" she asks.

"Well, that's why I'm ringing…"

Chaz always smiles when Doug says *ringing*. Although he moved to England from Iowa nearly half a century earlier – first to study, then to practice, then to nest – certain words and phrases still sound cutely *ironic* in his American accent.

"Some material I wanted to discuss – a client who amazed me. Are you busy?"

"Not particularly. I was only going to stop for a sandwich or a boiled egg for dinner," Chaz answers. "Do you fancy a glass of wine, by the river? We haven't been to The Pilgrims for a while."

"Feast Bridge it is," says Doug. "Sounds *lush*."

Decades earlier, a professional rivalry had developed between them, and grown teeth. In a town in which psychoanalytic material was in abundance, neither analyst could have claimed that the reason for their mirrored animosity was a struggle for analysands. There was plenty of work for both psychoanalysts. Indeed, there would have been room to move and air to breathe if the town had been a fraction of its actual size.

Instead of a spurious claim of other's wrongdoing in the securing of clients, therefore, both Dr. Bruce-Sange and Dr. Stegmeyer had relied on slurs regarding the other's technique and peer-reviewed contributions to academic journals. On the very rare occurrences that they had treated an analysand who had previously paid for the services of the other, a certain gloating note had been detectable in their sporadic email correspondence, which (in turn) would have seemed to be about something altogether different.

A potboiler novelist of the nineteenth century could not have contrived a less believable locus for the reconciliation between Chaz Bruce-Sange and Doug Stegmeyer. Of all unlikely places, they met by chance at a group therapy session, for the benefit of "the survivors" of problematic marital or long-term relationship breakdowns. Chaz had separated from her first (and only) husband, Kieran, and their daughter – although it was several years before she would fall under the spell of heroin – had displayed, with regularity, the early warning plumage of a wayward, self-defacing and ultimately problematic young woman as she had prepared herself to enter university.

Meanwhile, Doug Stegmeyer had twisted when he should have stuck, conjugally speaking. That final affair (of his wife's) had convinced Stegmeyer to ignore the advice that Marie had given him *gratis* at the commencement of their lifetime commitment to one another, six year earlier:

Never nag me, Doug. In fact, don't even prepare yourself *to nag me. I'll smell it on your breath.*

It was fair to say, therefore, that Marie had given Doug fair warning not to complain when he inevitably learned of his spouse's flings. But he *had* complained: he had given Marie notice of the termination of their marital contract. In addition to complaining, Stegmeyer had raised the emotional ante.

Regarding her husband's willpower as betrayal, Marie had packed two cases and phoned for a cab to take her to the docks. She had insisted that her reason for wanting to go there was no longer any of Doug's concern. After half an hour of intro-spective castigation, Stegmeyer had appreciated that Marie was right. In a far-too-jolly mood, he had leaned towards the driver's window and paid for his wife's twenty-minute journey upfront.

Marie was Doug's third wife – and the wife of the longest relationship duration. Vowing that there would never be a fourth, Stegmeyer had visited the therapy session for the sur-vivors of breakdowns, where he had been both appalled and appeased to encounter, no more than four chairs away around the arranged parabola, Chaz Bruce-Sange…

"I was just thinking about that time we met in the group therapy session."

"Our grand reconciliation," Chaz agrees with a nod of her head. "Sorry, I'm late. I couldn't get a taxi. Half the fleet is at the Bowl for the Springsteen concert."

"No problem, Chaz; I only just arrived." Doug stands up. "Is it warm enough to sit outside? Might be nice by the river for half an hour or so."

Chaz nods her head again. "Yes, it's just about okay. We can come back in if it gets chilly. Let's watch the narrow boats."

"And the ripples on the water! And the stars! What are you drinking?"

Chaz chuckles. "More to the point, what are *you* drinking? That cocktail is as *camp* as a pink handbag full of rainbows. What's in it?"

"No idea. It tastes like bubblegum. It's disgusting. I'll get a pint when I go to the bar."

"Brandy Mac, please," Chaz answers. "I'll nab a table."

Outside, the air is cool but not yet cold. Eddies of darkness coalesce above the river; the darkness hovers in trapeziums and parallelograms. A bat, either lovestruck or impossibly lost, makes helix shapes in the gloom between windproof candles under glass domes, on The Pilgrims' outdoor tables that lead down to the water's edge.

"Cheers," says Chaz.

"Cheers." Doug places the glasses on the table and takes a seat. "It wasn't far from here, was it?" he asks Chaz. "The reconciliation, as you put it. A building nearby, as I recall."

"It was somewhere in Raulton," Chaz concurs. "I couldn't tell you where, exactly."

Doug takes a sip of his ale. Chaz takes a sip of her Brandy Mac.

"You mentioned you had something you wanted to discuss," Chaz reminds her friend.

"I did. Picture the scene. The patient is a forty-two-year-old professional woman; she works in the HR department of an electronics firm. Mild narcissistic tendencies. Anxiety disorder with bouts of overeating and purging. Hates her mother and her teenage daughter. Not much to write home about, so far, would you say?"

"I would. How did she amaze you, Doug?"

"She wanted to establish a nationwide network of *Apology Centres*. People would go along, individually or for Group Apology Sessions, and say Sorry. For whatever it was in their lives. Even if he or she hadn't actually done anything to apologise *for*. Contrition be Thy name. Self-punishment the cornerstone."

"And the hair-shirt, presumably, worn as a uniform," Chaz adds. "Okay: unusual. But you said she'd *amazed* you – your word. I don't see ..."

"I agreed with her. I thought it was a brilliant idea. Confession for the non-religious," says Doug. "To tell you the truth, I was rather envious."

"You want to set it up yourself?" Chaz sounds mildly incredulous. "In the full comprehension that it might put us out of business?"

"I'm too long in the tooth, Chaz, to dedicate energy to something like that. But it *resonated* with me. I couldn't help thinking I'd heard it somewhere before."

"How would it work, though? You can easily see its limitations, presumably. Simon Psychopath finishes decapitating his mother and thinks: *Oh, I am a silly sausage; I've done it again! Another old lady on my list. Better high-tail it down to the Apology Centre before the Law arrives.* Wouldn't it be the opposite of the Nanny State that we all pretend to despise? No punitive superego to keep us in check. The Id running wild and free ..."

Doug's face expresses cumbersome disappointment. "I happen to think it's a good idea," he reiterates quietly. "It sounded *peaceful*."

Chaz has not finished.

"And what about the frequent flyers? The people who become rather *addicted* to the social whirl at the Apology Centre. *I'll do something naughty just to get a ticket in for next Tuesday.* Wouldn't it create *more* things to apologise for, rather than fewer?"

"…Maybe this is the reason we stopped being friends," Doug tells her.

"No it wasn't," Chaz replies; "and don't threaten me with that, please. Defending an idea is part of what we *do*. I'm sorry I cannot see the benefit in the National Apology Network; let me think about it some more, perhaps."

"Apologising for a notional place of apology is probably ironic."

A truce is silently agreed upon.

Later, as Chaz and Doug are preparing to leave, Doug brings another previous analysand to mind. They are walking away from the water when he says:

"I had a client once who went through a satisfactory romance but couldn't bear the idea that her partner wouldn't feel crushed when it was approaching an end. She couldn't handle it. And I don't blame her. I probably couldn't handle it either, knowing that you've made less difference to another person than even a squall of tears. So she kept it going, week after week – disastrous month after month – making it worse and worse…"

"God, it wasn't my daughter, was it?" Chaz asks. "That sounds familiar."

"No, it wasn't Jemima, Chaz. My client's name was Hazel. She ended her life." Doug pauses. "But I think there *is* a link of sorts. Nine years ago, Hazel was caught up in that nastiness in Edlesborough…"

"The Horror House."

"Indeed. And you told me once that one of your clients had been trapped there too."

Despite the fact that Chaz had expected something like this, Doug's utterance serves to chill her, in body and spirit both. She has no recollection of sharing a detail like this with Doug: what might this suggest? Had she also shared the name *Phyllie Reydman*? Or even *Phyllie*? Either would be regarded as a breach of protocol.

"When did I tell you that?"

"Recently."

By now they have arrived near the rank of taxis. Apart from proffering a farewell, Chaz discovers that she has no more to say. A worm of sickness wriggles in her gut.

THE WHIP OF HONESTY

Indignation stenched the air.

"I have no *idea* how to produce a poster," stated Phyllie Reydman. "I've spent quite a few years on the planet successfully *avoiding* the production of a poster, and I tend to think you can't teach an old dog new tricks."

Claire Carey was seated nearby – not so much "checking her phone" as using her phone as an alibi – an observable distraction. Although, generally, she enjoyed Phyllie's company, there were times when the older woman stomped on her chips. Constant displays of negativity – with the wings stretched wide – always reminded Claire of her mother. She was looking at the news feed on her phone as a means to absent herself from Phyllie's court. Other members of the group that had gathered in one of the university's cafeterias – other postgraduate students and doctoral supervisors – constituted Phyllie's audience.

Dr. Alex Gordon was one of the seemingly devoted. Calm, authorial, and speaking through a mouthful of sausage sandwich, Dr. Gordon provided what would be written up in the reflective journals as a "problematising challenge".

"Surely, when you were a teacher, you asked *your* students to produce a poster, from time to time."

"I'm *still* a teacher," Phyllie responded. "And yes, I most certainly did. But the direction of travel is clearly implied in your question. *They* did it. Not me."

"Well, now, in case it hasn't been made clear," Dr. Gordon continued.

"Allow me to interrupt. I know what you're going to say," said Phyllie. "I even *agree*. But that doesn't mean... And even if I *did* somehow work out how to put a poster together – to what end? Who'll even *notice* it?"

"The simple fact is – sorry, Phyllie! – you were late to apply. The presentation slots have been taken. It's a poster to show your work or nothing at all. You procrastinated."

By now, other conversations had developed and were underway. Dr. Gordon started talking to one of the other supervisors.

"I hope you don't mind me saying this, Phyllie," Claire ventured, having slid her phone into a pocket on her backpack, "but you sound livid."

"And *you* sound like my psychoanalyst."

"I don't know if that's a good or bad thing."

"You sound *even more* like my psychoanalyst." Phyllie laughed.

After a beat, during which Claire weighed up her options, she joined in. Later, she would record this agreement to share a light-hearted moment, in her journal, as paying her dues to join the club.

"Well, cast your mind back," Claire suggested.

"I do very little else these days."

"What skills did you teach the students, back in your Geography days? How did you teach them to start *their* posters?"

"I think I let the Teaching Assistant handle that. No, I didn't. I taught them the importance of research, brevity – the use of images and colour for the visual learners. That kind of thing."

"There you are then. You're a natural."

Dr. Alex Gordon had stood up. From the way that he tapped his jacket pockets, it appeared that he was about to take his leave. Hands waved. "Till our next tutorials," he said to Phyllie, Claire, and another PhD student named Bev.

"How do you find him," Phyllie asked Claire, "as a supervisor?"

Taking the question seriously, Claire hesitated before answering. "Pretty thorough, I would say. On the whole."

"And when he's not being pretty thorough?"

"… I suppose he can be rather distracted at times. But that probably goes with the territory. We should be grateful he's not the kind who leaves his glasses everywhere and has gravy stains all over his groin."

Phyllie smiled. "On balance, I suppose you're right. Does he ever do the one about the ten thumbs? *Play like a man with ten thumbs.*"

"*Oh* yes. Not so much now but he used to all the time. He's started to write new material for the next album. He keeps Ten Thumbs for the encore – one of the greatest hits."

"A crowd-pleaser," Phyllie added.

"Cigarette lighters held aloft." Claire agreed. "Is Alex your first supervisor?"

"Far from it," was the answer. "Do you know the mnemonic people use to remember the fates of Henry VIII's wives?"

"Not really," Claire admitted.

"Divorced, beheaded, died. Divorced, beheaded, survived," Phyllie explained. "Though don't ask me which was which, all the names were too alike! Henry had Catherine issues, for sure. *Catherine Envy*. Well, I always say, about my history of being supervised: I sacked the first one. The second one sacked *me*. The third one was sacked by the university. Alex is my fourth – my last-chance saloon."

"Really? Your third supervisor got the boot from the University?" Claire replied. "I thought you had to get your penis out in a seminar or set fire to a faculty office to get the push from here."

"Maybe he *did* those things! All I heard was, he was demanding this and that, and his contract wasn't renewed. I exaggerate somewhat with the word *sack*, I suppose. Nonetheless, the wanker left me high and dry, along with other PhDs and some Masters students. Greedy behaviour, at best."

"I agree. Have you ever met any of them, to swap disappointment stories?"

Phyllie nodded. "One or two, in passing. Cecil had a wide portfolio of academic interests. I think he used to be a dentist or something."

"Cecil is a good, trustworthy academic name. Very *dreaming spires*."

"Professor Cecil Joseph – with his odd way of speaking. You know, I don't think he called me by my first name more than once, just to confirm who I was. I was always '*Sister*' to

Cecil Joseph. Men were 'Brother' and I was 'Sister' – or *occasionally* 'Sister Reyd' for some reason…"

Phyllie paused.

"I'm getting angry just thinking about him," she continued, "and his flimsy standards. *Sister Reyd* indeed! I thought it odd I was assigned his dubious services in the first place… though he made it clear about thirty times that he'd read Freud. I think he wanted me to say: *Well done, Cecil…*"

"Or Brother Joe, it could have been," said Claire.

"How do you mean? Oh, I see…"

"He called you Sister Reyd and his surname is Joseph…"

"Yes, I get it. No, never," said Phyllie.

"I wonder why an ex-dentist would want to supervise PhDs. A bit of a come-down, salary-wise."

"Well, he taught on the MSc in Dentistry as well. There was a link. And maybe they made him an offer he couldn't reglue. A little orthodontic pun for you there, ladies."

"You'll make me look down in the mouth if you're not careful," Claire added.

"*Anyway*. He left behind his Masters' students – his abandoned dental clinicians – and me and I think two other doctorals. I hope his satisfaction helps him *rot*."

By this point, other members of the group had drifted away; respectful waves of the hand had been proffered. The cafeteria's noise had increased; the air was scrummy with the aromas of beef bourguignon and baked flapjacks.

On seeing Claire smile, Phyllie copied the expression.

"I'm glad my indignation has kept you happy."

"You've reminded me of something, that's all," said Claire. "I've been wondering about a way to say this for a week – we have someone in common."

"Who's that?"

"Her name's Amanda. As in: your ex-husband's wife."

The surprise that visited Phyllie's face could not have been feigned. "You know Amanda? How come?"

"I buy from her. She sells old dental tools on an auction site."

"Christ. What are the odds?" Phyllie replied. "I hope you won't be offended if I say that sort of coincidence turns my stomach a *tad*. I'm not sure I could manage lunch for a while."

"But don't you think it's wonderful, those little *clicks* in the universe?" Claire asked. "The things that lead people together, almost as if our physical space is shared by more than the people you can see there."

"Saturated spaces. My psychoanalyst has said something similar." Phyllie paused for a few seconds. "You don't know her as well, do you?"

"What's her name?"

"Chaz Bruce-Sange."

"No," said Claire; "but I've got another coincidence for you to chew on, if we're not going to chew on anything else. Amanda talked about the travelling group your ex-husband's part of. I swear this is true. There's a guy who goes by the name of Brother Joe. He calls everyone 'Brother' or 'Sister.' Just like your Prof. Cecil Joseph used to."

SCENT OF KNIFE

———•○•———

"A baboon is not a rabbit. Only a fool would expect it to behave like a rabbit."

Brother Joe

MEN ABOUT TOWN, 1

"Here she is, brothers! The Hotel Harlequin!"

Brother Joe slid the van into a diagonal space near the hotel's entrance and braked with unnecessary violence. Along with several others in the vehicle, Twennyfour was shunted forward in his seat; the safety belt pinched into his shoulder.

Disregarding the discomfort, he remembered the story that Bruno Amitrano had told him about the events that had followed a family wedding.

"Hey Bruno, my brother!" Twennyfour called. "Do you believe in coincidences?"

"I'm not with you, mate," Bruno replied, unfastening the seatbelt around his waist.

"The name of the hotel! Same as the place your girlfriend found the phone! At the wedding that you told us about."

Bruno smiled. "That's bizarre. I hope I get a decent-sized room this time. I had a poky little matchbox with Sheelagh."

It appeared that the establishment was not at anything like full capacity: plenty of car parking remained available. In addition, to strike something of an absurd note, at least three of the parking spaces were occupied by a donkey apiece. As far as

Twennyfour could tell (peering from one of the van's side-windows), the donkeys were not tethered to a hitching post... or indeed to any anchor at all. The donkeys had been parked in the same way as a vehicle would have been. Furthermore, each donkey seemed content to be in a specific place – and to rest. It was Twennyfour's contention that several of the animals were talking idly among themselves, like old men over a park chessboard.

"We've arrived!" called Brother Joe. "Fresh air is our friend once again!"

Joe leaned back in the driver's seat and rolled his head on his neck in a serpentine configuration. Everyone on board heard the man's neck *clicks*.

They had arrived in the town of Scent of Knife. As the men piled out of the vehicle, several of them noted that the atmosphere had a brown tinge.

Check-in at The Hotel Harlequin was an efficient affair. Twennyfour ended up on the third floor (of four), in a comfortable corner room, sharing with Roger Billie. One of the members of staff had left two windows on each of the corner walls ajar while making up the room; the resultant cross breeze had had plenty of time to clean the air and establish a comfortable temperature.

"I'm tempted to have a nap," said Roger. "Look how beautiful those white sheets are!"

Twennyfour clicked his tongue. "We've been on the road for seventeen hours, brother," he countered. "You've had plenty of time to close your eyes!"

"Why, what are *you* doing?"

"Hitting the town! Such as it is... See the sights, grab a drink."

"I'm hungry. What time did Brother Joe say for dinner?"

"Seven. We have two hours to fill our boots. Wanna come?"

Roger nodded his head. "Sure; why not? I can sleep when I'm dead."

"Is it me, or do a lot of these towns look very similar to one another?" Roger asked, looking through a window onto the street. They were sitting in the saloon of the first bar that they had encountered, a place called The Pilgrims. "Brown tones. Sepia lenses."

"It's not only you, my brother. It's something to do with low salaries and low expectations," Twennyfour answered.

"Can I speak frankly with you?"

In truth, Twennyfour had already come to regret inviting Roger Billie out for a stroll. He had done so for the right reasons, but if this was going to turn into a walk-and-talk confessional, Twennyfour could live without the burden of a secret shared.

None of this, however, did he articulate. Instead, he smiled and replied, "Of course, you can speak frankly with me! I'd have it no other way!"

"I'm not always sure we're making a difference," Roger offered. "We travel for mile after mile, and our hearts are in the right place – we *mean* well – but I'm not..." His voice drifted off. "Let me ask you. Do *you* feel like we make a difference?"

For Twennyfour, this was an easy question to answer.

"If I didn't think we made a difference, I'd have no hesitation in making my way back home somehow – even if it was on the back of one of those donkeys for an extortionate price – and I'd go and work on my Cousin Earl's pig-and-chicken farm. He made it plain the offer of work is wide open. It's only pride – up to now – that's blocked me from taking him up."

"Pride?" said Roger. "Pride because you don't want to work with poultry?"

"No; pride that I want to bring something *into* the family, rather than subdividing what we're got in-house, in a rob-Peter-pay-Paul way. My dad always told me not to pay someone in your family and not to take money from someone in your family either."

"Do you transfer what you earn to your family?"

"Of course! Why else would we endure this chaos? *Why else* would I want to sit in the back of a van, in the smelly-feet fog of a bunch of pseudo-desperate men? None intended."

Roger held up a hand. "None taken. Would you like another beer?"

Bellies full and heads pleasantly light (after a further two glasses of lager), Twennyfour and Roger exited The Pilgrims and moved on foot a few blocks to a bath-and-sauna establishment. Both men paid for a weather-appropriate brutal haircut; a close wet shave; and a luxurious wallow in a van-sized box of Venusian heat.

"I used to have a peculiar reaction in a Turkish bath," Roger admitted. "I'm opening myself up to ridicule here, I hope you understand."

"I'm reluctant to ask, but what *kind* of peculiar reaction?" asked Twennyfour.

"You're quite right to sound suspicious. I'll apologise in advance, just in case it happens underneath my towel. A full erection."

"Brother Joe!" called Twennyfour, as if for urgent assistance.

"But it wasn't a sexual reaction, I assure you. I'm not gay. I've never had a homosexual experience. I'm happily married a second time to my wife Amanda. But I couldn't help it. As soon as I stepped into a sauna or a steam room – hello, ding-dong, and *boing*. There she blows, as it were. Like a Pavlovian experiment."

Processing this unwanted information, Twennyfour nodded his head.

"I can honestly say I've never seen another man's erection," he mused, "and I can honestly say I have no wish to do so either. The moment you feel a stirring, would you do me a favour, Roger Billie? Let me know and I'll *cartwheel* out of here."

The two men laughed.

"I wouldn't want you to feel falsely *flattered*," Roger added.

For the next two minutes, both of them were able to hear the sound of steam as it climbed and curled. It had a voice: no doubt about that; a low *clish-ma-claver* quality.

"Well, this isn't awkward at all," Roger said finally.

"You started it, brother."

"I know."

Had the two men evolved from acquaintances to confidantes? If so, it had happened rather suddenly. Certainly, confessions could magnetise people together. The truth of confessions must never emerge. The truth was worse than chickenpox; worse than undergrowth smoulderings in a forest, after a month of timber-dry days.

On leaving the baths, Twennyfour and Roger found that they still had a quarter of an hour on their hands before the dinner rendezvous at The Hotel Harlequin. They strolled to a small lake, where gulls swooped, and midges throbbed in auburn clouds that appeared first opaque and then deliquescent. They took a bench. Boat captains called out to elicit the men's interest in an evening trip on the water. Briefly, a bat darted from sail to sail. Near a flotilla of banked canoes, a group of children wearing life-vests were being instructed by an adult.

"I wonder if I can draw you on something you mentioned before," said Roger. "I didn't feel comfortable talking about it at the time."

"What's that, brother? As long as it's not your erection."

"It's not. You said you found an abandoned clinic. With a child inside it."

Twennyfour sighed. "I know what I witnessed, Roger Billie. The prerogative to believe me or not is entirely yours."

"I don't doubt you. Nine years ago, something similar happened in my life. My first wife – Phyllie – was dragged into a nightmare. It broke the marriage in the end."

Twennyfour paused before asking: "What happened?"

"A man named Benny kept people as hostages, including Phyllie. He had them wired to machines and doped up – all sorts. The weird thing was, when they were zombies… they started to share their dreams and inhabit these fantasy worlds. Phyllie found it really hard to return to normality when she was released. She believed in what her mind had told her. *All* of the prisoners did."

"…I appreciate your honesty, brother; it must have been a difficult time. But I am afraid I don't see the connection with my own experience."

"You said there was a child in the clinic."

"Yes."

"On her own, with teeth embedded in her skin."

"Yes, that's right. I know it sounds implausible."

"But that's just it: *it doesn't* sound implausible to me. I couldn't admit it to you before now – or even to myself. But I wasn't being honest. There's *no doubt in my mind* you saw what you said you saw, like a haunting. I just wish we could go back there, so I could tell you what *I* saw in the same space."

"Maybe you'd see exactly the same thing," said Twennyfour.

"That's it; or maybe not. When those prisoners were released from that house of horror, they *totally believed* where they'd been. It didn't matter that in *our* space they'd been in a dungeon. In *their* spaces, stories had unravelled. I saw it with Phyllie. She was never the same again."

Twennyfour stood up. Nearby, one of the children had been invited into one of the canoes. The instructor was rocking the boat from side to side while speaking to the group.

"We should get back to the hotel," Roger said.

"Yes, brother. What happened to Phyllie? Did she make it through?"

"She's fine now. She teaches part-time at a university near us; she's doing her PhD. Well, she *seems* fine now..." he amended.

The two men started walking back the way they'd came.

"Who can say for sure?"

The following day, it did not take long for Twennyfour to locate what must be the town's strongly-beating heart: the street-wide entrance to a bazaar, into which floods of pedestrians of all ages poured. Accordingly, in something like an instructive reflex, Twennyfour jammed both fists into his trouser pockets, to protect himself from unwelcome thieving attention. Everywhere he looked there was movement, there was sound; who would know until after an event if any of this crowd happened to be a pickpocket, with eyes open to the possibility of fresh tourist blood?

Twennyfour entered the bazaar. Men and women hurried past with straw containers on their heads; a motor-scooter rattled past under the power of an engine that sounded even less healthy than that under the bonnet of Brother Joe's van. Smiling unselfconsciously to himself, Twennyfour granted that this bazaar – this accumulation of energy, this boiling pot of bubbling conversations, the bouts of haggling – was as beautiful a place at which he could imagine having accidentally arrived.

Then again, perhaps there was no such thing as an accident. Twennyfour had friends who had served military terms, who had had it drummed into them that the concept of an accident was a retrospective construction, a means to find reason in a pattern that appeared unfamiliar in the moment. With adequate planning (these friends of Twennyfour's insisted), an accident was impossible: you would have taken into consideration any factors that, when amalgamated, construed to cause a body harm.

Had this summary of a theory occurred to Twennyfour now because he happened to be walking past a dental clinic? Perhaps he had glimpsed its sign from as far back as the first intersection inside the bazaar, where Twennyfour had turned right on a whim. Yes, that must be it: he had snatched an unconscious look at the sign...

JOHN HODGINS, DENTIST
"Caring for Your Careys!"
"Feeling for Your Fillings!"

...and his thoughts had catapulted him back to the abandoned dental clinic where he had encountered the girl Carey, with the thousands of extracted or decommissioned teeth, embedded in the skin of all visible parts of her frame. (The fact that the dentist had the same name as the village where Twennyfour lived seemed no more than amusing.)

It wasn't an accident, Twennyfour concluded now, in the bazaar (though not for the first time). *I was led there...* As sure of this notion as he was of night following day, he stepped between two stallholders' plots – a young woman selling bottles of perfume and bathroom products, and a much older woman selling mobile phones and their accessories – and climbed the three steps to ascend from the compacted dirt of the road itself onto a covered metal walkway that ran the length of this collection of businesses. Not only had Twennyfour moved closer to the dental clinic, he had moved into a cooler space. The walkway was protected from the sun's glare.

The dental clinic was closed and Twennyfour walked on.

Every time he saw items for sale that might be offered to someone elsewhere as a homecoming gift, Twennyfour reflected on how far he had travelled and how far he was from home. The intervening distance was more than a matter of miles. Roads were markers and systems of measurement; the far greater distance was inside the skull. The sight of souvenirs on sale made Twennyfour nostalgic and raw. He continued onwards.

In due course, Twennyfour stood in front of a general store; and even outside there was plenty on display – a tray of loose pieces of cutlery; a clutch of gardening tools in plastic containers; kitchenware and washing-up liquid, tins of soup, packets of boiled chicken for pets, and furry trays of fresh purple-shelled eggs. A pig oinked nearby.

"You strike me as a man who likes a postcard," a voice suggested, a few metres from Twennyfour's ear.

As Twennyfour turned his whole body towards his new interlocutor, he noticed a revolving rack loaded with postcards, near the door to the general store itself.

"Or am I wrong?" the same voice continued.

"Pardon me, friend, I don't think I caught what you said," Twennyfour answered.

Its owner was middled-aged, male – as thin as a butcher's dog, as the saying used to be, back in the old days – back home.

"You're in town with the troupe, I reckon."

"You reckon right. What were you saying about postcards?"

"That you seem like a man who might appreciate a marker in time, like a postcard."

"I thought that's what you said. What made you say so?"

The store-owner smiled: such teeth as remained were the brownish hue of distant mountains. "Come take a look at the postcards," was the response. "Decide for yourself if I've guessed correctly."

The rotating rack on which the postcards had been displayed was dusty with sand and grime. Despite the volumes of people on the streets, travellers seeking souvenirs had not ventured through in quite a while, it would appear. The postcards themselves – now that Twennyfour had strolled over to pay them attention – ran the gamut of coastal scenes and cute images of cats and goats. Emerging from the animals' mouths were speech bubbles, inside which messages were printed in a language that Twennyfour could not read.

"Maybe I was wrong after all," the store-owner mused.

Twennyfour did not wish to cause offence. "It's not that I don't like your postcards, friend..." he began.

"My name's John Hodgins – I own this place, for now at least. Call me John."

"Thank you, John. My name's Twennyfour. And it's not that I don't *like your postcards* – it's that I just don't understand them." Twennyfour was still rotating the rack. "None of them are of this place, are they? Aren't postcards mementos of where you've been?"

"See if you think that on your way out of town when you're finished! An *armpit* of a town, so it is! I'm about the only thing it has going for it!"

Twennyfour smiled out of politeness.

"I jest, of course. Come in for a coconut drink, Twennyfour, and I'll pierce your ears free of charge – I need the practice. Everyone's already pierced around here."

This time Twennyfour chuckled for real.

"I don't need my ears pierced, thanks, John. I've come this far without wearing earrings, I think I'm fine."

"Are you sure? Nipples? Tongue?"

"No thanks."

"The end of the old chap?"

"*Definitely* no thanks. But your offer of a coconut drink sounds nice. I'll take you up on that one."

Twennyfour was led through a yellow-and-brown striped curtain – one of three doorways that led away from the shop's customer area (which was currently un-troubled by a single customer). Spice was in the air: the appetising aroma of something cooking. In the dimmed room beyond – at first glance, a stockroom – the shelves were crammed with sink detergents, boxes of light bulbs, and bulk packets of toilet rolls and kitchen wipes in transparent plastic. Water boiled in a kettle in the corner. Standing on the draining board adjacent to a deep sink against the room's far wall, a monkey dipped dishes and cutlery into sudsy water that steamed with its high temperature.

"Is your monkey doing the washing up?" Twennyfour asked, amazed.

"Well, he's not *my* monkey; but yes, he's doing the washing up. It's a punishment for being cheeky to my sister."

"And this monkey has a name, by the way," the monkey added.

"Sorry!" said John Hodgins. "But I *did* say you weren't my monkey…"

"Quite right as well!" the monkey went on, his tone petulant. All of a sudden, his paws now empty, the monkey leaped from the draining board to the overhead fan, the blades of which circled gently. One paw caught hold of the edge of a blade; the monkey rode a few rotations, calling "*Wheee!*"

Also abroad, perambulating his way from shop front to shop front, occasionally stepping to one side to avoid a chicken or a monkey, was Bruno Amitrano. Bruno was contemplating a bar and a drink when he encountered Twennyfour. The other man was emerging from a store that seemed, from its outside displays, to sell as wide a range of bric-a-brac as Bruno had yet to observe. In his hand, Twennyfour carried a small brown paper bag.

"What caught your eye?" Bruno asked.

"Postcards."

"Of this place?"

"No; of *no* place," Twennyfour answered. "A fascinating establishment. They have a sensory deprivation tank round the back."

"I thought your hair looked damp. What happens?"

"You buy a few postcards and concentrate on the images for a while. Then you take the images with you into the tank. You can't see or hear anything; you float and dream. It was the most relaxing thing I've done in years!"

Bruno nodded. He was on the brink of saying that he would act on Twennyfour's suggestion… when he felt a cold shiver sprinkle against his spine. A premonition reached for his attention. He was suddenly certain that if he looked at the postcards on the rack, they would show images that he did not wish to view. They would show the photographs that had been on the phone that Sheelagh Carey had found at the wedding.

He and Twennyfour would see different images on the postcards. There was no doubt of this in Bruno's mind.

Later…

"You seem to have a good bond with Brother Joe," said Twennyfour.

Paper Jake O'Donnell nodded his head. "I owe a loyalty to that man. I don't think I would be the man I've become – and still want to improve on – if not for Brother Joe."

Paper Jake was the youngest of the work group. Twennyfour would have guessed the man to be in his early twenties, with skin so pale and white that he had formed an assumption that the 'Paper' part of the name was a reference to it. How long had Paper Jake been under Brother Joe's leadership, for such a confident bond to have formed? Not for the first time, Twennyfour wondered if Paper Jake O'Donnell was somehow related to Brother Joe, despite their differences in appearance.

"Do you mind if I ask you why?"

Paper Jake considered the question for a few seconds – for long enough to spur Twennyfour on to add: "I'm sorry if I've accidentally touched a nerve. I don't mean to pry; just making conversation."

"You haven't touched a nerve," Paper Jake tried to assure him. "I'm trying to think of an adequate way to begin. What can I say? He taught me not to lie. He made me understand the value of honesty. The *whip* of honesty..."

"I can't help but ask, Jake... what were you like before? Did you lie a lot?"

"I lied all the time. It's because of Brother Joe I resist the temptation of unsubstantiated gossip. Joe taught me that the line that splits gossip and truth is a bifurcated cut – it slices *lengthways*. And it's not split entirely. The components live on either side of the cut, alongside one another, as if on either side of a psychic river. They wave at each other like the members of friendly tribes."

Twennyfour smiled and attempted to conceal his confusion. The concept of friendly tribes waving at one another made sense, but Paper Jake's metaphor was stretched too far for him to comprehend.

"That's nice." And he tried to imagine Jake's backstory. Apparently, Jake had been a man so accustomed to spilling untruths that another man had cracked (what he'd referred to as) the *whip of honesty* against his soul's rump. Well, that was believable, Twennyfour supposed; but where would their paths have crossed in the first place?

In Twennyfour's opinion (and experience), when people changed their natures, there was usually one good reason for doing so.

"Am I right to assume that your lies got you in trouble?"

Jake acknowledged the comment with a raise of the chin. "My lies almost got me killed. But that's enough about me. Tell me more about the orchestra you want to conduct."

Twennyfour smiled. Conversational boundaries were something that the work group had swiftly learned to respect. If a brother wished to close down a topic, that topic was closed down. They had miles to travel in each other's company; a falling-out would be worse than awkward, possibly for all seven of the travellers.

"Even as you mentioned the two tribes across the river," Twennyfour answered, "I thought of them singing as well as waving. A ritual to bless the river; a thank-you choir. Arms wave; water waves; voices pulsing and merging and rising to the sun."

Riffing now; the story was a blatant lie. But then again, Twennyfour had never made the same sort of promise to Brother Joe that Paper Jake O'Donnell had claimed to have made. Lies were fine if they made the time pass faster.

A hiatus followed.

"My dream is to own a hotel by the sea," said Paper Jake O'Donnell, eventually. "Three storeys and a cellar full of rooms for ping-pong and chess and pool. Sleeps seventeen or eighteen, that kind of thing."

"Sounds good," Twennyfour agreed with a nod.

"I sleep in a different bed every night."

"Once upon a time, I checked into a lodge. It overlooked a lake." Jake smiled briefly. "It was a work environment and I had no idea I'd be put into a lodge. I had imposter syndrome the whole time I was there."

Twennyfour recalled the evening that Bruno Amitrano had told the story about the phone his girlfriend had found in the bushes at a wedding. Paper Jake had added that he had a comparable tale of his own to share. On the principle of there being no time like the present, Twennyfour asked Paper Jake a curveball query.

"Was that where you had the spot of bother you mentioned the other night?"

For a second or two, Paper Jake's eyes moved quickly, as though tracking the inward trajectory of a wasp. Not a muscle of his body did he move, but his eyesight was lost in a tempest.

"Bruno told us about the hotel prank."

Jake nodded. "No, I meant a different hotel." He grinned. "Do you want to hear a good 'un, Twennyfour? A nice little *fairy tale. A hotel anecdote.*"

FAR-FLUNG HOTEL SMOKING BAYS (PAPER JAKE O'DONNELL'S STORY)

"Did they put you in a writer?" he believed he'd heard.

"...Did they *what* now?" he replied, simultaneously exhaling a truncheon of cigarette smoke that appeared blue in the mid-afternoon air. The climate felt stormy. He was proximate to a heavy metal table with an ashtray upon it the size of a hubcap.

His interlocutor was in her early thirties; *big-boned,* in the young man's jetlag-simplified lexicon. Big-boned, blonde, and attractive, the young man continued with his inventory, searching for words that the flight and the train journey seemed to have edited into mush. Standing at the next table along in the hotel's smoking bay, she had just torched the end of a cigarette. She sipped its end with a squeaky pucker; then posed an additional question while nodding her head with brewing comprehension.

"You haven't checked in yet, have you?"

"No; just arrived." He tapped at his solitary hold-all with the round booted toe of his left foot. Immediately he reviewed this gesture as redundant; his interlocutor had not noticed the bag.

"Ah. That's why my question meant nothing. I shouldn't spoil the surprise. You have a treat in store at the Reception desk."

"Go on – spoil it," he answered. "I'm half asleep; I wouldn't want to miss it."

"Some of the bedrooms have a little plaque on the doors – the names of the owner's favourite writers, I assume."

"*Did they put you in a writer?* I see what you mean. A cigarette seemed more important than checking in. Whose brain have you been assigned to?"

"Kurt Vonnegut's. For the gulag sensory experience, no doubt."

The young man chuckled holes into a temporary face-pack of exhaled smoke. "What's the room like?"

"It's delightful. The full heated toilet seat vibe."

"I can't wait. I hope I get a hardly-known writer with a fanatical fanbase of twelve or thirty people. Whose name is questioned every time someone arrives."

"Some of the names I walked past were unfamiliar, I must admit. Then again, I'm no literature buff. I'm Amanda, by the way."

"Jake. Nice to meet you. Are you here for the convention?"

"The main one, yes. Not the farming machinery one."

"It's a nice venue."

"Yes, I've been here before," Amanda added. "The last time I was here, I was in Dorothy Anthony – the room, I mean. I said that at the check-in desk half an hour ago and the guy gets snooty. *We have the Dorothy Anthony Memorial Room, madam, but it's not available this week.* The author passed away several years ago, apparently. He gives me the look you can only reply to with: *Never mind.* So that's what I said. Never mind."

Jake nodded. "Well, maybe I'll feel inspired to write something while I'm here."

"You and me both. Where are you from?"

He named the university town.

"We're virtually neighbours," said Amanda. "Are you presenting tomorrow?"

"No, the next day. I'm the keynote to kick the day off – amazingly."

"Oh, you're Jake *O'Donnell.* Very nice to meet you." Although Amanda did not move from the side of her own smoking table, she shook hands with the air as if the two of them were within reach of one another.

"And a virtual long-distance hand-shake to you too," said Jake, copying the gesture.

Sometimes you can pinpoint the pivotal moment, and it amounts to a handful of words or actions.

Paper Jake O'Donnell is a committed reflective journalist. This sentence was captured more than once, both on screen and in a file.

"Where are you from?" *she asked me.*

The four words that changed my life.

The verdict is for Paper Jake O'Donnell alone. His reflections have no audience.

"Long story short," said Paper Jake O'Donnell to Twennyfour, "we went to her room. I mean, she didn't have to invite me twice, right? She was lovely. Then I said to her: 'I wonder, if you pay extra, do you get a palpably different room experience?' '…Value for money, do you mean?' she asked…

"Not so much value as *luxury*. Do you see an obvious change, is I suppose what I'm saying – because we usually see inside *one* hotel room, don't we? – unless we go back to the same hotel another time. You don't really know if you'd have been checked into a flasher room if you'd spent the extra fifty or whatever."

"'I suppose so. Do I detect you're impressed?'

"'I'm impressed all right,' I told her. Then she asked me if I had a fridge in mine – and I said no. My room was fairly basic."

"'Well, mine's over there,' she tells me. 'Why don't you open it? You'll find a bottle of sparkly.' And I'm thinking – well, why not? How jolly *civilised*. 'You'll also find two glasses catching their death of cold in there. Why not rescue them and do the honours while I'm freshening up?'"

Trying gallantly to suffocate a yawn, Twennyfour said: "Long story short, eh?"

"Yeah. Then our *clothes dissolved*."

Although Twennyfour was successful at refraining from shrugging, he was not at all impressed with having lost the time he'd spent so far listening to a simple tale of a foreign affair – a hotel romance. *Big deal!* he wanted to contribute. A good upbringing had left him self-censorious during moments of inadvertent boredom or awkwardness.

Twennyfour sensed disappointment. Evidently, Paper Jake had expected a full fanfare – or at the very least, a sturdy *Bravo!*

"Anyway," the younger man continued (somewhat sheepishly), "It's the next day when the weird thing happens. The *next* day… Amanda was a big old bag of nerves."

Amanda made a sort of gulping motion, as though she had found something difficult to swallow. With jittery, raised fingers, she smoked in a no-nonsense manner.

"You know there are two wings to this hotel, right? Well, last night I went into the casino at the back, just to explore. And I thought: *I can sacrifice fifty quid if need be. If I lose, I lose – not the end of the world.* I've hardly spent anything on this trip. So, I played a few hands of 21 and won thirty pounds."

She laughed.

"The long and short of it is, if I hadn't won the thirty pounds, I wouldn't have treated myself to two glasses of champagne at the bar."

Telling the tale was improving her mood: she seemed less jumpy with every completed sentence; her smile appeared more natural.

For me, it was having the opposite effect: I couldn't help but dread what must have happened for her to have been so nervous in the first place. In her tipsy state, had Amanda lost the reins on her inhibitions and done something reckless?

No; I didn't think so. Someone had hurt Amanda in some way. She had been assaulted.

"What happened?"

Both of us had reached for our packs on the table. It was a sign to mark the end of the first scene and the commencement of the second.

"I wasn't falling-down drunk, you understand," Amanda went on; "it might have been better if I had been! I don't know about you, but in the past – on such occasions, as they say – I've managed to find my way home almost in spite of myself."

"A survival instinct kicks in," I offered – pleased to make a contribution. "You have to get back to safety. You owe it to yourself."

Amanda nodded; she rarely leaked smoke from her nostrils, but with the brisk motion of her head, on this occasion, two rival streams of grey demarked parallel check-symbols in the air between us.

Paper Jake O'Donnell read the runes embedded in his new lover's silence.

"You went to the wrong wing. Is that what you're saying?"

Amanda nodded. "I should have gone north and I went south. Or the other way around." She shrugged. "I went to the wrong wing. And it looked – please allow me to emphasise the point! – exactly the same!" She sniggered snottily. "I think that's my only line of defence. *The two wings look exactly the same.*"

"You went to the equivalent room."

"Yes! Entirely flying by batwing radar, my dear boy. Even the *door* looked identical – bearing in mind I was in no fit state to read whatever might have been printed on the nameplate thing. *I didn't read it.*"

"But surely your key card didn't let you in."

"No, it didn't; that's the thing. I asked a woman with her cleaning cart – she was down the hall a bit, servicing the rooms. She'd seen me try the card and get nowhere. She used the magic one and bowed. I think I even did that shop-soiled thing, you know? Putting my hands together and nodding my head? A walking, talking cliché: that's me. *Open Sesame…*

"The bathroom was on my right, just like in my own room… but I thought: *it smells different.* It wasn't my room – I knew that. The way an animal identifies a *lair.* A few more steps… and we're together, the woman on the far side of the bed and me. She looks up from stuffing her bag full of clothes and clocks me. And then says: *Where have you been? You're late. They'll be here any minute.*" And then goes back to packing, like the *building's* about to burn down. On the pillow was a revolver."

Paper Jake bit into the information. "A *revolver?* Like a *gun* revolver?"

"*No.* Like a *door* revolver. Like The Beatles' *Revolver…*" Amanda pouted. "Yes, a gun, you silly goose. She had a gun on the pillow and she was packing her bags in a hurry."

"And she expected a woman to arrive she'd never seen before," Paper Jake added.

"Exactly. What had I stumbled into? Sobers you up sharpish."

A crinkly smile worked wonders on Amanda's features. "Out of interest… what do you imagine *you'd*'ve done. In a similar predicament."

"Well…" said Paper Jake, taking time to perfect a response that he knew would also constitute a test of their fledgling relationship. "*Obviously,* I don't know if you and I – or you and me – are going to go anywhere after this conference…"

"You and I. And no; no, we're not."

I was crestfallen when she let that drop, he would type later.

"Gosh, your *face,* Jake! *I* don't know. I only met you yesterday!"

"Well, anyway; one thing I should be clear about, whatever happens. Are you ready? I am truly – I mean completely – a one-hundred-per-cent, dyed-in-the-wool, *spineless cunt.* There aren't many things I *won't* do to get out of a pickle."

"That doesn't quite answer my question," Amanda told him.

"…I would've backed my way out of the room."

"That's precisely what I did as well," Amanda answered.

"I only knew her for the duration of the conference, as it turned out. We didn't keep in touch after that – even though we were virtually neighbours – though I did try to email on a few occasions. But one of the last things she did type before the trail went cold for the last time was this. Amanda said something like: *There's not a day goes by when I don't wonder who that woman thought I was and who she was expecting to arrive. And what side of the law was she on, anyway?*"

SESSION 11

I return to the house I used to live in when I was a student for the first time.

It's early morning; I'm only wearing a pair of Father Christmas boxer shorts that Roger used to wear. I enter the kitchen. One of my housemates has left spaghetti in the kettle. Pans on the hobs are cooking vegetables and rice; the lids are jumping like they do in cartoons.

I find a small pan to heat some water in. A woman trying to be aloof (like the barmaid in The Pilgrims) eventually tells me she's passed her cycling proficiency test.

I'm suddenly aware I'm wearing nothing but boxer shorts; I fold my arms across my breasts, but it seems too late. In the corner of the kitchen, really tiny – like they're trying to hide – Roger is with a nine year-old girl.

He's pushing teeth into her skin; tooth after tooth he's collected in a bucket. I don't know if the girl is happy or if she wants him to push teeth into her skin or not; her face is expressionless.

Then the girl notices me and smiles. She says: "Don't worry… " – Roger keeps going – "… Benny's already dead."

"I kept my maiden name when I married Roger Billie."

Dr. Chaz Bruce-Sange arrives at a swift conclusion. "You didn't want to be Phyllie Billie. I don't blame you."

"I convinced myself that's what it was at the time; but really? A name? The *sound* of a name?"

"Names are very important. For some, a name is a way of keeping the source material at full strength. The change of a name can be both empowering and a fast track to identity dilution."

Phyllie nods her head and pauses.

"I think that's what was really behind my objection," she adds: "the *importance* of the name, not the sound of it. I could have gotten used to Phyllie Billie. Even the children I used to teach would have stopped smirking eventually. *Miss's name sounds like Silly Billy*. Does it now? Well done, you. Now, shall we learn something about CBDs or tectonic plates?"

"What's a CBD?"

"Oh. A Central Business District. I was a Geography teacher before my breakdown."

"Yes, I know."

"But the *envelope* of the name: what it *contained*. I look back on my decision and realise, I would have betrayed what my two names had collected up to that point."

"Your identity?"

"And my place on the planet. I'm sorry if I'm going on about this too much …"

"Not at all."

"… a full name is more than a simple storage system. Or even a complicated storage system. Our names are a badge of entry. A badge of honour, in some circumstances… I'm not sure I'm making sense."

"You're making perfect sense, Phyllie. What happened when you were divorced from Roger?"

"What do you mean, what happened? We sold the house and decided on an amicable way to share the responsibility of raising Claire."

"With respect to your name."

Again, Phyllie pauses. She pushes her fingertips together; the end of each finger develops a ramp and the thumbnails are side by side.

Dr. Bruce-Sange speaks again. "This is a church, this is a steeple…"

"Pardon me?"

"Your hands, Phyllie. You've unconsciously made a place of worship with your hands. *This is a church, this is a steeple…*"

"Let's go inside and here are the people… So I have. My daughter plays that game sometimes, with her friends."

"All little girls want to get married in a church."

"To their dads. I know."

"Not necessarily… and certainly not after a certain age. I've questioned, from time to time, if the position of the thumbs is meant to be the happy couple, outside the building."

"Coyly and nervously awaiting their fate."

"Or are the thumbs the heavy church doors, I wonder? You said, *My daughter.*"

Phyllie feels stapled onto this page of self-appraisal. In this moment, she remembers her wedding day (not a church, but a beautiful ceremony in a registry office); her mental gaze

sweeps the faces of attendees, every man, woman, child…
and even animal. (An infant niece on Roger's side of the family had thrown a tantrum on the day of the celebration, until
weary permission had been granted for her to take her beloved
pet guinea pig, Guinea Paltrow.) Everyone had smiled for the
happy couple.

Phyllie remembers a nervousness about keeping hold
of her original surname; and now Chaz had asked about her
name when she and Roger had divorced. What had Phyllie
experienced? Relief, perhaps; relief at not having to go through
the rigmarole of deed poll. And vindication? A sense of having
known she was right all along in not having sailed into Roger's
named waters.

"I said, my daughter. Yes."

"As opposed to *our daughter*."

"Well, all right, *our* daughter then. It's the same girl."

"But it's not the same dynamic. You excluded Roger from
the relationship, with that one simple substitution. Were you
pleased when the marriage ended, Phyllie?"

There is a pause. Has Chaz found an avenue into Phyllie's
introspection?

"*Pleased* is not quite right." Phyllie stares off into the
middle distance. "I hated him for not trying harder to keep us
together. It was childish. I wanted him to want me more."

Chaz mirrors the hands-together pose that Phyllie had
modelled. Another church; another place of worship and rev-
erence, but with skin older than Phyllie's own.

"Are you showing me your church, Chaz?"

"I think I am. In a manner of speaking."

"It's just occurred to me: I very rarely see your hands move. Or to put it in more commonplace English, you very rarely move your hands."

In the exaltations of a peak moment, she might conclude that she is a copy of herself, being watched by a hard-to-please audience.

The words are those of Dr. Chaz Bruce-Sange. She is typing onto the screen.

However lovingly she has been copied from reality, she knows that there is gravel in the projector; the performance is momentary – crystalline in its perfection, but losable, replaceable, and already sinking slowly.

"Do you feel you stare into that momentary darkness?" asked Dr. Doug Stegmeyer. "I'm keen to understand. Nothing else intended."

Dr. Chaz Bruce-Sange rolled her pen around her fingers like a drummer might a drumstick. "I think you've hit the nail there," she replied. "Staring into the beam of intense darkness – if you like – is important, to balance the things that went well the first time."

COLLECTOR STORIES

"I've sometimes wondered if vendors ever tell stories among themselves," said Claire Carey.

"Who's done well – that kind of thing?" asked Amanda Billie.

"Yes; the killer sale."

"Honour and dishonour among thieves? Not that I know of. I'm not included if they do. We keep ourselves to ourselves. Occasionally I'll receive a professional enquiry about something. Have I heard about a Hollenback someone's read about."

"What's a Hollenback?"

"Oh. It carves interproximal overhangs," Amanda replied. "Or someone'll say there's something for sale, am I interested; that kind of thing."

"I just wondered."

"You hear the odd story, mind you. Nothing to do with dental tools. It was books. Let me see. She had a rare book she didn't know was rare and a commonplace book someone had left something important inside as a bookmark. Call it a treasure map – it wasn't. She has a good weekend of sales, gets flustered..." Amanda raised her hands.

"She sends the books to the wrong people?"

"She does indeed. The one who gets the rare book is suddenly indignant about *caveat emptor* and all that – let the buyer beware, bought in good faith, yadda yadda. The *other* buyer starts wondering what this *treasure map's* all about. Completely by chance, two people have received something of value – but different *sorts* of value."

"Two *men* by any chance?"

"I think so, yes. Why do you ask?"

"I wonder if anything like this would've happened if two *women* had received the wrong books."

"Anything like what?"

"Well, greed. Isn't that what you mean? Let me guess. The first guy says: it's *my* book now, if you want it back here's what it's worth – cough up. The second guy gets himself involved in a criminal plot. Am I close?"

"You're close," Amanda admitted, "but it's the other way around. The *first* guy – who now owns the rare book – not only does he refuse to return it, he gets violent about it. He goes past the righteous anger bit. He obtains the vendor's phone number somehow and starts to call. *I've done my research, I know what it's worth. Pay me or shut up about it. Or I'll drive over and set fire to your car.*"

Claire whistled. "Talk about escalation. But wait a minute. Did you mean the two men had *each other's* books... or were there other disappointed buyers involved in this auction?"

"I'm not sure. I doubt it was only the two of them; it's too large a coincidence."

"So, someone else bought the rare book and had to be refunded."

"Presumably. But don't forget, the seller didn't *know* it was rare; it was listed cheap as chips."

"Yes, you're right. I wonder what Marx would have said about this."

"Deirdre Marx?"

"No, *Karl* Marx. Commodity, value, exchange… I was trying to be amusing. Who's Deirdre Marx?"

"She taught supply chains to undergrads when I was doing my Masters. The Business School. That's why I made the link. I actually *do* wonder how she might've interpreted the facts, now she's in my mind. But you meant Ol' Beardy Karl."

"Sorry. What happened? Threats to the car…"

"The vendor reported him to the police. It all went quiet for a while, while Big Man formulated his strategy. Then one morning, there's smoke in the air, and the vendor wakes up to find her boyfriend's car on fire on the drive… *Meanwhile…* the second guy, with the treasure map in his book, needs to find whoever it was who sold the book to the *vendor*. The treasure map's only valuable if the missing piece is restored – whatever that might be – so *he's* bombarding the seller as well, saying *we could all be rich!* He's returned the book but he's kept the bookmark."

"Crikey. Scandal and intrigue. The moral of this story being – I guess – be very, very careful when you're processing your parcels. Perfect your postcodes."

"Or don't sell anything in the first place," Amanda replied.

Claire smiled. "Except you couldn't do that if you tried."

"Except I couldn't do that if I tried. Part of the *pleasure* is selling it and buying it all over again. Losing on the deal.

Winning on the deal. The whole thing about collecting – for me – is knowing when to let it go and when to want it again."

Some days later, Claire would question how much of Amanda's story could be believed. By nature, Claire veered between susceptibility and suspicion.

What I believe, she would type slowly, *is always my choice and no one else's. It is time to turn the soil of reality.*

SESSION 13

I've written a new TV drama and I'm on set. A baby hangs from a ceiling, dead, in a plastic bag on a rope or a piece of string. I know it's fake… but it looks real. Then I'm in a lower floor flat, somewhere overseas; it's my flat, though I never lived there really. People keep visiting, uninvited. Seven men in a crapped-out old van cross a desert to get to me. One of them has a number for a name. Another one is my third PhD supervisor, the one who left the University: Professor Cecil Joseph – only the others call him Brother Joe.

"We're here for the funeral," Brother Joe tells me.

I think he's talking about me and I start to panic.

"I'm not dead yet!" I complain.

Brother Joe says, "Finish your thesis; then I'll find you again."

The funeral procession arrives and people offer their condolences for the passing of the old lady who used to live in the flat before me. The lead mourner takes off his top hat and it's Benny. He grins at me and asks if there's any room at the inn; his teeth are brown.

I slam the door in his face and wake up coughing.

In her mind, Phyllie summarises her most recent therapy hour with Dr. Bruce-Sange as a question that had not been asked but had been hinted at, with reference to Roger Billie.

Did you enact one another's fantasies?

"This is probably the last time I'll talk about this," Phyllie had proffered. "I reckon there's a limited time we say *anything*. Repetition burns the message to cinders." She had paused; her upper lip had wrinkled with a smile that was not to be – it did not *set*.

"When I was a child, I apologised so much that people started to create misdemeanours that had happened just to pin them on me. They knew I'd say sorry. It didn't matter how illogical the thing was. It didn't even matter if it was *impossible* I could have done it. I said sorry. I've been saying sorry all my life."

And…

"I used to be frightened of the dark. But more than that: I was scared of going to sleep in case the world stopped until I woke up again. I was worried people would be angry with me. And I don't mean when I was a child. This happened *well* into my twenties."

SESSION 14

I was the only person travelling on a busy train who wasn't crying. Around me, everyone was grizzling or weeping. I couldn't stop apologising. I felt I should cry; I needed to cry. Everyone was staring at me through their tears, but I couldn't join them. The train was racing... too fast.

"I have to ask – I hope you don't mind."

"No, I don't mind," Phyllie Reydman tells Dr. Chaz Bruce-Sange.

"With respect, you don't know what it is yet."

"With respect, I think I do. With *respect,* I've expected you to ask questions about that house for at least the previous ten therapy hours. It's an anchor in my unconscious."

"Well, I agree with that much," Chaz agrees; "how could it be otherwise?"

"How could it be otherwise indeed? I'm a current survivor of a nine-year-long post-traumatic depression. I just disguise the *shit* out of my current situation; that's what I do. I hide and lie – everywhere but here. Go on, Doctor, hit me baby one more time. What tickles your psychoanalytic fancy this fine morning?"

"Perhaps a simple one to start with. What do you remember?"

"... I remember *sailing*. That's how it felt. I was on an inflatable vessel, with a mainsail; sometimes it was a raft, sometimes something more ambitious – a rowboat..."

She remembers a moment that occurred nine years earlier: a moment that had spread like an ink stain. The moment in which he had understood – with spotless clarity – that everyone that Benny had imprisoned in the chambers beneath his Edlesborough house had been *connected*. A bond had stretched between the captives. A bond – indeed – had constituted the reason for the captives' very existence.

When I woke up, Phyllie remembers writing shortly after, *the world seemed still asleep.*

In truth, when Phyllie had awoken – or *been* woken – the world to either side of her bunk had seemed to bristle with activity.

From time to time, in her wee-hours panics, she tries to imagine if she would fall for it again. If someone like Benny, a sadistic sexually motivated predator like Benny, tried to trap her again, would she fall under his spell?

"I'm trying to understand," Phyllie says aloud. "But if I understand – by definition, I think – I cannot forget..."

She wants to say this to Dr. Chaz Bruce-Sange; however, something holds her back – with a restraint that feels physical. It is as if there are two hands on her shoulders, applying force; the two hands do not want her to enter a particular room.

"I can't talk about it," Phyllie states, as if to a mirror. "But I can't *wait* to talk about it either. I'm standing in a spotlight of my own creation."

"You've got stage fright," says Chaz. "You've forgotten your lines."

Phyllie's face brightens. "Yes, I like that a lot, that feels natural." And then she pauses for nearly three minutes; both women await a minor breakthrough. "I remember a hill. I was trapped under a house in Edlesborough – and at the same time I was striding."

"You mentioned it once. Benny Hill."

But there is nowhere to go after this has been recalled. Phyllie is suddenly uncertain if the memory is hers or if she has borrowed it from someone else. She experiences the uneasy impression that someone else is sharing her mind.

"Perhaps you could ask me a simpler one for now. Not forever. I feel *bunged up*."

"Okay. Let's go back to your marriage to Roger."

"That's easier. I can tell you about our sexual escapades, Chaz. We used to get up to all *sorts* of shenanigans! We were what people call *broad-minded*."

"Did you talk about fantasies?"

"Not often, to be honest. We sort of *fell into* each other's fantasies and merged our minds on the subject. It all felt fairly organic – and *normal* at the time. Who's to say what's allowed and not allowed between two consenting adults, after all?"

"No one. Yet you did eventually say to yourself, enough's enough. Which makes me infer that either something happened, or something felt *close* to happening."

"Well, *Benny* happened for a start."

"But what do you mean by that? Without using the word *Benny*, try to describe how your life changed – or threatened to change."

"Well… I fell into the web of a man who turned out to be a sociopath. As did plenty of other people. I'm not sure I can state it any clearer than that."

A silence descends. At length, Chaz adds:

"Thomas Ogden mentions a case study called Dr. F (I think). What our American cousins might refer to as a pompous *asshole* – although Ogden doesn't actually say so, of course. Dr. F starts his analysis with Ogden by saying that he won't be the one who speaks first, not in any session. And that Ogden should not attempt to wait him out. Ogden must be the one who speaks first."

"To ask the first question."

"Or to provide the prompt. To unblock the pipe, as it were. My point is, what if Ogden *hadn't agreed*? How long would the silence stretch? What might analyst and analysand create in an atmosphere without words? And I say *without words* as opposed to *in silence*, because there is always a sound. A clock ticking. A digestive bubble in your chest. Blood moving. A headache changing shape, perhaps."

"Perhaps we should try it one time."

"Would it frighten you?"

"Not *frighten* me so much as it would annoy me for the money I'd wasted."

"In which case – correct me if I'm wrong – you would have regarded the exclusion of conversation as something negative."

"Well, it *is* something negative!"

"With the option of becoming something positive. Tell me, Phyllie: how do you feel about embracing change in general?"

"I feel like it's a leading question – the word *embracing*. You've made an assumption."

"Based on our work together: yes. But if I may suggest, Phyllie, the question remains."

Phyllie gives the words some space before replying. Momentarily she believes she is being canny when she answers with a question of her own: "How would you expect me to feel?"

"Does it worry you, Phyllie?"

"You've used my name twice in the last half a minute. You're re-personalising the encounter."

"I use your name all the time," answers Dr. Bruce-Sange, before spotting another line of enquiry. "Do you not always hear me use your name?"

"I do not. Because you *don't* always use my name. Or would you suggest that I edit it out of our discussions? Perhaps *you* edit it out of our discussions!"

"I asked about your responses to change."

"You asked me about my responses to *embracing* change, which is not quite the same thing. But I'll answer, of course, because that's what we're here for. I don't think – on a conscious level – I *embrace* anything at all."

"Are we back on the subject of intimacy?" the psychoanalyst wants to know.

"Did we ever leave it?" Phyllie replies.

MEN ABOUT TOWN, 2

In a ruminative mood, Paper Jake O'Donnell had also marked the odd coincidence of the name of the hotel: the *Hotel Harlequin*. It was where he'd stayed in Japan; where his fellow convention-attender-turned-lover Amanda had gained access to the wrong bedroom, in the wrong wing of the building, and had seen the revolver on the pillow.

Names are important, he typed; but he could type no further – his fingers had turned traitorous. He felt paralysed in the glare of his three words' ineptitude; he felt stunned by their obviousness and lack of ambition.

Paper Jake had joined what he called "the caravan of goodwill" before a space had been found in the van for Twennyfour. He had been in place in the rickety vehicle since nearly the beginning of the expedition. Two or three days before Brother Joe had eased the van into a brown filling station to pick up fuel and Twennyfour, just inside a *village* named John Hodgins, they had stopped for the night in a much smaller town – and Paper Jake had met a *man* named John Hodgins...

At first, the man had seemed aggressive.

A squat, bald, aggressive fuzzy bundle; and for why, for what reason? Because Paper Jake O'Donnell had been taking photos of some farm machinery. The fuzzy bundle made the position clear with a pointed finger and a statement:

"*I'm* the only Pose-Yourself Man in this town, young feller."

Once Paper Jake had explained that he was a visitor and had not known of the town's restrictions on photography, the man seemed appeased. In Paper Jake's memory, days later, here in Scent of Knife, he and his accuser had become quite amiable. Before he knew what his mouth constructed, Paper Jake said, "And what's your name, Pose-Yourself Man?"

"John Hodgins. Now I offer you a coffee and a rum to say sorry, Paper Jake O'Donnell. I see my mistake as clear as day – and it's National Apology Day, exactly one month from today." John Hodgins sniffed and chuckled.

"… It's National *Apology* Day?"

"We explore our shadow sides and our consciences. We breathe deep in the sweat of the anger and sadness we've caused, even if it was accidental. One of my favourite bars is three streets from here."

Paper Jake O'Donnell grinned. "I'd be delighted to accept your apology, John."

For the first time in Paper Jake O'Donnell's life, he entered an establishment through the sort of batwing doors that used to represent the Wild West reality in a cowboy film, along with the horse tied up outside, its nose in a trough of food. Instead of a parked horse, however, the accompanying wildlife on this occasion was a solitary mule, outside a bar named Sevens & Nines. The mule ate monkey nuts from the palm of a little girl's hand. The little girl was about seven; her smile as piercingly white as freshly fallen snow.

"I have a question, if I may," said Paper Jake O'Donnell.

"What's on your mind?"

"Your name, my friend. John Hodgins is also the name of the next town we're stopping in. We're picking up a man named Twennyfour."

John Hodgins nodded.

"A sorrowful town. Attacked by bandits. That poor man be blessed."

"Twennyfour, you mean?"

"Yes. His sister Twennythree ended her own life. I know of him vaguely; we've met at trade fairs over the years."

Paper Jake O'Donnell nodded – both to John Hodgins, acknowledging what had been said up to this point; also to the waiter who had swerved a held-aloft tray through a medium-density crowd, to bring the two men their chosen drinks. This waiter's teeth were as exquisite as John Hodgins' teeth.

"Thank you."

"Thank you, Arthur." John Hodgins lifted the coffee cup to his generous lips; he sipped his beverage. Then he added: "You wish to mention the chicken and the egg, do you now? A question of which arrived first?"

"Something like that," Paper Jake O'Donnell admitted. "The town's name pre-dates your birth, I would guess. But even that makes me wonder... if it's not you, who *is* the John Hodgins the place was named after?"

John Hodgins shrugged. "I'm afraid I don't know the folklore, but I wouldn't read too much into the coincidence." Brightening visibly, he said, "Let's talk photography! I rarely meet a kindred spirit!"

"And if you did, you'd threaten to sue him."

"I don't need the competition."

"You don't need an outsider undercutting you on price."

"That's true, but there's something else in my mind. When I say I don't need the competition, I also mean I try to keep the art form mysterious. If there's only one photographer, it must be that photography is a calling that one is drawn to. Wouldn't you agree?"

"I suppose so. It's like the Wise Woman of a village – the rarity is what makes the position important."

"We have a Wise Woman too. Carey. By name and by nature, as they say. She's said to be over a hundred years old – *two* hundred if you believe the children's skipping rhymes. Not bad going; considering we've had droughts and vegetable famines. It was Carey – again, rumour has it..." John Hodgins smiled. "...who saved lives by suggesting we eat the floor."

Paper Jake O'Donnell had concluded his drink and was seeking Arthur to order another. "You ate the floor? What do you mean by that?"

"It was when I was a babe in arms," John Hodgins answered. "Lapsus was starving; no one had more than a single drop of spittle in their mouths. Carey spoke to the skies and communed with the ground."

"You ate the *earth*? Yes, please." Arthur had arrived at Jake's left shoulder; the second utterance was for the waiter's benefit. "The same again for you, John? Another coffee and rum each, please, Arthur." With the other man retreating, spinning his empty tray on an upturned forefinger, like a basketball player showboats with the ball, Jake added: "Are you hungry now? Should I have offered you a snack?"

"I've put the thought of food in your head, Jake," John Hodgins said as he flashed his flawless parade of teeth. "No, I'm not hungry now, but thank you; and nobody ate the *earth*. I said, the *floor*. In those days a lot of homes had floors made of dried cow-hide patches stitched together. Carey said desperate times require desperate solutions. People tore up sections of their floors and boiled this old leather for hours, in vats in the sun."

"…That *is* a desperate solution. Did it work?"

"People were sick for weeks," John Hodgins replied. "You could hear the vomiting from half a mile away, the rhymes say. Imagine little girls skipping along. *You might not starve but you might get sick / If you stop your skipping and you eat up quick.* A wave of madness went through the population. But the strangest of all – I think – was the periodontal disease that struck the town."

"Teeth?"

John Hodgins nodded. "Their teeth fell out. Like they do in a bad dream. People woke up in the morning with a mouthful of molars. You'd boil water and lose an incisor while you waited – that kind of thing. The town stank of gum rot."

After a moment, Paper Jake O'Donnell summed up with a whispered "Gosh." Louder, he then added: "At least it wasn't hereditary, the condition. Your own teeth are the ticket."

"Thanks to Carey. She told everyone to keep hold of the teeth they lost and take them to her. She pushed every tooth into her skin; embedded them right in there. Her body became a collection of surrogate *mouths*. She was orderly – one contributor, one part of Carey's flesh. My own great-grandfather's teeth were planted in Carey's left shin. Then Carey went on a walkabout."

Arthur returned to their table, his tray once more aloft. "Here we are, fellers," he announced; and for Jake, this was a welcome *entr'acte*. He wanted to listen to the thoughts in his head for a few seconds. It was not that the story's plot had disturbed him – with folklore being what it was, it seemed that civilisations competed for the most outlandish chapter in the Book of the World's Mythologies – it was more that the personalised touch in the last sentence had unnerved him. The mention of a great-grandfather brought things close to home.

Paper Jake O'Donnell stirred sugar into his coffee. Noise levels rose; he was finding it hard to think in anything other than poorly lit sepia images – a still of a woman thumbing a tooth into her leg, for instance. The only way to break the spell would be to request to hear the remainder of what had to be said.

"Walkabout for Carey lasted nine months, the story goes," said John Hodgins.

(Later, into camera, Jake would annotate this part of Hodgins' recital with the words, *The same length as a human pregnancy*.)

"She walked through the nights in a fog of prayer. During the heat of the day, she found shelter if she could, and rested. The teeth in her skin came from the people of the town, and all of those mouths on her body talked to her in her dreams. Sometimes they spoke all at once – or cried or screamed. Sometimes, the only sounds in the wasteland were the wind and the voices coming out of her pores."

Paper Jake O'Donnell smiled. Although this was not the first time that he suspected John Hodgins had relayed the story, he could not help but admire this most recent embellishment.

"The teeth in her skin protected Carey from harm and for nine months the entire population of a town was embedded in her skin. A few wild dogs had circled her from time to time, but she frightened them off with the combined voices."

Nearly halfway through his coffee, Jake understood the source of what had puzzled him since he'd arrived in Lapsus. *We only see patterns long after the event,* he had written somewhere; perhaps he had opined thus to camera too.

While focusing his attention on John Hodgins (and the sentence-by-sentence striptease glimpses of his heavenly orthodontics), Jake recalled the seven year-old girl outside the bar, the one who fed monkey nuts to a mule; Jake remembered her dazzling *smile*. Not that John and the girl were the only two *in situ* to experience the privilege of luxurious teeth. Arthur was similarly blessed; and now that Jake glanced around the increasingly busy bar at Sevens & Nines, the exposure of beautiful happy expressions was like fireflies, blinking, incandescent in any gloom.

A whole town with splendid teeth? Paper Jake O'Donnell would question himself via the camera's unblinking eye.

"What's wrong?" John Hodgins asked. "Is it the rum? It's quite a high proof."

"It's not the rum. I like the rum. It's like when I intuited my sister was pregnant... before anyone else did." Jake's voice sounded distant.

"You've lost me."

"Lapsus is full of people with ideal smiles. Your teeth are magnificent," Jake continued. "There's not a single person with so much as a yellow stain."

Helping to corroborate Jake's theory, John Hodgins proffered another lambent example. The white display in his very dark face was like day and night.

"That's what Carey did," John Hodgins explained. "She threw herself off a bridge to be consumed. Try to imagine the pain. A place called Feast Bridge."

INTERSECTIONS

———•○•———

"If it feels like Winter and Summer put together,
we must learn to compromise on it being Autumn.
There is no point pretending that it's Spring."

Brother Joe

THE CHICKENPOX PARTY
(PROFESSOR SIR GRAYSON TWIVY'S STORY)

"All violin players are beautiful," said Twennyfour. "All cellists look like they've been struck on the beak with a shovel."

As ever, the men were trading stories; it was par for their very long course. The weather had cooled dramatically, with wholly unexpected ramifications. In defiance of meteorological odds, for the previous nine minutes, it had been *snowing*. The snowflakes made notes of music in the air. Everyone was able to read the score of the afternoon – its crotchets and semi-quavers – and if it happened to be a film score, they knew what genre of film the men had become actors within.

"But personally, I prefer a cellist every time," Twennyfour continued. "You don't have to work so hard with a cellist."

The other men nodded, not necessarily in agreement, but perhaps for something to do. Voicing nonsensical opinions was a different way of theirs to pass the time.

Into the ensuing silence, Gray cleared his throat.

"I've got what I hope'll be an interesting one for you," he announced. "Back in John Hodgins, you used to have chicken-pox parties; am I right?"

"Yes, that's right," answered Twennyfour, bewildered by the change of direction, but happy enough to recall certain scenes from his childhood. Once more he remembered the time that Gray – as *Professor Sir Grayson Twivy* no less – had visited his school.

During the weeks that followed the Chickenpox Party, the illness robbed Peter to pay Paul; transmission occurred with a rapidity that bordered on the oneiric. Family members stepped aside from loading the dishwasher or feeding the dog... only to find their children or siblings, of normal appearance scant minutes earlier, now all-but *luminescent* with fiery-looking rashes. The skin conditions were the temperature of oxters. Spots that appeared as permanent as tattoos now combusted on children's cheeks and foreheads, their shoulders or their chests. Symptoms ranged from "feeling grotty" to lethargy and a washed-out sensation, the only treatment for which was twenty-four-hour continuous bed confinement. A prominent (nervous) joke among the parents revolved around a wish to have bought shares in dermatitis creams and Lucozade. And oh, how the adults indulgently smiled! Albeit with a smile that is usually reserved for the grudging acceptance of a racist quip.

Despite the fact that the local schools had enforced a strict no-spots embargo policy, the chickenpox spread. Any child with so much as a tickly throat or pale complexion was ordered to stay at home.

By the third week after the Chickenpox Party, all the local schools had closed, and the children were forbidden from leaving where they lived. Parents were encouraged to work from home – and not mix with one another unless a meeting was unavoidable. The afflicted children looked worse and worse; they *felt* worse and worse. Archipelagos of facial spots – by now the colour of roses – had evolved and joined together to form land masses. On some children's skins, no original tones remained: every inch of the body appeared bathed in blood.

Between four and six weeks after the Chickenpox Party, a sense of competition had broken out among the town's children. While adults – parents and medical experts alike – debated responses to the outbreak and tried to analyse its virulent right-to-life, the children had, under its cosh, begun to share videos of their fresh-and-fresher tribal markings. If circumstances had conspired to make the children ill, the next stage of societal development was to determine ownership of the superlative. Who was the sickest? Whose body was the best covered? Whose rash was the most startling *red*?

It had long since become clear that those neighbouring towns – or the children who lived within their boundaries – had not caught the chickenpox. Not a single case of it; not a rumour of its existence, not even in gossipy and lazy social circles.

"Can a town be damned?" people asked.

A matter of metaphysics that was debated on night-time local stations – radio and web – until the subject returned home one day, exhausted by senseless overexposure. The idea that there could never be an explanation grew beautiful wings. The town members sided towards a preference for ignorance and acceptance.

Meanwhile, one young boy prayed for his inaugural spot. One boy of nine years of age could not feel ill, though he wanted to. Not so much as the first spot had crept onto his brow. Not so much as a chest-itch bothered his sleep... although his sleep was most definitely compromised. The boy felt stigmatised.

Twennyfour was waiting; this evening his impatience felt hair-triggered.

"What happened to the boy who couldn't get sick?" he asked.

"You're talking to him," answered Gray – or perhaps, given the context of the story, it was not Gray but Professor Sir Grayson Twivy, with his faded skin tones and his professional reminiscences, who had told Twennyfour the tale.

SUBMISSION

During this coda – as we stretch towards completion – it is human (no less) to reflect on our project's successes and failures – as indeed it should be to reflect this on a daily basis.

These words are Claire Carey's. She approaches the end of her thesis. She prepares herself to jump philosophical ship and flail in the pedagogic waves.

She is *ready*.

We approach a denoeument of sorts, she types further. A red line on the screen scolds her inadequate spelling, from underneath the phrase's fourth word. "I know, I know," Claire tells her laptop's deity. She right-clicks the offending monstrosity for a spelling suggestion. "Well, I was *close*," she offers defensively as she accepts *denouement* into her draft.

Claire recalls the words of her supervisor, Dr. Alex Gordon: "The basic idea is to play with ten thumbs and then wonder what fingers to slide a ring on."

By now she knows no other way of working. It's ten thumbs or not at all.

"And I hope you'll take this in the spirit it's intended," Claire said into the phone. "I'd like to say thank you for your contribution to my thesis. We're allowed an Acknowledgements paragraph – or page if we like – that doesn't affect the overall word count. I wanted to check the spelling of your surname."

"That's very kind of you, Claire. It's bee-eye-elle-elle-eye-ee. Billie. I'm not sure I deserve it though. I only provided – what? – *chit-chat*?"

"*Vital* chit-chat, Amanda," Claire responded. "You helped me form some crucial amendments. I'll always be grateful."

"Thank you. So, what are you going to write?"

"… How do you mean?"

"In what language will you frame your generous appreciation of my services?"

"… I wasn't expecting a question like that." Claire laughed into Amanda's ear. The plosive sound returned to Claire's own ear, as if it had been repelled by her interlocutor and returned to sender. "*Throughout the composition of this.* No. *Throughout the drafting of this thesis, I have experienced fierce support from my friend Amanda Billie* … How about something like that?"

"Very flattering, if you're sure. *Fierce support* – that's generous. The way I look at it is, I've continued – in my *small* way – to help you to construct an argument – even if it's on the level of a simple phrase or sentence. So the way you write it on the Acknowledgements page is equally important. I do like *fierce support,* the more I think about it."

"Maybe you could say more," Claire did not quite ask her.

Amanda picked up the challenge.

"Well, the Acknowledgements page is part of the *submission*, after all – even if it's *not* part of the overall word count. It sets a tone. The reader wants to know who the people are who are being thanked – beyond a name and the description of a task executed, I mean. What are they *really* to the author? Then they set about detecting the parts of the submission that refer to what the person is thanked for. Becomes like *The Hunting of the Snark*."

Claire paused… before taking dictation from her future self. "*In addition, I would like to thank Amanda Billie for a number of useful. No. A number of illustrious conversations?*"

"Illustrious is lovely."

"*… conversations that led to several important rethinks during the final drafting.*"

"Well… I like *illustrious*. I'm less keen on *rethinks*. But ultimately, it's your choice. I'd only say, be careful you don't make it sound like I did any of the heavy liftings for you. You don't want to sound too humble, in case it gets picked up by the examiners."

A meeting had been scheduled for one p.m. in one of the lecture theatres in the Postgraduate Centre. The attendants were to be all doctoral candidates, their supervisors, and various administrative members of the Research Graduate School. It was time for the once-a-semester Doctoral Board Meeting, a forum for the doctoral candidates to present any advances in their work since the previous meeting, each report strictly timed to seven minutes long (five minutes for content, two minutes for questions from the audience).

After Claire had set out her academic stall, she received an intelligent question from Phyllie Reydman. They had long been in cahoots to pose the other a question in the embarrassing silence that sometimes ensues when no one else can think of something to say.

"What warning signs," Phyllie asked, "have you identified for when a person with a collection morphs into a person with an obsession?"

Although the contents of the question had not been rehearsed, Claire had expected something along these lines. After all, they had discussed obsession recently. They had also discussed – somewhat tentatively – what had occurred in the Edlesborough house, nine years earlier, to Phyllie and the other captives.

"What happened to you there?" Claire had asked on that occasion.

"What *didn't* happen to me there?" Phyllie had replied.

Taking the deflection as unwillingness to elaborate on or share painful memories, Claire had opted for a softer tack.

"I mean, I hope you don't mind my bringing it up," she had continued. "I don't want to rake up difficult ground for you."

Phyllie had smiled. "I promise you, Claire, if I didn't want to talk about it, I wouldn't. I've spent nine years not-talking about it and look where *that's* got me. Another few minutes won't hurt. I even don't-talk about it with my psychoanalyst – or at least I don't talk about it properly. What am I afraid of, in a psychoanalyst's room? A full-scale nervous breakdown? Hers or mine? And even if that *did* happen, so what? That's sort of what I'm paying her for, I think: to endure my full-scale nervous breakdown."

She had sighed. "The truth is, Claire, I think talking about it would help me immensely, in the long run. I just don't know how to do it."

At the time they had been seated in one of the rooms dedicated to silent study on the third floor of the Postgraduate Centre: by sharing their thoughts they were technically breaking the rules of the room itself. The fact that there had been no one else present was likely to have been a catalyst. The room had been too warm; they had both found it hard to work on that day.

"You said there was media interest at the time," Claire had offered.

"And plenty of it! But I tried my very best to keep *schtum*." Phyllie had performed the mime of turning a key in front of her lips. "I was offered twenty grand – I wouldn't even have to *write* the damn thing! All I had to do was sit with a reporter for an afternoon and she'd do the heavy lifting."

"And you told them no."

"I said no-*thank-you*," Phyllie had replied. "I've made it a point in life – as far as I can – never to slam a door in people's faces. You don't know when you'll meet them again."

Claire had nodded. "You might still tell the tale."

"Well, I *am*, really. That's sort of what the PhD is all about: our psychogeographies – the places where our memories merge with our landscapes. Whether they happen to be *true stories* is another matter entirely."

"I'd love to read what you've written so far," Claire had told her.

"And vice versa. But not today."

On a different occasion (one of many when Claire and Amanda would meet, sometimes as planned *rendezvous*, other times by chance, drawn like flies to the light bulb of the University; these meetings would eventually blur in their memories into a handful of occasions for each of them, but there were plenty more), the two women discussed collections and obsessions using different examples and different language still.

Phyllie said: "Your surname always makes me think of a friend I had when we were girls. Her name was Carey – which was pretty unusual for those days. We also had an Elton *and* an Elvis in our year. I wonder whatever happened to her."

"It's just the name that reminds you of her?"

"I think so. We had a Whisper Club. You could tell each other anything you wanted as long as you whispered it into her ear. There were other girls allowed into the club but at no point could everyone know everything about everyone else there, by definition. You had to choose your allies."

"It sounds like politics. How old were you?"

"Eight or nine."

"I don't remember anything about my life at that time," Claire added in a sad tone.

Phyllie chuckled. "Carey and I used to collect teeth. We thought the Tooth Fairy was a monstrous creation and we decided to make it our lives' work to thwart his endeavours."

"*His* endeavours." Claire smiled. "I always thought of the Tooth Fairy as a girl. How did you go about collecting teeth? Bit of a seller's market, I would have thought – scarce commodity."

"Limited distribution networks," Phyllie agreed with a nod. "But it turned out, Carey and I had saved our baby teeth, coincidentally. They'd fallen out when we were five or six. And we'd convinced our parents to give them to us – or perhaps we lied to them and said we'd lost the tooth, I can't remember. We each had a small collection of some of our baby teeth. What better way of cementing a friendship than by stockpiling a collection of baby teeth?"

"You pooled your resources?"

Phyllie nodded. "It's all coming back to me now. We took a doll – a girl's doll, a normal doll of a girl, with that skin tone that no child actually has in real life – and we ... embedded our collection of teeth in the doll's skin. We talked about where we would push in every tooth. It was a serious business for a nine year-old!"

"I bet it *was*."

"God knows how we kept it private from our parents, but that's another thing. We knew we'd need help with building the collection; by then we'd decided – don't ask me why – to cover the girl's skin, from scalp to soles, in teeth. Well, we needed more teeth – clearly."

"Supply and demand."

"We started a business, on the hush-hush. The younger siblings of the members of the Whisper Club – their baby teeth when they fell out. A Dobermann's tooth from a family pet. Whatever we could lay our hands on. Goods exchanged for pocket money or sweets – or a kind word about someone passed to a boy, to set them up."

Phyllie laughed. "The things we remember!"

"What happened to the doll?" Claire asked. "Did you complete the mission? To cover it in teeth from head to foot."

"Probably less than my memory tells me we did, to be honest. What happened to it? We changed its gender, for one thing; and we named it – named him. Carey and I started calling the doll John Hodgins, after a boy we liked in school." Phyllie took a sip of her drink. "A boy I've been obsessed with ever since, if I'm honest."

"John Hodgins, you say?" Claire chuckled.

"Yes. You're not going to tell me you know him, are you?"

Claire shook her head. "It's a weird coincidence, but five years ago, I dated a guy on my Masters course with that name." Again, she shook her head; more vigorously this time, to rid herself of the memory. It was as painful as a blister. "Obsessed with, in what sense?" she asked. "The one that got away?"

"But he wasn't my age, was he?" Phyllie asked, her voice uncertain. "It surely can't be the same man I knew when I was at school with him."

"Please don't panic, Phyllie; it wasn't the same guy. Hodgins was twenty-four when I was twenty-one. And a *man of colour*, if that helps you to settle your nerves."

Phyllie smiled. "Obsessed in what way," she reflected on Claire's query. "In a more literal sense than you probably mean, Claire. I've always been a bit more than *interested* in how his story turned out. Yet not quite interested enough to do anything about it. Not even search social media."

"He's the cat in the box – the psychology cat. Both present and not-present at the same time. And maybe dead and maybe alive."

"Ah yes, good old Erwin… Erwin Schrödinger."

"And John Hodgins trapped in a box the size of a planet. He could be milking cows in French Guiana."

An expression of panic flashed across Phyllie's face. Although her normal expression returned, Claire had noticed the effect that her attempt at a joke had had on her friend.

"They seek him here, they seek him there," Phyllie agreed.

"Except you don't seek him at all, of course."

"The last I heard – you might think I'm making this up – he was about to go to this very university – where we're sitting right now – to start an undergrad degree when we were eighteen. I've even managed to convince myself he wanted to be a dentist. I might've retrofitted that last bit."

"Do you think of him often?"

"Surprisingly so. I wonder what he looks like. I wonder what contribution he's made to his society, wherever that might be. I see him – sometimes – in a desert, in sepia tones. Browns and yellows. There's nothing much around apart from a solitary building. It's a health centre of some sort… or it used to be. It's abandoned. Conflict has wiped out any reason to stay."

"And you see Hodgins *there*? In the wasteland?"

Phyllie nodded. "Sometimes. He's the last remaining worker in this abandoned dental clinic. No one needs treatment but he stays anyway. It's a funny fantasy. Your mention of French Guiana a moment ago really hit home, by the way."

"I thought it had. Not offensively, I hope."

"Oh no, nothing like that… though you *could* do me a bit of a favour on that score. I'd be grateful if you used his full name and not just Hodgins. It's *John* Hodgins, please… if we ever even mention him again."

"No problem," Claire told her. "What happened to him, as a doll?"

"My parents encouraged me to throw that manky old doll away, but I wouldn't have any of it. It's in a box at home."

Claire raised her eyebrows. "Maybe there and not-there at the same time."

"Simultaneously dead and alive," Phyllie agreed with a nod.

"Speaking of which… there and not-there. I've thought about another way to approach *how to* talk about what happened in the Edlesborough house," Claire said. "There's something about approaching the end of the thesis – it's freed up other ideas in my head."

"All right, don't rub it in." Phyllie was currently making heavy weather of the methodology chapter in her thesis; she was a long way behind where she had hoped to be by this point in the year. "What's your brainwave?"

"When you think about what happened to you…" Claire collected her words and inspected them (Phyllie thought and would write in her journal later) with a diamond cutter's precision. "…do you see it like a film? Does it have an order?"

"Sort of. I see parts of my life as if they were filmed by an earnest but amateur cameraman: someone like Tim Branston."

"Who's Tim Branston?"

"Sorry. Branston was a lecturer in Film Studies at Barnfield College. I don't know the details, but he got involved with Benny. He filmed some of the experiments on us." Phyllie paused. "I'm surprised you don't remember some of that wonky footage they used on the news. Most of it they weren't allowed to, of course."

"I do remember it," Claire countered.

"In those days I was a Geography teacher about twenty miles from here. I was married to Roger Billie, a social worker at the time. What we lacked in adventure in certain parts of our lives, we made up for in the bedroom."

"*Ooh la la*," said Claire, wrongfooted by the change in direction. "You'll make me blush."

Not in denial of Claire's statement – more against the wave of memories – Phyllie shook her head. "Or anywhere else for that matter," she added.

Phyllie turned her attention to a member of staff who was pushing a wheeled set of shelves through the cafeteria. Most of the shelves carried trays of leftover food, crumpled napkins, and drink bottles on their sides. For a few seconds, as this parade rattled past their table, Phyllie found something more interesting than anything else on the planet in the meals, tools, and containers that people had left behind.

When she returned to Earth, she said, "It was all a block against reality, all that dirty stuff – I can see it now. We were hiding the fragility of the marriage from ourselves. There was always someone else in my head … even before there was *actually* someone else in my head. Before there was Benny, I mean."

"A particular someone, do you mean?"

"Very much so. His name was Vig. The one that got away." Phyllie smiled again but the display was brief. "In every possible sense you could imagine."

"What happened to him? Was he with you in the horror house?"

Towards the close of the nightmare, Phyllie had spoken to her child; a child named Claire. In the world that she had left behind, without knowing she had done so, the baby had not even been born; Phyllie had been heavily pregnant. But there, inside the world of connections that Benny had helped to create, the baby had been born; Claire had been four years old.

"Is that where Vig is?" Phyllie had asked Claire, "at the Overlap?"

The child had declined to answer. Her colours had seeped into the air and risen like will-o'-the-wisps, a multitude of them; the lines that defined the girl's face had blurred and smudged, lost distinction.

"Where is it? Where's the Overlap?" Phyllie had demanded, furious at the girl's silence. She had shaken Claire hard. "Tell me where."

"It's near the sea," the girl had answered in Phyllie's voice… and then the skin had aged and tightened.

"Which way?" Phyllie had rattled the wraith once again.

Phyllie had started to rotate one of the bracelets on her right wrist. "I'm getting emotional, Claire," she answered.

"Sorry."

"It's not your fault. We used to work together in the same school. Then he won it big on the Lottery and moved to a country pile…" She cleared her throat. "I don't think I ever stopped loving him."

Claire had sensed a bulb burning brightly; she'd stepped close to its heat and light. Now, both had dimmed. It was time to change the subject.

"Shall we get to work?" she suggested.

"Yes, let's get to work," Phyllie agreed.

SESSION 15

I'm at an academic writing retreat, as a delegate; it's a hotel in the country – lots of land and hills. We are trying to write our theses. I can hear a clock ticking; then another. All the clocks have different accents. I'm staring at a grandfather clock with a Polish accent... when the library door opens. In walks Benny, the mad sadist; he's carrying a clipboard.

Well, obviously I fly into a state of disarray and unease. He's standing there, dressed in the attire of a funeral's lead mourner – even the top hat on his head.

"I'm Benny, your new PhD supervisor," he states to the whole library – maybe another eight candidates. "I want you to play like men with ten thumbs."

I have to get out of there.

I run from the hotel building and across the grounds. I hit the foot of a hill and say "Benny Hill" – like an Open Sesame! command – and I start to climb.

There's a bus stop on the crown of the hill. The bus arrives quickly.

Professor Cecil Joseph is behind the wheel, and he tells me to get in; if I'm quick I can have the whole bus to myself for the *journey's duration. I'm trying to say thanks, but all I can do is compliment him on his novel The Ninth Village.*

He smiles at me and his teeth are missing.

"I didn't write Scent of Knife," he tells me, really angry now.

"I dreamed I was the only person travelling on a busy train who wasn't crying. Around me, everyone was grizzling or weeping."

Dr. Chaz Bruce-Sange pauses. The nod that she offers is modestly shallow. "Where were you travelling to? Do you recognise the scenery?"

Phyllie sips on what she has heard. "I always wonder when you start to use the present tense. But I like it. It feels like a validation of some sort."

"Including now?"

"Why not now?"

"Where were you travelling to? Did the dream tell you?" Chaz pushes.

"Not everything must be a direct refusal to cooperate, Chaz. I think the place was called Thin Snake. I was trying to find John Hodgins. I don't know why."

The psychoanalyst smiles.

"Oh, I think you *do* know, Phyllie. You might need to use different ears to hear the message, but I am *fully* of the belief that you know."

For almost a minute, Phyllie sits in silence. She listens to her pulse. "I sometimes dream I'm part of a group of men, travelling in a van. We're driving towards a place called the Ninth Village."

"And how do you interpret this dream? What's the significance of the number nine?"

"Well, my daughter is nine. There are nine months in the adult female's gestation. It's a long road to satisfaction – the mother's satisfaction, of course. And the baby's satisfaction."

"Am I right to think, in that case, you're approaching a deadline?"

"Partly. With my studies. And with our relationship – you and me," Phyllie continues. "I'm swimming towards two finish lines. *At least* two finish lines."

"May I throw an oar in?" Chaz asks.

"Before you do – no, I don't mind – but before you do, there's something else. I have a friend at the university: Claire. She's doing her PhD as well; she's nearly done. I think it was Claire who put the months idea in my head. Onto my psychic apparatus, you might say."

"In what way?"

"She worked backwards from the day her funding was due to run out. She counted nine months back from that final date and referred to those nine months as her pregnancy. She's determined in a way I can only dream of. In the first month of her pregnancy, she'll do *A*. In the second month... I don't know... she'll do B and C. You get the idea. She's treating the year leading up to her final exam as a build-up to a *delivery*. One way or the other, she aims to bring it into the world, kicking and screaming if need be."

"I seem to remember similar ideas of my own, way back when," says Chaz.

"Really? You counted the months?"

"Well, not in the same way as your friend is; but I was determined to sing from the centre of upstage, as it were."

The idea of such confidence piques Phyllie's interest.

"You had no doubts? No perfectly reasonable qualms?"

"Not that I can recall. All I wanted was to talk about my thesis. I was impatient. I've been a Doctor for thirty-two years now. You don't need me to tell you how corruptible the human memory is if we don't stretch it like violin strings."

Chaz joins her hands together. In the back of her mind, Phyllie starts to recite: *Here is the church; here is the steeple –* and as if on cue, Chaz's forefingers rise and connect.

"I was thinking about your ex-husband the other night," Chaz states. "You've painted a picture of him in a van, travelling from one remote spot to another; and I wrote in my journal – and I quote myself from memory – *her ex-husband's caravan of souls.* It made me wonder, what does he actually *do* out there? Wherever 'there' might be…"

Phyllie shrugs. "I don't know what he does out there," she answers. "And no, I don't know where 'there' is either. Claire Carey might know."

"Why's that?"

"Well, it's odd… but Claire has formed a connection with Roger's second wife, Amanda – on a professional basis. I *really* didn't like it when Claire said Claire sends her love, to me. Claire, my daughter, I mean, sends her love. You tend to think of yourself as an *absentee parent* when your own daughter employs the services of an intermediary."

For a few seconds Chaz says nothing at all; she taps together the buxom fingertips on her forefingers. "That's quite the small world," she offers eventually.

"Isn't it just."

"May I offer an interpretation?"

"That's what I'm paying you for."

"It's not uncommon for someone who has suffered a trauma to turn her back on the place and the people who were in some way associated with that trauma."

"Because she blames them."

"Yes; and because there are imprints on that place and those people. For some survivors of trauma, there's an unconscious wish to share; to dilute the experience."

"To project?" Phyllie asks.

"In a sense."

"Whether or not that place or those people actually wish to be projected into."

"That's right. If the link is made, we may have a case of projective identification – Melanie Klein."

"And if the link is *not* made?"

"The survivor hosts broken pieces with no means to plant them elsewhere."

Phyllie pictures a constellation of scattered segments – some shaped like jigsaw puzzle chunks, some sharp, some roughened down and as smooth as pebbles on the shore – and tries to imagine a little girl of nine years old, attempting to catch those that swim past her. She closes her eyes. As if what Chaz has said is now determined to prove its point, the image of the girl excites a memory. *Am I identifying?* The scattered segments circle the girl... but now she is not trying to catch them. They have found her: the girl is the eye of this storm. The segments swirl closer – and start to embed themselves in the girl's exposed flesh, on her arms, on her legs... on her face. The pieces are as tiny as teeth.

On opening her eyes once more, Phyllie begins a question without knowing where she might run to. All she wants is to rid her conscious mind of the picture of the girl with teeth-sized pieces embedded in her skin.

"From your *professional* point of view, Chaz. Doesn't it seem to you like a selfish thing to do? To want to rid oneself of these unhealthy pieces? Onto some poor sucker who mightn't have anything to do with the traumatic incident in the first place?"

"Well. It's a lot worse for the person *not* to share them out," Chaz answers.

"That's not what I'm asking. I appreciate that the one who projects feels a need to do so. What I mean is, what about the sap who gets lumbered with the negativity?"

"He or she must learn to decline the invitation."

"That's an interesting way of looking at it. In that sense, when my mother used to wail at me on the phone, I could have chosen not to lift her burdens?"

"It's more complex between mothers and grown-up daughters; but yes, in theory."

"I think I would have felt cruel to ignore her."

"I'm willing to bet you felt cruel listening to her, too, at least from time to time."

"So what's the answer? And please don't say: *the answer is you.*"

"You want something concrete."

"I want a *plan*."

"You're living your plan already, Jemima! You've chosen to recover; you're healing! How? By selecting the option of growth. In the literature, it's sometimes referred to as PTG – post-traumatic growth."

"… Are you aware you just called me Jemima, Doctor?"

"I must apologise for that. I must be tired."

"And now," says Phyllie, "as we approach the end of a session, I can't help but wonder who Jemima might be."

"The slip on my part is most regrettable. I would like to stress how sorry I am."

"Please don't beat yourself up about it, Chaz; but tell me – did something just happen in the countertransference? Why didn't I experience it?"

Chaz straightens up in her chair. "It's not your job to experience it. Job as in responsibility. But to answer your request – yes; I had a moment of clarity."

"When I was discussing my mother."

"As it happens; yes."

"You felt a surge of something protective, didn't you, Chaz? Is Jemima your daughter? I think she is."

"Maybe protective. Maybe murderous. What does my face give away?"

"Nothing at all. Your expression's inscrutable; you could be a Japanese poker sharp! But all the same, I think I accidentally found something."

Chaz nods her head and gives her analysand a crumb. "X marks the spot," she says. "And there we must end for today."

"I hope she's not in trouble – your daughter, I mean."

"All daughters are always in trouble, Phyllie. It's time to close shop."

"Do you mind if I read you something?" asked Dr. Chaz Bruce-Sange.

"Not at all. It'll give me something to listen to while I'm busying," replied Dr. Doug Stegmeyer. "Let's test this new phone's loudspeaker function. It should be good; it costs me enough per month. Go for it!"

Chaz heard him settle the phone on a hard surface. She imagined him in a generic kitchen: a lot of white goods; plenty of space. She could only imagine because although she had been to Doug's house in Raulton, she had never been in her friend's kitchen. Every time she had visited, they had talked in his office, usually with contemporary classical music whispering in the background.

"What are you doing?" Chaz wanted to know, her voice slightly raised in volume.

"Dinner!" Doug called back. "Can you hear me okay?"

"Loud as a bell. What are you having?"

"A poor unfortunate animal's internal organs. Sweetbreads."

"Yuck! Why *do* that to yourself?"

"We're psychoanalysts, aren't we? We *thrive* on complaint and misery!" Doug laughed... and Chaz hoped that he could hear her smile through his flashy new hardware. "What did you want to read to me?"

"I quote: 'It is very important to be aware that you may never be satisfied with your analytic career if you feel that you are restricted to what is narrowly called a *scientific'* – in inverted commas – 'approach. You will have to be able to have a chance of feeling that the interpretation you give is a beautiful one, or that you get a beautiful response from the patient. This aesthetic element of beauty makes a very difficult situation tolerable.' I like that."

"*... have to be able to have ...*" Doug repeated. "It's a live talk, I reckon. Wilfred Bion?"

"Wow. Yes."

"The one in Paris? Late 70s?"

"For the bonus. Yes. 1978."

"I remember reading something about it. Round about the time of 'Making the best of a bad job' – the tone is similar... What are you up to tonight? Apart from testing me."

"Quiet night in. Too tired to read or write."

"Have you eaten?"

"No; but thanks in advance – I won't be taking up your offer of offal."

"I'm not busy either, if you want some company. I've got pizzas in the freezer. The only thing I don't have much of is wine."

"I'll pick up a bottle on the way. Thanks!"

"But Chaz? It's Saturday night."

"Yes? So?"

"Make it *two* bottles – one of each."

THE WEDDING RING

Phyllie is early for her next appointment with Chaz Bruce-Sange. While reading the news on her phone in the waiting area, she hears someone outside the building's front door utter something to a putative interlocutor, who remains silent.

"I'll have a sandwich in my car while I wait," the man says, his tone irritated and longsuffering.

Will someone else enter the house?

Phyllie wonders if she has made a mistake with the time of her session – her *therapy hour* (a phrase that she always finds amusing). She regards the door through which she had entered.

It does not open.

Suddenly she remembers an experience from seven years earlier. Her companion had attempted to justify his breaking-off of the relationship – with a deposition concerning how *good she was* compared with him.

"I never lied to you, Phyllie," he had told her (truthfully enough, she had had to acknowledge). "I never said I was single, did I? I was clear I had a partner."

"Yes, you were clear," Phyllie had said into the telephone.

"You deserve so much better than me," he had continued, having sensed (presumably) an advantage in Phyllie's acquiescence (but then, what had he expected? Histrionics? Not her style). His voice had brightened, or had Phyllie imagined this?

"Please don't tell me what I deserve," she had told him. "Anything else is fair game, but don't tell me what I *deserve*. You have no *idea* what I deserve – no one does. And I *mean* no one, by the way. I'll accept your rejection in good faith, don't worry. You're not the first to cast me aside after you've had my clothes off – please don't imagine you ever could be."

The companion had not been sure how to respond. Was Phyllie scolding him – or letting him off the hook gracefully? Was it possible to do both? Or – Heaven forfend! – was Phyllie reducing him in erotic stature, by mentioning the fact that he'd been only one of the boys? An also-ran.

"I didn't lie," he had repeated – it had sounded somewhat helpless in Phyllie's ear.

"You didn't. That's right."

"I enjoyed myself."

"Thank you."

The companion had paused. Perhaps he had sensed defeat. His final retaliative flurry would suggest as much, or so Phyllie believed. He hadn't been praised and he understood that he was not about to be praised either. Rather than end with a goodbye, it had seemed more gratifying for the companion to raise the emotional temperature.

"I've got a child!" he had shouted.

"You've mentioned her," Phyllie had replied.

And then of course – as sure as night follows day – the accusation.

"What's wrong with you, anyway? Why can't you get a proper boyfriend?"

Instead of answering the insult (because she had known that he'd want her to defend herself in some way, even if that way was via an attack), Phyllie had disconnected the call. She had imagined her interlocutor's mouth, as it formed a suitable retort. To Phyllie, the mime had resembled a child blowing bubbles.

From time to time, Phyllie asks herself the question that her companion had demanded of her seven years earlier: *What's wrong with you? Why can't you get a proper boyfriend?*

The married man had been an experiment, perhaps: to see if she was ready for something for herself, after the horrors of the Edlesborough house. The clear answer had been: *No.* She hadn't been ready then and she is not ready now.

Phyllie Reydman would remember an anecdote like this for decades. It was the kind of conglomeration that people deployed as a retrieval cue.

"Psychodynamically – transference works in terms of *emotions*. In Lacanian terms, it operates in the imaginary register. But in his Seminar 4, Lacan works in imaginary *and* symbolic registers, and this was radical at the time."

Dr. Chaz Bruce-Sange pauses. By no means certain that she wishes to continue, she continues anyway, clutching at a variety of straws.

She is dictating into her mobile phone. Part of her believes that she is writing something; part of her believes that she is the most fully-formed fraud outside of crime circles.

"The Real is the trauma that cannot be symbolised. It cannot be *articulated*. As soon as we attempt to articular it, it moves into the imaginary or symbolic."

She hunts for breath. Something is forming.

"Once you articulate anything, it moves into the imaginary or the symbolic. If it's chaotic or madness – for instance, the fragmentation of the body – that's the Real."

Chaz leans closer to her keyboard.

Phyllie Reydman is her next appointment. She should be here any minute.

"On my mother's life," Phyllie remembers saying to a different bristly male face, "I didn't lie to you once."

"You deserve a medal," she'd been told.

"Come on now – you know what I'm getting at. You haven't developed amnesia, presumably. Half of it was fantastic and half of it was disastrous. I honestly wish the balance had been otherwise, but what do we do, this far along the track?"

"I don't remember lying to you either, for what it's worth. If I recall correctly, it was my honesty that got your knickers in a twist in the first place."

It doesn't matter what he looked like. She cannot recall him in any detail.

"Is that so?" Phyllie had asked. "What exactly were you being so honest *about*?"

"I met someone when you told me you'd had sex with your ex."

"You don't mean *met*."

"And *you* clearly didn't mean *ex*."

"And here we are, years later, with a pungent taste in our mouths. At what point does the past actually *qualify* as the past? I don't mind admitting, I've grown tired of all this."

"I don't doubt it. But what can I say? You were the air I breathed."

"Wonderful. Sarcasm next."

"Not at all, Phyllie – you misunderstand me. I would've given you a lot, I promise you – maybe everything. Yet, it's impossible to paint a canvas with yesterday's paint. But what I will say is this, mate: I loved you like a limb. Like a *thumb*. I imagined you'd be around a lot longer than you were."

"Story of my life."

"You're being flippant. Fair enough – we've probably gone as far as we can go. But may I offer this, please? I have no choice but to accept I lost you; but I won't accept your behaviour was decent. You treated me like a clown."

Phyllie remembers the option that she had had – of using the *Story of my life* line again to end matters once and for all – and how she had lapsed into silence again.

She looks up at the expected mention of her name.

"Morning, Phyllie," says Dr. Chaz Bruce-Sange. "Would you like to come through?"

SESSION 16

An old man's talking to a group of other men of all ages. He says, "I don't know what happened at the Chickenpox Party. Maybe the bouncy castle sprang a leak. There was a couple there no one could identify. They stayed apart from everyone else – they didn't say a word, even to themselves." Then I see them – the couple. They're wearing summer clothes – whites and pastels. They are watching the children catch chickenpox. They both have very white perfect teeth.

"Let me try to understand this. This group of yours…"

"No. Sorry to interrupt you immediately, Chaz, but no: not *group of mine*. That's part of the point. They were in place before me and they don't need me to exist," says Phyllie Reydman.

"All right then. I suppose knowing one more thing about what something *isn't* is a good way of learning about what that thing is. The group we're discussing… is that okay?"

"That's fine."

"Moves from place to place in an… *imagination* you think of as Africa."

"Kind of. As non-specific as that sounds, yes. I've never actually been to Africa – apart from a holiday cruise down the Nile once. Oh, and I took students on a trip to the Valley of the Kings when I was still a schoolteacher – but Egypt isn't the Africa I see when I'm able to tune in. It's further south, for a start. I see a lot of dust and desert; a lot of browns and sepia tones; and a lot of *boredom*. They'll rock up somewhere and do their work, whatever that happens to be; then they'll move on somewhere else. As far as I know, my observations don't influence what I see; but can a psychoanalyst ever be absent when he's conducting an observation? The ones observed need to '*forget*' – in inverted commas – forget they are being observed. Work conducted by Bruno Latour, then others."

"I know the strand. 'How does a psychoanalyst know what he knows?' Do you think they're aware of you then?"

"Not obviously so."

Phyllie seems to apply her full attention to the possibility. The truth is, what she sees, hears, and feels, from across many waters, is an application of the idea of saturated spaces. There is too much to contain in a space of its own: as children do, we must all learn to share. Sharing the locality – however much it varies from perception to perception – must surely be a noble ambition.

"And do you write down anything you see or hear?" asks Dr. Chaz Bruce-Sange.

"Occasionally; a snippet here and there."

"I see. Tell me something, going back to Brother Joe…"

"Cecil Joseph, as I briefly knew him."

"You mentioned his parlance, always calling you Sister…"

"Yes. He used to come out with one- or two-liners of wisdom and profundity. Just dropping them into the conversation." Phyllie grins – wryly, as they say. "There was one about seven angels…" Her intonation is flat and her pace is authentic: Phyllie has spoken these words aloud many times before, as if she has learned a script.

"If you are chosen to hold seven angels in your arms," Phyllie recites, "do not wish for an eighth. Seven is enough to hold – don't be greedy! It's six more than blessed! And what's more, do not complain that seven is a prime number…

"Copyright Brother Joe. All rights reserved," Phyllie concludes.

"And you have these… *bon mots* from Brother Joe on post-it notes in different rooms at home?" Chaz asks.

Phyllie nods her head.

"Seven angels is on the inside of my bathroom door. I read it every time I need the loo… I watched Cecil – or Brother Joe, I suppose I must call him now – as I'd watch Pooh sticks in a stream."

"That could almost be one on its own," Chaz answers. "Do you recall any others?"

"*When he shouted for his mother, the ocean roared back in a different language.*"

"What happened when you wondered where these transmissions had arrived from? I'm assuming you *did* pause to wonder."

"Yes, I did; though never for long. Words came to me – actually, I like your choice of term there – as *transmissions*. I wrote them down about three years ago." Phyllie smiles briefly at the recollection. "In my best calligraphy!"

While Chaz is absorbing what she has heard, Phyllie asks if she can have five minutes. She needs to use the bathroom; would Chaz mind?

"Do go ahead," Chaz answers, though in truth she is far from comfortable with allowing an analysand to use her facilities.

"There was a time towards the end – with me and Vig. *Physically* we were in Benny's dungeon, but we were also on a kind of expedition. I said something like: *Only one thing could make this moment more perfect. It's been a while since I had you alone…*"

"You were flirting with him."

"I suppose I was. No, I *know* I was because I even tried to justify it to myself. I said: *Technically, it's not cheating, I mean if we're not actually here. We're in a room somewhere, not even touching.*"

"I do love a good *technically*," Chaz Bruce-Sange replies. "What did Vig say?"

"He said: *As far as you know.*"

"… He didn't want to?"

"And it might have been so perfect. The wind was blowing through my hair in streaks of orange and gold. I felt threatened – and alive. We were explorers. It felt *dangerous*. We had to find a place – or a thing – or a state of being – called the Overlap. And I said to Vig: *We're still no closer to the Overlap.* And he said to me: *But I think we are, Phyl.* He stopped walking. *What if it's not a place? What if we're being too literal? This* occurs to me from time to time, even now."

Phyllie smiles. "Well, obviously it does or I wouldn't have mentioned it."

Closing her eyes briefly, she recalls Vig's voice – and his message.

"The Overlap is something that we made up, right? Or you did, to be accurate.'

'My daughter did, to be more accurate still,' Phyllie had answered.

"But how would the other people Benny's got know about it, other than through our words?" Vig's voice, as he thought out loud, had moved from a slow, quiet, almost shy mode, to something more direct and with greater volume. "Benny said his prisoners, some of them, under the influence of… whatever we've got coursing through our veins at the moment – he said they share parts of whatever existence they create, right? And then talk about things – the stuff he records, right?"

"Yes," said Phyllie, failing to see Vig's point entirely but not wishing to halt his excited flow.

"It's telepathic; it's got to be! It's more than words, Phyl… or less, I should say. Words are too direct. It's thoughts we need to create the Overlap. The people who are representations of those in the dungeon – and those who are – you know – the ones we make up ourselves. The moral of the story being…"

("Stop chatting and start noodling," said Phyllie.)

"We are not really here!" shouted Phyllie, her voice riding a wave of murmurs – agreement and dissent in equal measures.

Running with the baton now, Vig added, "We're all prisoners – in a man's home! We're in the dungeon he's built, under lock and key! Under sedation! But we can escape! If we all fight together… there's a lot more of us than there is of him!"

"The murmurs became cheers, in parts of the congregation at least," said Phyllie. "People gathered around us."

She opened her eyes to see Dr. Chaz Bruce-Sange nodding gently. It was a very rare moment in which the psychoanalyst seemed not to know the next thing to say.

Remembering past events is not like watching a recorded film, even if we believe it to be so. Remembering past events is a process of reconstructing what may have happened, based on the details the brain chooses to store and is able to recall. Recollection is triggered by a retrieval cue, an environmental stimulus that encourages the brain to retrieve the memory: be it a smile, a tone of voice, an aroma… or a photograph, perhaps. Why else do we take photographs, after all, if not to stockpile memory material for the future?

Chaz stopped typing. She read what had entered her consciousness and what she had transcribed from a source unknown. She was pleased to note that although it did not obviously connect with any of her other deposited gobbets, it was the first thing in a while that she had written in one go, with no breaks for a congratulatory sip of green tea at the conclusion of every sentence.

She stood up and stretched, a mild pain in her shoulder reminding her of the anti-inflammatory medication off which she hoped to wean herself. Midway to the kettle, she had an alternative thought to the thought of green tea.

"What's buzzing in your brain right now?" she asked Doug Stegmeyer on the phone.

"*Having taken my* open parentheses *obedient* close parentheses *place in the pungent countertransference, I must be honest with regards to the ramifications.*"

"You've got me; I don't recognise it."

"The authorship, good lady, is mine."

From her long experience, Chaz knew that Doug tended to get frilly with his utterances when he was feeling randy and proud with his prose.

"Your work in progress?"

"Indeed. I'm touting my metaphors from page to page. *Was it the fact that I felt blunderbussed? Was it that I had become misunderstood? –* I quote directly."

"…*Pungent's* good. *Pungent* is pungent, in context. What does *blunderbussed* mean?"

"Get thee to a dictionary, Chaz. Or I'll tell you over drinks in half an hour's time."

"Do you fancy The Pilgrims?"

"*Don't you* dare *attempt to understand me, I remember thinking. I don't want to be understood,*" Doug continued reading. "I thought you'd never ask," he replied at length, in his normal speaking voice.

SESSION 18

Hendrix is walking on his back legs, like a human. He knocks on my bedroom door – in the house I had as a girl. Or lived in as a girl, at any rate. Hendrix has only been pretending to be a dog. But the door turns transparent for a second and I see him for what he really is…

"And what is he? You said hind legs."

…"Sorry. He's a dog…" Phyllie smiles; considers. "What *else* would he be?"

"A cat, a tiger; a bear…"

"Or an elephant. Yes, of course. No, he's a dog."

"And what does he reveal himself to be?" asks Dr. Chaz Bruce-Sange.

"My ex-husband, Roger Billie. Just for a few seconds. And he tells me I have to be careful. Benny will be released from prison and is on the warpath."

Interesting use of the surname, thinks the psychoanalyst.

"Tell me if you ever think of Roger – consciously, as it were," says Dr. Bruce-Sange. "Not in your dream life."

"Yes, of course. We were married under the magic cloak of happiness for a while there. It's inevitable I'll remember my ex-husband from time to time. Not least because, we were two of the lucky ones. We parted as close to friends as we're allowed to, given the intrusion of ego and spite."

"What characteristics does Roger have – or *exhibit*, is probably better – that you can see in someone else in your life, right now, male or female?"

Phyllie inhales with considerable volume; her nostrils flare. Her eyelids descend.

"That's a tough one…" She pauses. "Well, he always wants to *help*; that's a defining characteristic. He's smart and he's curious."

"And who shares those traits?"

"A girl called Claire. I say *girl*. She's doing her PhD with me; we're study buddies. I reckon she's about a year ahead of me, which is galling, of course."

"Why *of course?* Chaz asks. "Are you in a race with Claire?"

"Not at all. I just don't want her to be a doctor before I am. She's too young and pretty."

"I'm swimming through concrete. The taste in my mouth is alien to any other flavour, and the experience leaves me exhausted. But the taste remains delicious for *months*."

"Inside the dream?"

"Yes, inside it. Not so long earlier, I mouthed through sand. These days, I mouth through concrete. Does that feel like progress to you, Chaz?"

"That would have to depend on how you're using your sand and concrete."

Phyllie sighs.

"Yes, I thought it might… I dreamed of my ex-husband a few nights ago. He was a long way from me, but I knew if our daughter cried, he could be with us in seconds. It was comforting, as dreams go."

"I can't say I *escaped*. It was rescue – pure and simple – like we were endangered animals. Which we were, of course. We were kept in *vivaria* – the plural of *vivarium*. I think I can remember the definition from what I tried to write about a year later. An enclosure, container, or structure adapted or prepared for keeping animals under semi-natural conditions for observation or study or as pets. That about sums it up. And sums *us* up."

"Close to *viva*, as we were discussing it a moment or two ago. Linguistically close."

Phyllie nods in acknowledgement but does not want to be distracted. Momentarily annoyed that Chaz has not picked up on the reference to writing, Phyllie elaborates – as it were – for an invisible audience.

"I got it in my head to write fiction. I wanted to write a novel. I thought – *I've all this material, the memories are still fresh*, even a year after I was released – *let's use it or lose it*. Little realising, at the time, I'd have nightmares for a decade to come. But that's another story."

A little hiccough of self-deprecating humour.

"I wanted to call it *The Mind: A Ghost Story*," Phyllie adds, once more grown serious. "Restore some order to my life. Make that awful experience *mean* something – or else what's the point? Why me? Cry-baby me."

"Do *all* experiences have to quote mean something unquote?"

Phyllie nods her head. "Or else what's the point, as I say? We should learn as we earn, shouldn't we? That was my guiding principle when I taught full-time and it's still the same now. If I learn from a hard lesson, maybe I won't be so *angry* with myself, all the time."

"Are you angry with yourself right now?" Chaz continues.

"Yes; and with you, to be honest. You haven't asked me to explain my school metaphor and I can feel it slipping away."

"Perhaps you'd care to fill me in now, in that case, Phyllie."

"I have a colleague – a fellow practitioner – called Doug Stegmeyer. We were rivals for many years... and then we seemed to hit a wall of common sense when we turned the corner at the age of sixty. We both have the same birthday, funnily enough. The twenty-first of February."

"That's today! Happy birthday, Chaz!"

"Thank you. I turned sixty-seven while I was asleep at three-thirteen this morning. Doug's was the first text I read when I woke up."

"And what did this old rival have to offer?"

"Oh, many happy returns – that kind of thing. I sent him something similar. The point is not necessarily our birthdays..."

"No; sorry..."

"It's the price of forgiveness and acceptance."

"... I'm not sure what you're leaning towards, Chaz."

"That's quite rare."

"What is?"

"That I'll say something as source material you'll find it hard to respond to."

"That's slippery. If I respond to what you've just said, I haven't so much proved you wrong as proved myself petulant."

"Can't you be both?"

"I should smile. You're in a most combative mood this afternoon. Are you enjoying the thrill of the chase, Doctor?"

"I don't think in those terms – as well you know."

"Are you ready?" Chaz Bruce-Sange asked Doug Stegmeyer.

"I'm *tumescent* with readiness. Shoot."

"*This founding moment of separation is both frightening and exciting, and to cope, the infant creates fantasies about the mother as a compensation for her painful absence...* Shall I continue?"

"I don't think I know it," Doug admitted.

"*Said otherwise, the infant reacts to the absence of the mother in reality by imagining her present in fantasy.*"

"You've got me. All I'll add is: *not only children.* The absence stays true a lot longer than that. The abandoned dental clinic in the wilderness."

"What do you mean?"

"I'm being metaphorical," Doug added.

"Yes I know, but what …" Chaz started.

"It doesn't matter – the details aren't important."

"On the contrary, darling – the details are *always* important."

NATIONAL APOLOGY NETWORKS

———• ◎ •———

"Our instinct for exploration will serve us commendably."

Brother Joe

NOTHING LIKE THE SUN

Clouds licked at the nose of the moon. Stars seemed as sharp as sprigs of metal on a barbed-wire fence. Night had fallen; Twennyfour was talking to three of the men.

"The box of matches is important in rural communities like ours. I mean, apart from the obvious use of setting fire to things. There's also a totemic value: you might even say a *spiritual* value."

"Give us an example," said Bruno Amitrano.

Twennyfour leaned to the left to collect the box of matches that had been under discussion. "I can use this box of matches to draw any rabbits in the area to our camp. My ancestors used the method as a hunting technique."

"The box of matches?"

"You doubt me. *All* of you doubt me." Twennyfour nodded his head; then shook it, as if with disappointment. "I can't say I blame you. But watch..."

Twennyfour breathed deeply for a few seconds. By now the box was balanced equally across his two upraised palms. A worm of concentration appearing on the bridge of his nose, he stared at the box and seemed to slip – like a pebble into water – into a trance.

Bruno and Paper Jake exchanged glances. Brother Joe had not taken his eyes off Twennyfour; Bruno would later describe Brother Joe's attention as that of the child at the birthday party, determined to pick a hole in the magician's trick.

Almost a minute had passed. Twennyfour's eyelids lowered for a further few seconds. His lips puckered into a *moue*, and he exhaled with sufficient force for Paper Jake to feel it on the back of one of his hands. Bruno, meanwhile, had started to scan the area for the sight of approaching rabbits. For him, there was no doubt that the ritual would be productive.

Twennyfour gave the box a quick shake; matches rattled inside it. He made a quizzical expression and shook the box again.

"Twenty-four, funnily enough," he announced confidently. "And twenty-four matches means twenty-four rabbits will be drawn to us."

Once more, Twennyfour devoted his gaze to the matchbox, this time turning it over slowly, as if reading its runes or seeking a way in. Very slowly he slid the tray out to expose a thumb-joint-sized gap. Seemingly reverentially, Twennyfour then removed a single match. He closed the tray so that the single match was trapped between the lower tray and the enveloping cardboard sleeve. The match stuck out, the strikable end most prominent.

Carefully, Twennyfour raised the box with the protruding single match to his right ear… and brightly he spoke into this mock telephone.

"Calling all rabbits. Calling all rabbits…"

A second passed before the impact of the joke was appreciated. The group was reduced to *molecules*. For half a minute Bruno laughed so hard that his eyes watered; stars became comet-long worms, wriggling in cosmic mud – these stars were both above his head and behind his eyes. Paper Jake snorted and snuffled. Leaning back against empty air, he held his ribs as if to keep them in place. When able to speak again, his breathing restored, he said, "I thought my *rectum* was going to capsize!"

Bruno's mirth had decayed to a half-life of blissed satiation. While silently summarising the experience, he had to blow his nose; the capacious yield resembled a small toad on the ground. For an instant, it seemed to *sizzle*.

"We all need to laugh, brothers," said Brother Joe – but he said it seriously, like a pearl of advice, like one of his mottos.

It was just another night before morning. Accompanied by good fortune and a following wind – and assuming the van held out – tomorrow would see the men rolling into the next destination on their itinerary: the town of Eden.

The rising of the sun found Brother Joe in a philosophical mood.

"We are cramped, my brothers," he said; "we are piled into spaces to such an extent, we cannot even see who else is present."

No one answered Brother Joe. Perhaps (thought Twenny-four) no one had heard him.

Twennyfour glanced at the van that they would board. In the early-morning light, the vechicle had appropriated the sepia tones of the morning itself.

"What about time, Brother Joe?" asked Roger Billie.

Immediately, Roger formed the impression that he had awoken Brother Joe from a fugue: he looked as if he had been *elsewhere*.

"Time, brother?" Brother Joe sought to clarify. "Time is the first thing your unconscious shovels up to crown the dung heap of your consciousness."

"…Wow."

"Allow me to expand, my brother. There is a house I try to occupy with my thoughts and understandings. There is also a town that I keep in the palm of my left hand and try to keep safe from the prejudices and violence of my right hand. There is a window I look through – and *I* am also that which *the window* looks through. The pane of glass is the medium."

Brother Joe interlinked his fingers and pushed his palms together.

"The bricks talk like cousins and the door knows every language. Every visitor's footfall tells a story, and when I am in the attic, I know who has arrived at the front door."

Hours remained before bedtime. All seemed shades of brown and grey.

"When you were a boy, did you ever imagine, when the sun is like it is this evening, you could tie it to its place, where it is right now? To keep it in place."

"I imagined it could lift me higher, like the boy on the end of the rising balloon."

"I thought about the sun having a life and a behaviour like a baby's. As soon as we'd finished looking at it for the day, it went into its nest of shade and shadows, like a very young pet that doesn't know any better."

"The sun is anchored to our vista like a ship in port; but the cruise must sail away, brother. Other harbours need the same sun."

"The sun sinking always makes me think of the dissolution of a friendship. I don't know why. Something majestic and colourful, swallowed up by darkness."

Elasticated, pulled-tight hours were still to come before bedtime.

Twennyfour wondered where the other colours went to, when everything appeared brown and grey; when one could read the world's sepia tones like a language, like a script.

Why did *so much* brown exist?

While nudged by the impression that he had been here before, Twennyfour wandered. He imagined the arc that the busty sun would describe in an hour's time. The air was as chilly as best linen. The blood, gold, and mud of yesterday's afternoon sky had long since been a prompt for Twennyfour's more obvious and more beautiful imaginings.

Twennyfour compared his footfalls with years: every stride was a span of three hundred and sixty-five days. Every fourth stride, three hundred and sixty-six for the leap year. Every now and then he gave a leap – or a skip – in recognition of time passing. Whistling low as he passed a graveyard, he wondered if anyone was watching. Feral cats kept their distance but observed him. Insects crawled the air adjacent to his face.

Decades past the circumference of the village (or so, at any rate, Twennyfour had deemed the distance), he sat on a rock the size of a space capsule, and decided to view the sunrise as a first-time observer might view the same.

Forget about what you know already. None of the above is relevant.

Take note of the natural, celestial phenomena; and breathe in what emotions this awakening furnace provokes.

Rick Shawdon concluded his lunchtime meal with a grandiose swipe of grainy white bread through a delta of delicious nutty gravy on his plate. He bit the drenched morsel in half and threw the other half up in the air, away from the picnic table. As he'd expected, the loaded contribution was caught in mid-trajectory by a swan that had assumed a place nearby on the grass, in what Rick interpreted as a spirit of respectful patience.

The swan's patience had been rewarded.

"I'd give it my plate to lick if I was allowed to," Rick told Twennyfour.

"I won't tell if you don't."

"What are you doing, brother?" Twennyfour asked Rick Shawdon.

"Pretending to fish by a river that does not exist," Rick replied. Then he chuckled. "And wishing I still smoked. Right now would be a perfect moment for a burn."

"I'm sure Paper Jake or Brother Bruno would oblige you."

"...May I join you?"

"Be my guest."

Minutes later, Twennyfour asked: "What's your strongest motivation, Rick? What gets you out of bed in the morning?"

Rick's reply was fleet-foot. "Boredom. I live for boredom these days," he answered. "Sometimes, I honestly believe it's my one true love."

Half an hour later, Rick asked: "And what do *you* play?"

"Nothing at all. I want to conduct; it's my life's ambition. To conduct an orchestra."

Twennyfour stared gratefully at something that Rick could not observe.

CRYING ON TRAINS
(RICK SHAWDON'S STORY)

"Okay, brother – I think I'm ready to talk," said Rick Shaw-don. "Are you ready to *hear* me? It takes two to tango."

Twennyfour wondered briefly what might be on the older man's mind. Why would Rick think that he, Twennyfour, might not be an attentive audience? Could it be common knowledge that he, Twennyfour, had exhibited impatience for Bruno Amitrano to conclude *his* story? Might Bruno have gossiped about him?

Too many questions.

"Be honest. Would you start a conversation with a man who was crying on a train?"

She asked me this when I was expecting her to say nothing.

"I was a man crying on a train," I told her, and she nodded her head. And you started a conversation with me, I did not add aloud.

"Exactly. But would you have started a conversation with yourself?"

"That's not the same dynamic," I protested.

"I didn't say it was," she replied; and then she told me that she had once been the only passenger on a busy intercity train who had not been crying.

I stepped onto the destination platform. I was wearing the gym shoes that my *condition* had led to my favouring, and accidentally I bumped into a woman in her late twenties – possibly early thirties – who had stepped down at the same time, to my side. My hip collided with her hip. I said sorry.

The problem on this occasion – or the observation I made – was the state of the young woman's face. She had been crying for some time; possibly for the span of the journey into the city itself. I was not sure where she had embarked. I did not recognise her from my station. But she'd wept for a while.

How could I do otherwise than to ask, "Are you okay?"

Perhaps it was naïve to narrow my lens to one young woman, given that the entire carriage had shed a tear. My gaze went up and down.

The *platform* was full of people wailing! Without a source!

"What do you mean, a source?" I asked. I was confused.

"I mean, there was nothing to whinge about!" she responded. "It wasn't as if the city had felt the deep gulp of a bomb detonation. Nothing of the sort!"

"What would have led to a train's-worth of people breaking down?" I asked Amanda.

"Disappointment on a cosmic scale?"

"That would do it!"

"A universal scale? Disappointment visiting from the nearest black hole? The ache of interstellar existence?"

SESSION 20

A man's saying something like, "I don't remember sunsets." Another man says, "I'm not sure they remember you either." Then I'm staring at a headstone. I notice a toad in the longer grass next to my mother's plot – a plump brown toad; alive, alive-oh. Just doing its toady thing; chilling in its toady environment. Good luck to you, I mouth to the toad. I look up from the toad and nod at the approach of the Celebrant.

"I see you've met Awesome," the Celebrant offers. "Awesome Load the Toad."

I don't know how she's seen the amphibian from so far away.

"He's something of a local celebrity. He only shows himself when the mourners' grief reaches a certain emotional pitch."

"And what pitch might that be?" I want to know.

The Celebrant smiles at me. "I'm not a scientist."

I'm not at all certain how to proceed, but a compliment usually moves matters along. "It was a very nice service."

"Thank you. May I ask how you knew the deceased?"

"A bit of a long story."

"I've a bit of a long gap between events if you need an ear."

Then she removes one of her ears and holds it out for me. Her teeth fall out, one by one, as I watch her. The ear she's holding out is embedded with tiny teeth.

"I had a dog when I was a girl. The thing I remember most is, I loved listening to her eat – the satisfaction she got from insubstantial origins."

"What was your dog called?" asks Dr. Chaz Bruce-Sange.

"Roger." Phyllie Reydman chuckles. "Named after my dad. And the same name as my husband, years later. Roger has always been a positive male role model for me, in one way or another. Was that something you wished to discuss?"

"It wasn't where I planned to begin. If you're willing to, I'd like to explore the nature of your relationship with Claire."

"The nature of the relationship is, she's my daughter. What else did you mean?"

"Not Claire your daughter. Claire your PhD study buddy."

QUIET EYES

Amanda asked Claire: "Would you like a refreshment? I have some herbal tea on the go."

"That would be nice; thank you."

"Take a perch." Taking three crabwise steps, Amanda exited the lounge that doubled as the home's hallway. She entered the kitchen. Seconds later, the hip-hop that she'd been listening to was squished flat into silence, the sound of water boiling replacing it.

"I did some research on your name," Claire called, "like you told me about mine. You probably know this already. Amanda is a Latin name meaning *loveable* or *worthy of love*… Can you hear me?"

"I'm listening!" Amanda called back.

"The name was first recorded in 1212 in Warwickshire."

A few minutes later, Amanda returned, carrying two cups of herbal tea.

"I knew it: I'm as old as *county records*." She chuckled. "As I get older, I find it tougher and tougher to take caffeine… Why are you smiling?"

"As you get *older*? Sorry – there can't be more than five years between us."

"I'm thirty-nine. I thank you for your compliment."

"*Thirteen* years between us," Claire calculated aloud. Perhaps that was not polite. "You have impeccable genes. I thought you were six or so years younger. What's your secret?"

"Settle comfortably into a life you can tolerate," Amanda answered without hesitation. "Don't aim too high, you'll end up disappointed. Don't sell yourself short, you'll hate everyone."

"Sound advice," Claire concluded. "You've reminded me of something. When I was a girl, from time to time a family member or friend of my parents would ask me what I wanted to be *when I grew up*. If you think about it, the question is *problematic* in a number of ways."

"Are you speaking your thesis to me, Claire?"

"I wonder if I am." She waited – either for revelation or instinct; possibly for a rebuttal.

"Do tell."

"First and foremost, a child is not aware of the range of possibilities. Second, however, the question suggests a transformation will take place at an unspecified point in the future. Could the thought of this change not seem *frightening*?"

Amanda considered the question; she rolled it around and bounced it against a brick wall, for a catch.

"A child is not aware of the range of possibilities," she repeated. "I like that. Claire's missing her dad at the moment – though God help me if she'd ever admit as much! I got a call from the school. She was rude to a boy about his ears, the little pansy."

"About his *ears*? What *about* his ears?"

"Wonky, or so I'm told. I've never met the boy in question. Apparently, his ears are on two different lines of latitude." Amanda shrugged. "I say sod the little prick, it's character-forming. I bet much stranger things happened to *you* when you were nine!"

"Early onset menstruation," Claire replied, "is what happened to *me* when I was nine."

"Ah! The gift that keeps on giving!" Amanda smiled wryly. "I wonder if we could talk about something else for a second."

"What's on your mind?"

"A friend of yours is on my mind. Phyllie Reydman – you've mentioned her a couple of a times."

"Yes, I have. You sound sheepish, Amanda."

"Well, I haven't *lied to you*, exactly, but I've kept a few things on the back burner. The first is how *I* know your friend."

"No, you told me that. You married her ex-husband; you're bringing up…" Claire made a quick decision to replace the word *her* with the definite article. "…the girl."

"More than that. We go back nine years, Phyllie and I. It's not only Roger we have in common. Or Claire, for that matter." Amanda swallowed. "Has Phyllie ever mentioned someone called *Benny* to you?"

"Quite recently," Claire answered. "And it was one of those memories in there deep – even when you don't know about them." She shrugged. "Home is where the hurt is, and all that. The house in the village."

"The Edlesborough House of Horror," Amanda agreed. "Benny had dozens of people imprisoned in the cellar

– drugged up, wires on their temples. A science experiment, he claimed."

Claire waited. She joined the dots.

"And you were there too?"

Amanda issued a brief nod of the head. "Though not in the way you think – not as a prisoner." Looking aside, she added: "Benny was never anything but delightful with me."

"Do I take your expression to be shame? Surely there's nothing to be ashamed of," Claire offered. *Unless you helped him…* "He couldn't have been cruel to *everyone*."

"He was loving to me." Amanda smiled. "He thought me *loveable* – or *worthy of love*. As all good fathers should regard their daughters."

The dots had joined into something realistic. Without so much as a hint of an interrogative riding the waves, Claire confirmed: "Benny's your dad. And you lived in Edlesborough when you were a girl."

"No. But I *visited*. I lived with my mum."

"You saw…" Claire brought to mind the word that Phyllie had used several times. "You saw the *vivaria*."

Amanda nodded. "Some of it. Not the depths. Some of the experiments with shared dreaming – that kind of thing. I even wrote about it for a school project once." Briefly she glimmered with humour. "The teacher ticked me off for writing a *story*. Mrs. McKenzie. She said we were supposed to write a factual account."

"What I Did on My Summer Holidays."

"That kind of thing. I learned a lesson from that, Claire, believe me. When something seems out of the ordinary – or even *magical*… like the idea of *sharing dreams* – then be very, very careful who you tell."

"Like now? This very moment?" Claire asked.

"Well, indeed. It's not quite chit-chat at the bus stop, is it? – confessing your dad's in prison for violations against body and mind…" Amanda laughed.

A sense of pride had gathered in Claire's bosom. "Thank you. I feel flattered. I'm grateful for your honesty… So how did it end? With Mrs. McKenzie, I mean: the project versus short story debate."

"She gave me a B+ and said I had a vivid imagination," Amanda answered. "I couldn't convince her I'd handed in a piece of *reportage*."

"You were penalised."

"Actually, no. At the time I was averaging Bs or B-minuses… I'd gone up the scale at least; but that wasn't the point – I hadn't been *believed*. I asked Dad if I could bring some friends with me the next time I stayed at his – to corroborate my findings." Amanda shook her head.

"He said no."

"Very *much* he said no. 'This is my place of work, darling. You don't go to your friends' dads' places of work, do you now?' No, Dad. 'This is just between us, darling.'"

"Which makes it more creepy, in retrospect," Claire added.

"To you, maybe… but to me, he was just *Dad*. And he could be a real charmer. Later on, I had a part-time job; I worked with pets and prey at the market by Feast Bridge. It's not there anymore."

"Pets and *prey*?"

"Sorry, but yeah. A rabbit for the granddaughter to look after, named Flopsy or Fidget… is the same price as a rabbit meant to be chased and munched by your snake called Satan-Big-Balls. Obviously, I switched to alternative employment."

Claire's eyes met Amanda's. In this moment, her friend's eyes seemed full of life, almost musical; her eyesight was *singing* – with joy, with relief, with memories shared… with *mischief?*

"And Benny was a customer in the market? Is that what you're saying?"

"Locally, he put himself forward as this generation's wealth of knowledge on the subject of which-animal-does-what-to-which-animal. Quite the expert, was how he portrayed himself. At first, it embarrassed me – like fathers do when you're that age, working illegally at fourteen on a market stall. But the punters liked him; my manager liked him – he came by so often he became a fixture."

"Your parents were separated at this time," Claire interjected.

"They separated when I was four," Amanda answered. "But he was there, I can't take that away from him, whatever he may have done later. Often he was there when Mum disappeared for a while. She had blackouts. Maybe once or twice a year, you could rely on her hitting the wine-and-vodka cocktails hard. But she *always* let Dad know what she was about to do."

"A planned blackout."

Amanda nodded. "An experiment of her own, you might say."

"And these blackouts…"

"Usually, a day or two. One notable exception. When I was nine, Mum blacked out for just less than a week. When she woke up, she'd applied for three jobs; she'd *attended one job interview*; and she'd enlisted to join the *Royal Navy*."

"A busy week!"

"*And* she got the job! They employed her! She's still there, years later, preparing for retirement. She works part-time in a hair salon."

"But not blacking out any longer, I hope," said Claire.

"Not that I'm aware of. I think Dad going to prison put an end to those habits… but I can't be sure. She struggled with his experiments."

Claire's eyes met Amanda's once more. This time her friend's eyes seemed quiet. Claire imagined that this might be the end of the discussion, at least for now. She wondered how much of what she'd learned she would relay to Phyllie, and how? – in what circumstances? How would one bring up the topic?

SESSION 24

A blonde woman comes to the house to sell something I don't want to buy, and won't leave the doorstep. Eventually, we invite her in. Then I'm cooking a massive dinner, but I don't have enough for someone who arrives late. The blonde woman leaves. Another blonde woman arrives, looking like the first. They recognise each other from their dress – the second one is also trying to sell something.

Then I'm in a big city, crossing a road at a light. The first blonde rushes by on a bike. Benny and I discuss various books by a well-known genre author, but I don't recall her name.

In the canteen, a man is reading books that I know, and I take it as a sign and talk to him. I meet Benny in the library later. Lots of people listen to our conversation. I talk about runes and shredded DNA.

"You've never mentioned anything about a physical relationship with John Hodgins, Phyllie. Did one exist?"

"Certainly not; we were nine years old."

"Even so. You show me yours and I'll show you mine. Doctors and nurses. Or *dentists* and nurses."

"I don't recall anything along those lines, no."

"And yet the question has made you uncomfortable."

"It has. The question's asking me about prepubescent sexual activity. I can't think of many subjects more guaranteed to make me queasy, though I bet you hear about it quite a lot in this office, don't you?"

"Quite a lot," Chaz admits with a tiny nod of her head.

"With people reaping the damage sown when they were kids."

"In a manner of speaking." Considering the contribution that Phyllie has just made, she nods her head. "That's a good way of putting it."

"The randy stepdad, and so on."

"Among other perpetrators."

"So how do you fix it?"

"Fix what?"

"Fix the problem those patients arrive here with."

"In the same way, I hope to help *you*, Phyllie. By talking and listening. Encouraging you to find tools that are already there but were left behind when you had to leave the clinic suddenly, as it were."

"All right, I'm ready." Phyllie exhales with the exaggerated sound made by some smokers. "You listen, I'll talk. Let's create some transitional space, why don't we?"

"Okay, Phyllie. Tell me how you feel about Benny right now."

Phyllie nods her head; she has anticipated this line of enquiry. "The honest answer is, I try *not* to think about him, right now or at any other time; as if I could avoid feeling *anything* about him if I don't allow him into my thoughts."

She waits.

"The implication being," Dr. Bruce-Sange suggests, "that he makes his way into your thoughts more often than you'd expect."

"Or appreciate. Yes."

"But that doesn't quite answer my prompt about how you *feel* about him now."

"No. I don't suppose it does." Phyllie waits again. "I try to tell myself, nine years is a long time to bear a grudge. He's going to die in prison. But when I say these things, I'm aware I'm just brushing them away. I'm *rationalising* the pieces – into a nice tidy jigsaw. You can see where the pieces join – but the picture is *whole*. But that's not how the mental apparatus works, is it, Doctor?"

"Not if you're still processing a trauma. Do you think you are?"

"I must be: I still dream about the bastard. And he's part of the reason I'm here with you, anyway; so yes, I must be processing Benny, to this day." Phyllie pauses. "What else can I do with him except keep him inside a prison wall – literally and psychologically? It's payback for what he did to me and others. Only at night does he roam free."

Phyllie stares up at the ceiling. She counts the stars that have been stuck to the plaster. When the light dims during an afternoon therapy hour, the stars take on a distant luminosity.

Phyllie had imagined that the glow-in-the-dark quality was for the benefit of the doctor's child patients. Now, she is not so sure.

Fiddling with her pen – its bright red clashing with her fingernails – Chaz nods her head. "Okay, Phyllie. Think for a few seconds before you respond ... If you'd *never* met him, and you could know what you know now, would you have *wanted* to meet him if you knew that he was responsible for helping you grasp what you now understand?"

These words have stowed away in the steerage of my consciousness for days, Chaz wrote.

She tried to count how many words had been spoken in this room, just today. Multiply that number by seven. How many words do we speak every week? Multiply that number by fifty-two. A year of words! In this one room! How many words did a street speak every year? How many words passed the lips of the conurbation? How chatty was the country in the terrestrial garden party to which all of the other countries had been invited? Was England an extrovert or an introvert? Did the country gather energy from those around it, or did the country prefer a quiet room?

"*The early stage of any writing project,*" Chaz said aloud, to an interviewer not present in her rooms – an interviewer constructed out of the deposits left behind by several hundred analysands over the years, "*is akin to spending loose change. You examine the coins in your pocket and pick through the bits of fluff and till receipts that have been redundant for months, and you see what you've got to spend. Your disposable income. You ask yourself how much you need to get out at the cashpoint, and what you hope to achieve with your money."*

An urge to write something more spoke volumes in her unconscious.

FORMER ACADEMICS
(BROTHER JOE'S PSEUDO-STORY)

"Brother, Joe is not my original first name, it's my adopted first name, borrowed from my surname, Joseph. My first name is Cecil."

Gray twinkled with mischief. "And presumably not 'Brother' either."

Brother Joe smiled. "*Brother* Joe was always an affectation."

"So… Mr. Cecil Joseph? It has a certain ring to it."

"Technically, it's *Professor* Cecil Joseph. I was an academic."

"Interesting! So was I, for a while," Gray told him. "I was a scientist – a virologist. As you say, *technically* I still am, in the sense that I never retired. The field seemed to retire away from *me*. I always thought 'Professor' was welcome but unearned. I dipped around in petri dishes and vacuum closets. I didn't deserve the 'Professor.'"

Professor Sir Grayson Twivy stopped short of mentioning his knighthood. He had decided that now might not be the best time to talk of when he had knelt in front of the Queen of

England and been tapped on either shoulder with a ceremonial sword.

"Imposter syndrome?" asked Brother Joe.

"It wasn't labelled as such in my day. But yes, I think so. What I enjoyed was working with small communities."

"In England?"

"Overseas too," said Gray. "When Twennyfour was a boy, I was on a vaccination tour, and I visited Twennyfour's home. Taught a day at his *school*… Do you believe in coincidences?"

"I believe in grander patterns. The mind opens. That's not to say that coincidences can't happen. Maybe it was a coincidence that you spent a day teaching at Twennyfour's school. And then you meet him again, twenty-odd years later."

"Twenty-*four* years, to be exact," said Gray. "Even that seems symmetrical."

Although Brother Joe did not respond immediately, he leaned back and laced his fingers together behind his head: a familiar sign of *acceptability*. He was ready for new wisdom. The curtains were wide open. Let the sunbeams splash on the floorboards!

"Symmetry," Brother Joe offered slowly. As expectant as Gray might have been to hear more, there was nothing more immediately forthcoming.

THE NINTH VILLAGE

—•◎•—

"Any midway point suggests a parenthetic breathing space, an offer of hope, and an invitation to a period of introspection. And wherever we are, at any moment in any day, we must be midway between two points, even if we haven't named them."

Brother Joe

THE AIRLOCK CONFESSION
(ROGER BILLIE'S STORY)

"Brother Joe," said Roger Billie, "it's likely a rumour will solidify while we're in Autumnal."

"*Solidify*, my brother?"

"There's no easy way to put it."

Roger tied the laces on his boot for longer than it takes to tie the laces on your boot. While Roger played for time in this way, Brother Joe regarded the other man's tonsure with superlative interest: almost as if he expected to make a spiritual connection by studying the tan-spots in the balding archipelago on the man's crown.

Roger sat up straight and stared out at a chorus line of chickens.

"I was here in this town before, Brother Joe."

"Did you commit a misdemeanour?"

"A young woman with certain issues I'm not sure I understand," Roger added. "She invited a group of men to disrobe her. And to disrobe ourselves."

"Imagine me with a lump in my throat, my brother," said Brother Joe. "What are you talking about? Are you saying you took advantage of a local girl?"

"She *invited* us. She *wanted* us! The invitation was to all and many. At the time, Carey was known to be a trifle *adventurous*." He cleared his throat. "Shall I put the matter as openly as *she* seemed to?"

"Not much has ever been achieved through confusion."

"The girl enjoyed group sex. She enjoyed being the centre of attention, if you don't mind the crudity of the language. There were seven of us," Roger added. "No witnesses."

"…To *what*? Or should I be nervous about asking?"

"We airlocked her. Accidentally," Roger answered. "She was plugged from sole to scalp with men's erections. Including mine."

"…What happened to Carey?"

Roger Billie sighed heavily. "Apparently, she stopped thinking cogently. She needed to breathe and we made her stop breathing. She ended up with brain damage."

"Because of an *airlock*?"

Roger nodded.

Making his scepticism plain, Brother Joe went on: "It doesn't make sense. You don't get *brain damage* by having group sex, for crying out loud, brother!"

SESSION 25

We're preparing for a Mott the Hoople gig in a smallish hall. People run around. Then I'm in an industrial kitchen of some kind. The kitchen is as tightly crammed as a lifeboat after a disaster at sea. Shouts wrinkle the air, and the noise is as hard to ignore as sinus trouble. The words are opaque and unfriendly. Some of the many people present are dressed in professional whites. Chef himself has a face like a cooking apple.

"I can be John Hodgins... if you'd like me to be," he offers.

"What I mean is," Doug continues, "how often do you physically move when you're with an analysand?"

"*Move?*"

"You sit in a chair and make notes. So do I."

"I don't make notes. I listen."

"They're the sort of notes I meant. Spiritual dictation. But apart from physically shifting to allow someone entry to the building, I'm willing to bet you don't move."

"Doug, that's nonsense. You've just said yourself, I have to let my visitor *in*. How could anyone think I'm paralysed?"

"I didn't say *paralysed*."

"I have to go," says Chaz, "as in *move to let someone in*. My next appointment's arrived. Will I see you tonight?"

"I'll dream a little dream of you," Doug responds.

"When you were married, what's the best piece of advice your husband ever gave you?" asks Dr. Chaz Bruce-Sange.

"Advice?" Phyllie pauses. "I'm not sure. I'm not convinced he ever gave me a single piece of what might be considered advice."

Hiatus. Caesura.

"Would you ever regard the process of psychoanalysis as a means of self-protection?" Phyllie asks, by way of deflecting the original question that she cannot satisfy.

"It's a very rare day that I think of it as anything else. Anything we can do is a way of comprehending something about the world we live in. If learning about our environment isn't a way of protecting ourselves, I'm not sure what is."

Hiatus. Caesura.

"I have a recurring dream about a man who dreams of a girl with teeth embedded in her skin. What can it mean?" Phyllie continues.

The psychoanalyst nods her head.

"I have a friend… associate… very much more interested in dream interpretation than I am. I'd be happy to ask him, if that would be of interest."

"It would. But in the meantime, I'd like to know more about what you *think. Just imagine I'm paying you for your expertise."*

"But you are *paying me for my expertise."*

"I was teasing. What's happening in the countertransference at the moment?"

"If you can't feel it, nothing at all."

"What's his name?"

"Whose name?"

"The dream interpretation expert."

"Doug," Chaz insists, as if she's struggled to recall her colleague's name.

"Doug. As in, once I excavated. Dig, dug, dug. Below the surface of consciousness. I think that's known as positive determinism – or is it nominism?"

"It's a loose connection, at best."

"But you can feel your power slipping away from the situation, can't you? You're sliding from Chaz to Claire… to Carey."

"I don't understand what you're saying, Phyllie. Which Claire? And who is Carey when she's at home?"

"Well, that's the problem, Chaz. She's never at home. She was lost a long time ago. And only a few people know how to remember her."

"Lost?"

"An abandoned dental clinic, Chaz," Phyllie tells her, with a smile that turns sharp and has a strange taste.

Chaz awakens in a bed that is not her own, breathing in a pillow's fabric and looking back at the dream as if on a ship heading out to sea, both wary of the journey ahead and keen to say goodbye to the shore of a foreign land. In her sleep she must have licked her pillow; it is wet to her left cheek.

"Good morning, Chaz," she hears. "How did you sleep?"

Of course, she recognises the American accent.

"Morning, Doug."

Sitting up, Chaz is relieved to note that she is still wearing a blouse and her wristwatch. Doug is not in the bed beside her: he is over at the window, breezily offering, "Don't worry," as he pulls a cord to raise the blind.

"You fell asleep moaning. As in *complaining*. Nothing happened."

"Did you carry me to your spare room?" Chaz enquires, wriggling slightly to experience the rub of her underwear on the under-sheet. It's the only way that she can think of to check that she's dressed without causing offence or raising suspicion.

Doug notices the movement anyway. "I said: don't worry. I was a gentleman. I even rubbed your back while you were being sick."

"Oh God, I wasn't, was I? I don't feel rough."

"I'm joking. You were exhausted. You had two drinks and started to get bad tempered. I danced you to the bedroom threshold and pulled back the duvet. Your sense of fatigue did the rest… You said my name just now."

"I mentioned you to a client. In my dream. In reality too, I think. Would you help me decode a dream?"

"Sure. I'll put the coffee on. Come through when you've had a lick and a fancy. I don't have anything spare for you to wear. The *en suite*'s through that door. You're in the main bedroom. I slept on the workroom couch – it felt like being a student again! You did me a favour."

Much later that day, as the hours face towards closing time, Chaz would pick up her pen and once again fool herself into thinking that she was writing a book.

What do you think it means, she would write, *to long for someone for thirty-odd years?*

"Do you realise something?" Phyllie asks. "We're in our ninth month. We've gone full term. What have we created? Is it a boy or a girl?"

Taking a chance on playing along, Chaz adds, "What will we call our offspring?"

Phyllie smiles.

"I did some homework," she says, "and brought you something. It's a reading from Freud. My equivalent of an apple for teacher. Because… what do you buy the florist on her birthday? You buy her a bunch of flowers. What else?"

"What's the reading?" Chaz asks.

"From *Analysis Terminable and Interminable.* I assume you know it well."

"Reasonably well. This is in response to what I said at our last session together: the awareness of our time together moving towards its completion."

"All good things must pass… Who was that?"

"Maybe Freud himself?"

"Mm. I'm thinking of George Harrison, randomly enough. *Well.* Are you sitting comfortably? Then I'll begin. 'Only when a case is a predominantly traumatic one will analysis succeed in doing what it is so superlatively able to do; only then will it, thanks to having strengthened the patient's ego, succeed in replacing by a correct solution the inadequate decision made in his early life. Only in such cases can one speak of an analysis having been definitively ended.'"

Dr. Chaz Bruce-Sange allows the recital to dissipate.

"Something resonated with you, Phyllie," she eventually offers. "Would you like me to guess what the resonating factor is?"

"I'll give you a million pounds if you select the correct word."

"You haven't got a million pounds – and your dare sounds childish. This is not meant as a criticism, of course."

"Oh, none taken."

"The words we speak are not always conscious choices. Lacan speaks of the mouthpiece."

"…Christ," says Phyllie.

"And change often brings with it a sense of dilution – of anxiety and loss."

"Indeed," Phyllie tells Chaz with a nod of the head. "But my headline since last we met? Are you ready? Benny's dead."

"Dead to you?"

"No, not dead to me: shovelling coal on the other side, whatever that means. *Passed away. Deceased.* A Family Liaison Officer called me two days ago. He had a heart attack in his cell during Friday afternoon prayers. He popped like an old bulb."

For a brief few seconds, it feels like the skin has tightened across Chaz's cranium. Momentarily she is lost for words. On recovery, she wants to know:

"How did you react? Immediately, I mean. You knew it would arrive one day – his age – and I imagine you'd planned a response, even if it wasn't the precise response you actually embarked upon."

Phyllie nods her head.

"That's perfectly fair," she replies. "I won't say I expected to cartwheel around the living room. But I thought I'd experience – at least – a sense of relief. Do you know what I did? I said thank you to the F.L.O. and made myself a salad sandwich on toasted wholemeal bread, with a pot of orange tea. I was hungry. I was numb too, but mainly I was hungry. I ate my lunch and had to force myself to chew every mouthful. Then I had an overwhelming urge to speak to my daughter. Even if I was sure I'd confuse her, I needed to hear her voice – to make sure she was safe. I can't explain it."

"You were worried that Benny's passing would take her with him somehow."

"As ludicrous as that sounds."

"It doesn't sound ludicrous at all, Phyllie. The three of you are tied together on emotional coordinates that no one else on the planet can comprehend. That's why you were hungry."

"The shock of it?"

"I doubt it. You've said it yourself, in the past, you knew it would happen sooner or later. My interpretation is, Benny roosted inside you these last nine years, like something you fed with your rage and darker feelings. You kept his memory alive. Then, as soon as you believe he's shuffled off, the space he occupied needed to be filled. It was time to look after your *own* nourishment for a change. And your daughter's. You wanted to feed her with something positive. The person you feared could harm her was gone. You could re-establish yourself in her life again … Does any of this sound reasonable?"

"It all does. *Now* all I want to do is take Claire to the funeral."

"Well, I wouldn't advise *that*."

"I wouldn't dare. It's a longing for closure, though; that's what I feel. I wouldn't put Claire through a funeral for *anyone*."

"But you asked the officer for details of the funeral arrangements, didn't you, Phyllie?"

"I'm ashamed to say I did. I thought about going. But I won't."

"Who else would be there, do you think? Did he have a family?"

"Doubt it. His goal was to create families from pieces of other people's. I only wish I could be happy he's dead."

"What are you instead?"

"Does *vindicated* work? I feel I can get on with things," Phyllie tells her psychoanalyst. "A sense of justice has prevailed. For years I've sauntered through the idea of existing as a collection of words piled into a script. Emphatically *someone else's* script: not my own. And now I feel *justified*."

Phyllie has stumbled against a wall of choices: embedded in the brickwork are three doorways. Which to choose?

"I think the stories carried on after we were released from Benny's home in Edlesborough. I think he set the dominoes clicking down – making links. He invited us to join our stories together, even *after* we were so-called *free*."

THE ORAL EXAMINATION

It is Claire's *due date*; the last ninth months of her "pregnancy" have come to this day of delivery. By every imaginable definition, there is work to be done: more specifically, objectively (and frighteningly) there is work *for Claire to do*.

Collectors exercise their right to accumulate, in the manner that a palette artist might blend pigments to enact the perfect smooth mauve.

Her consciousness is haunted by her own words and sentences.

On the morning of the viva – the oral examination by which she will defend the thesis submission of her PhD – Claire wakes at 5:45 a.m. and undertakes her exercise regime. During the twenty minutes that she takes to cycle 10K, she reads a few poems in *Ariel* by Sylvia Plath. During her squat thrusts and bicep curls, she pumps out old-school 1980s album tracks by Tina Turner, Nik Kershaw, Howard Jones, and excerpts from the soundtrack to *Purple Rain* by Prince. She feasts on a bowl of porridge with sunflower seeds and diced dried apricots. A bowl that she had prepared the previous evening and left to chill in the fridge.

Her backpack is already laden with books and papers: she intends to reach the university town, to leave her car in her usual car park, and to walk to the university, with the heavy bag nudging her spine as she moves through the streets. She will take a seat at her favourite desk in the 24-hour University Library, for a cramming session that will take her to 9:30. At this time, Claire will re-pack her bag for what she confidently expects to be the final time, and stroll over to the Postgraduate Centre to meet Alex Gordon, her PhD supervisor, to hear from him any last-minute tips or nuggets of invention, before the two of them are invited into the room that will represent the viva's nexus.

Fate scraps Claire's plans for the morning, almost from the word Go.

No sooner is she on the road than she notes the heaviness of the traffic. However, she has allowed herself plenty of time to make the thirty-minute car journey; Claire is not at all worried by the congestion. One long road will take her from where she lives and through the first town that she must encounter; a second long road will take her to the fringes of the university town; and a series of much shorter roads will lead her to the obliging salute of the car park's horizontal barrier.

It is only when the traffic draws to a halt in both lanes in front of her that Claire starts to feel uncomfortable. She has scarcely breached the first of the two towns, about eight minutes into what ordinarily is a half-hour trip. A few horns honk. *Don't panic*, Claire instructs herself silently, before repeating the instruction out loud.

Collecting affirms a state of personal identity and serves to reverse any sense of individualistic dilution to which we are subject during times of upheaval or change.

Claire starts to recite lines from her thesis. The two lanes in front of her contain multitudes of vehicles, frozen in a moment. While attempting to count the cars ahead, Claire brings to mind an image of siblings holding hands as they proceed towards the church on the a summer afternoon of a relative's wedding. She stops counting vehicles at one hundred and twenty-two: sixty-one in each lane. Further than that, the road bends; only mysteries await the drivers this morning. There is very little traffic approaching in the two lanes on the other side of the central divide. Claire notes her sloth at deducing the obvious: there must have been a road accident in the distance; it has blocked the artery through the town.

"Don't panic. Plenty of time," Claire counsels herself, in the intonations of her supervisor.

I spoke to collectors who said that the moment of abandoning the search for their chosen object did not represent the summit of their pain. Abandoning the chase was described in terms of mortal loss – "bereavement", for example, or "divorce".

Claire's brain tunes into the sound of the engines idling around her. Nothing has moved in six minutes. Horns honk like the mating calls of barn owls chancing their odds.

"I'll call Dr. Gordon," Claire decides out loud.

It cannot be the first time that a viva has had to be put back half an hour or so. (Claire has started to sweat. Her oxters could blow *bubbles* with the surplus of perspiration.)

Don't be presumptuous. Or panic either. It's only 7:48 by the dashboard clock. The examination is not until 10 a.m.

These interviewees informed me that not collecting what they had used to collect felt like needing to establish a new persona. It was not only that collecting had provided a purpose; it was also that giving up meant that someone else would win or earn the same object that should have been theirs.

Claire's phone is in her handbag on the passenger seat. She fishes for it as the brake lights on the car ahead extinguish. *Thank you,* Claire breathes; there is movement; she engages first gear and taps on the accelerator. Like a conga line on a societal level, everything in Claire's vision starts to wriggle forward. Unfortunately, the procession lasts only for the length of five cars, then everything stops once again.

Claire prods the screen to awaken the radio. While her temperature soars, she searches for a local radio station; news of the traffic hold-up might help her at least consider a different plan. She resumes her search for the phone in her bag. Not wishing to take her eyes off the road, she asks her fingers to identify the items therein – her purse, a compact, a notebook, a pen, a lipstick, and three tampons. She cannot find the mobile phone. In a fluster, she replays what she can recall of her last steps before leaving the house. She can picture herself in the bathroom, primping; she can remember the donning of her favourite boots; the swish of her scarf as she had flung it over her left shoulder on her exiting the property.

What she cannot recall is picking the phone up from on top of the microwave, where it had been charging its battery.

"Don't panic."

Collecting forms a defence against anxiety that in other areas of our lives might be organised via the erection of social structures, in the domestic setting, or the workplace.

Claire decides she will have to walk to the university. At the next opportunity, she will signal left and leave the main road. She will find somewhere to park and undertake the journey on foot. Although she has never needed to walk from this, her hometown, to the university town – and the centre of the university town to boot – she estimates that even with a bag of books on her back, the trek cannot last longer than an hour.

The traffic has been stalled for twenty-eight minutes when the conga line starts to wriggle again. For Claire, the engagement of second gear is a source of optimism, albeit one rare and sweet. There is one chance close by to turn left off the principal artery, just before a pub called The Ewe & Lamb. Although the traffic has not stopped moving, Claire seizes the opportunity and depresses the indicator lever. Outside a row of shops, she finds a space to leave the car; scarcely pausing for breath or to explore her choices, she removes her backpack from the boot (it weighs about the same as your average cabin cruiser), and places her handbag in the boot for storage, after transferring her purse from the smaller to the larger piece of luggage.

She starts to walk to the university town.

It does not take long before the backpack's straps start digging into Claire's shoulders. An uncomfortable tightening develops across her chest. Parenthetically (and far too late) she wonders if she is physically fit enough for a walk from one town to the next, against the clock, to sit the most important exam of her life, even without a space station's-worth of the finest field-specific analytic writing known to humankind wedged to her back. But it is far too late now to reconsider. Going back to the car to dump the backpack in the boot would constitute a retreat. Claire is not certain that she would be able to start all over again. Abandon the bag itself, in that case...

No. How could she? Write whereof you know, and all of that. Claire has spent a small fortune of hard-earned part-time waitressing and bartending pay packets on the books in the backpack. More than physically crammed against her spine, the monographs and editions are fused with her on an emotional level too. The collecting of these books has been more than a labour of love: it has satisfied something hitherto absent in Claire, on the levels of productivity, efficacy, and psychology. To abandon the collection by the side of a public rubbish bin (it would never fit through the slot to go inside the receptacle) would feel like a self-betrayal – and a betrayal of the hundreds of thousands of hours that went into the writing and the production of the books. Despite the accumulated timespan in question – which continually bumps against her back and strains at her cleavage – the books have not yet completed their work; this completion will be the viva, beginning at ten this morning, and apparently due to finish two hours later. Claire owes it to the writer, as physically close to her body as lovers would ever get, to be present and correct at the start of the exam. She owes her PhD to their erudition and tenacity and skill. They deserve to be shown, by Claire, these very same attributes.

So deciding, Claire picks up her pace. She straightens her back and begins to think less in a panicked way of arriving late, and more in a determined way of proving to her examiners what she knows – what she has digested. She can deal with any pulled muscles later.

Claire turns a corner and stumbles upon a sight that rings distant bells, deep within her sternum. Despite believing that she did not know the way to the university town, other than on a railway line built with the materials of navigational instinct, she appreciates that she has been here before. The memory is as deep as a seventh birthday; however, there is no doubt about it – she was here in the past, as a girl.

This place is called Lewsey Farm…

The name skids into her consciousness (with a squeak of brakes). There is a park up ahead; a public swimming pool is to the left, with the working man's club behind it (if Claire's memory serves). A ruckus from the middle distance suggests a garbage collection truck, chewing away on its breakfast of plastic and glass.

Claire climbs through the park – she thinks *climbs* is a suitable verb. The effort of lugging the backpack seems to justify the selection. Then she hears a sound that she hasn't expected to hear until she returned home: the chirrup of her own mobile phone. Although she knows there will be muscular hell to pay, Claire stalls by a bench and unburdens herself of her planet-mass backpack. The phone has been in the bag all along – it was never in the handbag in the first place.

For the full five seconds that Claire needs to locate the mobile phone, the absence of weight on her shoulders feels like sliding into a bathtub of the perfect temperature. The relief is both physical and emotional.

The caller is Dr. Alex Gordon.

"I just wondered if you'd like to meet in the S.U. for a coffee before you went in," he begins. Then adds: "What's the matter, Claire?"

She tells him about the traffic jam and the assumed road accident. She tells him about her progress on foot through the Venn diagram between the original town and the university town.

"What's the traffic like there?" Gordon asks. "I could pick you up."

"But I don't know about the main arteries; they might be as bad as earlier – then we'd both be late. No, I'll walk. It's a mission now – it's a point of pride and principle."

"You could've called me. I'm at the gym most mornings before work."

"I thought I'd left the phone in my kitchen. I'd better saddle up and hit the trail."

"Okay. Would you like to talk as you walk? Would it help?"

"I doubt it, but I'd be grateful for one favour if you're offering."

"Name it."

"I stink like a javelin thrower. Would you buy me a can of spray, please? I'll pay you back."

Gordon laughs. "I promise you, there's no need to pay me back. One deodorant coming up. I'll meet you in the Union, for a coffee and a bagel. Or a sausage sandwich, if you'd prefer."

"A coffee and a bagel sounds champion."

The talk has given Claire courage. Oddly, so has coming across this swimming pool from her childhood given her courage. A quality connected with the processing of familiarity has sunk charges of energy into her limbs. Though her backbone, breastbone, breasts, and even cervix feel bruised and strained, Claire is certain that there is an achievable path towards her destination.

While laboriously negotiating the backpack into its former position (with her breathing rate and blood pressure once more ascending), Claire notes an absence from the environment: the absence of chlorine. Childhood recollections inform her that the air, at the time, had been saturated with the scent of chlorine. She wonders when last she had smelled the chemical, other than when having taken to the water.

Convincing herself that she has made sufficient progress to justify a five-minute break, Claire leaves the peripheries of the park and walks over to the building that had used to house Lewsey Park Pool – the swimming baths. It is clear on her approach that the building had changed its function some time earlier: these days the building houses a collection of health and wellbeing private practices. The structure has become a local health centre.

Claire is conscious of time – conscious also that this stroll towards the addresses board might qualify as an anecdote to talk about light-heartedly in the viva (opportunity permitting). Something seems absurd (and absurdist) about the names attributed to some of the building's business units.

UNIT 1: HIGHSIGHT & WHITES, OPTICIANS

UNIT 4: STRONG & LIMZ, PHYSIOTHERAPISTS

Claire also sees a notice that has been cancelled out by an opaque red sticker bearing the single black-lettered word ABANDONED. Under this sticker and partially obscured by it, are the words CAREY something – ORTHODONTIST SERVICES. Claire says to herself: *It's an abandoned dental clinic.*

"Hello, Claire," she hears, and she turns her body to one side as swiftly as the tonnage on her shoulders and back will allow. The voice that addressed her is already familiar; only a glimpse of her interlocutor is required before Claire feels confident in saying, "Good morning, Amanda. Fancy bumping into *you* here – it's a small world!" Making light of the coincidence seems as good a way as any of removing herself from it. She cannot stand around chit-chatting; there is too much at educational stake.

"But what are you *doing* here?" Claire cannot stop herself from asking Amanda.

Although Amanda is dressed casually, Claire notices that she is wearing makeup. She cannot remember Amanda having worn makeup before. Who is she here to meet? And why *here* of all obscure places?

"I wondered how long it would take you to find me," Amanda replies.

Collecting is an activity through which we are able to balance our current status quo against where we'd hoped to be by the juncture in question. The activity of collecting represents a point at which we might adopt a reflective stance.

"I don't think I did find you, did I? I'm here by chance."

"Well. We can argue the toss on matters of probability, Claire, but if I repeat I expected you to come here, what can it mean? That you're readable? That I'm wrong?"

"I'd prefer the latter. But I have to get to the University. It's my oral exam at ten."

"You can say the word *viva*. I know what a viva is."

Is Claire correct to infer an element of tension? Certainly, she defers to an internal unwillingness to stay in this stultified moment any longer than she needs to. However, she has already bid her farewell to Amanda and it is surely up to her – to Claire – to exit stage left.

"I'm parked where the bowling club used to be," Amanda suggests, giving Claire a glimpse into something that she'd hoped for on an unconscious level.

"I'd be happy to accept a lift," Claire tells her.

"Of course you would. It's the very last stage of the play."

Could it be (Claire wonders) that Amanda has been drinking? Although there is not so much as a subtle alteration to the other woman's customary tone and timbre, an irrefutable peculiarity in the semantics and word selection persists. But surely Amanda would not drive all the way out here if she had alcohol in her system.

Perhaps she stayed in the area last night. After all, Roger Billie is far away, overseas.

They have reached Amanda's boxy red Citroen.

"I can't thank you enough for this," Claire tells her rescuer.

Amanda smiles as the locks *clunk.*

"Thank me when you've sailed through the exam."

When the engine fails to catch the first time, Claire's breath holds still. It cannot *really* be happening, can it? Today is simply a joke: one gigantic, cosmic, banana skin *pratfall.*

"Needs an MOT," Amanda explains. "The garage keeps nagging me to get it done."

The engine catches the second time.

Great, thinks Claire. *I'm also a passenger in an unsafe, uninsured vehicle…*

As a hobby, collecting goes back to our earliest days. Many of us remember what we used to collect during our childhood years, whether the collectibles were sports memorabilia, cards, cars, clockwork toys, or dolls.

"Or dental tools."

"Sorry?" says Amanda.

"Nothing. Just rehearsing," Claire tells her.

Although the traffic is far from threadbare, it is at least moving. Amanda edges them along in the Citroen, while Claire lowers her eyelids and rehearses her breathing.

"Do you want to practise what you're going to say?" Amanda asks as she drives. "Tell me what your thesis is *about.*"

All of a sudden, Claire's mind is a box of dense fog.

The room into which Claire is shown is one she has been in many times in the past. She has led study groups in this room (when it was her turn to do so); she has typed her password into a box and displayed a slide deck of her bullet-pointed findings to a small group of supervisors, as part of their professional development. Claire knows this room. And yet, today, this morning, it is as if she is stepping onto virgin soil. The furniture is subtly different. As she had been told would be the case, one table has been moved so that Dr. Alex Gordon can sit behind her eyeline and neither distract nor influence her in any way. The blinds are drawn against the sun. An identical plastic cup of water is in place for everybody present. A visual sweep of the room reveals to Claire a diamond of prepared drinks. The cup nearest the far end of the room has no one sitting by it – this must be where she is expected to take a seat.

"Good morning, Claire," is said three times.

"Good morning, everyone," Claire replies.

The three academics in the room have stood up to bid Claire welcome. One is from the Business School; he is here to chair the proceedings and to ensure academic fair play. The other two – facing one another across the table – are Claire's examiners. The external examiner is Dr. Louise Reardon, from a university in the north. The internal examiner is Dr. Something Something. Claire will need to wait for the introductions to be reminded of his name and his area of work, though she knows him.

Claire takes her seat and breathes her way through the shallow waters of a mild anxiety attack. Suddenly, she does not wish to be physically present; surely there must be another way to test her knowledge of her own work.

"Are you comfortable and ready to roll?" the chair asks Claire.

"I'm not sure *comfortable* comes into it," Claire replies. "This has been a strange morning already. I won't bore you."

"Then let's do some introductions," says Dr. Louise Reardon.

"Could you start by telling us a bit about the evolution of your research? How did you get from nowhere at all to here?"

It's a question very similar to the one that Amanda had posed in the car. Claire feels ready. Nevertheless, she pauses; she takes three deep breaths, for fear of appearing over-eager or cocky.

"It's been with me a long time, Dr. Reardon – or Louise, if I may."

"Yes, we're all among friends here, Claire."

"Thanks. Though I won't lie. I've practised calling myself *Doctor* since I got my diary appointment for today."

The room breaks out in a rash of smiles.

"That's understandable," says Dr. Reardon. "I did the same thing when I was in your position. It shows initiative, as far as I'm concerned."

"But that's not what you wanted to know. I've been interested in what I call the emotional equipment that helps us understand collecting ever since I was a girl. I think I comprehended, even then, the system of weights and measures that goes into buying and storing a physical commodity."

"Psychologically speaking, you might mean."

"I do mean – yes. Psychologically speaking. The way we put our money where our hearts are, as it were. I hope that doesn't sound too trite."

"It doesn't sound trite at all, Claire. But it doesn't entirely seem clear either. Would you care to expand on what you've said?"

Claire thinks again of Amanda; her face swims into the room and transplants itself over the features of the viva's Chair. The mask takes a few seconds to settle, but when it does it is snug and tidy.

Leaning forward, Claire grips her plastic cup of water.

"I understood from an early age that one of the cheapest things to collect is stories. When I was at school, I remember conducting interviews with my classmates. What did they collect and why? And I started to see patterns developing, even then. One boy collected coins. He went on holiday with his dad on the Jurassic coast a few times a year – just the two of them, father and son, with a caddy of tools and a metal detector. But he was a rare one. The rest of them – who showed any interest whatsoever, that is – talked of books and music and posters for their bedroom walls."

She sips her drink.

"We all collect something, is my submission," she elaborates. "Even if it's not the thing we honestly *believe* we're collecting."

THE BROKEN VEHICLE

Twennyfour imagined that the Ninth Village was surrounded by an oil slick: an enormous quantity of oil, not only on the rutted road that ran through it, but also in the *air*. Something *slippery* about the place, he had decided; something dark and deep; a quality that merged the evasive with the menacing – perhaps, in addition, with the *corrosive*.

Parenthetically, Twennyfour wondered when he had last looked at his watch. When had he last had a clear idea of what time of day it happened to be?

What time is it now?

As the men left their hotel, their bills settled, a piece of classical music played in the small foyer, near a worktop on which a jug of coffee steamed and a plate of doughnuts, with pink and green icing on top of them, coaxed closer a phalanx of bluebottle flies. The music was Mahler; the doughnuts seemed unapproachable at this hour of the morning.

What hour, Twennyfour?

When Twennyfour glanced at his wrist, he was not much surprised to note that his watchstrap did not circle it. He must have lost his watch.

Outside, the air was oil-slick-rich, as always – in Twenny-four's opinion, at least. None of the seven men spoke; nor did they so much as look at one another.

They were alive in a moment that existed somewhere vague: somewhere between the chilly rising of the sun and the morning's low-energy origins. The air had about it a smeared brown-and-tangerine smeared

Alive but lost, thought Twennyfour. *Alive but lost and uneasy.*

They walked to the van that had served them well. The same van: the same galaxy spray of bullet holes on either flank, as if it were wounded safari prey; and the same broom handle holding shut the vehicle's rear doors.

Yet something felt different.

For the first thing, Brother Joe was suddenly in a hurry to leave the Ninth Village. His forearm flapped like the wing of a wounded raven; inexplicably cranked up in a matter of seconds, he was ushering the other men aboard their rattling dice set on wheels.

The second matter of note was the deepening, darkening weather. Within the last few minutes, the Ninth Village seemed to have taken the stage, and had become the centre of climatic attention. Far from being feathery, now, the clouds had taken on new shapes, and appeared to be *breathing*.

"Storm's brewing," said Paper Jake O'Donnell. "Shouldn't we stay put?"

"We have to be on the road, my brother," said Brother Joe.

"Why?" asked Rick Shawdon.

"I like chasing twisters," was Brother Joe's somewhat miffed response.

Either needing no further encouragement, sick and tired of disputes, or just sick and tired with their mutually exclusive hangovers, Roger Billie and Bruno Amitrano stepped on board the jalopy. They had loaded their bags into the back of the van an hour earlier.

Rick Shawdon was not so easily persuaded.

"I don't know, Brother Joe; driving into a storm seems a bridge too far. Wherever we're going next can wait for us for an hour longer, surely."

Slope-shouldered and with his head twisted sidewards, Brother Joe regarded this latest statement of dissent with evident disgust; he met its maker eye-to-eye.

"We are leaving now, brother," he told Rick, "…because we are not *welcome* here in this village. If you disagree with me, that's your prerogative. Act as your conscience advises. You're welcome to stay here if you wish – it's your decision."

Rick Shawdon felt – and acted – chastened. He dipped his chin a few degrees.

Whether it was intended as an act of solidarity or not, Gray made a contribution of his own. To Brother Joe, he said: "Brother Rick meant no harm, brother. Can you at least tell us where we're going next?"

"But of course I can!" Brother Joe piped. "The next town's known as Eden. Less than a hundred klicks due north-east."

A hundred kilometres? wondered Twennyfour. *We'll never make it in this hunk of junk.* He looked out at an environment that seemed dulled by sepia tones.

Brother Joe sniffed the air. "We snout our way into the unknown!" Saying which, he executed quite the pirouette…

and gambolled his way over to the far side of the van. He jingled the keys in his hand against one another.

"Last one in's a spotted *dick*. No returns!"

Twennyfour experienced an instant of gastric discomfort.

We've already been to Eden; it's been and gone, he remembered. *Why don't the others remember where we've been? I'm* sure *we've been to Eden already...*

Later...

"It won't start, brother."

Brother Joe was discussing the state of vehicular affairs with Gray and Paper Jake. It was Paper Jake O'Donnell who said, "It is an ex-vehicle."

Brother Joe shrugged his shoulders.

"Imagine," he began, apropos of nothing, "if every dental clinic that had ever closed had left one dental tool in the soil beneath the premises. Then imagine a resident of a universe other than ours – a collector of these tools and how they depict our current human geography. This resident has no interest in what purpose our oceans serve, or how our continents have formed. The hobby of this resident is to visit and to collect the tools left behind at the sites of abandoned dental clinics. Imagine that for me if you'd be so kind."

Twennyfour turned away. He wondered what the dirt on the horizon tasted like.

Do all horizon wastelands taste the same? The air smells of something like combusting timber.

Maybe a fire was alight across the plain, at a right angle from where he and Brother Joe had found themselves reminiscing earlier.

What are we doing? Twennyfour had enquired.

Right now, or in life in general? Brother Joe had replied.

Bright-focussed though the moon might be, it provided the men in the van with little more than token illumination; the landscape spread in sepia tones. Not far from where Twennyfour waited (seated), an armadillo scratched through the dirt and sand. A sight to behold! Up above, bats sewed the night air together; the air smelled of effort and price.

BOOK TWO

LEWSEY FARM

… say whatever goes through your mind. Act as though, for instance, you were a traveller sitting next to the window of a railway carriage and describing to someone inside the carriage the changing views which you see outside.

Sigmund Freud, 'On Beginning the Treatment'

I believe rather that I discover – that I prove – the direction I am moving in by moving.

Georges Perec, 'Notes on What I'm Looking For'

THE ORGANS OF BUILDINGS

—•◉•—

"Every shark is a smiling shark. The shark has no choice but to smile."

Brother Joe

RETURN TO THE AREA

The most recent time that Claire had visited Lewsey Farm had been for a very good reason: on the morning of her PhD viva, a traffic jam had delivered her here, humping a backpack so heavy and cumbersome with books that she had ached for the following week – a powder-trail of pain from shoulder blade to lower thigh.

Today she drove all the way to Lewsey Park; no nomadic trudging with a cargo of vital literature had proved necessary. If anything, the traffic from home to here proved jokingly light. On a different day, Claire might have recorded (in her journal) a different adverb. *Facetiously* light, for instance. But today, the word deployed would be *jokingly*: it might only take a paranoiac to imagine the roads to be sniggering at her carefree progress.

Am I here because she wants me here? Claire wondered, aiming the Fiat into one of the many empty parking spaces that faced the park. For no obvious reason, she found herself gripping the steering wheel. She felt both panicked and peculiar.

Although it was mid-morning, plenty of children were using the playground facilities. *Why are they not at school?* It was not a public holiday; nor a half-term break either. Dangerous antics were being undertaken by some of the children. One game seemed to be to jump from the top of the slide and land on their bottoms, roughly halfway down the metal slope. Squeals of delight rose like birds and bats. Despite the fact that the sounds of kids at play had always lifted Claire's spirits, this morning a grating quality was all the rage. Even watching them riding the roundabout made Claire uneasy. She was not at all certain why.

Unfastening her seat belt resembled the crossing of the Rubicon. Instinctively Claire understood that she had entered a drama that was not of her own making – someone else adjusted the scenery and organised the blocking. Claire's role was strictly that of spear carrier.

Breathing through her nostrils, Claire exited the vehicle. As yet she had paid no attention to the building at her back: the one that used to be a swimming pool, two decades ago – maybe much more recently than that. Now, she turned to face it.

What had brought Amanda here on the day of the viva?

Claire walked from the car to the building's entrance. Many windows at ground level had been broken or boarded over. Graffiti artist Spyblood had been here and had used his time busily. He had sprayed his moniker and spiky doodles on walls the colour of sand.

What did I expect?

Claire tried the front door – the door that once had opened to a fee-paying public. It was locked. *Of course* it was locked. Why would it *not* be locked?

The choices were to give up or to persevere. Determination had carried her this far. Would a drive back home not feel anticlimactic? For a reason that Claire had yet to determine, she wanted to go inside the building, even if it meant trespassing.

Before she had taken two strides, she had made herself a promise.

Somewhere on this building's perimeter, at least one door would be unlocked. Why? Because Claire was *supposed* to be here; she felt certain of this. What was more, she felt absurdly *welcome*. She started to explore.

Weeds and hollyhocks necklaced the brickwork. A scent of wild garlic reached Claire's nostrils; it bombed its way into her consciousness with the lubricity of the uninvited guest.

Following the edifice was to trace a path parallel to the edge of Lewsey Park. Nothing moved – neither vehicle nor pedestrian – along the drive that separated the building from the children's area and the bookable tennis courts and bowling lawns. In the full awareness that she might see nothing of interest, and that someone might bark a comment at her, Claire noted the various isthmuses of cigarette butts and plastic sandwich sarcophagi.

When there was no more wall for Claire's shoulder to trail, Claire turned and started her trek through grasses that had not acquired a path through them recently, if ever. By taking this expedition, Claire stepped away from the driveway parallel to Lewsey Park, at an angle of ninety degrees. Claire kicked and trampled through some nature as dense as societal neglect. Every step took her further away from the children's play structures.

Bending forward at the waist, Claire peered through the shadowed and smudged glass; she right-angled a paw against her temple, as if in prolonged maritime salute. The attempt was to blot out daylight, to discern what was on the far side of the pane, to determine what dwelled beyond.

An office, was it?

Claire squinted into the inspissated gloom within. Through a jigsaw-shaped gap of missing glass, she sensed an unexpected aroma. Her nostrils distended, Claire acknowledged the fragrant reality of anaesthetic.

Or so it seemed.

The room looked like a mouth. The benches inside resembled a set of gums and teeth.

When Claire tried the door, it opened inwards.

It was brown-and-grey-dark inside the building; as Claire stepped forward, the gloom condensed into the consistency of margarine. Once upon a recent time, had the lights flickered on as soon as the first person stepped over the threshold? If so, it was no longer the case. Nor could Claire find a manual switch on the wall. With every cautious step, Claire kicked through debris. Was that *chlorine* that she could smell?

The phone!

Claire reached into a coat pocket, by her hip. The phone had a torch function. Immediately relieved to watch the shadows curtsey and retreat, Claire deployed the torch; the shadows waved goodbye, and a sea of bats fluttered through Claire's consciousness.

Even an abandoned building has a sound about it.

The sound was not quite a throb, but that was close. The hum of... what? A generator? A nocturnal grind (even if the world outside remained in the hours of daylight); a low-pitched consistency.

Claire shone her phone's flashlight at the floor through which she rowed... or so it seemed. There was paper on the carpet; discarded clothing; webs of cables; extension boards for plugs. A phone charger had been left behind. A rodent had donated its droppings onto the area's carpet.

What was that sound?

Claire's chest tightened as she ventured, step by careful step, into a building that had once been her childhood swimming pool. She recalled those visits now as she attempted to decode what was buzzing in the structure's bowels.

On her current trajectory, the pool had been to Claire's right, the changing rooms at the end of a wide corridor. Once (and only once) Claire had entered the wrong changing room. She had not been paying attention.

My shoulder muscles ached, Claire recalled.

A man who had chosen not to occupy a changing cubicle had been drying himself with a Tottenham Hotspur towel. It had been Claire's first viewing of a non-parental penis, sheathed as it had been in a wallet of hair as dark as the corridor's interior, as Claire now traversed it.

Back in those days, the door that Claire now faced had borne a plaque reading GENTLEMEN CHANGE. Claire imagined that the man who had been towelling himself dry would be waiting for her. He would be frozen there in the

Noughties (as it were); never having been able to escape the changing room.

Claire had gasped at the sight of the man's physiognomy: a shallow, brisk inhalation. To the swimmer's credit – a young bearded man who had seemed old to Claire at the time – he had shielded his groin from observation, using that very same towel. He had asked the child if she happened to be all right. Did she need any assistance?

On recognising her mistake, Claire had backtracked swiftly. Several years would elapse before she'd stop blaming herself for a misdemeanour worthy of incarceration.

"Sorry, my mistake," Claire said into the darkness, as she had babbled to the bearded young man eighteen years earlier

Claire moved the phone's torch in a rough approximation of the sweep of a lighthouse's beam. What she saw was a reception desk and a suite of waiting room furniture. Claire imagined that two of the magazines on the coffee table curled their corners on being addressed by the phone's illumination, the shiny pages reacting like slugs in salt.

Moving deeper into the building, Claire was surprised to note an improvement in the quality of light. Somewhere up ahead, a lamp was on. This must mean that people were present; wildlife had no use for the overhead bulb. The thought both troubled and appeased her. *Who was here, and why were they here?*

Don't be a sausage, Claire answered herself immediately. *If you hadn't thought someone was present, you wouldn't have entered the building – illegally! – in the first place.*

The next step that Claire took crushed glass under-foot. Whatever the source of light happened to be, Claire approached it. No longer did she need her phone's torch function; she could save the battery.

From somewhere up ahead came the muffled sound of voices – simple conversation, it would seem; no raised emotional pitch, no anger or hatred. Three – possibly more – interlocutors, in conference.

They were in the next room, Claire thought. Her chest slammed shut; an inhalation clicked in the back of her throat.

She expelled another breath – and entered the room.

The source of illumination that Claire had detected corridors earlier was easy to identify. She had stepped into a dentist's surgery, and an overhead light the size of a shield – on a moveable crane-like apparatus – was on full beam above the patient in the chair. This patient, however, had not been instructed to open wide or rinse, or warned that she might feel a brief scratch. The girl in the dentist's chair was nine years old; her skin, bleached arid by the overhead light, showed the remaining hints of the chickenpox that had recently afflicted her.

The girl in the chair was Amanda's stepdaughter, Claire.

"Hi Claire!" the girl offered.

"Hello to you too," the adult Claire replied, summoning a jollity that tasted phony.

Five adults sat in more modest chairs, surrounding the girl's adjustable leather throne. One of them was Amanda

Billie, who had smiled as soon as Claire walked in. "Welcome – and well done," she said now.

The second was a man who might have entered his eighth decade, in Claire's estimation; he was portly, white-haired, full-bearded – and when he added "You might be Claire Carey", he did so in an American accent. He was probably in his early seventies. He was wearing a summer suit close to the colour of his hairdo and Dickensian sideburns, and a plump cravat the colour of blood. "My name's Doug Stegmeyer," he confirmed, rising to his feet and holding out his right hand for Claire to shake.

Too normal… were the only words that swam into Claire consciousness.

Claire shook his hand by leaning towards this stranger over a child's sternum. Their palms met in a handshake directly above the invisible umbilicus of the girl's navel.

The third adult present in the room was dark-skinned; his mop was cropped close to the scalp. While smiling as he was, his lips seemed poised on the brink of an unspoken and fatally hilarious quip.

"They call me Brother Joe," the black man taught Claire. "Real name Cecil Joseph. And a pleasure to meet you finally, my sister."

The heavily accented construction meant something to Claire's memory. Where had she learned of someone who said, *My brother* or *My sister*?

The image of Phyllie Reydman surfaced.

"*Professor* Cecil Joseph?" Claire asked, taking psychic inspiration from the back of her talented skull.

Brother Joe rocked back in his chair as if he'd been called a saviour. The smile had not deserted his face: if anything, the man appeared more pleased than ever.

"Why, yes! Have our paths crossed in the Academy?"

"Not exactly," Claire answered, "but you might remember a PhD candidate named Phyllie Reydman. You goosed her and let her down when you jettisoned your responsibilities. You hurt a lot of people, *Brother* Joe," she continued, shifting the angle of her gaze by a couple of degrees. "Still, if you *hadn't* left the university, I suppose there's a good chance the two of us wouldn't have ended up with *you* as our supervisor."

The fourth adult present was Dr. Alex Gordon. Perhaps it was perfectly in keeping or perhaps it was ironic that Dr. Gordon nestled in his lap the empty plastic remains of a late-lunch sandwich. Although Claire did not guess if the packaging had contained a pallid sausage between triangles of white bread, the option jostled in her mind.

"And who might you be, if I may be so bold?" Claire addressed the fifth adult present in the dentist's light. He was probably mid-forties; harried and emotionally bustled.

"My name is Roger Billie," the man replied. "I won't shake hands if you don't mind – this place is ghastly. But I believe you know my ex-wife, my current wife, and my daughter Claire. What took you so long to *find us*?"

Collecting is a manifestation of a person's individual psychology and frame of reference – her window on the world. It straddles the division between extrinsic and intrinsic motivation. It introjects our fundamental desires and leads us to expect a favourable outcome. I will buy this object and through the act of exchanging money for an object, I will merge with the object. I will not "own" it. I will become it.

Temporarily crippled by Roger Billie's accusation, Claire might have taken a seat if one had been available. Seconds elapsed with Claire standing near to the jamb. She felt neither happy nor sad; neither threatened nor comfortable.

What she had not expected was a deposition to emerge from the mouth of a nine-year-old girl.

"To business."

In one fluid movement, Claire wriggled to the left side of the dentist's chair – the side closest to Claire and the door – and hopped down to the ground.

"Where are my manners?" the girl asked rhetorically. "Would you like a refreshment, Claire? We're not stocked up like a bar, but we can offer you a tea or coffee."

"Do you know what I'd *really* like?" the adult Claire responded, her gaze making its way around the room. "I'd like to know why you seem to have been expecting me, for starters."

Brother Joe clicked his teeth in a gesture that sounded to Claire like disapproval. "Beneath you, sister," he confirmed, with a ruminative shake of his head.

Dr. Alex Gordon piped up.

"Shall we call this your celebration drink after your viva? We didn't quite make it to the caff or a pub."

"What's happening, please?" Claire attempted from scratch, looking Alex point blank in the eye.

"They'll talk when I tell them I approve of them talking," said the nine-year-old girl. "Follow me to the staff kitchen, as was. There's herbal tea as well."

Stunned, Claire Carey filed into the line leaving the former clinical setting. At a height of less than one metre, Claire Billie led the procession. Roger Billie followed his daughter. His second wife Amanda was next. No words were spoken. Claire Carey slipped into the queue after Amanda: it seemed fitting. Following the older Claire were Doug Stegmeyer, Alex Gordon – and bringing up the rear, the most academically rewarded member of the group, Professor Cecil Joseph – or Brother Joe to his friends.

"To the vivaria!" announced Roger Billie, his waspish attitude of a few moments earlier having been replaced by an air more melodious.

Although Claire was content to acknowledge the shift in Roger's emotional weather, it was the last word of his utterance that rang a bell through her memory. *Vivaria* was not a word heard often.

Benny had not used *cages* to imprison his human experiments. Nor had Phyllie described the subterranean cells as *torture chambers* (though torture chambers was how Claire had visualised Phyllie's former reality).

Feeling shaky and increasingly nervous, Claire followed the procession – to the vivaria. Lights blinked on as they walked along a corridor.

They knew I would come here. How did they know?

The solution had to be that Amanda had told them. But if so, how had *Amanda* known? And what was the connection between Amanda and Dr. Alex Gordon?

The answer is me.

The prevailing emotion that Claire experienced now was not fear; it was a sense of feeling *betrayed*. She had clearly been a subject of their conversation; perhaps she had also been a subject of their experimentation.

The party stopped; evidently, the destination had been reached – an unremarkable-looking blue door, similar to at least five others in this corridor alone.

It was Roger Billie who stepped up to a keypad. Claire watched his finger prod a code.

999.

"How ironic," Claire thought aloud. The phone number for Emergency Services, used as an entry code.

Claire's primary emotion had shifted once again. For the moment she felt absurdly enraged by the group's preening hubris.

The door swung inwards. Through the doorway crept a smell like camomile tea.

"What's ironic?" asked Amanda.

"I was just wondering about dialling the same number," Claire answered.

"Why? No one's broken your leg yet," Roger offered in a reasonable tone.

"Don't tease her, Roger," Amanda continued, chuckling a little and slapping her husband's forearm in mild reproof. "He's only joking with you, Claire."

"I meant the Police Force," Claire replied; "not the Ambulance Service. You *are* squatting here illegally, I take it."

"Squatting!" said Dr. Alex Gordon. "We're *working*, Claire! Squatting indeed."

"After you, Claire," added Dr. Doug Stegmeyer.

Claire Carey stepped over the threshold.

The room that they entered was dimmed but not dark. No overhead illumination flicked into action, revived by the explorers' motion. All the same, it was plain for Claire to see a collection of narrow trolley beds – the kind found in a doctor's clinic – within.

The beds had been arranged around the walls; there were five in total. At approximately ten o'clock (as Claire read the room) was another doorway.

There'll be more through there, Claire surmised.

Each trolley bed supported a sleeping and recumbent human form – either a patient or a captive. Snores were shallow. Claire squinted into the brownish gloom.

"Take a closer look, by all means," said Roger's daughter, speaking at a level that was mature beyond her years. "They won't bite."

What do they want me to see? And where do I start?

Claire turned her torso and moved to the right. Stepping closer to the nearest of the trolley beds, she saw a young black man in predictable (and unremarkable) young man's clothing – gymwear and boxy fresh-white trainers. The beard on his face was dark with no hints of grey or white in the bristles. Claire imagined him to be about thirty. Lying as he was above the trolley bed's solitary blanket, it was simple for Claire to notice the young man's most prominent feature. Beneath his grey gym trousers, he sported an unignorable erection.

"Do you assume I know him or something?" Claire enquired (of nobody in particular). "I'm not cracking the code here…"

It was her PhD supervisor who took the question.

"Keep looking, Claire," said Alex. "Inspect the evidence. Do what you did in your viva. What have you researched for the last five years?"

"The psychology of collecting. You're collecting human beings?"

"Not particularly inspiring," was Doug Stegmeyer's contribution – though Claire was unsure if he was offering a review of the quality of her submission, or was putting down the idea itself, as low-hanging fruit on the tree of ambition.

Claire moved to the next trolley bed. The occupant on this one had fallen asleep (or been rendered unconscious) facing the other way. He was older and whiter and taller than the first man; his feet, inside their mud-and-paint-spattered heavy workman's boots, almost touched the younger man's pristine footwear. There were lines on his face; his beard was unkempt and two-tone; his hairline had receded into twin asymmetrical lagoons.

In Claire's judgement, the man approached what she'd heard referred to as the Bullseye Club or the Half-Ton – the milestone age of fifty. Perhaps he had reached that age already. Although this second man looked exhausted, there was no way for Claire to determine his current state of sexual arousal. He had slipped away from consciousness beneath what seemed to be a regulation blanket.

As had the woman on the third trolley bed. Where the two men's bunks had occupied the wall on the right of the room as Claire had entered, the third occupant's sleeping arrangement was at a right angle to theirs.

Claire estimated that this woman was the oldest so far. Such had been the length of her tenancy up to now that the caramel-coloured dye in her hair was betrayed by her silver roots. Her skin was dry; crenellations on her lowered eyelids made Claire think of someone she might have passed in a corridor at the university. Although Claire had never been taught by this woman in her sixties or early seventies, she might have been served by her in a different capacity.

"I don't know her either," Claire admitted.

"Keep working the room," said Doug Stegmeyer.

"Keep playing like a man with ten thumbs," added Alex Gordon.

Parked end to toe with the older lady was another man of well-advanced years: possibly older still. No sound did this man make, but he was crying, with tears oozing from under his puffy eyelids. At some point in his life, he had suffered from a skin condition whose name his observer did not know. The bone structure made Claire think of an elderly black man, but the pigment had leaked from his facial skin; and although small patches of colour remained in a frecklish archipelago, what Claire could see of the man's face and hands was as pale as the old lady's or the middle-aged man's.

"Is the university the connection?" Claire asked. There might have been a note of panic in her question.

And then, on turning to the final trolley bed in the room, pushed up against the wall to Claire's left...

...seeing Phyllie's well-made face on the woman lying there...
Claire gasped.

The last of the room's unconscious occupants was her friend, Phyllie Reydman.

"And to think," said Dr. Doug Stegmeyer, "you might have travelled from left to right. Phyllie might have been the *first* you saw. I wonder why you made that decision, Claire."

Claire faced the man and proffered an interpretation.

"Phyllie's seeing a psychoanalyst – Chaz Bruce-Sange. If everyone's linked..." Claire faltered. She switched her attention to the lady of more advanced years. "Is that *her*?"

"Well done," said Doug. "That's Dr. Chaz Bruce-Sange – my peer, friend, and colleague of many years."

"But why is she here?" Claire asked. "Why are *any* of you here? Or maybe a better question is: why are you *keeping* them here?"

"We're not keeping anyone anywhere," Doug answered. "That door you see? That leads to a simple communal lounge area. Couches and armchairs. Go and look if you don't believe me."

Aggravated tension flared in Claire's shoulders. The PhD pursuit, in many ways, was a solitary occupation; nevertheless, there were people she could have told that she was coming here today: people at the pub where she worked sometimes; or people at the university... faculty staff, support staff...

I would have told Phyllie, Claire admitted to herself; *and she's already here.*

"And there's a kettle and a microwave," Doug had continued, defending the amenities in such a way that made Claire infer that he had set this arrangement up.

"What Doug is proudly boasting," interrupted Professor Cecil Joseph, "is the door that lies *beyond* the communal area – the door that leads to the outside air."

"Don't stand on ceremony," Doug continued.

He didn't like being interrupted… Claire interpreted from the exchange; but she almost did not hear that side of her brain as it spoke.

That's not Phyllie. It can't be.

Of all the people present, it was the nine year-old Claire who adjudicated the two doctors' sub-academic dispute. Her logic was perfectly childlike – and thorough.

"Claire. Do you see any restraints on these five people? No, you don't."

Despite her reservations, the adult Claire had taken up the invitation to inspect the far room, beyond where the five people slumbered.

"No, I don't," the adult Claire agreed. What she saw – as promised – was a simple but functional lounge and kitchenette. Two doors led off from this area, which might have seated ten or twelve people.

Phyllie would have told me, she promised herself. Phyllie had been open about her psychoanalytic therapy hours; why wouldn't she have been as candid about this setup?

On the far side of the lounge, a door similar in appearance to many in the building bore three universally recognised symbols: the one for a man's facilities, the one for a woman's facilities, and a decal displaying a shower head and water spritzing from it.

They eat here. They wash here.

Indeed, the lounge showed vague sensory clues as to recent usage. Claire could smell coffee; a washed cup and spoon looked wet on the draining board.

She would have told me if she came here voluntarily, Claire insisted to herself. She remembered her friend's description of Chaz Bruce-Sange's style of conducting the psychoanalytic session: in particular, the efficacy of the unexpected question, intended to keep the interlocutor slightly off balance.

"Why do you keep the room dark in there?" Claire asked.

The second door leading off from the lounge was supposedly the one that led outdoors. Perhaps it was one of the doors that Claire had tried while prowling the building's exterior. Although cream-coloured sun blinds covered the window, lending the room a tranquil sepia air, there was no denying that it looked like daylight around the window frames, where the fit was not snug.

"Shall we all take a seat?" Doug suggested. "We wouldn't want to wake our guests."

"They're just *napping*?" Claire wanted to confirm. "They can leave whenever?"

Roger laughed when his daughter replied: "I'm nine years old, Claire. Do you think I could stop five grownups from leaving if they got *bored*?"

"That's a good one," said Amanda.

"And *you*," said Claire Carey directly to the speaker. "I thought you and I had formed at least the basis of a friendship."

Amanda appeared puzzled. "Whatever gave you *that* idea?"

Yes; whatever gave me that *idea? The best question posed so far.*

"*You* bought *your* collections and I bought mine," Amanda continued. "Different objects; different currencies – but the processes are not unalike."

I was an object to her... and so are the five in the napping area, Claire thought to herself. *Things to be traded and moved.*

The mechanism continued to make no sense, but at least Claire had warmed to the idea that this group of misfits meant her no unequivocal harm. What they *did* mean for her was as vague as pawprints in mud; some of the aggravated tension had risen wraith-like from her shoulders and slipped away.

Claire Carey sat down in the communal lounge. She cast a prim figure, perched on the edge of one of the four armchairs, her spine as straight as a telegraph pole, her hands loosely crossed on her lap.

What followed might be steered by a pungent question. Looking into herself and rallying, Claire asked aloud as the group filed into the lounge and took their seats: "How does this connect with Benny and that house in Edlesborough?"

ABANDONED DENTAL CLINIC, 1

"You mentioned a network," Claire offered with what felt like suitable humility. "I assume you wanted me to join it. On what side of the divide?"

"...What divide?"

"The operators versus the nappers."

The expression on Amanda's face might even have been pained.

"There's no *divide*. We are all in the National Apology Network, Claire – the NAN. The people you saw napping were having their conversations, or carrying on about their stories... *or*... " Amanda made a gesture of helplessness. "...they were simply *snoozing*. It's a free-for-all. Some stay longer than others. It's all about how the individual views penance."

"I have nothing to apologise for," Claire stated.

"Really? When was the last time you called your parents?"

"Oh, come *on*... "

"The last time you called your friends, come to that."

"The PhD's a solitary road," Claire attempted to defend herself.

"Please don't try to be slippery, Claire. You shifted your focus, and that's fine – but please don't give me the *isolation* nonsense."

"I spoke to Phyllie a lot."

"Yes, you did. While you were here," Amanda informed her, with the caesura between clauses punching home a relevant point. "When was the last time you called your sister, Sheelagh?"

Perspiration broke out over Claire's body. A reference to Sheelagh was damning evidence. However, Claire had not devised a methodology for interpreting the data.

"I have to say sorry for what I'm about to tell you," Claire confessed.

Amanda indicated with her arms the two women's general surroundings. With a beam of good-natured light on her face, she said: "Claire? You're in exactly the right place to say sorry."

"Not to you. To myself. For having to ask a question. I'm terrified at what you'll answer."

"Ask away, Claire. You're in a safe space. You always were."

Claire paused; her throat tricked her – clicked and refused. Then she managed to ask what she needed to ask.

"Did I honestly submit my thesis and sit my viva?"

FEAST BRIDGE & THE PILGRIMS

The most obvious person for Claire to phone was Phyllie Reydman. Not entirely unexpectedly, the answer message was triggered.

"Phyllie, call me, *por favor*," Claire said. A bluff seemed useful. "I've something for you for your thesis. A little trick of the trade. Maybe meet in the Student Union tonight? I'm happy to drive. I'm not drinking."

"Phyllie, it's Claire," she said half an hour later. In those intervening thirty minutes, she had *physically* moved between rooms in her modest flat – from the kitchen to lounge to the bathroom (she had not stepped into the bedroom) – but had *mentally* moved miles ... and moved mountains.

"Ring me, would you? It's urgent. Please."

(Claire Carey would leave a message like this at nine a.m. the following day. Then at 10 a.m., 10.25, 10.37, and noon. Throughout the afternoon she would drop a bundle of similar pleas into Phyllie's phone storage. It was not the content that would change: it was the mounting sense of desperation.)

She's still in Lewsey Farm, Claire knew. She committed the opinion to her journal, writing much earlier than normal at half past two. *I have to go back.*

If she could not rely on Phyllie for the moment, who should Claire consult next? For now, Amanda was out of the question: she could not face Amanda right now. The lingering pong of depression was mingled with something yet harder to inhale: the stench of perfidy. Had she gone as far as to love Amanda? No, not really; but Claire had liked her a good deal. Worse still, she had *trusted* Amanda; that was the foulest stink of all.

Claire toyed with the notion of tracking Roger Billie down through his place of employment. Perhaps leave a cryptic message at every roadblock on the sonic map – every time someone else said: *He's not here right now. Can I take a message?* Claire knew that Roger was a social worker; there was bound to be a link with the local council or the government offices. How hard could it be to find him?

Yes, Roger was a possibility.

Around 3 p.m. Claire headlocked herself into a deferred lunch. It involved grainy bread and salad cream; beyond those basic ingredients, Claire would have been unable to elaborate, less than ninety minutes after the repast. The meal was fuel – nothing but fuel. Claire needed to think. Fuel greased the cognitive cogs.

A bottle of red wine – drained to an inch remaining over a period of three non-consecutive evenings – stood on Claire's draining board. The afternoon's sun had warmed the glass. Picking it up by its neck, Claire took something like comfort from the heated bottle. She poured its fluid into a Tina Turner mug that her father had given her the lion's share of a decade earlier. The material was chipped from dishwasher use; it didn't matter. It had been a gift from Dad. It said: YOU'RE SIMPLY THE BEST!

How long had it been since she had called her parents? How long had it been since she had called Sheelagh?

Several minutes ticked past. By now, Claire was sitting on a stool in her kitchen, at her breakfast bar, watching the stilted sweep of the minute hand on the cooker clock. Her first sip of the red wine felt comforting; the sun on the kitchen window had ignited the Tempranillo to the temperature of a pancake.

"But I'm *not* simply the best, Dad," Claire remarked to Tina Turner's 1980s image on the mug. "They let me walk away. Why didn't they try to *stop* me?"

She tried to call Phyllie again.

You've reached the orbit of Phyllie Reydman. You can leave me one or try later.

Claire was close to uttering another request for a return call, when she realised – and said aloud – *What's the point?* If Phyllie remained in the derelict healthcare building, presumably so did the other four sleepers.

Let's test that theory. How hard could it be to find the contact details of a local psychoanalyst? One of the other nappers had been Dr. Chaz Bruce-Sange.

On the doctor's website was a mobile number, an online form, and an email address. When it came to hooking new work, the woman left few stones unturned.

Claire tried the phone number first. Predictably enough, no reply. Claire assumed that Dr. Chaz Bruce-Sange remained in the building as well, near Phyllie. Claire did not know the names of the other subjects. But she *did* know the names of the people who purported to work there. She knew the names of those who had shared the lounge area with her.

Once more, her thoughts drifted over to Amanda and Roger. Trying to capture what she knew (or believed that she knew), Claire made notes on pages of her journal. Where appropriate, to pledge her belief in a specific connection, she drew an arrow in a different colour of ink, using a whiteboard pen or a highlighter. This style of annotation was how she had marked up many of her research notes.

Amanda Billie BLUE ARROW *Roger Billie* BLUE ARROW *Claire Billie.*

A family connection, in more ways than one. Amanda claimed to be the daughter of a psychopath named Benny. Roger was the ex-husband of a woman who had been imprisoned in the Edlesborough house, nine years earlier. Roger was also a social worker. Was it possibly true, the story that Amanda had told Claire (and the story that Phyllie had corroborated): that his *caseload* had taken him into Amanda's environment? Had Amanda ensnared Roger too?

For Claire, it felt like *too much* to believe; it was too *big*. Even appreciating that a social worker might have had his priorities challenged and realigned by the incarceration of his first wife in a house of horrors, it was still a tall rampart to climb.

Shuffle the deck.

Dr. Alex Gordon and Professor Cecil Joseph... otherwise known as Brother Joe... Phyllie had told Claire that Alex was her fourth supervisor. She had sacked the first one. The second had sacked *her*. The third had been sacked by the University. His name was Cecil Joseph. The academic connection.

And then, Dr. Doug Stegmeyer, whose occupational link to Dr. Chaz Bruce-Sange had been established while Claire was still in Lewsey Farm.

(... though who knows, they might have been lying...)

The *psychoanalytic* connection.

Friends and comrades. Professionals in their field. Peers and colleagues.

Although Claire had no way of knowing how Doug spelled his surname, she found his website swiftly enough. It resembled Chaz's.

Absorption of the slug of red wine helped. Claire's consumption was just enough to make her feel confident and not cocky.

"This is Dr. Doug Stegmeyer," the American's voice announced – in such a way that Claire believed she would be invited to leave a message. But no: a silence followed – a moat across which to swim.

A deep breath.

"I'll call you Doug," Claire told him. "Your standards defy any code of professional ethics. I reject your title of doctor."

"...Who is this, please?"

"Who *is* this?" Claire repeated. "Who do you *think* it is?"

"I really couldn't say, Miss. I get a lot of calls."

Could this be happening? Claire had fluffed her feathers in the expectation of a confrontation. The last thing she had predicted was memory loss.

"I visited your laboratory in Lewsey Farm as recently as *yesterday*. I met your colleague Chaz Bruce-Sange. Again, I'll omit the professional recognition."

"Ah! Thank you," said Doug Stegmeyer. "You must be Claire or Deonne."

Deonne?

Claire's heart tipped over and leaked its contents into the brook. Not once had she considered that there might be others like her, in a similar position. Humbled by the psychoanalyst's failure to recognise her voice, Claire confirmed her name.

"I'm pleased to hear from you, Claire, but is it a quick one? I have a client at four and I make it a point of principle to be on time."

Second by second, Claire's sense of self-importance – and means of self-propulsion – were draining into the same brook… or into the river at Feast Bridge. Having noticed Stegmeyer's work address, Claire added, "You must know The Pilgrims."

"The pub? I go there often."

"You'll meet me there at five-thirty this afternoon. Bring a notebook if it helps."

"Why would it help?" Doug Stegmeyer asked.

"In case you want to make notes. I'll be talking a lot. Five-thirty."

The Pilgrims looked and sounded the same as it always did. Upon her entry, Claire wondered why she thought it might have changed. After all, it was not *reality* that had altered; what had altered were *contributions* to that reality.

Pseudo-swiftly, another assumption of Claire's was battered to the ground. She had anticipated finding all of them present – Stegmeyer plus his cronies, including the Billie clan. But no, this was not the case. As Claire arrived, Doug was sitting by himself in a booth, reading the small print on a tomato ketchup sachet. The fact that his arms were extended suggested that he had issues with his close-up vision. Claire deduced that the man wore contact lenses with a distance vision prescription.

The important (and striking) thing was, Doug was alone. He had not arrived at The Pilgrims armed with the goodwill or backup of others in his band of brothers and sisters.

Without a word, Claire slid into the booth that Doug had occupied.

"Tell me about your relationship with Chaz Bruce-Sange," she said.

"Would you like a drink?" Doug replied.

"...Yes."

"Honestly, Claire – the ballbreaker act is only going to make you feel embarrassed. Every bully requires the reciprocal actions of a victim – and vice versa. What would you like?"

"Half of bitter shandy, please."

Doug rose. Due to his bulk and his age, this was not a gymnastic display. With what seemed like difficulty, he shuffled out of the space in the booth.

"My relationship with Chaz," he told Claire, "…is none of your business."

With which he strolled to the busy bar.

On his return, carrying a half pint of shandy in a thin glass and a concoction that almost defied description, Doug placed the drinks on beermats.

"You have salad in a fluid," Claire informed him. "Would you care to elaborate?"

"Tequila, lime juice, and vodka." Doug settled back into his seat; the effort to do so was audible in the chugs of his breath. "Stick of celery. Some other *mauve shit*. It's called The Pilgrims' Tooth, for some reason. Pilgrims plural. Either it's a punctuation error or a group of different pilgrims shared a solitary tooth. Which do you think is the most likely?"

Ignoring the question (it might have been intended as rhetorical), Claire said: "There's more foliage in there than a stick of celery and some mauve accoutrements."

"Who knows? Maybe it contains *diced otter*. You had a question to ask."

"No, I didn't. *You* did."

"*I* don't, Claire. Are we both here under false pretences?"

Claire nodded her head. Deliberately she took her time taking two sips of her shandy. Equally deliberately she ignored Doug for at least a minute; she glanced around the saloon. Deposited kids noised playfully in the soft-toys corral. The kitchen coughed out piquant clouds of beef madras.

Play like a man with ten thumbs.

"You must have known Chaz for a long time if you were able to convince her to stay in the old swimming pool."

While sipping his cocktail, Doug seemed immersed in something like a jungle safari. Peering through the gaps between what looked like two fern leaves, he said: "I don't have to convince anyone of anything. It's not my *bag*… Claire."

"But I'm right about the length of time. You've known each other a good while."

"Oh, indeed. Decades."

"She's part of your fruitcake network."

"No. She's part of a National Apology Network," Doug replied.

Claire hovered over the spoils of the material, wondering whether or not to swoop. She did not want to ask a question; she wanted to make a statement – to strut it out.

"I assume she doesn't know she's a research subject."

The articulated assumption amused the psychoanalyst; his beard quivered like a cat's back on being stroked. "What makes you presuppose that?"

"The roots of her hair," Claire answered. "Different colour, you see – a point a geriatric old *bully* wouldn't notice. She's *classy*, Doug. She wouldn't be seen dead in a place where her scalp showed the greys. I bet you haven't looked after her legs or oxters either."

"…What are oxters?"

"Armpits."

"*Me?* You expect *me* to keep an old girl shorn?"

"Your mob."

Collecting is a matter of gaining the upper hand…

Doug shrugged. "You have a point, Claire… Now. As I add *oxters* to my lexicon, can I mention another Anglo-American difference? In the States, the floor of a building is called a story, without the E before the Y… Story – as in a creative narrative. Every floor is a story – of so-many chapters. Every high rise a book. An anthology!"

Where's he going with this?

"The characters slip from novel to novel," Claire added, playing along; "and it's your ambition to join the stories together. You call it a network."

Doug appeared to lose focus. Having sipped his drink, he spent half a minute combing the end of his grey-and-white beard between two fingers.

Claire was on the brink of adding something when Doug said: "To be specific? *Roger's* ambition – and Amanda's and Claire's. Originally, at least. You know Roger's a social worker?"

"I do."

"I've never in my life met someone more intent on helping his fellow man. Not even me! Not even *Chaz*…"

When Doug brought his beard back to Claire, it was wrapped around a broad grin.

"He says – he's achieved more through the curative powers of people sharing and creating stories than he's managed in two-decades-plus of social work. Can you *imagine*, Claire? – the combination of pride and *disappointment*. Imagine you reach your forties – well into your forties, in Roger's case – and your career has been *humdrum*."

"Well, at least you and Chaz have your next cohort of analysands," said Claire.

"Because they're bored? That alone?" Doug considered the proposition. "It's not impossible – but it's not likely either.

There's usually a cosmos of debris to navigate through, on board the Spaceship Unconscious."

Claire smiled; she recognised the style of delivery. "You're quoting from yourself right now, aren't you, Doug," she told him.

"Guilty." The smile had taken root in the nest of Doug's facial hair. "What we're doing – without harming a soul – is inviting people to say sorry and to share thoughts and form structures… if they *want to*, Claire. Including you. And if you don't want to, that's fine. Walk out the door, as Donna Summers advised."

"Gloria Gaynor. I don't know what you want me to apologise for."

"Neither do I. How would I? But *someone* does. Twennyfour talked about you after you'd gone, for example. They knew you were there in the room."

Claire had not anticipated a contribution such as this.

"Really? What did he say?" Claire asked, bluffing further. "Assuming Twennyfour's one of the men who were sleeping."

"The first one you looked at," Doug confirmed. "As in, like attracts like. Young black male; twenty-nine years of age, given what he sings out loud like a canary. He's in a band of brothers, in a van. They sleep in the desert sometimes. They drive from town to town."

"Yes, I heard about them from Phyllie. Brother Joe at the helm. Professor Cecil Joseph to his friends, if he has any."

"Brother Joe's a good guy," Doug added in his colleague's defence.

"Why does the black guy call himself Twennyfour if he's twenty-nine?"

Doug nodded; he'd expected a question such as this. "I must resort to the theoretical," he stated. "Something happened to that young man when he was the age of twenty-four. That's my suspicion. It stunted his growth, emotionally speaking. A trauma."

"And he's lived in a post-traumatic depression ever since."

"I believe so."

"What's his real name?"

"He's never shared it – never *divulged* it." Ostensibly delighted by his choice of synonyms, Doug Stegmeyer turned aside his head and grinned, his features netted in a mesh of zygomatic lines.

"And he spoke about *me?*" Claire waited to clarify. "Are you sure it wasn't Phyllie's *daughter* Claire?"

"I am. Because he didn't use the name *Claire* at all," said Doug. "He used your surname. In Twennyfour's world, you're a nine year-old girl named Carey. You have teeth embedded in your skin. Does that mean anything to you?"

Something cold and toothy howled its way through Claire's body. This monster chewed the years of Claire's life and chewed her organs within its icy breath. One second, Claire Carey was a twenty-six year-old PhD student; the next, a nine year-old child, cast aside by her father in favour of his new girlfriend. Panic riffled through her pages. Breath felt harsh against the back of her throat.

"Would you like to discuss anything, Claire?" Doug enquired, deploying for the occasion his richest, lowest American brogue.

It can't be Hodgins.

"Claire?"

"I had a boyfriend named Hodgins – when I was twenty-one, five years ago," Claire told Doug. "We had a silly thing – where we called each other by our surnames. He'd call me Carey."

"You think Twennyfour might be John Hodgins?" Doug asked.

"It was dark in that room. I couldn't see him properly..." Claire regrouped. "How did you know his first name was John?"

"Phyllie's talked about him. So's Chaz," Doug replied.

Claire thought back to the man on the first trolley that she'd inspected. The man she'd glimpsed in the gloom had been heavier of build, but five years was plenty of time to bulk out a physique. And although John Hodgins had always dressed better than the man on that trolley (Claire gulped)... yes, it might have been him. "It's possible," she conceded.

"Thank you. *Now,* I have to ask you something that might sting. Are you ready, Claire?"

"I'm not ready, and I'm ready at the same time. Ask it."

"...Were *you* the trauma in John's life that stopped his development?"

"I might be," Claire answered. "I damaged him deliberately."

Dr. Doug Stegmeyer leaned back against the wall of the booth. "And so I'm clear… you knew John when you were nine?"

"No, not at all. I met him at the University – we'd started our Masters. The reference to the nine year-old must be to his older sister – bless her soul."

There were no divides, Claire had been told when she was in the abandoned dental clinic. The fact that the stories were being shared – and that their authorship could not be validated – was surely proof that the network's ambition was well and truly underway.

"What happened to Twennyfour's sister?" Doug asked. "Or *Hodgins'* sister, I should say. Twennyfour's older sister took her own life. When they were adults."

"In real life – don't laugh – the poor girl didn't make it that far. Her name was Susan. She died of sepsis when she was nine. Understandably enough, Hodgins found it hard to talk about; but from what I recall, she had poison trapped in a gap behind a tooth. A dentist accidentally released the poison into her bloodstream. It's a tragic story."

"It is indeed," Doug agreed. "Do you read anything into what you've told me?"

"Isn't that supposed to be *your* job?" Claire replied. "And besides, you still haven't told me what Twennyfour actually *said*."

An unmistakeable twinkle embedded in his eye – like a nugget of precious metal in a stone – Doug shifted his bulk. He leaned towards his interlocutor.

"What do you think he *might've* said?"

Instead of protesting that she could not possibly know, Claire gave the question some appropriate attention.

"I find myself thinking of a conversation I had with Amanda. I hadn't known her long…" Claire snickered. "If indeed I ever knew her at all."

"What did she say?"

An assumption, here: that it had been Amanda who had spoken first, or who had uttered the foremost message. The fact that Stegmeyer was *correct* in this assumption rankled richly – albeit briefly.

"She'd researched my name for me – something I'd never done. She told me I was a contradiction: *Claire* from the French, meaning *clear* in the feminine form. Origin: bright – or light. Then *Carey*… Irish – an Anglicized form of the Gaelic Ó *Ciardha*: a Leinster family name meaning *descendant of Ciardha,* meaning dark or black. Amanda told me I was her Bright Dark or Light Black. She told me I was her *favourite contradiction.*"

The tears that formed in Claire's eyes arrived without warning. A deep appreciation of what she had lost was uppermost in her mind.

"I hope I don't sound abrupt," said Doug Stegmeyer, "but what's your point?"

"I have the feeling you're going to tell me something about myself."

"You might be right." His eyes sparkled with disobedience. "But not right now. Let's finish our drinks. The evening is still *Claire* – it's a fine old time for a final walk across Feast Bridge and along the river. Before it gets too *Carey.*"

"You told me Feast Bridge doesn't exist."

"Feast Bridge is another story, Claire," Doug replied. "It's as real as any other story; or as real as you'd like it to be. But if we're going there one last time, let's do it before the sun sets on the water, shall we? Illumination on ripples is good for the soul."

ABANDONED DENTAL CLINIC, 2

"**D**o you expect me to say: *I've been expecting you?*"

"Like a Bond villain, please," Claire answered.

"In that case, Claire … I've been expecting you."

"I love what you've done with the place," Claire added, her voice saturated with sarcasm. "Tell me. Do you intend for me to stand until I cease the menstruation process? Offer me a seat, for God's sake! My legs ache."

Amanda smiled. "Please take a seat. Make yourself comfortable."

"You first came here four months ago," Amanda informed Claire.

"I most certainly did not," Claire replied.

Undeterred by the objection, Amanda pushed on.

"Your satnav had run out of juice; you got a bit lost … You were thinking of the run-up to your viva as a pregnancy. You were five months pregnant, so to speak."

Claire frowned in stretched concentration. "Do you mean the first time I bought something from you? That wasn't here.

I drove to your bungalow in Raulton. We met in a café called Back to the Eggy Bread. We walked to your lock-up."

"You were *here*, Claire. We both were."

It had taken Claire the full span of twenty-four hours since leaving the dental clinic before she had screwed up sufficient courage to buzz Amanda Billie on their online platform.

Amanda had given Claire her postal address. *You really don't need it, though,* Amanda had finished the call by saying. *You found me the first time. It's the same address.*

I drove to Raulton, Claire had protested.

Compare the postcodes. The one I just gave you to note down. And the one in the satnav in your car. The postcodes are the same.

The concentrated expression on Claire's features had been replaced by something more candidly baffled. She double-, triple- and quadruple-blinked… Amanda waited. Amanda counted Claire's blinks and would later merge this minor finding into a master file. For Amanda, every detail was eventually part of an archive; every action of her own, one of collation, collection, and filing. Amanda regarded herself as a societal *cleric*. Where her father had been a researcher and a scientist, reaching out into the chaos, Amanda liked to keep matters in tidy order.

"I drove to Raulton, Amanda. I remember the journey clearly. I've returned a bunch of times!"

"But do you though?"

"…Do I what?"

"Remember the journey clearly. For the benefit of a visitor to Planet Earth, how would you describe Raulton?"

"I'm in no mood to play games."

Amanda had taken on that sly twinkly air that Claire remembered had first impressed her – and then, in retrospect, had *attracted* her.

"Did you compare the postcode in your satnav with the one I gave you yesterday?"

"I was frightened to, I must admit," Claire told her.

Experiencing this sly air again now, Claire could not shake the feeling of admiration, nor the mild, vague attraction; but new developmental material had been added to the mix. Claire now hated her for it as well.

"Humour me," said Amanda. "The visitor to our planet…"

Submission to the greater spirit of inquiry might be the most direct route to self-perception.

Claire thought of her own words, which had travelled a substantial distance aboard the damaged van of her thesis – from being discussed in an academic milieu, to being submitted as part of her examination, to being *defended* as part of her viva.

The sentence had performed much heavy lifting… for its author's benefit. Surely it was time to live by its code.

Treat this as another viva. If the question makes you uncomfortable (Dr. Gordon had counselled her), *then regard the discomfort as a gift. Answer everything. Get comfortable with being uncomfortable.*

"Raulton is a town of mixed socio-economic realities. There's poverty – sorry, but there is – and there's a small central business district."

Amanda was nodding her head. "A bit like Lewsey Farm, wouldn't you say?"

"Yes, a bit. We sat in your bungalow, Amanda. Claire had chickenpox. We walked near a pub called The Pilgrims, on Feast Bridge."

And now Amanda was shaking her head. "You were here, Claire. There's no such town as Raulton. There's no such bridge as Feast Bridge. No river runs through Lewsey Farm."

"I was *there*, Amanda!"

"Look it up if you don't believe me. You won't find Raulton on any map of the area. It doesn't exist."

Claire knew this to be the case. She had (of course) tried to find Raulton and Feast Bridge on an online map. Their absence on the screen had been felt in the hollow of her stomach. She'd felt sick for hours; on the brink of an uncertain style of emotional breakdown, but above all, *very sick.*

"I live seven streets from here. When I walked you from home to the storage lock-up... I walked you *here*, to this building. To get the more expensive tools. Just look around. There's *loads* of guff left behind from when the businesses folded. They never cleared the building."

An alternative way of regarding reality now sat like an anvil on Claire's chest. There was no need to censor herself from asking a question. On the contrary, Claire had discovered that she no longer had a single comment to utter.

If this terrible interview was an effect, there must have been a cause. Claire forced herself to recall what had led her into Amanda's web.

The answer, of course, was the Web.

"I found you on an auction site," Claire told Amanda.

"Well, you found some interesting items on an auction website."

"Don't split hairs."

"I'm honestly not, Claire. I advertised some items that were lying around."

"Yes, I know – to lure me in."

"Not at all."

"Oh all right, to lure *somebody* in – it just happened to be me."

"No, that's not right either," Amanda protested. "I was selling stuff no one wanted."

"As part of your experiment," Claire told her coldly.

"You overestimate me, Claire. As a way of *making money*." Amanda shrugged. "Girl's gotta eat. So's her stepdaughter and husband."

Claire experienced the twinned sensations of deflation and depletion. Had she vastly overregarded her role in the scheme of things? Surely not. Whatever else had happened or been said, Claire had warranted the presence of a welcome committee when she had driven for the first time...

(*or* consciously *for the first time*)

... to Lewsey Farm, a few days after the successful viva. Those seemingly unrelated adults – and a child! (let's not forget the ethically-chewy involvement of a *minor* in all of this) – had invited her in, to show her their wares.

Any sense of agency had deserted Claire. If she obeyed her own vow and refused her interlocutors the power shift of a voiced question, her options – suddenly – had been reduced to one. Claire was left with the opportunity of stating facts, in the hope that one of her launched arrows found a mark.

She recalled a comment that Phyllie had made about someone named Branston. Nine years earlier, Benny had wanted a Film Studies lecturer named Tim Branston to record the experiments in the vivaria. Benny had employed an archivist.

"You want me to write about your experiment," Claire guessed.

Amanda winced visibly. "I'd prefer to think," she answered slowly, "of our *services* … the services we offer. Rather than an *experiment*." She straightened, equally visibly. "But no: we have writers. Doug's a writer. One of the amusing conversations he has with Chaz is about what they're writing. They talk on the phone or they go to The Pilgrims to discuss psychoanalytic literature. Each to their own. But what he's *actually* writing – in *our* time – is something called 'National Apology Networks' – and I doubt he'll want to share the credit."

One arrow flown from her quiver, to no great effect. That said, Claire now comprehended that her skills as a social scientist, soon to be a Doctor (once her amendments had been approved), were not in the group's demands.

(She acknowledged a sting to her pride at this realisation, and it perplexed her. Had she *wanted* to write something?)

"You wanted to show me what you're doing," Claire stated, backtracking slightly and grasping again for what seemed obvious.

Amanda shrugged. "Well, you or a number of other people."

THE POSTGRADUATE CENTRE

Phyllie was first to arrive at the university café that she and Claire favoured. She ordered a Turkish coffee without sugar and a chocolate bar to redress the sucrose balance. She saw Claire in the distance; it was only as the younger woman strode closer that Phyllie saw she sported a face like thunder.

A mere ten minutes earlier, Phyllie had turned her phone on for the first time in seven days. Her one-and-only charger had become faulty and unreliable; the blob that attached the plug to the cable had frayed, probably due to carriage in Phyllie's bag. She'd needed a new one. It had taken a day each to determine which kind of charger she required; to find that charger on various websites; to conduct a price comparison that took into account her preference for supporting small local businesses; and to order the item. This morning she had charged her phone and seen nine missed calls from Claire (and none from anyone else). Phyllie had assumed that Claire might be cross at not having her calls returned, but she hadn't expected Claire's current expression.

"What's up?" Phyllie asked her, rising to her feet to proffer what had become a customary peck on the cheek.

Although Claire accepted the kiss, there was no alteration to her expression. "We're not safe here," she informed Phyllie without preamble, and in a voice that brooked bullshit quotient *zero*.

It took Phyllie a double-blink to process the words. "Not *safe*?"

"I have to tell you something about your ex-husband and your daughter, Phyllie. And Roger's wife. And our supervisor. And others."

Immediately, on sitting down, Claire started to cry.

"None of this is going to make much sense," Claire warned Phyllie; "but I swear it's true – every word of it."

Mention made of Roger and their daughter had served its unconscious purpose: it had poured benzene onto Phyllie's lap – and threatened to strike a match. Mention made of Alex Gordon, however, had served simply to bemuse.

"Are they all right?" Phyllie wanted to know.

Claire tilted her head to one side and dabbed the sleep deprivation bulbs under her eyes with a blue serviette. She issued a sigh that seemed to have no theoretical lower level.

"We'll need to define our terms," Claire answered, "in the Socratic fashion." What she issued next was a chuckle of garlicky bitterness.

"Don't mess me about, Claire. Is my family safe?"

The seconds that swept by turned a screw on Phyllie's nerves, tightening them efficiently.

"Claire, please…" Phyllie's tone had changed: it had slipped from accusatory to conciliatory. "What's going on?"

"You and I are not having coffee in the university café."

"I don't care about *coffee* for God's sake! What did you mean about *Claire*?"

Leaning forwards slightly, Claire gripped the end of Phyllie's fingers. "I saw her in Lewsey Farm, with Amanda and Roger," she replied, her eyes widening in anticipation.

Phyllie shook her head. "So what?" she demanded, pulling her hands free. "You told me you went there to buy things. The hell's this *about*, Claire? Why did you ring me nine times?"

"I told you I went to Feast Bridge to meet a woman named Amanda."

"…Where's Feast Bridge?"

"In Raulton."

"…Okay. And where's *Raulton*, when it's at home? No pun intended." Phyllie did not wait for an answer. "Roger and Amanda live in Lewsey Farm, Claire." She paused before continuing. "Is everything okay with you?" she asked… but this time in a kindly manner.

Claire had to step out and fight.

"We're seven streets away from Roger's bungalow, right at this minute – swear down. The coffee we smell was brewed in a communal lounge area in an abandoned dental clinic."

"You're making me nervous now, Claire. Go slowly. You went to Roger's house in Lewsey Farm. What happened next?"

"No; that's the point, Phyllie. I've *never* been to anyone's house in Lewsey Farm. I went to their house in *Raulton*… when I went to a house at all – or a bungalow… They *do* live in a bungalow, don't they?"

"Yes."

"I thought so... My gosh." If it was possible to pull off an expression that homogenised horror and appeasement, Claire Carey had just achieved the unlikely.

Everything that Phyllie had confessed about what happened nine years ago, in the Edlesborough house, had severed to convince Claire that face value was a redundant commodity. A more or less redundant *concept*, too. It was what occurred in the *intra-realities* – in the overlaps and the links; the palimpsests and the saturated spaces – that screamed importance. The *irony* was, Phyllie had been there at that time, and was physically present in an equivalent set-up *at this moment*.

And she's blind and deaf to the truth of it, Claire summarised. Just like last time, nearly a decade earlier, the poor sow Phyllie knew nothing about what was occurring.

Claire watched Phyllie as she leaned back in the cafeteria's booth. Leaking carbon dioxide from between her teeth – like a silky *femme fatale* exhaling smoke in an ancient black-and-white picture – Phyllie seemed to settle into what had yet to be proposed. Had she secretly assumed that the postman always rang twice; that lightning, likewise, executed a second strike? Was Phyllie resigned to a return of the repressed?

Claire would never commit to her journal what she saw in Phyllie during this café scene. But what she imagined was something like a mother hen, plumply *settling*: establishing herself inside her functional coop.

"Tell me why you said we weren't safe," said Phyllie, calmer now than she had been so far. She gave Claire the impression that somehow... she was *ready* to hear this.

"I can't pretend I haven't been waiting," Phyllie mentioned. She and Claire had switched to a different set of seats, in the Postgraduate Centre, on the second floor. Dr. Alex Gordon shared a staff office behind a (currently unmanned) Reception lectern where postgrads could leave messages in a pigeonhole structure – or request an ad hoc appointment.

Standing shoulder to shoulder, Claire and Phyllie had asked for a quick word with Dr. Gordon. They'd been told he was in an online meeting with a Masters study group and would join them as soon as.

"Let's hope there's no back door," Claire had mentioned, "for him to escape out of."

Conversation between the two PhD students was scant. From elsewhere on the floor came the murmur of small group tutorials or action learning sets underway; nimble fingers tapped on keys; a student was taking a few lines of his dissertation out for a walk, reciting them just about out loud. A water dispenser hissed into someone's bottle.

Dr. Alex Gordon eventually emerged from the staff room.

"What a pleasant surprise," he must surely have bluffed. "What brings your path to cross with mine?"

"We are here to play you like men with ten thumbs," Claire advised him.

"You're my fourth PhD supervisor," said Phyllie to Alex Gordon. They had taken seats in one of the empty classrooms; they were about to have an impromptu tutorial. "And I can't believe it's a coincidence that my third and you are associated."

"It's not. Cecil felt guilty about leaving the University in limbo. He had a project in mind to redeem himself."

"The National Apology Network."

"That's right."

"Did you know him before he left?" asked Claire.

"Only vaguely, by name," Alex answered. (Phyllie felt a prickle of irritation at Claire's question; both at its content and the fact that it was not Claire's turn to speak.) "He had a broad portfolio before he threw his toys out of the pram. He had Dentistry Masters students, PhDs – he had a mix. I'd meet him occasionally at a supervisors' thing about changes in the regulations – or something like that."

Alex turned back to Phyllie.

"Talking of redeeming himself, Phyllie, shall we talk about Roger? We'll have to at some point, after all. It should go without saying I wouldn't want to embarrass you."

"I'm not embarrassed," Phyllie answered. "Roger's about the only person I know whose first instinct is to protect and serve."

"Well, yes; I agree. Roger's only goal *in life*, I think, is to do good for people." Alex shrugged. "He's a social worker, after all. So, when his marriage to you ended…"

"He married a madman's daughter," Claire interrupted, with the timing of a comedian. "Makes perfect sense," she added, in a tone from which you could have titrated pure sarcasm.

Dr. Alex Gordon made the universal gesture of hopelessness in the view of greater odds, the palms of his hands rising significantly.

"I can't explain why two people get married, can I? I haven't pulled off that trick myself. But my understanding is, he went to Amanda's house for professional reasons."

It was Phyllie who picked up the thread.

"A neighbour of Amanda's was hoarding. She'd had a breakdown. I empathise."

"The *neighbour* had a breakdown – or Amanda?"

"Neighbour."

"All I'm saying is," Alex resumed, "I don't think you should think ill of anyone in our group – but in particular, not Roger. Roger's still the man you married, I would guess."

The academic guide had become a guide of physical spaces. *Come with me,* Alex had said to Phyllie and Claire. *I'll show you somewhere you've never been.* One by one they had ascended to the third floor of the Postgraduate Centre, where the banks of computers remained largely unused – not so much abandoned as never found – and where lectures and presentations were underway in rooms with glass for walls. The third floor was where Alex's supervisees delivered their own classes, occasionally.

Now they stood at the foot of the next stairwell. As always, it was barred by a simple admonition – AUTHORISED PERSONNEL ONLY – on a metal sign hanging at thigh height between two stands that resembled oversized candlesticks.

"Anyone can ignore the sign and go up," Alex offered, "so why don't they?" A pedagogic follower of fashion, Dr. Gordon was *problematising* on his students' behalf. "Why do you assume you're not authorised?"

"Why do *you* assume I haven't ignored the sign?" Claire retorted. "Maybe I've been up there for picnics."

Phyllie wished that Claire would stop talking: their supervisor was giving a lesson; it was just like Dr. Gordon to provoke with enigma and elicit his learners' responses. *So what is my response?*

"This reminds me of something," Phyllie interjected before Alex could respond to Claire's taunt.

Dr Alex Gordon pointed one of his two thumbs at Claire in a gesture that was meant to appear firm but non-confrontational, but which appeared phony and vaguely uncomfortable.

"Because you'd've been on camera. It's a protected area – but protected by a flimsy rope a child could step over – or two poles the same child could move to the side to walk past. The physical deterrent is irrelevant: it's the word *authorised* that holds us back. A symbolic deterrent. But what if you don't *know* you've been authorised? What if the administrator forgot to click Send on the email? You've *got* your access badge – but at the same time, you haven't. You've been granted authorisation – by Lacan's big Other… but you're the only one who doesn't know that she doesn't *know*."

Dr. Gordon's eyes had begun to sparkle, Phyllie noted; she had always enjoyed watching him sear his brand onto the rump of the class. These private excursions, however, were all the more thrilling.

"We're going up there now, aren't we?" said Claire.

"What would you hope to find in such a restricted area?" Alex asked, involving Phyllie in the question (with his eyes) in what felt (to Phyllie) like an afterthought.

Claire rose to the challenge. "What would you hope we'd hope to find?" she replied, smiling defiantly.

To Phyllie, the brief exchange contained a convincing flavour: what had happened felt like a therapy hour with Dr. Chaz Bruce-Sange.

Phyllie threw a pebble into the dark, hoping for a gentle plop as it fell into a lake or a pond in the unknown.

"Is *Chaz* up there?"

Alex frowned. "Chaz Bruce-Sange?"

"Well, I don't mean Chas from Chas & Dave. Yes, *of course* Chaz Bruce-Sange. Is she up on the next storey?"

"No," was the answer. "Why would she be?" Dr. Gordon stepped over the rope.

Unwilling to lose ground, Phyllie ran with an improvisation. "Because she's just learned she's been authorised."

"Well, let's find out, shall we?" Alex answered, beginning the ascent.

"After you," Phyllie said to Claire.

They climbed to a landing that looked nearly the same as all the others in the Postgraduate Centre. The only difference was the door in front of them, with its calculator-sized pad of numbers standing as a more effective obstacle than two candlesticks and a metal sign ever would.

Surprising both Phyllie and Alex, Claire leaned in and said, "Allow me." If everything else was interlinked and overlapping, why would a passcode be any different? The passcode inside the building in Lewsey Farm was 999. With confidence, Claire tapped 999 into this similar pad.

The resultant electronic no-no was suitably derisive. It even sounded like *uh-uh*.

"…Oh."

Dr. Alex Gordon tapped in something more complicated than the number for Emergency Services, and too quick for the human eye to follow.

This time the electronic payback was as if a robot magician had pulled a rabbit from a hat: *ah-hah!* – in an Abracadabra! fashion. In such a way, agreeing with the visitors' permission to enter, the door popped open, and Alex pushed it wider still.

They stepped into the very hat of the building; parts of some of the walls leaned inwards to reflect structural designs that were probably visible from the ground but which neither Claire nor Phyllie had ever noticed. (The building was not likely to be a perfectly elongated cube, after all.) Around the walls and across the ceiling trailed insulated lengths of cables. Resembling insects at dawn, hidden circuitry buzzed and clicked.

"The brains of the operation," Alex announced.

Claire wanted to know: "How come an academic like you is considered authorised?"

"Follow me." Alex set off, on an expedition into this crepuscular man-made jungle. "And mind your head… Why *wouldn't* I be authorised, Claire?"

"Because it's an engineering area," Claire replied immediately; then felt the need to expand, as though to a PhD examiner who was either attempting to entrap her or whom she had not heard correctly. "And you're not an engineer."

As a group they walked through the overhanging branches of wires, on which lights occasionally winked like the eyes of camouflaged creatures; past an alcove area of throbbing machinery (Phyllie felt menaced); to a door that led out onto the roof. No passcode was required this time.

Images from the time she'd spent under Benny's spell returned to haunt Phyllie now. A self-protective instinct fluttered; while here on top of the building, she would stay away from the edges – four storeys was a long way to fall.

"What do you see?" Dr. Alex Gordon asked his supervisees.

Claire and Phyllie looked each other in the eye. Silently they bargained to attend this extended tutorial with their full attention.

Claire turned to Alex and said, "The surrounding area."

"Specifically."

"Businesses, flats ... the overpass," Claire continued.

"Sundon Park in the distance," Phyllie helped her, having to face in a different direction.

"The motorway?"

"Warehouses – near the slip road."

"People?"

"The Student Union. The halls of residence. The area where Chaz lives and works ..." This last utterance came as something of a surprise to Phyllie as its speaker. It had bubbled up from elsewhere.

Claire changed the direction of her vantage point again.

"Lewsey Farm," she realised aloud.

"And all roads lead to Lewsey Farm, as we know," Alex added, either as a quip or as a statement of truth that meant nothing to his audience. "We're looking at a few miles'-worth of businesses and domestic settings; would you agree? Several thousand people? The only obvious connection is the geographical space inhabited. But we know differently, don't we?"

"Do we?" asked Phyllie.

Alex nodded. "You of all people know! Where we sit or stand is only a tiny footprint in the wet sand. What we say – what we think and dream – *these* are our coordinates. *These* are our major contributions to society. And they're all connected. Why? Because *we're* all connected, even if we don't happen to know it."

Was it the fresh air that had cleared Claire's thinking? Was it the view, which was scarcely more than a townscape, but unimpeded by cloud or poor weather? Claire found herself able to see and think for *acres*.

Can you focus that gaze inwards? one of her examiners had asked.

Claire concentrated on a bench outside the sound labs, where the students of radio production and broadcast techniques spent their days. On one bench, a man (she thought it was a man) was feeding bread (she thought it was bread) to a polite and respectful gaggle of geese (she thought they were geese). The birds waited their turn as their benefactor doled out chunks from what appeared to be a hot dog bun. While unable to recall another time when she'd seen geese on campus, Claire considered the variables in this one sight alone. Three main variables: man x bread x geese (going across the probability chart in her mind). Probability fraction of one-sixth… if the other options were not-man, not-bread, and not-geese.

She shook her head.

"We went to the National Apology Network in Lewsey Farm," said Claire, "Phyllie and I; but neither of us remembers going there."

"I think I'm starting to," Phyllie interjected.

"I'd like to know how you gained our interest. I can't think of anything I need to apologise for, so why did I visit in the first place?"

"You were Phyllie's plus-one," Alex answered. He turned to the older of his two supervisees. "You needed some moral support. You said you wouldn't go unless someone took you."

"But why me?" Claire persisted. "This hasn't just happened overnight; we're talking the better part of a *year*! We hardly knew each other back then."

Once more, Phyllie interrupted; but this time, not with a statement supporting her vague recollection of a past event; this time, with a quotation.

"In our Year of Moths, we must learn to expect no butterflies," Phyllie quoted, staring into space that had come to feel saturated. When she returned her attention to her interlocutors, it was into wide-open expressions that she peered. "One of Brother Joe's *bon mots*. I have it on a post-it note at home."

Dr. Alex Gordon smiled. "Playing Devil's Advocate for a moment, Phyllie…"

"Yes?"

"Who's Brother Joe?"

"He leads a group of six other men from town to town, in a rickety rocket of an old van."

"From town to town in what country?"

"... I've always imagined in Africa. *Rural* Africa. Lots of deserted spaces. Browns and sepia tones. Yes, Africa."

The satisfied grin had lingered on Alex's features. "Africa's not a country, Phyllie," he reminded his sparring partner. "The dark continent, to borrow from Freud in a different context. It's a rather vast place."

"Then I can't answer your question, Alex," Phyllie told him impatiently.

Alex set off on a trot towards the door. The wind caught his hair and the flaps of his corduroy jacket, and the result was a choreographed *bye-bye* wave that stirred ancient echoes of abandonment issues in both Phyllie's and Claire's core. Instantaneously panicked, Phyllie was about to shout *Wait!* – when Alex said:

"Shall we go back inside? It's getting a bit on the *nippy* side."

The trio retraced their steps, back past humming machinery and circuitry, ducking under items of building maintenance that would have appeared out of place in any other setting, but which seemed just right, here in the very brain.

On their descent from the fourth floor, they met a middle-aged man, ascending the same staircase, dressed in overalls of university colours, with a toolbelt worn gunslinger style athwart his ample waist. His confused expression was met with a cheerful "How do you do?" from Alex Gordon; a look of embarrassed concern from Claire Carey; and a nod of conciliatory acknowledgement from Phyllie Reydman. Of the three, Phyllie was the only one who wanted to show this employee that she knew they should not have been up there.

They kept on with their descent, step following step, occasionally passing a student or a member of staff. The thought crossed Claire's mind that Alex would take them lower than ground level, to a basement area that she had not known existed: a complex of interconnected environments that she pictured, first, as the interior of a submarine; then as the chambers of what Phyllie had called Benny's *vivaria.*

No.

Ridiculous! There was no conspiracy here, Claire told herself. The University was not hosting a subterranean torture chamber! A derelict building that had once housed medical businesses, was one thing; a seat of higher learning, quite another!

But what if? Claire's mind continued. What if *even more* people were involved? What if the arrangement had been endorsed by the Vice Chancellor?

On the ground floor, Alex, Claire, and Phyllie turned and repaired to one of the smaller coffee bars on campus.

"I'm in the chair," offered the supervisor. "Would either of you like a sausage sandwich? Best in the neighbourhood, I'd say."

The PhD candidates declined the offer, somewhat to Alex's visual disappointment. He wanted to break bread, both figuratively and literally.

"I'll have a cherry muffin if you're buying," said Claire.

Phyllie plumped for a bar of chocolate and an espresso. Given what she had learned, it seemed ironic to sense the need to *stay awake;* but Phyllie longed for sugar and caffeine, in no particular order.

Once they had seated themselves, Phyllie became uncomfortable at the proximity of a student at the next table, who was reading her laptop screen over a steaming bowl of noodles. Not even belatedly noticing the buds in her fellow student's ears was much of a reassurance.

Phyllie had told Claire about a friend named Carey that Phyllie had had at the age of nine. *We had a Whisper Club,* Phyllie had explained. *You could tell each other anything you wanted as long as you whispered it into her ear. There were other girls allowed into the club but at no point could everyone know everything about everyone else there. You had to choose your allies.*

These words (and the emotional censorship behind them) seemed important to Phyllie at this moment. How much easier would the work of the world flow – if only we whispered to one person at a time and never shouted!

All the same, the timber that had been dumped in her yard was not going to magic itself into a shed. Phyllie had to do some carpentry of her own. She could ask permission now – or seek forgiveness at a later date. She picked up a hacksaw.

"I don't need to wonder what it was I wanted forgiveness for at that time," Phyllie announced. "Abandoning my daughter, for one thing. Wiping out the batteries on my marriage. You name it. But there's no such thing as *coincidence*, Alex. What happened to me under Benny's coercion left me susceptible. Didn't it?"

For Claire, her choice of snack – the cherry muffin – tasted as appealing as a handful of river stones. Within the thick-ply pages of her reflective journal, Claire would record that the muffin tasted *flat*.

"It's chaos on the table time, Alex," Claire submitted. "Don't make two ladies beg."

"Say what you will about Benny and his experiments, he reached a human conclusion," said Dr. Alex Gordon

"Did he now?" asked Phyllie. "And what *human conclusion* was that?"

"Look, Phyllie: I'm not defending the actions of a self-affirming – and rigorously committed – sadist and pervert. Honestly, I'm not. Benny's in prison..."

"Benny's *dead*," Phyllie stated firmly. "I won't have it any other way – I don't *care* what else is happening. In *my world*, Benny's left me alone, finally. That's a wrap."

"...Okay, Phyllie, but what I'm saying..."

"No. Repeat it, Alex: I want to hear it from your lips. Or God help me, I'm going to walk out of here, and the only stop I'll make before the Police Station is the office of the Ethics Committee, to make sure your name is on their next agenda."

"All right, Phyllie," the academic conceded, "have it your own way. Benny died in prison. Of old age."

"Thank you. He bequeathed me a gift in his will, didn't he, Alex?"

"In a manner of speaking; yes."

Phyllie turned to Claire. "If you take away the violence, what Benny's *experiments* taught us was how to tell each other stories."

"And the power of stories," Claire added. "The social adhesive of stories; their societal vitality – and their psychological *currency.*"

Claire took her friend's hands in her own; she noted the thick meniscus of unshed tears in each of Phyllie's eyes.

"The stories *didn't stop*, Claire," Phyllie explained. "I can see that now. I was in the mesh that Benny created – maybe we all were."

Here, Phyllie looked at Alex for some sort of support or reassurance. After a few beats, he nodded and asked:

"What happened in your marriage after you were rescued?"

Phyllie's face turned cold. "The marriage failed, Alex. There was nowhere else for it to go. I couldn't cope with what had happened, not for a long time."

Claire squeezed her fingers. "And it's fair to say, you couldn't cope with what you'd left behind in that house either? You experienced a sense of loss."

Phyllie nodded. "I experienced a bereavement," she agreed.

"The way Amanda tells it," Alex continued, "you talked to each other in the Edlesborough house…" He doled out his amazement expression, in a fair fifty-fifty, between Phyllie and Claire. "…and *created worlds.*"

"We? Me and Claire?"

"No, you and the other specimens."

"Oh, I *do so* love being thought of as a *specimen*," Phyllie told him.

Alex bowed.

"Subjects, then. It wasn't simple sleep natter. You constructed timelines and plots. You had parts to play in narratives with strangers and with people you loved." Here he stopped sharing; he settled his attention on Phyllie. "Your friend and colleague Vig, for instance. You did more than work with him in a secondary school. You worked with him and made a *planet out of clay.*"

Sitting back in her chair meant releasing Phyllie's hands, but Claire wanted to be alone and framed adequately. The student at the next table turned to face her momentarily (the chair legs had scraped on the floor). The coffee machine hissed – in admonition or in relief.

"This is my best shot, Phyllie. May I?"

Having received her audience's signs of approval, the great theatre actress Claire Carey strode back onto the stage.

"Benny's experiments – including you – didn't know what they were moulding, from the power of the imagination alone. The stories went around the vivaria. You were all both blind and with perfect vision, at the same time. When you were released, you *continued to tell the stories* to those around you – in your case, to Roger and Claire, when she was born.

"Whether you hate Benny or not, what he did with you opened a different window in your mind. It allowed you to posit *choices*: so we don't need to see – or experience – the same realities… Before you fly off the handle, let me say I hate him too, for the distress he caused – you and others. But I can't help admire him for what he *achieved*."

Claire paused. Her breaths were very slightly faster than normal, as though she had completed a modestly paced length of the swimming pool. A flashback slapped her across her consciousness. She remembered the man she'd stumbled in upon when she'd entered the wrong changing room.

Why is this significant? He hadn't harmed her in any way; he had only seemed embarrassed at being on show. Metres of wet floor had stretched between the nine year-old Claire and the man whose body she had seen in all its perfect imperfections.

"Amanda is Benny's daughter," Claire stated; "or so she claims. I don't know if he kept her in the vivaria with prisoners. Either way, she got involved with Benny's work. So did Phyllie's husband … or *ex*-husband by that point. And of course, so did their daughter."

No one hurt me. I'd remember. Claire's inner voice was insistent. *And why would I need to apologise if someone hurt me anyway? Why did I return to Lewsey Farm?*

Eye to eye now with Alex Gordon, Claire said: "You've brought the experiment up to date – as a service. A National Apology Network – with the emphasis on *Network*. You don't sit around in an Alcoholics Anonymous circle. I'm not even certain you *speak*. But you connect, don't you, Alex. We all *connect*."

Claire remembered what Phyllie had told her about the Overlap, during the latter's experience nine years earlier. The Overlap was the name given to (or conjured for) the imaginary confluence of dream-worlds. It only existed behind the eyes.

"We all overlap," added Phyllie, as though she had read her friend's internalised script. "I have to tell Chaz."

Alex was nodding his head. "*Overlap*'s good. Same spaces, different realities – or perceptions. Good."

It did not matter to Claire that the viva had been and gone. All learners crave the vindication accomplished on hearing their educator say *Good*.

Feeling that she had just sat a further exam, Claire beamed from ear to ear.

THERAPY HOUR, 1 (PEDESTRIANS)

Although Phyllie and Claire covered (on foot) the distance between the Postgraduate Centre and the home and office of Dr. Chaz Bruce-Sange in the fifteen minutes that the former said it would take, the latter was several times disturbed by the fact that Phyllie appeared lost. The streets might look similar to one another, but Phyllie had said that she had walked to her psychoanalyst's place on numerous occasions. What variant of fog had crept into Phyllie's brain, for the woman to lose her way?

Easily, Claire recalled the drive in her Fiat, five months earlier, on a search for Feast Bridge Road, in Raulton. Streets could disguise themselves, perhaps at will; not only during one's oneiric interludes, but also in times of confusion. A troubled mind transformed a conurbation into Anagram City – no letters stayed put; patterns reiterated themselves in complicated formations.

Very little conversation was shared between the two women *en route*, the wordlessness as thick as custard; such that it was almost overwhelming.

Sometimes Claire had wondered what conversing with a psychoanalyst might feel like. Perhaps she could benefit from the treatment herself: a therapeutic hour of the talking cure; a pseudo-hypnosis, the better to unearth the repressed.

On arrival at Chaz's, Phyllie prodded the buzzer – the *familiar* buzzer. Never having been one to stand on ceremony – nor to kowtow to security precautions – Chaz pressed something at her end a mere second later. (Had she even had time to check who was calling?)

The door made the sound of a nine year-old girl's sigh. However, with this granting of access came a warning – a shot across the bows.

"I'm with a client. Take a seat in the waiting room, please. I wasn't expecting you."

Claire and Phyllie stepped into the house. "Does she know who we are?" Claire asked.

"How do you mean?"

"Or was she saying, she's not expecting *anyone*?"

"I've no idea, Claire. This isn't my appointment time."

The waiting room seemed its familiar, friendly self to Phyllie. To Phyllie it said: *Hi! How're things? Long time no see!* The building itself was almost a home away from home, she realised: via the payment of her fees to Chaz, Phyllie had probably spent more on the décor in *this* house – Chaz's home – than she had on her own. *That throw rug,* Phyllie listed silently, with a pointed finger not physical but only in her mind; *those cushion covers; that antimacassar… I bought all those furnishings.*

Chaz bloody well owes me!

Phyllie sat in her favourite chair. Claire, meanwhile, had been unable to shake a similarity from her memory: Chaz's waiting room resembled the communal lounge area inside the abandoned dental clinic in Lewsey Farm, minus the kitchenette. Instead of a sink, work surface, and microwave oven, two jugs of water sat on a wooden tray on a sideboard. But the furniture configuration was similar, from one business to the other.

"She couldn't have expected *me*, could she?" Claire continued. "The only time I've *met* her – if that's the right word – she was asleep in a room with other people."

"But you entered her narrative at that moment, don't forget, Claire. The stories overlapped in Benny's dungeon; why not here too? Realities *interfering* with one another. What larks! It's what we're talking about, as far as I can tell. I'm here with you right now; I'm also on a trolley in an old swimming pool. Left behind like a broken umbrella."

Phyllie sniggered; something bitter sang through the sound.

Sitting down briskly, Claire felt a chill brush down her spine. She stared at the jugs on the sideboard. She required a fixed focal point – or the memory demanded the same. Or both.

"He left me there, Phyllie – at the swimming pool in Lewsey Farm."

"Who did?"

"My dad, when I was nine." Claire's recollection took baby steps. "He took me for lessons… and he was always there when I came out of the changing room. He bought me a hot chocolate and a packet of Monster Munch."

Phyllie waited. She followed Claire's line of sight, hoping for comprehension on the wall *beyond* the water jugs.

"Then one day, I dried myself and got dressed and went out – and he wasn't there. I must've panicked. I'm sure I did; I think I remember it – the sense of loss."

Claire cleared her throat. The waiting room waited for her soliloquy.

"I needed to find my father. I thought he must be in the men's changing room, and I couldn't see why I shouldn't go in there."

Claire shrugged.

"So I did. And a man was there, getting dressed. I saw him naked – I remember him to this day."

Leaning forward in her comfortable armchair, Phyllie wanted to know: "What did he look like?"

It was on Claire's breath to respond: *What does it matter?* – but then she checked in with herself.

Everything matters.

"He was thirty-odd. Full head of dark hair." Claire closed her eyes. "Lightly muscled. Hair on his chest and pubis. Stubble."

"Does he remind you of anyone, Claire?"

The man in her mind *should* – he *should* remind Claire of someone. But no one would swim into Claire's cognisance.

"I tried to find my dad," Claire summarised. "I ran through the men's changing room – but Dad wasn't in the showers or any of the cubicles. I ran back out the way I went in, past the man who had put some clothes on by then – probably over wet skin. Dad wasn't in the pool observation area, looking in at the next class. I walked outside. Maybe he was waiting in the car, even though he'd never done that. I couldn't see him…

"By now there were tears in my eyes. I didn't know the way home; I couldn't *walk*. So what could I do?"

"What *did* you do?" Phyllie asked.

"I went to the desk and said I can't find my dad."

Claire breathed as if through jungle oxygen, the atmosphere in Dr. Bruce-Sange's waiting room suddenly damp and warm, like the breath of a mammal.

At the opening of the door into Chaz's consulting room, both Phyllie and Claire started.

A smart woman in her mid-fifties stepped out from under the umbra of her treatment, back into the space where the two supervisees waited their turn. Neither of them recognised Chaz's analysand.

The psychoanalyst stepped into the doorway between the two rooms.

"Would the two of you like to crawl in?" she asked sweetly.

SESSION UNNUMBERED

John Hodgins is reassembling his shredded DNA in the flowerbed of a country hotel. "I don't mind if I'm white or black," he tells me. I tell him that's fine. Then he goes on: "Do you know the old saying about travelling and returning to the place where you started? If you get far enough away from home, you must be on your way back. The world is finite, after all."

"What surprises me," Claire Carey tells Dr. Chaz Bruce-Sange, "is why you let us in."

"I didn't have an appointment for this hour."

"You said you weren't expecting us."

"I wasn't!"

"Which suggests, on a different day you would've been." Claire appears satisfied. "Do you *recognise* me, Chaz?"

"No, I don't think so," the doctor replies. "Though I should *append* – in a spirit of candour – you bear a physical resemblance to my daughter Jemima. Many young white women do."

Phyllie Reydman remains quiet. Her mixture of moods is a complicated cocktail.

"Why would you have gone somewhere in Lewsey Farm to say sorry?" Claire Carey asks Dr. Chaz Bruce-Sange.

Chaz grins; her eyes sparkle.

"*I have no idea* – is that what you're expecting me to say? Well, tough luck. I have *plenty* to apologise for, trust me. My daughter got involved with heroin when she was at university. We could start there if you like."

Daughters, thinks Phyllie.

Daughters, thinks Claire, recalling the difficulty that she had represented for her own mum and dad at one protracted time in her life.

"I was abandoned at a swimming pool when I was nine," Claire tells Chaz in a matter-of-fact tone. "My dad was having an affair with a part-time worker there named Amanda."

Claire thought back to minutes earlier, when she'd stared in a trance at two jugs of water on the waiting room sideboard. Seventeen years in the past, as a nine year-old child, in a different waiting room altogether, she had stared in a trance at different glass: not the glass that separated where she was from poolside, but the smudged grey glass that separated the waiting room from the outside world.

"What do you think is the significance of Amanda having been *part-time*?" Chaz asks.

"Excuse me?"

"Her part-time status is something you've seen fit to bring into our consideration of your dad's girlfriend. I wonder why that might be. Phyllie? Do you have a view on this?"

Phyllie has had months of not-expecting her analyst's questions; this example is no exception – she believed she'd be safe in her silence. Called on by the teacher in this manner, the effort makes Phyllie squint.

"*That's* what you'd like to take from my confession?" Claire complains, the pitch of her voice climbing from foothills to peaks.

Phyllie has spent hours in Chaz's company; she knows how to hold the analyst's attention.

"It's something about her being *part-time* and therefore of a lower class. Someone Claire's dad shouldn't have bothered with, perhaps."

"She could've been the manager, Phyllie," Claire argues, "I was still *left alone*."

"She was younger than your dad; that might be worth noting," Phyllie continues. "Early twenties? Closer to *your* age than your dad's age. A rival *sister* for you on the unconscious level."

"*Anyway*. A lady behind the counter where you bought tickets tried to calm me down," Claire persists. "She came out front and sat me in the space where you watch your children swimming. She bought me a hot chocolate from the machine. I can remember thinking: *I can't taste this*."

"Were you alone?" Chaz asks.

"Was I *alone*? What've we been talking about!"

"I mean, in the waiting area."

"No." Claire frowns. "Well, in my head and heart I was, of course. But I'm sure there were other people there talking. I must've noticed them without noticing them. I was willing my dad to come and *find me*. That's how it had to be, right? I thought: *he's lost me; he doesn't know where I am* – it didn't matter we'd been there a hundred times. He must've thought I'd gone outside for some reason. *He's gone to look for me in the park…* So I stood by the window, with my wet hair and my plastic cup of chocolate, staring out at the park across the road."

Claire clears her throat again.

"Then I saw him. Or *them*, I should say – Dad and Amanda, though I don't think I knew her name then. Walking back to the building, not exactly hand in hand but *close*, you know? – too close for strangers. Not in any hurry either: they'd lost track of time. Then they kissed." Claire shrugs her shoulders. "And I knew he'd left us. They'd only been for a walk, but I think I knew it was wrong. The kiss was wrong."

Claire stiffens her shoulders in a moment of gelid comprehension.

Of course the girl had to have been Amanda Billie. Of *course* she had – albeit with a different surname in those years.

It is all connected, Claire remembers writing, somewhere close to the denouement of her thesis. *Collecting is connecting – and connecting is collecting. If you lose Ns you are left with loose ends. You need Ls to make up the space; you need something or someone else. You need the Ls – the Else – and the Ns – the ends – to complete the whole.*

"Abandoning you was wrong," Phyllie adds. Claire acknowledges the statement of support with a threadbare smile. "So how did you punish him, when you could?"

During less tempestuous months, Claire might have plumped up proud at the assumption that she had taken revenge. But such months seem on the wane. Claire feels testy with emotion; almost feverish; as though, if something – even water – were to touch her skin, she would experience soreness.

"I damaged a boyfriend, years later," Claire answers. "Deliberately."

Although Phyllie is not certain that Claire's self-analysis is the right road to travel right now, she cannot deny that Claire has gained Chaz's professional interest. Perhaps it is best that they see this through, in this strange group therapy session that they seem to have entered – and co-created.

"What was his name?" Chaz asks.

Claire swoops a look in Phyllie's direction that says both *sorry!* and *we've talked about him before, so I hope it's okay to mention him again.*

"John Hodgins," Claire replies.

Something as heavy as gold drops through Phyllie's emotional storage system. Chaz leans forward (puzzling Claire), and says: "An interesting caesura."

"I don't understand," Claire tells her.

"John Hodgins was a boy I knew at school," Phyllie explains. "Chaz and I think I've anchored a lot of psychic material in John – and his absence from my life."

The shake of Claire's head is like a twitch. "We've talked about him, Phyllie. Your schoolfriend was white; my ex was black. It's not the same guy. It's a *name.*"

If she had been in her audience's seats, Claire would have wanted to know, *straight away*, what it was that she had done to her boyfriend at the time. Claire is mildly disappointed that she must share the attention with Phyllie – because of a young man's name!

I'm ready to broadcast, thinks Claire. *Hear my story! Collect me!*

"I think I said it before, Claire," Phyllie offers, "I don't believe in coincidences anymore. Their value has very much … how shall I put it? … *diminished* in my mind."

"I'm confused. You *do* think it's the same man? Despite the age difference alone?"

"Not the same man," Phyllie answers, "as we usually *understand* man."

"And what's *that* supposed to mean?" Claire sounds miffed.

"Well, they're talking among themselves, aren't they? Aren't *we*? You say I'm there – and I can't doubt you. But so are you, I'll bet. There's no *one person* in *one space*. Benny's experiments taught me that loud and clear. Consider Roger."

"What about him?"

"Well, up to a few days ago, he was part of a group of men in a van, moving from town to village. Starting point and destination unknown. Him and that Brother Joe." Phyllie turns to Chaz. "I've mentioned them plenty of times, have I not?"

"You have," Chaz confirms.

"And yet… you say you saw them in Lewsey Farm."

"I don't *say* I saw them. I *saw* them."

"Poor choice of words – sorry. You saw them there. So, are they present in a living breathing existence, or are they present in a fantasy existence? And which is which? I think the stories are bleeding into one another. *Transforming.* Being told and re-told; re-*created*, the idea of *authorship* becoming more or less redundant. That's what I think. We have shared ourselves out among our communities – our *audiences*."

Having declared which, Phyllie sits back in her chair.

"I heard a bit about them from Amanda," Claire reminds herself.

"And there you go then: the proliferation of tale and gossip! The oldest school of social media – the one without any kind of platform required!" Phyllie turns to Chaz and invites her in. "What do *you* know about the group of pilgrims?"

Although Chaz understands that she has been asked to comment to prove something of Phyllie's point, this is no reason not to respond. It's all material.

"There's a young man named Twennyfour," Chaz answers. "Twennyfour's about twenty-nine. His older sister was called Twennythree, but she died after bandits raided their home. I don't think I know much about Gray... they call him Gray," she adds by way of explanation; "that's not just me being over-familiar or *chatty*. Your ex-husband, of course – Roger. Someone called Jake..."

"Paper Jake O'Donnell," Phyllie tells her with a nod.

"Then Bruno, with the photos and the postcards..."

Another nod. "Bruno Amitrano."

Back in the clinic in Lewsey Farm, Claire had seen at least two of the men mentioned. She interrupts at this point.

"When I was there, I saw Twennyfour – or the man who uses that name, at any rate. Gray is an older guy with a skin condition: Sir Grayson Twivy. He was knighted for his *work with germs*."

Claire tries to remember Twennyfour. She had no more than glanced at the man; illumination in the room had been furry. A nugget of nausea in Claire's gullet suggested that she should have paid closer attention.

No one hurt me.

"Are you on an even keel, Claire?" Phyllie asks – into the expectant hush.

It was me who caused the pain, Claire teaches herself. *I wanted to say sorry for breaking him – for breaking John Hodgins.*

"What's the taxicab situation around here like?" Claire asks. "I'm parked a twenty-minute walk away."

"Where do you want to go?" Phyllie wants to know.

"I have a client at four," Chaz Bruce-Sange interjects.

Phyllie fixes her psychoanalyst with the twanging tightrope of a gaze.

"Cancel the bitch," she demands.

THERAPY HOUR, 2 (PASSENGERS)

Dr Chaz Bruce-Sange was mentally preparing a paper that she would write – or at least type the title and first paragraph of – on the topic of shared delusions. *Gustave Le Bon. Charles Mackay.* So intrigued had she been at the story that Phyllie and Claire had *literally* brought to her door, that she phoned her four p.m. appointment – a middle-aged man named Rick Shawdon – with her apologies. Rick had sounded relieved at the contents of the call, in a way that had made Chaz reflect on whether anyone actually *enjoyed* her therapy hours.

Chaz could not wait to tell Doug Stegmeyer about her day.

When Phyllie and Claire started to discuss metaphysics, Chaz darted glances at the side of their driver's face. Someone had probably written about what taxi-drivers eavesdrop on and pick up; even so, Chaz hoped to catch a surprised expression – at least! – on the man's facial features. *It's all material.* However, the driver's emotions remained mumchance.

"Before we go in," said Phyllie, "you don't think I'll see myself asleep, do you? Whatever else is going on, I can't *physically* be in two places, can I? I won't see myself with my hair roots showing."

Instead of answering the question, or even attempting to manage her friend's expectations, Claire turned to Chaz.

"Don't you want to ask me something similar, Chaz?"

"No I don't… but I can't deny," said Chaz, "…I'm fascinated to see who's inside."

"You've decided we haven't lured you here to murder you, then."

"I've *decided* you wouldn't be able to overwhelm me," answered Dr. Chaz Bruce-Sange.

"Seriously?"

"Kung fu, mate. I'll break a middle finger just to convince you of my intentions."

Although both Phyllie and Claire laughed, neither of them knew to what extent to take Chaz seriously.

The taxi was a standard four-seater. Chaz had slipped into the passenger side.

"Lewsey Park Pool, please," said Phyllie.

"I don't understand," said Phyllie, a matter of minutes later. "And I'm almost scared to ask this… but when you say you *damaged* him…"

"I accused him of something he couldn't refute." Claire laughed bitterly. "It was the perfect crime."

Phyllie had to know. After a pause, she gingerly went on: "Something… like rape, you mean?"

"Worse… I accused him of plagiarism."

"Plagiarism's worse than rape?"

"It is if you're transitioning from a Masters to a PhD! Not in general."

"But why? What did he do to you in the first place?"

Claire needed a moment before she replied. "He was too nice," she answered with shame.

The taxi dropped the three women at Lewsey Park Pool at a dig-and-a-scratch after four p.m. The afternoon's good weather had rusted; through moustachioed cloud came a sunlight orange in tint. The air felt refrigerated; a perky wind huffed and puffed across the jagged surface of the slide and the roundabout in the children's playground. Shivers of aroma writhed in the environment; something sweet – maybe candyfloss – from the Mr. Whippy van; something beefy from the Miss Barbie-Q van. The major food groups to sustain children's recreation – ice cream and burgers – were on offer this afternoon.

THE COORDINATES OF JOHN HODGINS

—— • ◎ • ——

"Back then I didn't have the vocabulary. These days I don't have the permission."

Brother Joe

PROUD CITY OF WASPS

"When he shouted for his mother, the ocean roared back in a different language," announced Brother Joe, at another pit-stop somewhere between place and space – a *negative* area; a nowhere-fast. Darkness drank at the well of their combined souls.

For the last ten minutes, Twennyfour had tried to remember a single piece of music – anything at all.

Nothing.

There was *in situ* not a single retrieval cue that Twennyfour could discern. Momentarily this had made him feel edgy and restless; this mood combination had given way to a sense of panic.

Imagine if this is my last night on Earth... and it's a night with no music.

He did not (in truth) imagine that it *was* his last night on Earth, but the thought persisted; and when he asked himself why his head was empty, he understood that he had broken his own spell. The very thought took him away from its lingering, threatening absence.

"Where next, brother?" Twennyfour asked.

Brother Joe responded with a sigh. "We seem to be driving a long way in one direction," he said.

"So we do."

"Has it ever worried you, brother? The miles we're covering?" Brother Joe continued.

Twennyfour was slow to consider the question; he chewed his answer over (without moving a muscle). "I've wondered how we'll get back home, from time to time."

Brother Joe nodded. "A reasonable concern," he added, non-committal in a way that rubbed Twennyfour's feathers the wrong way.

"Could you add to that, brother?" Twennyfour prompted.

"The honest response is, I don't know we will. I don't really have a home to go to anyway." Brother Joe paused before adding: "Do you?"

Twennyfour thought back to the village of John Hodgins. Then he thought of his mother, and of how they had conducted classical music together. They had conducted Franck's *Symphonic Variations*, all sixteen minutes of it, with the Royal Philharmonic Orchestra. Once upon a time, Twennyfour and Mama had played the piece twice, one time straight after the other. During the first recital, Twennyfour had conducted Mama, watching her long brown fingers as they had tickled notes and struck chords from the edge of the kitchen sink. For the encore, they had swapped roles and responsibilities: Mama's baton had been a toothbrush...

Grief seasoned Twennyfour's eyes. Perhaps the most important question was not where John Hodgins was placed in relation to where they were; its coordinates could be determined at a later date. Perhaps the most important question was whether Twennyfour had any plan to return there at all. What was left for him there?

"All roads are home," he said to Brother Joe. "I'm in no rush."

Indeed, recent days aboard the van had seen Twennyfour in something close to a philosophical mood. He had started to believe that the brown-and-yellow deserts through which they chugged displayed their fingerprints, for all to observe from above. Every dune bulged with marks of identification, of one sort or another. Seen from on high, the patterns of sand and shrub would resemble faces, an ear, parts of the body. It was a matter of scale.

Everything was revealed – or revealed *itself* – in sepia tones.

Brother Joe smiled. "You astonish me, brother. The van doesn't bother you?"

"Not really. The worst part of being in a van with six other men is not the flatulence – or even the pointlessness of it all. It's the *homesickness*…" Twennyfour shrugged. "And yet, here I am, telling you I'm in no rush. I must be a split personality – a *hydra*."

Before long, more of the group had joined Twennyfour and Brother Joe.

"Mind if we grab a pew, lads?" asked Bruno Amitrano.

Amitrano, Professor Sir Grayson Twivy, and Paper Jake O'Donnell borrowed seats from tables nearby and scraped the chairs' legs over to where Twennyfour and Brother Joe had settled for the late afternoon. In place of verbal welcomes, casual uplifts of chins were proffered. Pleasantries complete,

Amitrano wasted no further time in rolling a cigarette. Aerodynamically, a waiter swooped like a buzzard.

Have you ever wondered how we'll get back home, my brother? Twennyfour heard Brother Joe ask either Gray, Paper Jake, or Bruno – perhaps each one in turn.

Twennyfour stared into the distance. From his earlier strolls around the town, he knew that the field next door had been dedicated to an outdoor museum of antiquated farm machinery. Each monstrous piece had been scrubbed of rust and dust – as far as possible – and decorated with garlands of meadow flowers. Shrines to Earth's Labour's Lost.

Not for the first time, Twennyfour considered himself a man of the soil, and he continued to stare in that direction, remaining silent, while the conversation poached in the hot damp evening air. Soon, drinks and snacks were delivered.

Inevitably, a standstill in the conversation arrived. Apropos of nothing in particular, Twennyfour chipped in: "You're full of wisdom, Brother Joe."

The other man took his time chewing and then swallowing his mouthful of soil-brown chips. Everyone else had stopped talking.

"But *am* I, brother?" Brother Joe replied. He nodded his head: to all intents and purposes. He saluted the zigzagging upward mobility of the restaurant grill's principal flame. "How do you know I'm not spouting nonsense? It would sound the same."

Brother Joe pointed a finger at another member of the group. "What do *you* think of me, brother?" he asked. "What's my purpose?"

Is he goading us? wondered Twennyfour and he went on to consider if others might be thinking something similar. Antagonism was a radio station to whose frequencies Brother Joe seemed tuned.

Gray smiled his delightful old boy's smile. "You want me to adjudge *your* purpose?" he sought to clarify. "I haven't even sussed out my own!"

Twennyfour remembered Gray as a much younger man, when he – Twennyfour – had still studied at school. Gray had paid an academic visit as a guest teacher. This happened long before the dark pigment had drained from his facial features, although the early signs had been present at the time, during his boyhood.

"You're right, my brother: I'm asking too much of you – or of anyone else, for that matter."

"Questions exist that attempt to nail us into a moment – to keep us noticed by the people who are present," said Brother Joe. "Or to use our words as a kind of bookmark in our current chapter."

BRAVEST MOMENTS

"The bravest thing you could do right now is nothing at all."

"Don't just *do* something. *Stand* there."

"Exactly. Your work is over, Claire. As painful as that might seem."

"Painful is not quite right. I feel I should play a further part."

"And do what?" Phyllie asked. "I'm not being deliberately obstructive – but do what? *Notify the authorities?* What good would happen? The police raid. You get your name in the local news – possibly the national. What have you *achieved*?"

Claire shrugged. "By that token, what have I achieved by watching? What's my *purpose*, Phyllie? What's my way of operating?"

"Perhaps these are questions for Alex."

"Perhaps they are."

"But I do know one thing, Claire, and I'll do my best to explain this without sounding like a middle-aged hippy *seer*."

"Or the wise woman of the village." Claire smiled.

"Nine years ago – nearly ten – it's almost an anniversary! – I left that house in Edlesborough, and I've always said to

anyone interested: *I was saved.* Or *I was rescued.* And my gratitude hasn't dimmed, Claire – I want to be clear on that."

"But?"

"But it was *my project*; something *for me*, however dangerous it might've felt. With hindsight, I know that I was kept in
a sort of dungeon, but hindsight's *not always* such a wonderful
thing. I didn't simply occupy a house: the house also *occupied
me*, including the other people there. It was a fully functioning
community, Claire."

"An unconscious community," Claire offered.

"Well, if you like …"

"Including Benny."

"Yes. I've been thinking about this as well. He was an evil
man – I'm convinced of that. Evil with a fringe on top. And yet …
I can't deny it, I was in his house, and if I hadn't been, none of
those thoughts and impressions would have come my way."

Phyllie's face brightened.

"I might never have slid close to Vig, for example!"

"Every cloud …"

"But you asked a genuine question… about Benny. Or
raised one, at least. The truth of the matter is, I still find it hard
to say his name, but I can't deny I was part of the system."

"And what has Alex told us about understanding a complex environment?" Claire asked.

"… Ten thumbs?"

"No, not exactly; the comprehension of an environment's
purpose – and its way of operating."

Claire was referring to a workshop that Dr. Gordon had
delivered, well over a year earlier. Alex had made a song and

dance (in Phyllie's view) about entering an environment's hubbub and chaos, the better to grasp its purpose.

"Brown font, purple font?"

"That's the one."

As a way of helping his students to remember his message, his slides had presented the information about an environment's purpose in a brown font; the information about an environment's way of operating, in a purple font.

"The key messages being?" Claire prompted.

"... Let me see now. Speak, Memory! Brown font: the environment's *purpose*. We must enter the environment to understand it."

"Step into the haunted house."

"And purple font: the way of operating. Learn the language of the new environment. But haven't we *done* that? We *went* there! We *saw* the people ..."

Phyllie's mind was taken from where she sat with Claire – and catapulted to the clinical space of Dr. Chaz Bruce-Sange. She saw Chaz producing the church with her hands.

Here is the church. Here is the steeple. Open the door... Chaz had flipped over her hands and wiggled her fingers. *And here are the people.*

"I'm *already* one of the people!" Phyllie continued. "If *that* bit's not established, I don't know what is! But I still don't know the environment's purpose – brown font – or way of operating – purple font."

"Are you sure you don't?" Claire asked her.

"I'm pretty convinced on that point, if you don't mind my *stinging tone* when I say so." When Phyllie smiled, her lips felt as thin and sharp as razor blades.

"Don't get angry, Phyllie – I'm trying, just like you are," Claire replied. "But it seems to me that two of the most important people to talk to are the two you *haven't* talked to – Roger and Claire."

"It's not my turn for custody," Phyllie answered quickly.

Claire tipped her head to one side and made a *Please!* expression of makeshift incredulity. "I think we both suspect you might be using that fact as a reason not to make contact."

"Don't tell me what I *suspect*."

Claire nodded her head, absorbing the wisp of her friend's anger.

"All I'm saying is, if you want an interpretation of a childish world... ask a child for it."

"A *childish* world?"

"Don't you think? Saying sorry as a suitable *modus operandi*?"

"I think I see what you mean, but how does it help us? I don't know how to connect!"

"Maybe not; but Roger does. Roger travels with the men in their beaten-up van. Roger knows their stories like the back of his hand, even if your daughter doesn't... though I wouldn't be surprised if Claire was in the mix as well from time to time."

"I'm not going to interrogate my own daughter!"

"No, of course not. But you could read your stories together, couldn't you?" Claire asked. "How often do you see her? Amanda told me once but I can't remember."

Phyllie frowned. "Amanda told you a lot of things, didn't she? Got quite *chatty*, the two of you."

Refusing to accept the rebuke, Claire offered only, "Yes. And look what *good* it did me."

A silence fell. Both women had sent a barbed contribution; neither of them felt better for having done so. The silence stretched.

Claire drove alone to Lewsey Farm – or rather, to a place to which she would always refer as Lewsey Park Pool. Having parked the Fiat, she thought back to the first time she had driven to a place named Raulton, in search of Feast Bridge Road. Although the truth was hard to deny, the spell was rather slow to dissolve. As difficult as it was to accept, Claire had driven *here*; perhaps to this exact parking spot. (It was mandatory to believe *something*.) Whether she remembered that journey or not was redundant. If anything, the defiance of her memory to allow in what had happened only served to support the theory of the stories gaining momentum, and the accepted wisdom of the curative power of the apology.

Sardonically, Claire grinned at herself. She knew that she was watching the children at play because she was stalling. She had to go back into the abandoned dental clinic, but instead, she found her brain asking questions. Were these the *same* children who had been at play when she'd visited before? Where were the parents or care providers?

And were the children present anyway?

What if I'm watching a film from the side of my car?

The children without their adult supervisors were child *actors*.

Claire shook her head. She turned her back on their joyous pastimes. She adjusted the backpack against her spine, for better comfort.

The building.

Claire knew how to get in; she was well aware of the door around the back… so what was keeping her anchored in place? She had come here to apologise to John Hodgins, and to a lesser extent to Twennyfour – assuming that he (or they) were physically present.

Only one way to find out!

Carrying the backpack, Claire crossed the drive and walked around the edge of the building. She discovered that tracing her deer track around the periphery had the effect of making her feel calmer. And was that *nostalgia* in the emotional admixture too? For a moment, Claire was puzzled; then she recognised the sensation.

It was how she felt when she was welcomed home by her parents.

Claire made her way through the building, following the same route as before: the image of a rat in a maze, chasing down the cube of cheese, occurred to her vividly as she walked through patches of darkness and spaces where her motion flicked on an invisible light switch.

On this occasion, there was no one in the dental clinic where she had met Claire Billie and the five others before. Little Claire was not – this time – barking out her orders to the courtiers. The room with the big dentist's chair and the overhead lamp was empty; and from the sense of relief that Claire experienced, she understood that she had *feared* seeing Phyllie's daughter again, perched up on her leather throne and gurning at the fearsome illumination.

However, dental tools were present, here and there, available to the eye; no attempt had been made to present them professionally. They lay on the work surfaces, abandoned like everything else. Here was a perio probe, which measured sulcus depth. There was an acorn burnisher, used to carve and burnish occlusal restorations… Tossed aside; left behind; unmissed. Who would notice if Claire slipped a few items into her backpack? If anyone saw her, so be it; they *owed* her. Let one of them get stroppy and they'd see how fast she could be at the doors of the local news office!

Without much further thought, Claire unshouldered her backpack and slipped into one pocket each a straight chisel, a condenser, and an amalgam carrier.

Then she was off again, back on her toes; the backpack against her spine felt hardly any different. Dental tools weighed surprisingly little.

Where the dentist's room had been empty, the waiting room that led onto it was busy with very quiet people, as if they were hanging on, on the off-chance that a dentist would turn up for work – to do some extractions or fillings. It took a moment for Claire to notice that half of the eight people present had their eyes shut. She experienced a prick of jealousy; she wanted to know what the people sharing their stories *felt*.

Two women (Claire noticed) were hand in hand.

Claire continued her way through the building, *en route* for the communal lounge. As she was about to enter the room, a woman in a supermarket tunic passed in the opposite direction; the smile on her face contagious; it made Claire copy the expression.

In the lounge were three people, all of whom looked at Claire as she walked in. The first was a woman in her thirties whom Claire recognised from the university but did not know; she was seated at one end of one of the sofas, a magazine on her lap. The second, standing at the kitchenette sink, was Roger Billie. The third presence, established on one of the armchairs – and looking as beautiful as he had when they had dated – was John Hodgins.

"*You* took your damn time, Carey," Hodgins said with a grin.

Claire turned away from her ex-boyfriend. To Roger she challenged: "I thought you were supposed to be a social worker."

"I *am* a social worker, Claire."

"Did you get lost on your way to the office? The only time I've seen you is here – and it's a work day. I bet you're supposed to be visiting some poor old girl who can't stop collecting empty peanut butter jars."

Roger shook his head. "My work appointments are none of your concern."

"But I bet your *manager* might have an opinion on your laxity. What do you say, Roger? I doubt your department'll be too hard to find online. How will your manager respond to an accusation of your *skiving your duties*?"

"Nice try. I was leaving anyway," Roger replied.

Seconds later, once Roger had exited the communal lounge, Claire said to John Hodgins in a sing-song voice: "I think we're alone now."

"There doesn't seem to be anyone around," Hodgins finished quietly.

An old exchange; a feedline-punchline that reached back half a decade. For both halves of the former couple, the words landed with a bitter-sweetness.

"Would you like to sit down?" Hodgins asked.

"I could. Or we could walk in the park? Get some fresh air?"

"Am I looking a bit pale?"

"No, not at all… Oh, I see. Ha-ha, John. But shall we?"

"Yeah, okay. I'll buy you an ice cream from the van – for old times' sake."

"Children's laughter is like music," said John Hodgins. "Don't you think?"

He and Claire had taken a bench near the tennis courts; the children's playground was across a pitch-sized stretch of park, but the children's joy was audible across the distance.

"I wonder where the parents are," Claire answered.

"Why?"

Claire looked at him. "Why do I wonder? Well, let me see. Because I'm *concerned* about them?"

"They're having fun. They have a bottle of water each – they'll be fine."

"I don't doubt they'll be fine, but where are the adults?"

"Maybe at the National Apology Network." Hodgins nodded in the general direction of the derelict building, before conceding: "I have no idea; I'm not their keeper."

"You're right; none of my business. Maybe I'm stalling… I'm not sure where to begin."

"You said I plagiarised you, Carey," said John Hodgins. "It was an unfair accusation."

"At the very least. I don't know why I did it."

"No. That's the one thing I won't buy. You've had five years – nearly six – to think up something more substantial than *I don't know why I did it.* Five years to work on your perfect thesis," John Hodgins coaxed her. "Your argument is watertight. You've even done the References section to a semi-colon-perfect standard. Your images are sharp and clear – or did you use any images in the end?"

"No images," Claire answered.

"You're even proud of your Acknowledgements section as a lasting work of art!"

Claire made a noise, somewhere between an inquisitive sniff and a derisive snort.

"Do you want to hear irony?" she asked. "I even mentioned Amanda in the Acknowledgements. I remember asking her for the correct spelling of her name!"

Hodgins looked confused. "Why's that ironic?"

"Because I'm *thanking* someone for causing me a miserable time; that's why."

"I don't agree that needs to be a tension. Did you think a thesis would be easy? The thesis I'm still waiting for from you, by the way."

"What thesis? Oh yes: my true confession. I'm working up to that."

Hodgins grinned his flawless smile; one of the characteristics that had made Claire (and reportedly, a good deal of others) fall for him. Almost despite herself, Claire smiled.

"Well, could you *work up to it* on the time clock, please?" Hodgins asked. "The sun'll be setting soon. There'll be bats in the twilight."

Claire appreciated her ex-boyfriend's attempt at sarcasm. Very briefly, she might have blushed. It pinged a response in her memory banks. She thought of him – then – as he had been, half a decade earlier. Before she'd stabbed him.

"When I went into that room where the five of you were asleep, I didn't recognise you."

"That much is apparent."

"In my defence, it was gloomy in there." Claire copied Hodgins' expression of mirth. "There was a bulge in your trousers."

"Oh, you noticed *that* easily enough."

"It was sort of hard to miss," Claire replied. "Long shot time. Did you recognise my voice in your unconsciousness?"

"And establish an immediate erection?" John Hodgins chuckled. "You might be accused of self-*flattery* with a question like that, Carey."

"I know. But that doesn't mean the answer's no."

"…Sure enough. Hey, what happened to *me* being in the power seat? I thought *I* was giving *you* your viva!"

Hodgins waited.

"I retract the question about the Honourable Member's member."

"Truth *is*, Claire – I've no idea. You don't necessarily remember *anything* about what you've shared. I couldn't tell you if you were there in the mix or not."

"But you *did* make up stories about a nine year-old girl called Carey. The one with the teeth in her skin. Left behind in the abandoned dental clinic."

John Hodgins nodded his head. "I remember her."

"You might have mixed me up with your sister, in the story. *I* hurt you five years ago. *Susan* left you… what?… Two *decades* ago?"

"Do you want to know something odd? Two decades to the very *day*."

"No way!"

Although John Hodgins shook his head, it was a gesture of disbelief and not denial. "You *both* betrayed me," he added.

"…Then why don't you take me to see her?" Claire demanded. "We can both say sorry to you at the same time."

John Hodgins' eyebrows climbed a foothill. "The cemetery, you mean?"

"No. I *mean*, why don't you pick me up in your dilapidated old van?"

"Because I haven't *got* a van, Claire."

"In your story with Brother Joe at the wheel. The van with bullet holes in the side."

"…You want me to be Twennyfour?"

"And I'll play the hitchhiker." Claire Carey showed her ex-boyfriend her teeth, in a friendly manner. "I have a feeling you'll find me… to offer me a lift."

"Not until you've answered my *Why* question, Carey. For the final time. Why did you do it? Seriously. As if you were telling your parents about a school detention."

"Okay, I'll tell you, Hodgins; but first I have to write it. Deal?"

John Hodgins made an uncomfortable face. "Well, I don't know what you're proposing," he complained. "I don't have sufficient information to spit-shake."

Claire puckered her lips; she blew the universe a kiss.

"How about this? I go home now and face the abyss of my reflective journal, as I do every day. And I try to write what I'm going to tell you about what I did and why I did it."

"And I do what? Wait here?"

"No; while I'm writing, you use my kitchen to cook us something nice to eat. You relax in my humble abode… and I do mean *humble*, by the way – don't expect too much. Then we eat. Then I read. Then whatever."

With what felt like physical effort, Claire closed her eyes. She passionately willed John Hodgins not to ask the question that might complete the sequence: *And then what?* To Hodgins' credit (in Claire's eyes), he did not ask *And then what?* Instead, he asked:

"Why would you invite me into your home after five years?"

And her answer was ready. Her answer had been ready for a long time.

"To say sorry."

Hodgins nodded his head.

"Shall we exchange phone numbers?" Claire continued.

"No; let's not," John Hodgins replied.

"Not?"

"No, we'll make plans and stick to them. I don't want you to call me out of the blue, Carey. You're assuming too much."

"I wouldn't. You'd have my word."

Hodgins' eyebrows expressed an emotion that might have been interpreted as *wryness*. "If you'd stayed away from me *now*, sister, I might believe you."

"Five years!"

"I don't care if it's five *minutes*. We had a deal: you'd stay away from my existence forever more."

"We didn't have a *deal*."

"An understanding, then."

"There was no understanding either! We *split up*, John!"

"After you'd accused me of stealing your intellectual property."

"I've apologised for that."

"Actually, you haven't. Not as much as *I* would if I said something that made someone homeless for a while."

"You were homeless?"

"I had to leave the University," Hodgins answered. "Out of interest – where did you think I might go?"

"Home?"

"Yeah right – with a poisonous allegation in the air. With *my* folks? Not likely." Hodgins made the *tsch* sound to denote abject disappointment: disappointment in Claire; disappointment in the universe. Then he turned to Claire again. "What do you think I say at interviews, by the way? When they ask about the five-year gap on my CV. *I went travelling*?"

Claire fell into a hole inside her head; she imagined that she'd tripped. This moment was the first time that she had considered John Hodgins' current state of employment. The revelation stunned her: even though she knew that he had left the University, she simultaneously believed that he attended the University. Schrödinger's Learner: either present or not, at the same time.

Considering her ex's alter ego as Twennyfour, Claire added: "You *have* been travelling! You've been to villages to help the people! You've had *adventures*, John!"

"Nothing I could prove with a stamp in a passport."

"An employer won't ask for *proof*."

"*I've been travelling. For five years? Yes, I've really explored the territory. And what territory would that be? Well, I don't really know – maybe Africa?*" John Hodgins made a multi-syllabic click sound with his tongue. "They'd laugh me out of the building. *And do you want a form to claim your travel expenses? Well, you can piss off with that idea too.*"

"Yes, I get the idea," Claire told him.

"I'm either a university course quitter… or I'm a sort of *dope-head* on a hippy commune for squatters in Lewsey Farm." With a languid wave of his left hand, Hodgins indicated the building beyond the trees and the playground.

"You're not a dope-head, John."

"Well, *I* know that! Try telling the dude with the iPad and the questions."

"So you're not working at all?" Claire asked.

"…I got a bit of part-time in the end," Hodgins conceded. "I work at the bus station; help the passengers with their cases – that kind of thing. General customer support."

"That's good, John!"

The man nodded. "It's nice; I feel like I'm doing something to pay back."

"Pay back *what* though?" Claire continued. "I'm still confused. If the National Apology Network is for people to atone for their sins – as it were – what did *you* do wrong? It's *me* who should be apologising."

"Yeah, *about* that," Hodgins interrupted.

The prompt served to irritate Claire. The man was like a dog with a meaty bone.

"Would owning me body and soul be sufficient?"

"No, *leaving me alone* would be sufficient."

What had Claire expected? To continue where the two of them had left off, five years earlier? Despite a scandalous caesura?

Naïve, at best.

And yet. She had yearned for the forgiveness that came with no emotional debt, at least. Not so much a completely clean slate as a slate with its identifying data duly smudged.

"When you say you were homeless for a while …." Claire invited.

"I bounced from sofa to sofa, till I outstayed my welcome. My privileges were cancelled. So yes: I spent a few weeks in Sundon Park – or at the business sprawl by the airport." John Hodgins grinned. "Different bedroom every night."

Claire shook her head. "I can't tell you how sorry I am, John."

"Try."

"This is like one of those nightmares you kick at in your sleep."

Hodgins' tone was one hundred per cent saccharine. "I'm alarmed to have caused you such distress."

"…Yeah, all right, John – I've said I'm sorry."

"Not much though … as I mentioned before."

"All right then." Something midpoint along Claire's spine clicked, such was the ferocity with which she now sat up straight. "Cards on the table. What would fix it for you?"

"*Fix* it?"

"Or make it better, then… I mean, come *on*, John – I'm flying a white flag here!"

The answer could not have been predicted in a month of Sundays.

"Help me with some graffiti," Hodgins said.

SPYBLOOD

"...*Graffiti?*"

Hodgins nodded his head. "I have another identity."

"Yes, I know."

"...*in addition to* Twennyfour. You might have seen my name on walls and fixtures. I'm Spyblood."

Claire looked aghast. "But why, John?"

Hodgins shrugged. "I'm spreading the word. I work in Marketing, you might say." He laughed deeply.

"There's no way I'm spraying your tag all over town," Claire told him.

"Then there's no way you're setting the record straight."

"You're asking me to commit a crime!"

"A fairly minor one, though. Who's the victim?"

"I'm astonished you'd ask me to do that."

"What, with you and your high-flying academic ways?"

"My high-flying social responsibilities, if nothing else. What if I got caught?"

"An eternity of atonement, Claire," Hodgins answered with a grin. "Consider the proposition carefully – as if it were an exam question... Besides. How would you get caught?"

"Oh, I don't know, John… because I'm not a criminal maybe?"

"And you'll therefore be banged to rights?" Hodgins crinkled with ongoing amusement. "That's low self-worth you have there."

Claire's temper jumped up like a performing animal. The same thing happened with Hodgins' palms: a gesture of defiant resistance.

"Relax, Carey; I'm joshing with you. Don't bust your chops."

Joshing? As in: *japing? Joking? Pranking?*

"You *wanker*," Claire assured him.

"I had you going!"

"You don't think I've suffered enough?"

"You?"

"For God's sake, why? Why lie to me? You're *not* Spyblood."

John Hodgins waved the suggestion from the air. "I'm not Spyblood… *Roger's* Spyblood. Amanda's Dogtooth. Claire, they're *busy* with their paints! Proselytising, I believe it's called."

Claire could not recall ever having heard of Dogtooth; she could not picture ever having seen the name on any wall or surface. A perplexing amount of contentment was drawn from this comparative anonymity of Amanda's; from Amanda's relative lack of success. It was good to know that Amanda was not good at everything.

Minutes before bedtime, Claire called Amanda.

"A question for my dreams, if you will," the caller stated. "Benny's not your father at all, is he? You lied to me."

Amanda chuckled. "Did I ever tell you the one about the budgerigar harness?"

"I don't care about the budgerigar harness. Your father: yes or no?"

"The answer's yes, Claire."

NOSTALGIA BOLOGNESE

"I'm not *frightened* to meet her in my dreams," said John Hodgins, "but I don't know how it's going to work out – and I'd rather not... like Bartleby said."

"There's nothing unusual about being frightened of your dreams, John," Claire replied, her back now to him in her small but pleasant kitchen.

"You didn't hear me. I said I'm *not* frightened."

Claire turned away from the stove; she'd been stirring the pasta sauce that the two of them had made together. Quietly, focussed on the task at hand, Claire and John had prepared their old-times'-sake meal of Spaghetti Bolognese. While Claire had browned the mince, John had chopped onions and peppers. Smiling proudly, Claire had remarked on how tiny he could still cut vegetables. *I'd forgotten you could do that,* she had said; but in fact, she had thought about his skills in the kitchen several times while she'd awaited his arrival.

Nostalgia Bolognese, they had called it, laughing nervously. Back then, five years ago, it had been one of the few dishes that they had both known how to cook. Right now, in Claire's flat, it was one of the few dishes that they both wanted to eat.

John smiled. "It smells *lishus*, by the way."

He was letting her off a hook, and Claire was grateful for that, but for a few seconds, she was not sure what was going on.

"That was something Susan said when we were kids. *Lishus* – for delicious. She said it as a baby and kept it going; she knew the right word."

Claire sat down at one of the two other kitchen chairs. When she had house-hunted in the area, two years into her Masters (and determined to move out of the family home), she had fallen in love with the triangular kitchen table. Now, with John, the shape had a bonus beyond the aesthetic: Claire could sit close to him. They could be two sides of the triangle, with the apex pointing at the pan of pasta sauce that marked the summit of their ascent.

The next thing she offered would be important. She took hold of John's hands.

"What other cute things did she say?"

John's eyes sparkled. "Bimnastics. Just a millet…" He was bringing his sister closer, Claire knew; he might have been bringing her back to existence.

"I feel like – sometimes – if I could only meet her one last time, I could say goodbye properly. And say sorry."

"Sorry for what?" Claire asked.

"I've never told a single person this in my life, Claire."

This confessional preamble did not arrive as anything of a surprise to Claire. Instead, it unearthed a revelation that had lain in a stratum of psychic debris for several months: the revelation that most matters from hereon in would be novel and original.

"I'm listening."

"She had a doll she loved when she was younger," John began, "I was jealous of it. Remember, she was an *older* sister, and I had no one else in the family. I was, like, four or five; Susan would've been six or seven."

"Still playing with dolls?"

John shook his head. "Not *playing* exactly; the doll had become her *diary*. She talked through her day – to the doll. Wouldn't leave the thing alone. And as I say, I was jealous."

"...What did you do to the doll?" Claire asked.

"Stole it. Almost *kidnapped* it. Then tortured it with stones. I pushed little stones into the doll's skin, one by one, in the back garden. Making her beg for forgiveness for taking my sister away. Then she died."

"Still the doll?" Claire wanted to clarify. She recalled a story that Phyllie had told her about having pushed teeth into a plastic doll's surface.

"Yeah. In my fantasy world, like – she died accidentally at the hands of her kidnapper." John laughed; then his face set in recognition of a tragic recollection. "I buried her."

Releasing John's hands, Claire said, "You have nothing to apologise for – to Susan. But *I* have something to apologise for – to you. It's time I wrote something down for you to read. Will you watch the sauce while I'm away?" She stood up.

"Where are you going?"

"Just outside, in the stairwell. Sometimes I sit on the stairs with my notebook. You'll have the run of the mansion while I'm gone."

John stood up and crossed to the stove. "That sauce looks ready. How long do you think you'll need?"

"Not long. It's only now I realise I've been writing my apology for five years, John." Claire tried to smile. "If I'm not word-perfect by now, I never will be."

John nodded.

"How about this? You go and write what you want to write. We eat our nice Nostalgia Bolognese. Then we drive to Lewsey Farm to find my sister."

"I'm sure we can find her here, John – together," said Claire.

"But I'm comfortable there. It's easy for me to travel when I'm there."

Claire waited to hear him out. "I propose a compromise. While we're eating, you tell me everything you can about the men in the dodgy van and what you've been up to on your travels. If it *doesn't work*… I'll drive us to Lewsey Farm. But let's at least try. Here."

"We put our heads together, you mean?" John asked with a smirk.

Although Claire returned his good humour with a smile, she did not recall the reference. Clearly, John was alluding to something in their past, but she could not remember what it might have been. It probably did not matter.

"Tell me Twennyfour's story," Claire said. "Take me in the van for a ride."

The Nostalgia Bolognese was *lishus*. The two of them having discussed what solitary meal would be on the menu, John had taken it upon himself to bring a bottle of red wine. He poured them each a glass while Claire dished up. By the time Claire offered John a second serving, they had drunk John's bottle of wine and had opened one of Claire's. Neither of them seemed surprised that each had chosen the same wine from a different shop.

John had hardly stopped talking throughout the meal. Claire had been happy to listen and not to ask questions. Now the conversation was slowing down.

"Where next?" Claire asked eventually.

"You've got the same map as I've got," John told her. "But you'll need to relax. Where's the most relaxing place?"

"My bed, I suppose."

"Then you take the bed and I'll make myself comfortable on the sofa."

"John, we're not exactly strangers. I think I can trust you to lie beside me on the bed. Like you all did in Lewsey Farm."

"I didn't want to seem presumptuous."

SESSION FINALE

Claire Carey's wrestling with her temper; she's talking to Amanda. "How did you know I'd walk past that dental clinic in Lewsey Farm?" she demands. Then she adds: "I can't tell you how surprised I was when I met you there!" – her voice a bit lighter, with less suspicion.

"I knew you wouldn't miss an important audition," Amanda tells her.

Then Claire starts to lose years from her face. She goes backwards. She becomes my daughter Claire and I have to tell her I've stopped being sorry. That I can't stay apologetic for the rest of my life. I'm tired of being contrite.

Later that afternoon, while contemplating a phrase that she has either read or written herself, on the subject of *maladjusted solitude* (and what it might feel like to experience this), Phyllie Reydman will spend nine minutes relaying between two rooms in her flat, solely to read two different post-it notes that have been in place for years.

In the lounge, attached to the record player lid that she no longer lifts to play vinyl (which sits atop a stereo stack system from a concluded millennium), is a yellow post-it that reads:

"Every shark is a smiling shark. The shark has no choice but to smile."
Brother Joe

Tucked into the top right corner of a windowsill mirror in her bedroom is a pink post-it that reads:

"Back then I didn't have the vocabulary. These days I don't have the permission."
Brother Joe

Phyllie will read one gobbet of wisdom and then the other; then walk the few strides between rooms and begin her studies once more, seeking a meaning that must be curled up dormant inside the inky curls of her handwriting.

She will not be able to recall how the afternoon's therapy hour had begun.

Neither will Chaz Bruce-Sange remember the same beginning of the session.

For years to follow, however, both partners – analyst and analysand – will recall how it ended. From time to time, both will see the other in her dreams.

In one such dream, Phyllie will say: *It's been nearly ten years, and every year I try to analyse my expectations. After the first year,*

*you go past the last-of-the-firsts. You go past the first bereavement
anniversary. You go past the other anniversaries.*

"I thought of something last night. I can't believe it's taken me
so long to notice it."

"What's that?"

"The fact that we are both strong, independent women –
independent in as much as we have no significant others to
tippy-toe and compromise around."

A nod of the interlocutor's head.

"Agreed."

"*Not* so independent in other parts of our lives, of course, if
Claire Carey's to be believed, and I can't see why she shouldn't
be; but we'll park that for a moment."

"You don't doubt the theory of ongoing alternative
existences?"

The question mark adorning the utterance is very faintly
inscribed; the words fall short of question status, but Chaz's
doubt remains in place, albeit scrutinised.

"Why should I?" Phyllie asks. "It happened to me a decade
earlier, don't forget. Perhaps I never quite…" She smiles. "I
don't say this to amuse, I promise. Perhaps I never quite got it
out of my system."

As far as Chaz is concerned, Phyllie's caveat is redundant.
There is nothing vaguely amusing in the idea of psychic and
emotional material locked fast in a bodily system. Recently,
Chaz had discussed the *rebus* with Doug Stegmeyer: the

subject's desire for lost objects. A memory of that discussion returns to Chaz's consciousness now.

"But there's something else," Phyllie continues, snipping her analyst's mental string. "If we're so independent, you and I, why do we both go by names derived from the masculine form? I'm a Philip and you're a Charles. I'm your *dad!*"

"You're my *dad?*" Chaz triple-blinks before snatching at the reference. "The Royal Family... Which makes you deceased, I'm afraid, Your Royal Highness."

"At the age of ninety-nine," Phyllie concurs. "But I *nearly* made the century."

"Nearly. Good effort."

"All these *nines* in my life," Phyllie adds, almost as a footnote. The regaining of her focus is the work of half a minute. Chaz waits for her with qualified patience.

"The question is a powerful tool, is it not?" asks Phyllie Reydman, adjusting the balance of her blouse's collars, either for effect in the presence of her psychoanalyst, or to protect herself from a draft trickling in from one of the office's windows. One of her collars had tucked itself inside the garment's material.

"If I had to narrow my range of tools down to one tool," offers Dr. Chaz Bruce-Sange, "I would choose the simple question. Specifically, the *open* question."

"Then one for you, if I may – given your positive endorsement."

"Certainly."

"What if we couldn't ask them? What if they were banned?"

"Linguistic censorship."

"No, not really; more like *ethical* censorship. There's a proposition in Nabokov – in *Pale Fire*. He asks us to weigh up the horrors of not being able to read, one morning. You wake up without the gift."

"And what would we do?"

"Exactly. What *would* we do? Our identity is an amalgam of skills and experiences, after all. So yes: the Question – capital Q – is stranded on a desert island. What does *anyone* do, robbed of talents and attributes? Robbed of curiosity and ambition."

"But we're not *anyone*, Phyllie," says Chaz. "It's not an insignificant point."

"No, it's not; you're right. But you know the one, don't you: if you ask me no questions, I can tell you no lies. My dad used to say something like that when I was a girl. It's not *true*, is it, Chaz? If you *do* ask me questions, I can still *try* to tell you no lies. I hope I've been a reliable analysand. I hope I've been as honest as I believe I've been."

"With me?"

"With the planet! Yes, with you. With Claire and Roger. With Claire Carey. With Alex Gordon. With everyone."

A moment passes. Chaz links her hands to make the church and the steeple; however, she does not show Phyllie the people. Instead, she raises the building to her lips and breathes through the nave and the congregation.

"We both know the end wriggles within our sight, do we not?" asks the psychoanalyst.

Nodding her head, Phyllie says, "We do."

"I would like to do something I have made it my business to avoid doing, where I can. Here we go. Your friend Claire Carey approached me. She told me I should end our professional relationship. I'm no good for you."

By flicking her two fingers briskly from her chest in the direction of Chaz's torso, then back again – four times – Phyllie makes the gesture that seeks to secure an answer to the question: *you and me?*

"*Our* professional relationship?"

"Yes."

"Or *hers* – with you?"

"You and me. I and thou ..." Chaz dissects the church and copies Phyllie's gesture with her left hand.

What Phyllie had hoped for (she comprehends in a beat of time) is a stringent denial from Chaz Bruce-Sange that she has any sort of relationship with Claire. It had only taken a second for Phyllie to feel envious: the thought of Claire having encroached upon her space with Chaz is stifling. Mentally signed codes of confidentiality, of course, will prevent Chaz from ever saying anything, not even in the negative. Denying that Claire is an analysand would be to affirm the young woman's physical dimensions. Chaz prefers to work with the wraiths and analytic thirds that she co-creates with her analysands. Phyllie believes that now Chaz has met Claire in the flesh, she will be less inclined to discuss her as part of the therapy hour...

(*... unless that meeting never happened...*)

It is just as well that the arrangement is heading toward its conclusion. *Analysis Terminable and Interminable.* The social scientists who have taken root in Lewsey Farm have it wrong (Phyllie opines). It is not an Apology Network that will move society along: what breaks any stasis is the action that we need to apologise for *later on*.

The tension is the key to unlock the scene, Phyllie quotes from her thesis – unless she is quoting from Claire's, which she had proofread in its penultimate draft. Ultimately, it doesn't matter. What matters is *not saying sorry*. Phyllie has said sorry for half of her life, and where has it gotten her? The important thing now – in general, not only in this psychoanalyst's saturated space – is to *make a scene*. To interrupt and to confuse. To be feisty.

"You told me once about Jacques Lacan – and the variable length of session," Phyllie remarks.

"Yes. Lacan imposed the variable hour on his analysands. Quitting the session at the point of client revelation: whether that's fifty minute or five. Do I take it that means you want to finish for today?" asks Dr. Chaz Bruce-Sange.

"Yes; and not just for today, Chaz."

"I see."

Phyllie will leave Chaz today, and she will leave the woman wanting more of Phyllie: more of the transaction; more of the countertransference; and more of the material that might one day be woven into words between hard covers.

Phyllie will not return. She has finished. She might even delay the payment of her final bill – a possibility that causes her to grin.

"…So it's probably bath time," one of the women present suggests.

"Oh, it's *definitely* bath time," the other one agrees.

THE DOUBLE BLINK

Of all the unexpected things… a text from Dr. Alex Gordon. *Unless you tell me you can't, usual time & space. V.v. urgent.*

Claire stared for moments at the inverted mountain range of the repeated *V*s. Once her heartrate had slipped back to its normal velocity, Claire took stock and demanded a response from herself.

Where's the usual place?

What was Alex Gordon talking about?

In the instant of recognition, Claire smiled. In recent months, she and her supervisor had pursued a nomadic existence around the cafes and coffee shops at the University. But to start with, for a couple of years at least, they had met in a bar in the Student Union.

Okey-dokey.

But usual *time?*

Heading towards the rack of coats and hats by the front door, Claire did her sums in her head. More often than not, she and Gordon had met either at ten a.m. or eleven a.m. The supervisor had often brought with him a sausage sandwich in its shrine of plastic.

It was best to be on time… or early. She would drive her Fiat to the university town and be sure that she was present from ten o'clock onwards.

Grey, determined – with a humourless expression glued *put* – the face of Dr. Alex Gordon remained all *student-debt* and *academic progress report* throughout much of the following exchange – and certainly when he said:

"We have something crucial to discuss."

Claire provided her supervisor with the double blink that she had long since regarded as a demonstration of idiosyncratic weakness. A pause for thought – for intellectual breath – was no admission of something lacking; but the double blink meant an empty vessel behind the eyes; a scream for nourishment and affection. The double blink was a gesture that she had avoided throughout her viva.

Dipping swiftly into a pool of conjoined perspectives, Claire imagined that Gordon was about to apologise. For Claire, it sounded like the future echo of an acknowledged confession.

"A serious allegation has been made against you, Claire."

Very little could have prepared Claire for this tidy collection of words.

"… Allegation?"

"… Yes. I'm not sure how to state this, to be honest."

Claire sniffed defiantly. "Play like a man with ten thumbs, Alex."

Gordon nodded. "As if I should've considered anything else. All right." His compromised morale now straightened its backbone. "You've been accused of plagiarism. You've been *accused* of stealing work for your PhD thesis."

"That's *nonsense*," Claire protested, climbing through the gears into a high-velocity panic.

"Hopefully so." Gordon nodded his head.

"It *sailed* through the text-detection software," Claire continued.

By now, Gordon was rubbing his neck. Claire wished (very briefly) that her supervisor would go back to his old ways of annoying her by cracking open a sausage sandwich package. Surely this had to be a joke. *Surely* this was another budgerigar harness story.

"Problem is," said Dr. Alex Gordon, "there's no accusation that you stole from internet sources. If a student steals from the internet, that's one thing. He sounded (thought Claire) a whisper away from *cheerful*. He sounded as though he was about to deliver a tutorial.

"I haven't stolen a word from anywhere," Claire told him slowly but firmly.

The academic was not about to have his lectern kicked over by a heckler.

"Push it through the recognition software – as you say – and it's Bob's your uncle and Fanny's your aunt."

Gordon stared at Claire until she said, "... Agreed?"

"Agreed. You get a percentage match – and if a student's lying, you can use the percentage to argue a case. This is different."

"You're being insulting, Alex. I promise you I haven't stolen a *punctuation mark*." Claire's voice was still in the controlled zone; both of them knew, however, that it might not remain there for long. "I'm about to be a *doctor*, for Christ's sake!"

The truth was, she felt sick to the stomach; her skull felt pricklish, as if with a fever. Thinking back to when John Hodgins had joined her for dinner at the flat, she added:

"Let me tell you, Alex – he was out of my sight for about five minutes. He said he was going to the loo. I don't know *what* he did – a USB stick in my bedroom?"

"Sorry, Claire – who are you talking about?" Gordon asked.

"John Hodgins! Who else?"

Claire halted.

"Who are *you* talking about?"

Dr. Alex Gordon's eyes were like fossils in flint.

"Who's accused me of plagiarism… if it wasn't John Hodgins?" Claire demanded.

"…Phyllie Reydman," was the reply.

The fear of being found out is a shared phenomenon. Everyone is guilty of something. In the moments directly following the accusation, Claire tried several times to rally; to find something in herself with which to retaliate – or at least respond.

The word hoard was empty. For the moment there was nothing to use.

On her drive home, Claire wondered how her flat would smell.

This notion was inspired, in part, by the deteriorating quality of the Fiat (it did not handle as well as it should; it did not *feel* right), and a very faint accompanying odour of something like human illness, which reached in from the air ventilation system. (Could a creature have died in the engine?)

Claire's noodling on how her flat would smell was also inspired, in part, by abstract considerations of revenge. Now that she had received Phyllie's accusation of plagiarism, it made sense that John Hodgins would have found a way to exact a revenge on *her*.

Only three nights earlier, Hodgins had been in her flat for several hours – for dinner, conversation, and storytelling… and no more than a good night peck when the taxi had arrived – and yet Claire had imagined that he *might* have planted a USB stick of his own work in her bra drawer (or something like that) while she had sat in the building's stairwell, busy with writing her apology letter to him. There was no doubt about it: as soon as Dr. Gordon had fumbled the allegation against her, Claire's mind had turned to Hodgins.

However, the finger-pointing belonged to Phyllie. What *had* John Hodgins done while Claire drafted her five-years-late apologia? How *had* he spent some of that time? Claire had heard stories of jilted lovers who had returned to a partner's home one final time… to sew a dead haddock into the curtain lining – or an act of similar ilk. As the fish decomposed, the stink ramped up. Had Hodgins had time to get out his embroidery purse?

Don't be stupid, Claire!

At a zebra crossing, Claire drew to a halt. Three seemingly unrelated adults squired a troop of eight children across the road, one of the latter group in a high-end buggy. To Claire's dismay, at least four of the children frowned!

Frowned at the driver who had legally paused to grant them passage... *Frowned* at her! Changing the posse's tack somewhat, a little girl of approximately nine years old blew Claire a kiss.

Claire drove on. She indicated left and pulled into the parking area. Her allocated space was occupied by an old pigeon – a bird who had seen better days.

"Join the club, darling," Claire whispered, subsequently feeling guilty when she had to toot the horn gently to make the pigeon move. When the bird had waddled away, Claire parked the Fiat... and *breathed*.

She walked around the building and let herself into Number 9.

The hallway did not smell of fish; nor did the bedroom or the lounge – nowhere did. If revenge had been on John Hodgins' mind, he had not acted out his wishes with the assistance of a river or sea creature. The flat felt calm; the waters were still; the flat was its normal self.

Resisting an urge to tear books from a shelf and haul them across the room, Claire steadied herself in the kitchen by making a cup of herbal tea. She was too disappointed to cry. She was exhausted.

Claire finished her herbal tea and called John Hodgins.

"I'd like to know if you wanted to make a final statement," she said.

"A *final* statement, Carey?" Hodgins asked – or perhaps Twennyfour asked. "Is this your societal swan song?"

"No, John; it's my final apology – the one I didn't dare give you the other night, when I read to you instead. I owe you one more item."

"I'm listening."

"I owe you my PhD."

"…I don't want it."

"The energy I put into my thesis was drained from *you*, in part. I think now. But I'm ashamed of myself. I *forgot* you, John. I let you go."

Claire remembered how she had crept into the Lewsey Farm building that first time. How many others present in that room, on that afternoon, had disgraced themselves with another?

"This is probably our final contact, Hodgins. I hope you took suitable revenge."

"I certainly did, Carey."

Claire waited. Then she laughed in acknowledgement of what had not passed but might have. "And you're not going to say what it was, are you?"

"What kind of revenge has an appointment date and agenda? You'll see."

Absurdly delighted with this transaction, Claire smiled like the girl who has thought through the worst case, only to judge it marginally negative.

"Thank you," said Claire, and she closed the call.

THREE NINES
(EMERGENCY SERVICES)

Nine *days* from now, John Hodgins will call her back.

"You had one final say, Carey, and now this is mine. Are you ready?"

"The revenge call?" Claire will ask.

"You decide. Five years ago, I helped you to forget something. And I convinced you you could have what you wanted."

"As opposed to what I *didn't* want?"

"Accidentally, yes." Hodgins will appear amused on the screen. "You *saw* us, Claire – and you flipped. It was all you could do not to rip the blade across your wrist. I had to tell you your future."

Hodgins will pause for a moment.

"I promised you I'd leave the University – and your life – if you agreed to forget what you stumbled in on. We had a deal," he will continue.

"And what did I witness, John?" Claire will demand. "Help me unlock it!"

"You know what you saw. I was twenty-four…"

"So?"

"... And your mum was forty-two, Claire." Hodgins will permit a moment to slide before continuing. "She has a birthmark east of her navel. Her shoe size is six-and-a-half."

Dreams and dreads will clog in Claire's throat. The desire to escape will somatise as an ache in her gums, chest, and lower back. Not a word will cross her bunched lips.

"It's always been me who should say sorry to *you*," Hodgins will tell Claire.

Claire will add: "And now you have."

"And now I have."

Nine *months* from now, approximately six months on from her graduation ceremony, Dr. Claire Carey will look into the eyes of an undergraduate student who is in her first year of a Bachelors degree. The student's major subject is business supply chains, but Dr. Carey will not be teaching Business. Having grudgingly accepted the best offer that she'd received, Dr. Carey will be teaching generic Research Skills to a variety of that year's academic subjects' intake. No suitable full-time position will have been established – yet – for Dr. Claire Carey, PhD. Very much for the time being, Claire will have accepted part-time hours on a temporary contract from Human Resources.

And Dr. Carey will find, in the eyes of one student, a world that she believes to be recognisable. There is something in the young woman's features that Dr. Carey comprehends. A perception of ambition, perhaps; something that might be appetite – an intellectual hunger. *Perhaps she fancies me,* Dr. Carey will write in her reflective journal that evening; but she will make the *tscsh!* sound of disapproving self-reproof. Physical attraction had had nothing to do with it.

While in the classroom at the university, Dr. Carey will imagine that she saw Claire Billie's features in the undergraduate's face and eyes. While writing in her journal, she will scold herself and admit: *No, it wasn't Claire Billie. It was me. I remembered who I used to be, and saw the undergrad ME in that girl.*

Nine *years* from now, and seven full years since securing her first and only academic post – a position that she loves dearly – Dr. Carey will be working in a different classroom, with a group of twenty-odd Psychology first years.

Dr. Carey will know that Claire Billie's name is on the attendance register. Claire Billie will be eighteen years of age, just starting her university days.

The two Claires will pretend that they do not recognise one another.

Claire walked as far as her Fiat, which was parked as ever in her allocated spot, before changing her mind. She did not want to drive; there was nowhere she wished to visit, there was no one she wished to talk to. On deciding to take a brief walk instead, Claire noticed the pigeon that had seen better days – the pigeon that liked to occupy a parking bay of her own. For a second, the avian eyes and the human eyes met; Claire fancied that there passed an instant of recognition. Perhaps a woman had a distinctive smell … for a bird.

Good luck to you, darling, Claire thought; and she turned on her heels. Back out of the car park and onto the road she walked; she turned left, in the opposite direction to the town. Hours from now she had a shift arranged at the pub where she worked; wanting something to do until then (something that did not involve reading or writing), Claire paced with a growing focus onto the trading estate. Something currently vague in her mind gained sombre and meaningful accrescence every metre or so that she travelled. John Hodgins left her with more than a parting shot, she was convinced.

Trucks and vans a-plenty were parked outside the row of hardware and plumbing supplies outlets, which were open for workers only. Claire once attempted to buy replacement light bulbs from one of these outlets; sceptically, she'd been asked to show her trader's ID – and asked how many hundred bulbs she required. A different business establishment advertised the servicing and repair of gadgets. A sign above the door read: "Ray's Against the Machine" – and it made her smile.

The Post Office's sorting depot contained its own enclosed car park; red vehicles crammed in behind chain link fencing, like red ants protecting a mound. Claire had been to the sorting office once but could not recall why. While trying to remember what brought her here – again, on foot – she understood what John Hodgins' gift to her was.

Claire would never be able to ask her mother if she and Hodgins were intimate – and this was Hodgins' revenge on Claire. The *filament of doubt*.

Hodgins knew that Claire needed to know everything. Curiosity and critical thinking (on a stratospheric scale) were part of her DNA: a fact of which Hodgins was likewise aware. What better way to sew a figurative haddock into her emotional curtain lining – than to leave Claire with a doubt that she would never be able to satisfy?

When Claire stopped walking, it was all she could do to refrain from applauding the man's acuity.

Feeling bright and cheerful, she ambled home.

AIRPORT CONCLUSIONS

"Hello, Roger. You look surprised to see me."

"That's one way of putting it. I *am* surprised to see you, Phyllie. Can I ask what you're doing here, please?"

"To greet you. Welcome home!"

The airport was hot and noisy, but Phyllie was certain that the heat and the din were not the only factors contributing to her ex-husband's sense of discomfort.

Phyllie could not purge herself of an impression: the impression that whatever else happened, she would always know more than her ex-husband knew.

She would always be able to help more people than he could assist.

"I'm already being greeted, I'm afraid," Roger told her, adjusting the weight of his carry-on luggage on his right shoulder. The straps bit into his clothes, causing dents.

"Amanda said she couldn't meet you."

"I wasn't referring to Amanda."

Phyllie waited for some sort of comprehension. Without any warning came the thought that Roger was cheating on Amanda; he had found another girlfriend – someone more than the accumulation of Phyllie and Amanda; someone *more*, someone additional, fresh, and new. Did Phyllie's facial expression give away her disgust at this notion?

"My brother said he'd take me home, in case you're wondering."

"I see." *Do I believe him?* "I wanted to do something nice."

"The timing's wrong, Phyllie, not the intention. Thank you. But I must skedaddle."

Tears increased in temperature in Phyllie's eyes. *How can this hurt me?* she wondered; *after everything that has happened, how can something as simple as a rejection hurt me now?*

"I'm here of my own volition, Roger. I thought I'd do a *nice* thing."

I've said nice *twice now. He'll think I've regressed to the vocabulary of a nine year-old. But I thought he'd be pleased to see me. I thought I still meant something to him.*

Roger nodded his head.

"At least acknowledge I did a nice thing, Roger," Phyllie said firmly.

"You did a very nice thing. Now I'd like to go, please."

Phyllie Reydman walked from room to room of her humble home, in each one removing post-it notes that had hung in place for years. Brother Joe's maxims had accompanied Phyllie through the chapters of her recent days, but now it was time to conclude and close her book. Disconnecting post-it notes from surfaces, mirrors, and cupboard doors – the post-it notes on which she had taken down Brother Joe's psychic dictation

– was one way of doing so, now. The occasion required neither ceremony nor an audience. Phyllie crushed the post-it notes in either hand, simultaneously.

It was finished. The last words that she had read were these:

"Our instinct for exploration will serve us commendably."
Brother Joe

AUTHOR'S NOTE

Although Des Lewis has always been this novel's dedicatee, back from the time when the book existed as no more than a title, I would also like to acknowledge those who once shared our saturated spaces: those who abandoned us, for reasons of their own, and those whom we abandoned.

One of the dedicatees of my novel *Ventriloquists* (about which, more below) was Sheila Furnell; the dedication was offered *in memoriam*. A year or so before Sheila passed, I responded by letter to a question she had posed about what I was writing. I told her that I was working on a fiction about two rival psychoanalysts; and now, as I complete *Abandoned Dental Clinics*, I can tell her that those characters finally made it *to* – and made it up *on* – the page. As a teacher of English, Sheila encouraged me to write stories. It is possible, therefore, that this book – or any of the others – would never have been written without Sheila's guiding light at Queensbury Upper School, Dunstable, Bedfordshire. Furthermore, it is *literally* in this moment of coda that I recognise I have been carrying Sheila's name through this novel, albeit with a different spelling.

A coincidence? Possibly; coincidences are certainly a topic of conversation in this book; and although a work colleague recently told me, and with energy, that there is *no such thing* as a coincidence, I would like to note the date that I write these last words: 11th February, 2023. Do I agree with my colleague Sam when I mention that today would have been my father's 78th birthday?

It is all connected.

I encountered the Pose-Yourself Man (as a synonym for a photographer) in a Truman Capote story entitled "Preacher's Legend". It is available in the *Collected Stories* (and I'd recommend it).

May I also express my appreciation for two books that I read as a child, each of which was useful to re-read while the first draft of this book took form? They are *My Side of the Mountain* by Jean George and *The Winter of the Birds* by Helen Cresswell. It occurs to me (in considerable retrospect, marking as I did my fiftieth birthday, late in 2021), how drawn I am, and how much I learned from, a boy in fiction who overcomes trouble.

Dr. Chaz Bruce-Sange refers to the work of the psychoanalyst Thomas Ogden during one of her therapy hours with Phyllie Reydman. The anecdote is from Ogden's book *Reverie and Interpretation*. On another occasion, Chaz tests Doug on the subject of separation. The reading is from *The Unhappy Divorce of Sociology and Psychoanalysis,* by Lynn Chancer and John Andrews – page 328.

Professor Sir Grayson Twivy quotes from Samuel Beckett's *Molloy.* The sentences are pincered between pages 19 and 20 in the Calder edition of the *Trilogy.*

Talking of Beckett, I am reasonably sure that the 'Scent of Knife' section was activated by my reading of Beckett's work. I acknowledge the debt, though I do not recall the specifics.

My psychoanalyst character Doug Stegmeyer bears no deliberate resemblance to the musician of the same name, may the latter individual rest in peace.

My thanks to Chris Baker for the story about the rabbits.

For readers interested in the events leading up to some of the references in this novel – for those, in other words, who appreciate the *full story* – a volume entitled *Ventriloquists* was published by Montag in 2014. Be advised, however, that each novel may be read independently of the other; furthermore, the order in which they are read is a choice for the reader. The same criteria hold for the other interconnected volumes in the "Saturated Spaces" library, most recently *Nostalgia's Boat* in 2020. This narrative universe might be haunted by overlapping themes, but there are no dictators in these whorls. Read the books in any order – indeed, in any *way* – that makes you happy. *Torso Redux* and *The Concrete Blush* will soon be on their way to keep these spaces warm.

For conceptual and clerical neatness, it makes sense that this book was written on various borderlines. Furthermore, it makes sense that the manuscript was completed as the train on which I travelled pulled into my destination station.

David Mathew
Leighton Buzzard, Rutland Water, Leicester, and Birmingham, England.
Marmaris, Turkey.
2020-2023